I0728694

Division One:
Trojan Horse

by Stephanie Osborn

Chromosphere Press

Huntsville, AL

Trojan Horse

© 2018 Stephanie Osborn

ISBN 978-1-947530-00-3 (print)

ISBN 978-0-9982888-9-5 (ebook)

Cover art © 2018 Darrell Osborn

Fiction

First electronic edition 2018

This is a work of fiction. All concepts, characters and events portrayed in this book are used fictitiously and any resemblance to real people or events is purely coincidental.

Chromosphere Press
P.O. Box 3412
Huntsville, AL 35810
www.chromospherepress.com

Table of Contents

Chapter 1

"Okay, guys," Echo said from the pilot's seat of the *Trojan Horse* as he set the course through the Solar System, "we're gonna take it a little bit slower than I did the first time I went to Edeptis. We're going nearly to the other side of the galaxy, and we're taking a longer route, to ensure we avoid that cosmic string from the collapsed wormhole. The Ennead already has an astronav hazards team out, mapping its location, to mark on galactic travel and shipping maps. And then they'll put up some special beacons to notify shipping and other travelers, if they accidentally get in the vicinity."

"You didn't get in trouble for it, did you, Ace?" Omega wondered from the co-pilot's chair, concerned. "Creating the string, I mean."

"No, they didn't blame me," Echo said, working out the route he wanted to take on the console. "Because, if the *Trindak* hadn't interfered, the wormhole would have collapsed normally and disappeared, once I exited near Edeptis. But," he added, looking up at his partner with a slight, grim smile, "it's just one more hash mark on the list of Cortian violations. Which, I gather, is getting kinda long."

"Serves 'em right, dammit," Omega grumbled, scowling for a moment. Echo grinned at her reaction. But the grin held more than a hint of wolfishness; he agreed with her entirely.

"So, everybody's okay with my proposed route, right?" he asked again.

"All right, Ace, yeah. I'm good. Makes sense to me," Omega decided.

"And me," Doron said simply, sitting in a chair behind the helm, on the port side of the flight deck. It was officially the navigator's station, but it was generally only used as such on special exploratory missions, when the navigation was performed separate from the piloting to better enable celestial mapping.

"Good," Echo decided, glancing up again as he hit the initiate button. "And there we go. Meg, are you ready for your first lessons in interstellar flight?"

"Oh HELL yeah, Ace!" Omega exclaimed, grinning from ear to ear.

"Doron, are you doin' okay back there?"

"Indeed, Agent Echo," Doron vouched, scrolling down a computer display on the nav console. "Thank you for arranging for me to obtain my personal messages before we departed. I can see what is happening at home, and prepare matters for my arrival on the morrow."

"Not a problem, Doron," Echo said, sobering. Beside him, Omega grew serious as well. "After everything you've done for us," he gestured to his partner and himself, "that sure wasn't any big deal."

"What he said," Omega murmured.

"It is what I do, heal," Doron said, serene. "I would expect that neither of you would consider profuse thanks required for apprehending a galactic terrorist, am I not correct?"

"Yeah," Echo agreed.

"Ee-zackly," Omega averred.

"It is a parallel, you understand. Simple thanks—which you have both provided, long since—is all that is necessary. Just as you do not require effusive thanks for the performance of your job, so do I not require it. And therefore I am simply glad to have helped, and to see you both healthy and happy, and working together once more." Doron offered the Edeptan equivalent of a smile; it was a cheerful expression, even to humans, and he waved them toward the helm console. "Get on with your studies, and I shall get on with my...I think Agent Romeo called it, 'email,' did he not?"

"Right," Omega said, her own smile returning. "Sounds good. Echo?"

"Okay, Doron. And to that end...Meg, have a look at this, 'cause it's nothing like the *SchmaltzBlitz*'s controls—this spacecraft is a completely different make and model, so it's a lot different; that's why I chose this ship. Right now, I'm gonna show you how to program the digital autopilot..."

"That's what we called the DAP, at NASA?"

"Yeah, and a lot of the Agency pilots use the same term..."

* * *

The *Trojan Horse* had departed Earth about 10 in the morning Chicago local time, or some two hours prior to first lunch, according to Division One time. By the time Alpha One finished their afternoon snack, just over sixteen hours later, Doron was exhausted; Edeptan days were slightly shorter than normal Earth days, and the little physician was not used to Division One days, having not bothered—or particularly needed—to adapt during his stay on Earth.

And while normally a partnership such as Alpha One would have left one member of the team at the helm while the other slept, Omega's trainee status made that impossible; nor could Echo remain at the helm continuously throughout a multi-day space mission. A few seconds of silent, coded, and surreptitious conversation between the members of Alpha One was sufficient to decide to call it a day, for the diminutive healer's sake.

So Echo set the sensors on long-range, activated the proximity and other alarms, ensured the DAP was on course, and Alpha One escorted Doron down the short passageway to the sleeping berths, darkening the cabin illumination as they went. Omega turned left; Echo and Doron turned right.

"G' night, Ace, Doron," Omega called over her shoulder as she entered the starboard sleep station.

"Good night, baby," Echo replied.

"Good night, Omega," Doron added. "Sleep well."

* * *

"Does it matter which bed I choose?" Doron asked as he and Echo prepared for bed.

"Nah," Echo said with a shrug, going to his overnight kit and fishing around in it. "Pick whichever one you want, and I'll grab another."

"Very well. Are the, um, the hygiene facilities, through here?" The alien indicated a door opposite the compartment's entrance.

"Yeah, that's one of the heads," Echo noted. "Er, a 'head' in this instance is a shipboard bathroom."

"Why ever is it called a 'head'?" Doron wondered, puzzled.

"Well, in my linguistics courses, we were taught that the term goes all the way back to Earth's ocean sailing ships," Echo explained. "Back in the day, sailors went up to the bow of the ship—the front, on either side of the figurehead decorating the stemhead—and took a, erhm, uh, they relieved themselves over the side, into the ocean. I suppose in the most ancient ships, they just went over the rail, but in later sailing vessels, there was a box with a seat, and a hole or slot in the bottom that, uh, well, it all ended up in the ocean. So whenever they had to relieve themselves, they simply told their companions, 'I gotta go to the head.' And I guess it stuck, even after indoor plumbing got developed for ships."

"Ah, I see! It has a very, um, colorful history," Doron decided.

"Yeah, it does, kinda. I never really figured out why they did it at the

FRONT of the ship; I'd have thought it was more logical to do that at the back, and leave it all behind, though I was told that, sailing being what it is, the bow tends actually to be downwind of everybody else. But I've never sailed; I grew up in a landlocked area with little water, so I dunno. Anyway, the term is several centuries old, and pretty well established. The other sleep berth has a head as well, and there's one on the deck below, too, but it's smaller, without the showers an' junk. Feel free to go do whatever you need to do before going to bed."

Doron toddled through to the head, where he washed his face and cleansed his mouth while Echo brushed his teeth.

"Echo? What else is on the deck below us, besides another hygenic facility?"

"Oh, I never took y'all around the ship, did I? I'm sorry; I shoulda done that. I'll do it tomorrow, first thing. The flight deck is in the forepart of the top deck, the sleep berths in the mid-deck, and the EVA prep room is in the aft. The middle deck houses the galley—where we prepared and ate our meals today, remember?"

"Ah, yes."

"Right. So it has another head like I said, storage and cargo, computers and electronics, shit like that. The very bottom deck is the engine room."

"Ah. I see. Thank you. I was, as you say, just curious."

"No prob. Like I said, I should have shown you and Meg both around," Echo said, offering him a grin. "I just got busy tryin' to keep Meg from liftin' off without the rest of us."

"Indeed, indeed!" Doron agreed, and they laughed.

Within about five more minutes, both males were in their bunks and asleep.

* * *

Across the way, a certain trainee pilot managed to damp down her excitement long enough to prepare for bed and retire, herself.

Then she lay in her bunk and stared at the darkened ceiling for a long time, a happy smile on her face. *'I'm here! I'm finally out here!'* was the joy-filled refrain that ran through her mind, over and over.

After several moments of this, she threw back the covers and climbed out of bed. Tiptoeing over to the door into the corridor, she peeped out long enough to verify that Echo had, indeed, gone to bed himself. Then she tiptoed out and made her way to the flight deck. There, she stood for long moments, just gazing out the forward port at the star field as it slipped past.

Suddenly she spun into an improvised, barefooted dance around the flight deck. Every dozen steps or so, she paused long enough to look out the port again, before whirling into a new expression of elation.

Eventually, worn out by the sheer exhilaration, she made her way back to her berth, climbing into her bunk once more with cold feet that she barely noticed, to resume a rapturous contemplation of the dark deckhead.

Finally she, too, fell asleep.

* * *

Echo and Omega strolled across a meadow on Krevit, a world quite similar to Earth, but less developed, and with a blue-white star. They had just finished a very successful assignment and had decided to take a much-needed break from work, and had concluded that Krevit made for a nice vacation spot.

He shot her a warm glance, smiling slightly, and she met his gaze with a look of such warmth and devotion that it nearly took his breath away. He held out his hand, and she grasped it, lacing her fingers through his. They wandered on, happy and content, joined hands swinging gently between them as they walked.

They paused under a purple tree, sheltering from the hot blue sun in its shade, and Omega turned toward him, sliding her hands up his chest and around his neck. He smiled at her and bent his head to hers, savoring the feel of soft lips, the sweet, honeyed taste of her mouth. He heard her sigh, and he gathered her close in his arms to deepen the kiss.

"Oh, I don't think so!" declaimed a cold, familiar voice from some-where nearby.

Echo and Omega broke the kiss, their heads snapping up in surprise as they looked around to see who had spoken.

Just outside the shadow cast by the tree stood...

Chase.

Clad in canary-yellow feathers.

Flanked by Cortians.

All glaring at Omega.

"Oh, no. You don't get MY man, bitch," Chase said to Echo's partner, striding forward. "Not now, not ever."

"You married somebody else. I don't think you get an opinion in the matter," Omega declared, turning to meet the advancing woman.

"The hell you say," Chase replied, aiming a slap at Omega's face.

"Yeah, I do say," Omega averred, calmly blocking the slap before throwing a flurry of punches and palm-heel strikes at Chase. Chase, somewhat to Echo's surprise, parried all of them, throwing her own, which Omega likewise blocked.

And suddenly Echo could only watch as the two women he had loved—past and present—fought fiercely over...him.

* * *

Meanwhile, the Cortians flanking Chase spread out and drew weapons, advancing upon Echo—

—Who suddenly found that he could not move.

"Aw, shit," he grumbled, fighting down an unaccustomed emotion, something akin to panic, as he awaited disaster striking once more. "Not again. MEG!"

"Comin' Ace!" she called, then returned to fighting Chase.

"NO! You gotta clear outta here, baby! GO! Before it happens again!"

"Enough!" Chase declared. "He's MINE!"

"You're DEAD!" Omega pointed out. "He's free!"

"NO! He'll NEVER be free! He'll ALWAYS belong to me!"

"Like hell!" And suddenly Omega had both blasters in hand.

"Meg! I need some help! We gotta get outta here!" Echo tried again, as the leering Cortians neared, breaking out flamethrowers as they came.

"I'm on it, Echo!" Omega replied.

Echo watched in horror as Omega leveled one blaster at Chase...and fired. The woman he had once loved dropped to the ground, most of her head gone, her body landing at the feet of the woman he now loved...

...Who turned and pointed the other blaster at Echo.

Omega shimmered, melted, and re-formed as a giant, iridescent green slug...with human hands. Omega's hands.

The chimera fired the blaster, point-blank.

* * *

Echo started awake with a grunt. He stared about himself in the dim lighting for a moment, confused, then remembered he was aboard the *Trojan Horse* with Omega, taking the physician Doron back to his homeworld of Edeptis. He raked an agitated hand through his dark hair.

At least I didn't yell this time and wake up Doron, he decided, glancing over at the sleeping alien being in the bunk opposite. *That's something. But damn. Where did Chase come from?! Like I needed THAT complication. I thought that was over and done with. Evidently my subconscious disagrees, though,* he decided, mulling over the dream. *Part of me must still be hangin' on to the affair with Chase, even though we broke it off a couple years ago; even though she's been dead a good six months or better now.* He shook his head. *Hell, it ain't like seeing Meg get torched didn't do a number on my head...and heart,* he amended. *I suppose it isn't surprising that it's stirred up a whole shitload of stuff that never really quite got resolved. I gotta figure out how to let go of all that mess and move on, or I'm never gonna manage to develop the kind of relationship I want with Meg. Assuming SHE wants one, I guess.*

He hitched around in the bunk, trying to adjust the pajama bottoms that he wore in deference to the little alien physician sharing the berth with him. *Mmph. Damn wedgie. Aw hell. I'm hungry anyway. At least gettin' up for a midnight snack will give me a chance to untwist this stinkin' straitjacket for the family jewels. I'm ditchin' the damn things as soon as we get Doron home.*

Echo rose, then spent several minutes adjusting his sleepwear until it was more comfortable on his body. Once that was settled, he stole out of the berth and down to the galley, where he grabbed a glass of milk and a couple of pre-packaged cookies. He wolfed them down, chugged the milk, stopped by the head, then swung by the flight deck, just to check on matters.

A blinking yellow light on the console drew his attention, and he moved to it, noting that it was an indicator of activity in the flight deck that shouldn't have occurred. *That's odd,* he thought. *Surely Meg wouldn't have tinkered with the flight settings.*

So he brought up the security video of the area, and watched as it depicted a barefoot, pajama-top-clad blonde, platinum hair loose and flowing, as she entered the flight deck and stood for long moments, just looking out into the universe. Echo gasped then, as she abruptly whirled into a kind of dance of delight, almost hedonistic in nature, uninhibited and jubilant and utterly delightful. Every few steps she turned and looked back out the main portal, before spinning back into her dance.

That's...adorable, he thought as he watched. *She couldn't stand it, so she came out here to take one more look and...* He shook his head. *Express herself, I guess. Vent a little of what she's kept pent up for so very long. Damn, it must have taken all the control she could muster to keep THAT inside all day, until nobody could see. Especially with Doron along for the ride. And it wasn't like she could whoop an' holler with me an' Doron asleep across the way—well, I guess she coulda, but she was considerate enough not to wake us—so she got it out of her system this way. At least as much as it's gonna get out, I bet.*

He smiled to himself, sending the video snippet to his personal tablet before erasing it from the security system. *No way I'm gonna let that go into the bit bucket permanently. It's too damn cute. But I'm not gonna embarrass her with it, either. She obviously didn't think about the security system, and she just had to let it out.*

He did a quick scan over the other controls, only to see green lights. *That looks good, then,* he decided. *I guess I'm done here.*

Ascertaining that all was well with their spacecraft and they were still on course for Edeptis, he returned to the sleeping berth he shared with Doron.

I better not have any more damn nightmares tonight, he thought, annoyed, as he climbed back into his bunk. *I need my wits about me tomorrow to keep training Meg, which means I gotta sleep. Though, you know, I think I'm glad I took Fox's advice and got a little counseling while Meg was in the regen pod. Not that I hadn't decided to, anyway. But it might not have been enough, after all.*

He pulled the covers up, settled into the bunk, and went back to sleep.

* * *

The next morning, Echo rectified his omission and took his companions on a brief, but detailed, tour of the *Trojan Horse.* The spacecraft wasn't huge, so this was swiftly followed by breakfast, which all three joined in to prepare, Doron having discovered during his sojourn on Earth that he liked bacon and eggs.

Then Doron settled down at the meal table in the galley, content to review some new medical information from Edeptis which he had downloaded onto his hand-held tablet from an email discovered the day before. Meanwhile Echo escorted Omega back up to the flight deck, there to give her a few more basic lessons in the capabilities of their spacecraft.

"Not that we're going to actually go off-course," he noted. "After all, Doron's people are expecting us to arrive at a certain time this evening. And I think they have some more official 'first-contact' sorts of events planned, as well as a welcome for you, baby."

"Oh?" Omega wondered, startled. "For me specifically? Why on earth? Er, on Edeptis?"

"Yeah. See, they know I came to fetch Doron to heal you, and from what I could tell, they were delighted to hear that you were coming back with us, all healthy an' junk."

"Aw, okay," Omega said, offering him a grin. "I get that. 'Local boy makes good' kinda thing. I'm Doron's trophy patient or somethin', I guess."

"Something like, I'd say," Echo agreed, "but I think they're curious to know what you're like, that I'd go flyin' across the galaxy to get him on your account, in the first place."

"Oh!" Omega blushed, somewhat to Echo's private gratification; he rather hoped that had been a nice, broad hint regarding how he felt about her. But if she considered it in that light, she made no outward sign, and, stifling a sigh, he turned his attention to increasing her familiarity with the spacecraft's operations.

* * *

"Ace, can I ask you something?" Omega said, watching him as he returned control of the spacecraft to the autopilot, nearly three hours later.

"Sure, baby, any time. You know that." He straightened up and looked at her. "You got a question about the training?"

"No, that all made perfect sense," she told him, chewing her lip in a bit of concern. "You're an awful good teacher. No, it's about my...promotion."

"Oh, the assistant department chief thing?"

"Yeah."

"Okay, shoot."

"Well, I was just wondering...see, in NASA, we had the whole multiple redundancy bit, so that if something went wrong, there was backup..."

"Right. And that's what you are, in addition to a kind of aide—you're my backup."

"Yeah, but...don't get me wrong, I don't WANT to do this, but... shouldn't we be on different teams, then? Let alone going on the same missions together. I mean, look at the President and the Vice-President. They don't fly on the same airplanes. They don't take shelter in the same emergency shelters. All that junk. I mean, if something happens to Alpha One..."

"Oh, I get it." Echo nodded. "You're worried that, if Alpha One gets wiped out, Alpha Line is leaderless."

"Yeah."

"Well, I'm happy to see you thinking like that; it's the mark of the leader you're turning out to be. But it isn't as much of a concern as you might think. See, we have enough of an experience base in the department now to where we actually do have that multiple redundancy. Alpha Two is Alpha One's backup overall, and I set that up with Fox at the same time as I put in for you to be my second. Specifically, Romeo is YOUR backup. I sat down and talked to him, to India, to Fox..." Echo shrugged. "India has no interest in being in the chain of command. She's content to be the department's medic, and a damn fine field agent, both of which are good things, and both of which are needed, especially in Alpha Line. But Romeo has some really great military experience, and he knows how to command if he needs to—and you've probably noticed, I've been giving him the opportunities to do so."

"Yeah, I have."

"Thought so; you pay attention to stuff. Anyway, he's smart enough to realize that he's still pretty young, and needs a bit of maturity, to be a good commander. But that IS where India comes in, because she's leveling him out, both professionally and personally. And he knows that, and appreciates it. So if it should fall out that he ever becomes the department chief, then she becomes his executive assistant...like you were, before the promotion to assistant chief. But," he added, "she made us specify that at no time was she ever to be put in the chain of command, any more than she is as part of Alpha Two."

* * *

"But...wait...then shouldn't HE...? I mean, Romeo?" Omega wondered, sapphire eyes troubled.

"No," Echo declared, shaking his head firmly. "For one, Romeo is also self-aware enough to know he's not in that place yet. And for two, you proved your leadership to me, to Fox, and to the entire department, the day the Cortians revealed just what they really are. Damn, baby, maybe you haven't stopped to think what you did, but you planned tactics, including multiple levels of backup plans, coordinated prep, organized AND COMMANDED no less than TWO different departments—Alpha Line, and Diplomacy—and did so seamlessly, as if they were all one unit. And that also includes the department heads for both: me, and Sugar. Hell, even FOX obeyed your direction...and he doesn't do that unless he's convinced that the planning and direction involved is up to his standards."

"Well, but he didn't let me distribute anything but stun guns..."

"But that was because of the diplomatic considerations. And wow, did he regret that later—he told me so, and was not happy about having to admit it." Echo paused, then added, "In fact, I need to tell you this; I've just been waiting for a good opportunity. See, he admitted it was the wrong decision, and he should have listened to you, should have trusted your judgement. Because your original plan was the correct one, he told me...and he asked me to pass on a discreet apology to you. It's like this: he's in a position, as Director, where he can't just publicly admit he screwed up...there was enough of a fruit basket turnover in the Ennead..."

"Oh. I get it. So he told his deputy in private, and asked him to pass it on to me."

"Right. With additional apologies for having to do it this way." Echo watched her, head cocked to one side, waiting to see what her reaction would be. "So...is he forgiven? Are...WE...forgiven?"

"Huh? For what?"

"...Not listening to you like we should have." His voice cracked slightly despite his best efforts.

"Aw hon," Omega murmured, face crumpling a bit in something that looked to Echo like sympathy and understanding, "there's nothing to forgive. I swear, Ace, there is nothing to forgive. I think I told you this, once before, but please tell Fox too—sure, it hurt that y'all misunderstood an' stuff, but it isn't like I didn't understand WHY. I mean, damn, Ace, what a mess." She sighed. "I guess...in the circumstances, in the future, I'd just ask..." She broke off, apparently searching for the right words, and Echo waited, somewhat tense, to see what was coming next. "If I ever come to you with something that's bothering me in future, take this sorta thing into consideration and look at it seriously with me. Help me figure out if it's something, or nothing. I'm always gonna be on your side, and sometimes

I...I just want..." She paused, then shook her head and looked up at him with a pleading gaze, and he understood.

"I know, baby," he whispered, laying a hand on her shoulder and rubbing lightly for a moment. "I get it. Working with you, especially since we found out what, what happened to you, what Slug did, has been a learning experience for me, too. But I think this last escapade taught me a really big lesson. And I swear on everything I hold holy, I will pay attention from now on, and I will NOT blow you off, and I will listen, and try to help you sort through this shit, if it's in my ability to do so."

"Then that's all I can ask, Ace. Look, I...I know it makes me a better Agent for all the tinkering...which is why I didn't have Doron do a 'reset'... but...I just get kinda tired of all the unexpected shit cropping up, ya know?"

"Yeah, I know, baby. But...you still haven't answered my question. Okay, I know you say there isn't. But WE, Fox and me, we see things that need forgiving, big things, but..."

Omega offered him a wry, affectionate, somewhat tired smile.

"Then yes," she told him, voice warm, "you're forgiven. BOTH of you."

Echo nodded in relief. He opened his mouth to speak, but found nothing would come out; he dropped his gaze to the deck instead. Omega reached out and covered his near hand, squeezing gently for a moment before withdrawing her hand.

"It's all right, Ace, I swear. You gonna be okay on this?"

"...Yeah. I am now," he responded, slightly hoarse.

"Go on, then."

"Right." He cleared his throat. "So...you devised, developed and commanded the whole operation. And you did all of it, successfully enough to thwart the Cortians, deny them their prize—me, if that doesn't sound too egotistical—and send 'em running as fast as they could go, off-planet and into hiding."

"Well...um..." Omega flushed. It was Echo's turn to smile, but he laid a light hand on her shoulder again, this time squeezing in encouragement. But instead of removing it, he left his hand there, providing subtle support.

"And we all followed you, baby. Once we knew what was really going on with you, we all followed you without question. Like Romeo said at the time, into hell and out the back. And it was hell," he admitted, "for you and me especially, as much as anybody. But you proved yourself a leader to the lot of us. And a damn fine one."

"O...okay," she murmured, stammering a bit as she flushed even deeper.

"And that goes all the way up, it seems. Pulgey pulled me aside after dinner the other night, and told me that when he showed up and started raising hell, the Ennead had insisted on seeing the security footage from the hangar, and as he put it, 'Every last Creator's child of them was damn impressed with that partner of yours.' He told me that Dulziv couldn't even meet anyone's eyes, after seeing what you coordinated and did. And that apparently it—Dulziv—had made some highly disparaging remarks, in turning down Fox's request to delay the departure some days before, that it profusely regretted in that moment."

"Oh..." Omega screwed her face into a frown of distaste. "Serves it right, I guess."

"Yeah. So when Fox ran my promotion paperwork up the NEW chain of command, there was absolutely no problem getting it approved. Especially since Pulgey was back in charge, by that point. Not a blasted one of 'em was even close to THINKING about turning THAT down. Not after everything you did. And believe me, I made sure, in the paperwork, that the full scope of everything you did was officially recorded."

"Um, wow," Omega mumbled. "Thanks, hon."

"Hey, baby, it was only fair. If it wasn't for what you did, I'd be dead or enslaved by now."

"Well, I wasn't gonna let that happen, no matter what," Omega said, jaw setting in determination, and he grinned.

"I know—but that's exactly my point. That's what a leader DOES—protect his or her people, at whatever cost. And you did, and are, in spades, and I am damn proud to be your partner, baby."

"But..." Omega began, then paused, apparently trying to figure out her wording again, Echo adjudged. He waited patiently, and finally she continued, "But...it was because...well, family..."

"Did you know that Fox halfway considers the entire Agency 'his kids'? I've heard him call us as much."

"No, but I guess that doesn't really surprise me."

"It shouldn't. So I want you to stop and think: Is there anybody in all of Alpha Line that you couldn't, or wouldn't, consider family of a sort? Okay, I know that there's at least one of the Firewall Team that still has an attitude problem, but isn't he kinda like an annoying cousin who keeps showing up at the family reunion?" Echo laughed. Omega snorted in response.

"Yeah, I guess so, when you put it like that," she agreed. "Some are closer than others, true. But all a kind of extended family, I s'pose."

"Good. And that's how many good leaders see it, so you fit in perfectly. Now, have you stopped to think about the future ramifications of that promotion?" Echo wondered. Omega frowned, patently puzzled.

"What do you mean?" she asked.

"Just this: When Fox has had enough of the bureaucracy that goes with being Director, he plans to retire from the Agency and go back to work for Entiyti," Echo explained. "He told me a few days ago that Pulgey has already made him an open offer...and Zebra is likely to go with him, as his mate, wife, whatever you wanna call it. He told me he'd already discussed it with her a few times, and she was not only open to the idea, but excited about it. So they'll head off-world and he'll go back to being the galactic traveler that he was when I met him...and maybe start a family of his own, to boot, if I know Zebra."

"Aw! That's great!"

"Yeah, it is. And you already know that I'm in line to be the next Agency Director."

"Well, yeah, of course," Omega said, nodding, a proud light in her eyes that sent a wash of warmth through her partner. "I've known that since a few weeks after y'all brought me in."

"Exactly. So...who does that leave in charge of Alpha Line, when I become Director?" Echo wondered, letting himself grin a bit, unaware that it was just as proud an expression.

Omega stared at him, expression blank, for long moments; Echo could practically see the cogs turning behind her eyes, and he realized that it wasn't so much that the answer hadn't occurred to her as it was that some part of her mind was denying it. Then she blinked, and the bright blue eyes got wide, as she was finally forced to accept her conclusion.

"Oh shit," she whispered.

"Right." Echo chuckled at her reaction. "I move into Fox's old role, and you move into mine. And probably by that time, we can move Romeo into yours."

"Echo—!"

"What?"

"I dunno if I..."

"Calm down, baby," Echo murmured, letting the hand on her shoulder rub in a soothing fashion. "All of that is still a few years off. We got plenty of time, you and me, to get ready for THOSE promotions." He slid his hand forward, letting his fingers cup under her chin, lifting her head to look into her troubled gaze. "And believe me, I'm as worried about being a good Director as you are about being a good Alpha Line department chief. But we'll have each other's backs then, just like we do now. I swear."

"Me too," she breathed. The statement was simple but succinct, and combined with the look in her eyes, told him all he needed to know about that matter.

Yeah, we got each other's backs, he thought, satisfied. *Now and always. And maybe by that time, it'll even be a life partnership. Damn, but wouldn't we make a power couple—the Director, and the Alpha Line Chief. I...could actually get into that, I think,* he decided. *It might even be fun.*

"Good. Not that I thought you might say different," he replied aloud. "But in the meantime, we can help each other get ready."

"Okay. That'll work, then."

"All right. Now let's go see about our passenger, and get him—and us—fed."

"Okeydoke. Sandwiches, pre-packaged meals, or fire up the cooker and make something fresh?" Omega asked, turning for the doorway out of the flight deck. Echo slipped a companionable arm about her shoulders.

"I dunno," Echo considered. "Let's ask Doron what he'd like."

"That works..."

* * *

The Edeptan defensive perimeter recognized the *Trojan Horse* immediately, a circumstance for which Echo was deeply grateful. The fact that it had been significantly upgraded already, with several shiploads of Pan-Galactic Coalition components, only served to deepen that gratitude.

Omega, having seen the automated recordings from the *Tour de Force*—it being an experimental spacecraft, such recordings were required, and the cameras hard-wired into the system—totally understood Echo's relief, and their spacecraft continued without hindrance through the system toward the principal inhabited planet.

* * *

By the time they reached Edeptis, it was quite late in the afternoon in the eponymous capital city, but Omega was sufficiently familiar with the *Trojan Horse*'s controls by then to be able to follow along in the process as Echo entered atmosphere, approached the same park where he'd landed before, and initiated the landing procedure. Echo hid a grin as he surreptitiously watched her watching him, realizing just how quickly his partner was catching on to piloting interstellar spacecraft.

Teknon, the Edeptan Minister for Offworld Affairs, was waiting, along with several other official-looking Edeptans, on the sidewalk just outside the multi-story administrative office building nearby...which was now bedecked with red and green banners. A crowd was gathered around the edges of the park meadow where the *Trojan Horse* sat, watching with eager curiosity.

But as the trio emerged from the hatch of the *Trojan Horse* and got a look around, a thunderous cheer went up, and suddenly posters, placards, and signs appeared throughout the gathered throngs. Teknon raised a device and pressed a button, and in response, three large banners unfurled from the roof of the administrative building—three pictures, whose images were reflected on the posters in the crowd.

One was a photographic portrait of Doron, the famed healer.

The other two...were Echo and Omega.

16

Chapter 2

"What the hell?!" Omega murmured to Echo, shocked.

"I dunno, baby," Echo muttered back, exceedingly uncomfortable at his sudden high visibility. "I'm not sure what this is all about, let alone why they got our pictures up there...or even how they got 'em."

"Oh, that is readily explained," Doron remarked, overhearing, as they walked slowly down the spacecraft's ramp toward the official welcoming committee. He paused, and Alpha One stopped beside him. "Echo, do you remember the coalition of local administrators who came through the field hospital, while you and I were using your spacecraft's power plant to manufacture the medication?"

"Vaguely, yeah, I think so. I kinda had my mind on other stuff, I'm afraid. What? You mean they got off a photo of me while they were there?" Echo wondered, chagrined. "Damn. I was so busy, I didn't even notice. That's bad situational awareness...shit."

"Indeed they did. Do not worry. You are a hero of Edeptis, friend Echo," Doron declared. "You helped to save an entire region from a terrible pandemic."

"Nah," Echo protested. "You did that, Doron."

"I could not have done so, had you not been there and offered the use of your ship's power source to run my equipment. So I am in full agreement with according you such honor."

"'Bout time," Omega breathed, surreptitiously elbowing her partner in the ribs. "You've earned a lot more than that, over the years, I'll bet."

"Meh." Echo waved a dismissive hand. "I get paid plenty well enough, and I've been promoted several times. I'm way the hell up the chain of command," he pointed out. "I don't need hoopla. And we can't 'do' hoopla on Earth, anyway."

"But this isn't Earth," Omega pointed out. "Here, they know who and what you are, what you do. And you did something really important here, even while in the middle of kind of a catastrophe of our own."

"True," Doron agreed. "And I know exactly how true, because I was at my wits' end before Echo arrived and helped. For a healer to have the medication to save lives, and be unable to access and administer said medication, is frustrating and painful in the extreme."

"Okay," Echo admitted, begrudging, "fair enough, I suppose."

"What I don't understand is why MY picture got plastered everywhere," Omega said then, "or even how they GOT it. I wasn't even here..."

"Oh, that is not hard to explain at all," Doron said. "Your picture was on the control console of your partner's ship; no doubt one of the administrators managed to copy it, while Echo and I were otherwise occupied."

"Oh, damn—I knew that photo of Meg looked familiar. Yeah, that's what they got hold of," Echo realized.

"Indeed. After all, we all knew why Echo had come for me—your condition, and its cause, Omega, was in the initial communiqué from my old friend Indak. And," Doron added, unassuming, "I may have let it slip that it was your idea, passed to your partner, that gave Echo the notion of doing what he did. I am certain that everyone was curious regarding the woman for whom this strong, honorable man traversed the Great Spiral, in any event."

"Wait, wait, wait. Ace, you had a picture of me in the *Tour de Force*?" Omega queried, startled, turning to Echo, who flushed slightly—both at her question, and at Doron's words.

"It was already there when I boarded her," he told her. "Evidently somebody got hold of some ID photo of yours, copied it, and stuck it in a corner of the console. I guess he or she—I dunno who did it—thought it would be a morale boost or something."

"Aw. And was it?" she asked, lightly touching his arm. He shot her a glance, and saw the slight smile on her face, the warmth of her gaze, and decided to allow himself the truth...and see what happened.

"Yeah, it was," he admitted. "I, uh, I kinda talked to it like it was really you, sometimes. Stupid, I guess, but...when the situation was tight, which it was a lot, it...helped."

"And he was able to show it to me, so that I might have a baseline knowledge of your appearance to work from, once I arrived and saw your condition for myself," Doron added, serene, diverting Omega's attention from further questioning, to Echo's considerable relief. "Now come. Take Echo's arm, Omega, and let him escort you the rest of the way. My people await their heroes."

Omega obeyed, slipping her hand into the crook of Echo's offered arm, and another ground-shaking cheer arose from the waiting crowd.

* * *

Once they had reached Teknon and his associated officials, Teknon quickly introduced the two Agents to his contingent, then turned to Doron.

"Rrt ta drr gbrl mm trg," he declared. Doron nodded with a smile, then bowed to the other officials.

"Trr ta gbrl trg," he replied, then waved them toward Alpha One. Teknon gave Echo a smile.

"Welcome back, Agent Echo," Minister Teknon declared. "And first welcome to your partner, Agent Omega, as well."

"Thank you, Minister Teknon," Echo murmured. Both members of Alpha One bowed in formal manner; prior to atmospheric entry, Echo had given Omega a quick primer on offworld diplomatic ritual, and she followed suit most carefully, not wanting to offend these people whose most prestigious healer had saved her life. Then Echo gestured at Omega, and she smiled.

"I thank you kindly, Minister Teknon," she told the alien being. "Believe me, I'm very glad to be here! And I could not be here—I would certainly be dead—were it not for your people, and the incredibly knowledgeable, skilled physician you allowed Echo to bring to me."

Echo pressed his lips together to hide a pleased smile at her deft, diplomatic—and wholly honest and heartfelt—response, even as Teknon beamed and Doron turned a darker shade of red.

"It is good, then, that your partner risked so much for you, to bring Doron to your side," Teknon agreed. "And we have enquired of the Pan-Galactic Council about you both, and are VERY impressed at what we were told. It is ever our honor to serve Alpha One." The other officials, who remained quiet, nodded vigorously. "Have you been told that we have an unwelcome familiarity with your assailants, Agent Omega?"

"I have," Omega confirmed. "And that we—the PGLEIA, that is, in addition to Echo and myself—intend to help protect your planet, your system, from further depredations by the Cortians."

"That is excellent; and we already have the paperwork ready for application to that organization. It only awaits yourselves as official witnesses, and then we shall transmit it." He paused. "We are not, as yet, formally signatory to the Sydys Concordat, though that is coming. It seems that Lord Entiyti, the head of the Ennead, wished to set an agreement in place sooner than such a proper signing ceremony could be arranged, in order to enable immediate aid to our system against the Cortian renegades."

"Very good," Echo said. "And that makes excellent sense."

"Yes, it does, and we are appreciative. Now," Teknon said with a smile, "would either of you object to participation in a few small Edeptan celebratory rituals? I can assure you, you will enjoy it..."

"I think you may safely participate," Doron murmured, beside Echo.

"Sure," Echo agreed then. "I'm game. Meg, you up for it?"

"I sure am, Ace," Omega said, grinning. "Celebrations sound great to me!"

* * *

The trio were led to an adjacent table set up on the grassy verge, where a small, traditional meal from the south continent of Edeptis—in which Edeptis City, the capitol, was situated—had been prepared. Media crews were set up around it, presumably televising—or whatever medium they used for broadcasting news—the event to the rest of the planet.

An involved and somewhat elaborate blessing ceremony was performed over the meal, with Doron quietly translating from standard Edeptan. Then the first two plates of fruit and some sort of cheese-like substance were given to Omega and Echo, the third to Doron. Everyone sat, then the Edeptan officials waited, watching their visitors with expectation.

"This is the breaking of fast with guests. As the honored, visiting guests, you are to eat first," Doron instructed in an undertone to Alpha One. "The fruit is drgl, and the hrgundr milk product is called grmf. Do not worry; based on my meals with you, I think you will like it, and it will not cause you gastro-intestinal difficulties."

So Echo and Omega each sampled the food on their plates, Echo trying the cheese, Omega the berry-like fruit.

"Mm," Omega murmured, tasting, "tart and sweet at the same time. That's really good."

"Yeah, it is," Echo agreed, picking up one of the berries and adding it to his sampling of cheese. "Oh damn, Meg baby, try both together. It's almost like a strawberry cheesecake or something."

"Ooo!" Omega exclaimed in delight, following Echo's suggestion.

20

"That's GOOD!"

Sounds of pleased approval came from the officials, who smiled and began to eat themselves. Another cheer went up from the watching crowd.

* * *

When the light meal—which Omega considered to be along the lines of 'heavy hors d'oeuvres'—had been completed, Teknon came to them once more.

"It would be our honor if you would take part in a ceremonial procession with us," he said with a smile. "We will perform all of the appropriate ceremonies throughout the evening, followed by a festival, and tomorrow morning, we have but the signing of the paperwork, with you as our witnesses, to become a protectorate of the Pan-Galactic Administration. Then there will be a small banquet to celebrate."

Echo and Omega exchanged glances, then nodded.

"We'd be happy to," Echo agreed.

"Then come this way," Teknon said, turning and heading toward a nearby street. Alpha One followed him, accompanied by Doron; the rest of the officials fell into the procession behind him. The watching, eager crowd surged toward the street.

* * *

"Agent Omega, in consideration of your so-recent injuries, we have provided a special conveyance made just for you," Teknon declaimed, as they arrived at the head of what was evidently some sort of parade route; the street in front of them was cordoned off, and the excited throngs now lined it. The little minister gestured at an antigrav chair, sized to human, rather than Edeptan, proportions.

"Oh, but I'm doing fine," Omega demurred.

"No, please, we insist," Teknon said, concerned. "We do not want you to unduly wear yourself; the rest of us will be on foot for most of the procession. And Lord Entiyti was kind enough to inform us, at least to some degree, of the extent of your injuries, and that you are only recently back at work from sick time."

"Go ahead, Meg, it won't hurt," Echo murmured. "After all, they made it especially for you. They want to make sure you're properly taken care of, given everything Doron did to patch you up. And I dunno about you, but I can appreciate that."

"All right," Omega acquiesced, and moved to the chair, sitting down. "Let me see if I can figure out how to fly it..."

"That's okay; I'll push," Echo said, moving to the rear of the floating chair. He 'unlocked' it, took the small handles at the back, and eased it forward. "Here we go. Minister Teknon, lead on."

Beaming, the offworld affairs minister did just that, moving to the head of the procession and gesturing Alpha One to follow him.

Behind them, Doron glanced about, watching as several large parade floats were moved into the street. He frowned, and developed an obvious case of anxiety, glancing ahead at Alpha One.

"Oh my," he murmured, "surely they did not..."

* * *

As the parade began, a huge, brightly decorated float eased into the front of the procession, in front of Teknon and the other officials, who grouped around Echo and Omega, smiling, greeting, and congratulating them. As the official group moved forward, and dancers and musicians filled in behind, the crowds lining the parade route began to cheer. More floats, of a similar design as the first, were interspersed between musical groups.

"Ooo, how pretty," Omega said, gesturing at the float. "Echo, are those some sort of Edeptan flowers, on that float? The big purple and red sculptures? They're lovely! They remind me of something from the Rose Parade, back on Earth!"

"I dunno, Meg," Echo admitted. "It sure looks like some sort of flowers to me, but I didn't really get much of a chance to look around, and the area around Doron's field hospital was kind of...decimated, from all the sick refugees camping out. But I see petals and junk, you know, the pollen stems and leaves and stuff, so I suppose so."

"The stamens and pistils," Omega supplied, "and petals, and the leaves form the calyx."

"What you said," Echo agreed, obliging. "Doin' okay there?"

"I'm fine," Omega averred. "All I gotta do is sit here and watch. It's not too heavy to push, is it?"

"Nah. I can hardly tell I'm pushing you, baby. It moves easier—and smoother—than a maglev wheelchair from the medlab. I think PGLEIA might wind up getting some seriously improved antigrav tech out of this new addition to the Coalition."

"That's good."

"You wanting me to ask somebody about the flower species?"

"Maybe later. I can barely hear YOU at times. It's a bit too noisy to try to carry on that kind of conversation, with all the people yelling and stuff. I'm not exactly used to it!"

"Tell me about it," Echo said, rueful. "I've always worked so hard over the years to stay in the background. But damn, are we out in front today."

"No shit. But like I said earlier, it's all right. Because here, they KNOW about the pan-galactic government, and the Ennead, and the PGLEIA, and all."

"Yeah, I suppose you're right. Kick back and enjoy it, for a change. Besides," he added, smiling at her as she glanced over her shoulder at him, "you've earned it, in spades, baby."

"No more so than you," she pointed out.

"Well, I'm just glad you're okay."

"That makes two of us. Glad YOU'RE okay, I mean. As opposed to what the damn Cortians had planned."

"Yeah."

* * *

As soon as Doron saw the float that led the parade, let alone the others that were added to the procession, he had become exceedingly agitated, practically hopping from foot to foot.

"No, no, no," he murmured to himself. "This will not do. It will spoil everything that they have worked so hard to set in place, and possibly force their hands, into the bargain. It could destroy it all. No, no, no."

He ran a small hand across his red face, yellow eyes blinking in anxiety as he tried to think of a way to circumvent what was happening.

* * *

Brightly colored confetti, flower petals, and streamers showered down upon the guests of honor as the parade moved forward. In the distance, past the red and purple floral sculpture, could be seen a platform rising above the crowds; Alpha One judged they were headed for it, and that the ceremony which had been promised would take place atop it.

Just then, Doron appeared at Echo's side, tugging gently but insistently at the Agent's coattails.

"Hsst! Echo! Agent Echo!" the little Edeptan healer hissed. "We must speak, you, and Omega, and I."

"Now's not a good time for it, Doron," Echo replied, trying to focus on not running into the security guard who flanked Teknon, and who was right in front of Omega's floating chair. "We can't stop in the middle of the parade, and it's damn hard to hear, anyway. We'll talk later, okay?"

"No! Later will be too late!" Doron exclaimed, hopping up and down in obvious concern, as he grabbed the armrest of Omega's chair.

* * *

"Whoa," Omega noted, seeing the healer's unusual behavior. "Echo, something's wrong, here. Let's hear him out. Doron, calm down; it's okay, hon—we'll listen. Tell us, what's up?"

"You must not go through with the second part of the ceremony," Doron informed them. "The parade, while likely embarrassing for you, is acceptable, and the first half of the ceremony is also unobjectionable, as you are already close companions. But...you MUST NOT do the second part! We must slip you away from here before that can take place!"

"It's just thank-yous and speeches, Doron," Echo tried to calm the physician. "Settle down."

"No, it is NOT!" Doron insisted. "You do not realize what is happening here! You MUST NOT perform the second half! For your own sakes! Promise me?"

"I don't understand," Omega murmured, as Echo continued pushing her floating wheelchair. "Why not?"

"Because this is a fertility rite, and the second part of the ceremony is a connubiality ritual!" Doron exclaimed.

* * *

"WHAT?!" Omega cried, and Teknon glanced back from his place at the head of the procession, seeming puzzled by the outburst.

Echo watched as Omega pulled a face, bit her lip, and offered the official a shrug and a wry half-smile by way of apology for the loud exclamation. Teknon saw Doron beside them and smiled back, nodding, apparently deciding that the three had shared a joke. Then he turned around and continued following the lead float.

"What do you believe these parade, um, 'floats' I believe you call them, to be?" Doron pressed.

"Meg thought they were pretty flowers," Echo replied, drawing his eyebrows together as he began to suspect the truth. "She wanted me to ask somebody what species they were. But they aren't flowers, are they?"

"No, they are not," Doron confirmed, flushing a deep crimson. "They are, ah, Edeptan copulatory organs."

Echo took one look at Omega's face—wide-eyed, jaw dropped open farther than he had ever seen it, face a mottled shade as she alternated between paling and blushing—and desperately stifled a monumental snort of amusement.

"Lemme guess. Because partners means mates here, right?" he asked, and Doron nodded vigorously.

"Huh?" Omega said, still confused. Then her eyes grew wider still, in alarm. "OH! You mean they think we're MARRIED?!"

"Well, uh, not exactly, baby," Echo explained, becoming increasingly concerned himself as he realized what was being planned for them. "It seems there's a semantics problem between English and Standard Edeptan, and the Binary Language Transmission didn't 'take' quite as well as I'd hoped..."

"You didn't tell me any of THAT!"

"It wasn't exactly like I had much of a chance!"

"So just exactly what DO they think?!"

"I don't know! Doron! It's YOUR turn to answer a question!"

"Agent Omega, I am uncertain as to what this 'marriage' thing is," Doron tried, "but I am afraid they do believe that you and Agent Echo are, erhm, well..." Doron glanced at Echo, uncertain of the word. "Is 'intimate' the correct terminology here, or is it f—"

"That'll do!" Echo interrupted hastily. Then the implications hit. "Waitaminit. Are you telling us that they plan on GETTING Meg and me hitched? Uh, married? Um, a formal religious ceremony uniting couples in matrimony?"

"Yes! A ceremony intended expressly for the two of you!"

"But...WHY?!" Omega wondered, shocked. "What ever gave them the idea that I...that Echo would want...I mean...?"

Echo released one handle of the floating chair to smear a hand down his face in sudden, complete understanding.

"We—Doron and me—had a little conundrum to work out like this, when I was bringing him to Earth, baby," Echo leaned down to murmur in her ear. "Like I said, there was a semantics problem. And since the original message indicated that I was coming to fetch Doron for my injured PART-NER, I'm guessing that the whole damn planet has now translated that as 'mate.' So they think you and I are, um, an item...THAT way."

"Oh," Omega said, flushing. "Oh dear. I see. So when they made the request for more information about Alpha One...they must have specifically asked if we were already married..."

"They did," Doron averred. "I have already verified this among some of my friends in the ministry. And, upon getting the word that you were NOT married, and that the Agency charter does not even have such provision, they are hereby providing such a ceremony for you, believing you will be gratified by the opportunity to make your presumed relationship 'official.' And then will celebrate your union by..." Doron broke off, and somehow managed to flush an even deeper red, "what I believe your people would call...an 'orgy'? In which, um, you would be expected to, ah, participate, if not outrightly lead..."

"Damn." Echo smeared a hand down his face again, then reversed the motion, raking his fingers through his hair. *Well, a marriage to Meg would be great,* he thought, *but not like this! And what happens later is PRIVATE, dammit! Okay, how do we get out of THIS one and maintain diplomatic relations...? You're the one with the degree in diplomacy, Echo—THINK!*

* * *

"This...wow," Omega murmured, utterly dumbfounded, and unsure what to say. "I'm...sorry, Ace."

"'Bout what?" he asked, seeming to come up for air from deep thought.

"Gettin' you tied to me, even just in the rumor mill. Not many guys would appreciate bein' romantically linked to Frankenstein's monster," she teased gently, trying to ease the tension with a bit of humor.

They just don't know I really mean it, she thought with a hidden sigh, turning to face forward once more and thereby missing Echo's wince at her joke, and the sympathetic glance that Doron gave the other Agent. *I'd love to be his wife, mate, whatever you wanna call it. Just...not like this. I want him to WANT to, not be forced into it. And that ain't ever gonna happen.*

"Okay, we gotta do something," she decided. "How can we get out of this without...?"

"Right," Echo agreed. "Causing a diplomatic incident. I've been racking my brains, but I'm comin' up blank. I just don't know the Edeptan culture well enough, yet. Doron? Can you...get us out of here, in a hurry, before things go in a direction we're not ready for? And somehow manage not to make everybody mad at us in the process?"

"Let me make some preparations," Doron said, "and then be ready to follow my lead, once we get past the actual speeches and such, which will occur up on the platform ahead, at the Speaker's Park. The matters of concern SHOULD take place at the Temple at sunset, so we have time."

The healer scampered off, farther back in the procession, and Echo and Omega both sighed, worried...

...And discouraged.

* * *

Doron made several contacts among friends in the entourage of administrators, quietly explaining the situation and asking for assistance. As understanding gradually began to emerge among those contacts, consternation, horror, and dismay filled their features.

"You mean...they are not...? They only work together? But...you think they...wish to be...?"

"Yes, I do think so, but the relationship has not progressed nearly far enough, as yet," Doron explained. "Neither is even sure the other cares in that fashion. And I am not entirely certain of Omega myself, despite how much she confided in me in the doctor-patient relationship; I THINK she does, but I cannot be sure. She simply does not talk about such things...to anyone, that I could ascertain. Even Echo did not ADMIT as much to me; I simply deduced it based upon observation and my prior, and very limited, knowledge of humans. Those two in particular are extremely reserved, so it can be hard to 'read' them. I will admit, both Lord Entiyti and Lord Levy believe it to be so, as well, for I discussed it with them both in private— but they are not totally certain, either. One thing I do know: Earth human courtship and mating is much different from Edeptan. But the fear is that, if matters progress too quickly, it may not only destroy such feeling ever developing between them, it may destroy their ability to work together as colleagues! And believe me when I say they are a PGLEIA team without parallel; destroying that team would be disastrous. So I—WE—must NOT

27

be party to forcing their hands on the matter, or it may ruin all! They need more time, and we must give it to them."

"But...Teknon is convinced that..." one began.

"Teknon is a dear friend, but he does not understand this," Doron declared, confident. "It is a semantics problem, a difference between their language and ours. I spent much time in discussion with Agent Echo over this very thing, for I made the same mistake initially. He found it...embarrassing, disturbing." He sighed. "I do not wish to hurt or anger Teknon, nor does Alpha One. He is a good man, a good minister, and deserves our honor—and they, Echo and Omega, agree. But I...no, WE, Alpha One and I...will need help in the doing of this. For events cannot be allowed to proceed as Teknon has planned it, though I—and they—know the intent was hearts-felt."

Nods of agreement began to go around the small group of administrators.

* * *

Alpha One had been concerned about how to get the floating chair up on the elevated platform, which was higher than even Echo's head, intended for those on it to be seen at large distances.

But it turned out that the Edeptans had given due consideration to the matter, and a comfortably-angled ramp, complete with roomy switchbacks, rose from ground level to the top of the platform, which was also equipped with low—for humans—railings. The pair of Agents had no difficulty getting Omega to the top, without her ever having to rise from the chair...which was, apparently, something that concerned the Edeptans.

Oh shit, Echo coded to his partner just then. *I think I just figured out WHY they want you resting and not walking this whole way...*

Why? Omega responded in kind.

Are you sure you wanna know? It's, uh, kinda risqué, baby.

Yeah, tell me what you think.

Well, remember how Doron said this whole shindig was supposed to end up in an orgy? With us leading the way? I think, given they know you nearly died, they wanted you well rested for...that. Echo pulled a face, but did so as subtly as he could, so that no Edeptans watching would notice. But he knew Omega would see and understand.

Oh geez, Omega replied, making a similar face. *Yeah, that makes sense. I take it, you never got an impression like this out of 'em when you were first here?*

Not at all, Echo told her. *Of course, we were surrounded by the dead and dying, so maybe it just wasn't exactly a priority at that point.*

I can sure understand that.

Yeah. Me too. Especially after what we just went through, you an' me.

Yep. But I never would have guessed they were so into, uh... 'doin' it,' Omega noted delicately, *based on getting to know Doron.*

Me either.

We are in such trouble.

I hope not. Be ready to jump up outta that chair and move out at a moment's notice, though. At either Doron's signal, or mine.

Roger that.

* * *

Once upon the platform, the erotica parade floats were interspersed throughout the crowd surrounding it, and Echo and Omega were given translation devices to hang around their necks, the tiny speakers resting against their heads on the bones behind the ears. Equally tiny devices, appearing to be microphones, suspended along their left jaws.

What Alpha One took to be some sort of portable media camera crews moved into position. Then Teknon stepped to a small device on the podium, smiled at the crowds and the cameras, and spoke into the device.

"Our planet's heroes have returned to us," he declaimed in Edeptan, and the translators immediately rendered it in English for Alpha One, even as the alien sound system projected it throughout the assembled audience. "The renowned healer, Krplekt Doron!"

Doron stepped forward and bowed slightly at the waist, holding his arms outstretched before himself. A cheer went up.

"The famed Pan-Galactic Division One Agent Echo!"

Echo shot a quick glance at Omega, then moved to Doron's side and bowed at the waist. Another cheer rose in the air.

Behind them, one of the other Edeptan officials quickly locked out Omega's floating chair. She threw him an appreciative look, as neither she nor Echo had expected to be introduced in such fashion.

"And his so-special partner, for whom he courageously traversed the Great Spiral, Pan-Galactic Division One Agent Omega!"

29

Omega rose from the chair, moved to Echo's side, and bowed in turn.

A thunderous cheer abruptly shook the platform on which they stood.

Echo and Omega exchanged subtle looks, and it didn't take codes or any sort of 'telepathic overlap' for them to know they were thinking the same thing: *How the hell are we getting out of this?*

* * *

"...It is our great honor to welcome these three, only one of whom is of our world, and to recognize them for their lifesaving work," Teknon continued. "Doron, whose medical skills made possible the ending of the deadly pandemic of Vegan hemorrhagic fever on the northern continent; Echo, whose presence, willingness to help, knowledge and skill made possible the manufacture of sufficient medications for Doron to use; and Omega, whose idea to use the power core of Echo's spacecraft to run the medical equipment, and which idea she communicated to her partner, made Echo's contribution possible."

Another roar went up. Various articles of clothing—not all of which resembled hats—were flung into the air. Another government official moved to stand beside Teknon, carrying three heavily-inlaid metal boxes, of a silvery sheen.

"Doron, would you step forward, please?" Teknon requested.

The little healer toddled to stand before Teknon; only then did Omega and Echo realize that Doron was considerably shorter than Teknon—shorter than any of the other Edeptans, as far as they could tell.

Do you suppose his height has anything to do with his choice of career? Omega wondered to her partner, using their secret codes.

Dunno. Could be. Maybe he had some problems as a kid, like I did with my leg, and the medical treatments to heal him made him interested in the subject.

Good idea. I wonder if we can find a discreet way of asking that wouldn't hurt his feelings.

Better to just let it go, baby. I know you got that insatiable curiosity, but this is one line of inquiry I think you better leave alone.

Eh. Good point. I'm sorry.

Not a problem. You discussed it with me in private, rather than acting on it, anyway. And you were concerned for his feelings, first and foremost. You got a good head on your shoulders. And a good heart.

I try.

You do just fine.

* * *

The Minister for Offworld Affairs took the first inlaid box, opened it, and produced a shiny, flat crystal of some translucent pink stone, inscribed upon both surfaces and suspended upon a ribbon.

"For your willingness to risk illness and death on behalf of our people, and your wonderful success in developing new treatments for ever more diseases and injuries, we present you with the highest honor our world can bestow, the Rtuwdk Medal," Teknon announced.

Omega turned and subtly coded to Echo, *The what kinda medal?*

Dunno, he coded back. *I guess there isn't a word in English for that. Maybe it's a proper name or something, such as 'Nobel Prize' or the like. Kinda like how they don't have different words for 'mate' and 'partner,' dammit.*

Yeah.

Doron tucked his head, and Teknon eased the ribbon over his head, settling the medal on his chest before presenting him with the case.

When Doron raised his head and turned toward their huge audience, applause, cheers, and whistles greeted him. Something that, to Alpha One, looked suspiciously like a pair of panties was flung onto the periphery of the platform; they noted that Doron studiously avoided looking at it.

"Doron, the podium is yours," Teknon decreed. The little healer stepped toward the microphone and smiled at the assembly.

"I appreciate this," he said simply. "But it was not necessary. It was ever my honor, my duty, and my privilege to heal. When I departed Earth, these two, and their OTHER colleagues," Doron indicated Alpha One, and emphasized the word, even as Teknon blinked in sudden uncertainty, "desired to honor me, as well. And Omega could not even find words sufficient to her gratitude. But it is as I told them then, this is what I do, heal. It is who and what I am. I see the gratefulness and joy in the eyes of my patients when once they are well, and in the eyes of their friends and loved ones, in addition. It is all the thanks I require." He waved, nodded, and fell back to the ranks of the other Edeptan government managers. Deeply respectful applause followed in his wake.

* * *

"Agent Echo? Please step forward," Teknon requested. Shooting a quick glance at Doron and getting a slight nod of approval, Echo did so. "Echo, to you goes our highest off-world honor, the Wrotfl Medal." He opened the second case, to extract a flat blue crystal, cut and engraved in similar fashion to the one Doron now wore.

But Echo was far taller than any of the Edeptans, and he immediately realized that Teknon could not possibly reach high enough to put it on him. So, before Teknon could be embarrassed by the situation, the male Agent quickly knelt before the diminutive minister, bowing his head and allowing Teknon to slip the ribbon around his neck.

As soon as he knelt before Teknon, a hush fell over the crowd, almost as if in awe. A soft "Ooo!" ran through the assembly as Teknon placed the medal on Echo's chest. Teknon stepped back with a smile, gesturing for Echo to stand and speak; the microphone which the minister and the physician had used would be unnecessary, as the translator would pick up Echo's voice, convert it to Edeptan, and transmit that translation to the sound system.

Echo drew a deep breath; he was unused to public speaking, and not at all comfortable with it. *And this situation,* he thought, *isn't helping MAKE me comfortable. What if something I say gets mistranslated? Well, lemme see what I can do here.* He cleared his throat; quiet fell over the crowd, a silence so deep that the hungry cries of a tiny baby, held by a couple far in the back of the audience of thousands, could be heard clearly.

"Greetings, people of Edeptis," he said, offering a hesitant smile. "I'm pleased to be back on Edeptis under much happier circumstances than my first visit. But I must admit to considerable surprise over this honor; I find I'm much like Doron in that regard. You see, it's my JOB to look out for others. On my world, not everyone knows there is a galactic government yet, so there is what you might call a 'regular' law enforcement system, handling everyday planetside crime, public safety, traffic accidents and such. And the regular law enforcement organizations have a motto: *To Protect and Serve.* Sometimes it's even part of their sworn oaths. And I get that, I understand it," Echo said, thoughtful. "I've been doing this job for all of my adult life, and I can't really imagine doing anything else, not any more. So when I got to Doron's base camp and saw how bad conditions were, there was never any other real consideration, but that I had to help him stop the pandemic before I took him offworld to save my par— um, Agent Omega. And while I was anxious and worried for her, I knew that Omega would have wanted, and did want, me to do exactly what I did, even if it had meant she...well. At any rate, what I'm trying to say is that I don't need thanks for doing what I considered was the RIGHT thing to do. I'm just glad Meg and I—uh, Agent Omega and I—"

A titter ran through the audience. Echo raised an eyebrow; silence fell immediately.

"—Between us, came up with a solution to the problem while there was still time—for your people, and for her."

Echo nodded, and returned to his partner's side, accompanied by a soft, impressed ululation rising around the platform.

* * *

"And speaking of whom..." Teknon said, returning to the microphone. "Agent Omega, would you come here, please?"

Omega stepped forward, but held up a staying hand. Teknon blinked, hesitating, even as he held out the medal on its ribbon, mate to the one Echo now wore.

"No, Minister Teknon," she said, and the translator picked up her soft voice, even as it had Echo's, and transmitted it through the speaker system. "I don't feel right about this. I wasn't even HERE when all this went down. You've awarded the medals to the right people; giving me one just cheapens what you've given to them."

"Meg," Echo said, the translation/sound system carrying his remark, "YOU thought of using the warp generator to power Doron's replicator, not me. And you, uh, got the word to me to do it. I wouldn't have thought of it, because a regular spacecraft's warp system doesn't work the same, and couldn't have done what the *Tour de Force* did. You earned it fairly, baby, and trust me, it doesn't cheapen ours." He gestured to Doron and himself. "Go ahead and accept it."

"I still don't feel right about it," Omega protested. *I'm giving you an opening, Ace,* she signaled, using their subtlest codes.

For what? he asked in kind.

To play the rank card. To show them we have a working relationship, not an intimate one.

Oh!

"Am I gonna have to pull rank on you?" Echo demanded then. "I will if I have to, you know."

"Pull rank?" Teknon wondered, curious...and not a little puzzled by the remark.

"Yes, Minister Teknon," Omega informed him. "Alpha One is the first team in a special department of Division One, the Alpha Line. We handle the really serious situations, the off-world terrorists, the would-be assassins, the planetary emergencies, things like that. Echo is the head of that department, and therefore he is my supervisor. We work together, but he's the boss."

"That is...interesting," Teknon noted. "But you are partners?"

"We WORK together, yes," Omega averred.

"On Earth, the term 'partnership' usually denotes a business relationship," Echo explained quietly, while signaling to Omega, *I sure hope this doesn't upset everybody.* She responded with a subtle nod. An uncertain hush fell across the crowd.

"But Echo and I are very good friends," Omega admitted, emphasizing the word.

"We are, that," Echo agreed.

"Ah! That will work," Teknon decided. Happy cries came from the assemblage.

Alpha One's gaze met and locked. *Oh, shit* was the message contained in blue eyes and brown.

* * *

In the end, Omega accepted the medal, made a few more comments in the same vein as her previous, and thanked all of Edeptis for this honor of her teammate and herself.

Then she publicly thanked Doron for the treatments which saved her life, and promised that Alpha Line and Division One would do all they could to assist the PGLEIA in protecting the Edeptan system, especially from the Cortian marauders.

Finished with her remarks, Omega returned to her floating chair, glad to have a place to sit down: She was as unused to such speeches as Echo, far less experienced at them, and her knees had felt a bit wobbly.

* * *

Teknon moved to the microphone again.

"It is our great joy to welcome the partnership of Alpha One to Edeptis. For, while Agent Echo has been here before, Agent Omega never has, and we are glad to see her here, healthy and happy beside her partner once more. It is almost sunset, and nearly time for the festivities! We would like to begin the festivities by offering a blessing of Alpha One by one of our chief priestesses. Will Alpha One please come to the podium to accept this blessing?"

Two quick sidelong looks at Doron were answered by one subtle nod, so Omega and Echo took the spotlight once more. A delicate little female, beautiful by Edeptan standards, her age indeterminate, dressed in robes made of some silk-like fabric and bedecked with live flowers and embroidered floral motifs—which, Alpha One now knew, actually represented Edeptan sexual organs—moved to stand before them.

"Kneel," she commanded in a high-pitched, sweet voice.

Echo and Omega shot another glance at Doron; again, he nodded. They knelt, Echo on her right, Omega on her left. The priestess crossed her arms, laying her left hand on dark hair, her right hand on silver-blonde hair. Then she intoned a blessing over them.

"Source of Being, we come today in joy and thanks, to celebrate your life-giving love," she prayed.

"Bless, Oh Maker bountiful and true, these Your children.

Bless everything within their dwelling and in their possession,

Bless the kine and the fields, the flocks and grain and fruit.

Ruler of the new-pink-time, we give you honor this day.

We are here; we are fertile and the land is fertile, ready to offer up gifts in Your name.

We pay You honor, our Maker, our Ruler, and ask Your blessing on this pair."

Something that the translator could not render, but that sounded very much like 'amen' to the humans' ears, rose in a murmur from thousands of voices around them. The priestess lifted her hands and stepped back.

"Come," she declared in ceremonious fashion. "Let everyone make way to the Temple of Creation."

Teknon smiled, then leaned over to speak surreptitiously to Alpha One.

"Leave the hover-chair here," he murmured. "It is not far to the Temple, and it is now desirous that you both should walk. Come with us."

He turned and headed for the ramp down to the ground, following the priestess.

But Doron and the other ministers hung back. Then the other ministers crowded into the ramp after Teknon, providing a buffer between the Minister of Offworld Affairs and Alpha One.

"Be ready now," Doron whispered. "Take off the translators and place them on the floating chair, and prepare to follow me, as soon as we get to street level. And..." he hesitated, "can you possibly crouch down a bit, so that you are not as obvious above the crowd...?"

* * *

Once on ground level, the crowds did indeed swirl around them, and Omega and Echo both hunched slightly, trying to walk with bent knees and stooped shoulders, in order to be less obvious—the majority of Edeptans only reached Echo's waist level; even the tallest barely reached the bottom of his ribcage. The Temple—a large structure of an unusual but attractive dark-red stone, looking vaguely like the Parthenon as viewed through some carnival mirror—had been apparent to them both from the speaking platform, a little more than a block and a half down the main street of the parade route, and Doron led them from the center of the street toward the sidewalk, declaring rather loudly that it would be easier for Omega to walk there.

But as they passed a little alley to the right, he caught Omega's hand in one of his, and Echo's hand in his other, tugging gently.

"Come with me, now," Doron said. "Now, while my friends are distracting Teknon. They will explain matters to him, so that he will not be upset by our actions, though he may be distressed when he realizes the truth. For now, we must escape before we reach the Temple. Matters will become...concupiscent...by then. And the people will want to see you properly mated, and then it will become even more libidinous."

So Alpha One, accompanied by the little healer, swiftly ducked behind a building from the rest of the procession. Thence they proceeded into another alley away from the crowds, and via a circuitous route that only Doron knew, the trio made their way back to the *Trojan Horse*. The park in which it sat was empty when they arrived, much to the trio's relief.

"You will be safe here," Doron told them as they reached the ramp to the hatch. "Stay inside with the hatch closed until the morning."

"Will you come in with us?" Omega wondered.

"No, I look forward to sleeping tonight in my own bed," Doron said with a smile. "My quarters at your headquarters were lovely and quite comfortable, but I am certain you both know how it is, when you have been away for a long time. My home is not far from here, in a suburb to the west. I will come in with you long enough to fetch my few belongings, and then I will go home."

"You're not gonna, um, participate in the, uh, ritual ceremonies?" Echo asked, curious. "Or are you, um, taking someone home with you, or meeting someone, or...?"

"Oh, no; I never do," the little Edeptan said, serene. "You see, when I became a healer, I took a vow to remain celibate, and faithful to my work, until such time as I choose to lay it down. At that time, I may take a mate if I desire."

"Vows? Like a monk?" Omega asked.

"Not precisely, but something like, yes. It is how the most dedicated of healers upon my world function. It is indeed part of...I think you call it theology, or perhaps religious matters. Here on my world, the ancient history is a story of hardship and privation; my race was nearly wiped out several times, in various ways—an asteroid impact, in one instance; I think you call it a 'supervolcano,' in another. A nearby supernova did great damage to the entire ecosystem. And there were more. The history of my world lists a total of at least five nigh-extinctions of my people, and possibly as many as eight. Procreation became extremely important for the continuation of the species, and thus it is now a part of our faith."

"But...then how do you, um, keep from having an overpopulation problem?" Omega asked, face turning a light pink.

"Oh, that has never been an issue, Omega," Doron said, seeming not at all embarrassed by the question. "Edeptans are relatively long-lived—I am myself fully one hundred fifty-one Edeptan years old, yet I am considered only what you would term early middle-aged—but for one thing, Edeptan years are only about two-thirds the length of an Earth year. Our star is cooler and redder, and the habitable zone therefore closer to it, than in your home system, so our orbit takes less time. So I would be...I reckoned it up for Lord Levy a few weeks ago; let me think...I am, I believe, not quite one hundred and three Earth years old."

"Wow. Older than Fox," Echo murmured.

"Yes. But only middle-aged," Doron confirmed. "I have many more years before me, Maker willing. But this factors into the next consideration, for evidently as a result of that longer lifespan, we are unable to breed as often. I suppose it is an equilibrium response, of sorts. Even when intimacy occurs, it rarely results in offspring. So..."

"Oh!" Omega said, realizing. "I get it now. So when some catastrophe decimated the population, you had to do everything you could, just to obtain a few pregnancies to offset the death rate..."

"Precisely correct," Doron confirmed her sudden brainstorm. "And thus it was that it became a part of our faith, as we prayed for our population—our tribes, our clans, as it was in those ancient days—to increase. And so it is, to this day. But I cannot take a mate and father children, and still maintain the ability to go hither and yon, into danger; it would not be fair to my family. So healers, and a few other professions with such considerations, often take vows of celibacy. It is not a universal practice by any means, but it is not uncommon. And since I have a mild genetic disorder—you may have noticed my shorter height, which is one result of that disorder—that I am working to repair, it would not be fair to produce offspring as yet, in any case."

"But that doesn't bother you? The being alone?" It was Echo's turn to ask a question.

"No, it does not," Doron said, calm. Then he offered Echo a smile. "For I know it is not for my entire life. But I have not found anyone suited to me as a mate as yet, either. I might perhaps feel differently, were that the case." He reached over, took Omega's hand, and patted it gently, all while speaking to Echo, and suddenly the male Agent realized that the physician was even more astute a student of people than Echo had given him credit for being.

He knows, Echo realized, *and he's kept my secret. Even protected the potential of the relationship, by getting us out of a situation, back there with Teknon not understanding. Damn. I take back every gripe I ever made about this guy's constant questions. Doron is a friend, without doubt.* He mentally shook his head. *And I didn't even realize it. Then again, I guess I was a little distracted.*

"Thank you, Doron, once again...for everything," Omega said, squeezing the Edeptan's hand.

"Yeah," Echo agreed. "THANK you." He met Doron's wide yellow gaze and allowed his full meaning to show in his own.

"You are both quite welcome...for everything," Doron murmured, seeming to pick up on Echo's intent. "But promise me something, both of you."

"What's that?" Echo wondered.

"Please to keep in touch? Both of you...and Lord Levy, as well, if he can manage it?"

"We will," Omega declared, beaming. "We promise."

"We sure do," Echo averred.

* * *

After Doron left with his little travel kit, Echo closed and locked the hatch while Omega closed the blast shutters, then the pair turned to look at each other across the width of the flight deck. Abruptly both let out long exhalations of relief, and two sets of shoulders slumped.

"Was that as big an ordeal for you as it was for me?" Echo wondered.

"Oh hell, yes," Omega mumbled, bone-weary from stress. "Chasin' down that Veelsi a few weeks ago didn't leave me THIS tired, I don't think." She sighed. "Listen, um, I'm sorry everybody here got the wrong idea about us. It... I, um..." She flushed. "Don't get me wrong; I'm honored that they'd think I was a suitable, uh, mate for you. I just..." Omega broke off, and Echo watched her, puzzled and hiding uncertainty. "Look. I will never get the image of your head in my gun sights out of my mind. Ever. I...can imagine what it must have looked like from the other side. Never mind all the...tinkering...that's been done." She shrugged. "So, you know, I'M honored, but...I don't expect the feeling to be mutual. And...I'm sorry." Omega dropped her gaze and stared at the deck.

"Hey, baby," Echo said softly, finally understanding what was in her head on the matter, at least in part. He moved to stand in front of her, caught her chin in his fingers, and lifted her head to face him. "It's okay. You know, I think in some ways, that whole 'your programming tried to shoot me' thing was way more traumatic for you than it was for me. From my perspective, I was watching it all go down kind of at a distance, you know, mentally and emotionally, and wondering what was going on with you, because

39

never mind the fact that I knew you wouldn't try to kill me, you weren't even moving normally. Do you know, for a couple seconds there, I actually thought someone had kidnapped you and substituted a doppelganger? We've talked about this before, at least a little bit, but maybe you never saw where I was comin' from with it." He offered her a gentle smile. "If I gotta be 'associated' with somebody, I'd say my partner is a pretty damn good choice. Nobody can accuse me of poor taste that way, for sure!"

That coaxed a wry grin out of her, and he chuckled.

"That's better," he murmured, smiling. "Now, what do you say we take these medal things off, stow 'em in our ditty bags—at least until in the morning, when I guess we better wear 'em to the signing—fix something to eat, and take some down time, you an' me? We can ditch the Suits, put on some loungewear an' get comfortable, and then we can read, or play video games on the computer, or just yak, something like that. Whatever you wanna do. And then we crash early. I'd say we've earned an evening like that, wouldn't you?"

"That sounds like a plan, Ace," Omega agreed, offering him a slight smile of her own. "Let's go change clothes first, then we can look at makin' some dinner. Or second lunch, or whatever the hell time it is now."

"Ain't it the truth."

* * *

The next morning after breakfast, when Alpha One opened up the *Trojan Horse* and looked out, the streets of Edeptis City were incredibly quiet. What few inhabitants were out and about moved slowly and stiffly, as one might after a night of far too much partying.

"Which isn't surprising, judging by some of the sounds I heard outside the ship last night," Echo decided. "Damn, but these guys are uninhibited."

"Well, I guess if your entire planet came close to getting wiped out— over and over again, at that—then there's a certain rationale to it," Omega concluded, thoughtful. "It's not exactly something you or I would ever get into, I don't think, but there's a logic there, even if it isn't to our taste."

"I suppose you're right," Echo capitulated. "And you're right about the other, too; it isn't to OUR taste. Meaning, 'Echo also says no way in hell.' But it isn't our planet, so I guess I got no cause to bother about it. You ready to go see about the official paperwork signing?"

"Yeah, but don't we need those medal things? They were gorgeous, by the way. After I went to bed last night, before I went to sleep I pulled mine out and studied it for a little while, trying to figure out what the crystal was." Omega dug the inlay box out of her travel bag, as did Echo, and they extracted the medals and donned them.

"I did the same thing. Is it natural?" Echo wondered, taking his in hand and turning it over to look at it. "I thought Doron's looked like, um, what's that stuff called...rose quartz? Only I dunno about clear blue quartz. Is there such a thing?"

"Not naturally, no. Well, there IS natural blue quartz, but the color's produced from inclusions, so it isn't transparent, it's mostly opaque. So...it looks like quartz, but it isn't," Omega told him. "This medal is a lot harder than quartz, for one thing—I checked last night. It might be a blue topaz, or even a corundum—a blue sapphire. It's a dark enough blue for a sapphire, for sure. And both topaz and corundum also come in pink hues, so that could be what Doron's was, too."

"Damn! They woulda had to come from some mighty big crystals, to make these things!"

"Yeah! Which might mean, if the rest of Edeptis is that gem-rich, Fox might get what he wanted from the Cortians, that the Cortians didn't have. If I can figure out how to run a few basic mineralogical tests without damaging it, I'll probably try that later. Otherwise, I'll wait until we get home and get the Geology staff from the Science department involved. If I determine what it is, I'll let you know, if you're curious."

"Yeah, I am, now," Echo admitted. "Because suddenly I'm thinking maybe we just figured out one reason why the Cortians kept bugging hell outta Edeptis. Okay, let's head out."

"Right beside ya, Ace."

* * *

An anxious, wan Teknon—his face was actually a dusky deep pink, rather than its usual crimson—was waiting with his equally hung-over assistant ministers, when Alpha One arrived in the foyer of the administrative building. As soon as he saw them, he made straight for them, a worried expression on his countenance.

"Agent Echo, Agent Omega," he murmured, seeming ashamed, "my friend Doron has explained the little mistranslation problem that we have had, as well as some...cultural differences...and I must apologize deeply and profusely. I assure you, we wished only to provide you with the opportunity to..."

"That's all right, Minister Teknon," Echo replied, laying a light hand on the Edeptan's shoulder. "Omega and I understand the honor you wanted to accord us."

"Yes," Omega agreed. "It's just...that's not what we are. We're really good friends, but...we're not lovers or anything." She grinned. "Now, if Alpha Two was here..."

"Yeah!" Echo agreed with a laugh. "Whole different situation, there. They ARE lovers and mates in addition to being working colleagues, and I expect it's gonna be permanent."

"And you are not angry? Either of you?"

"Nope," Echo assured him.

"Not at all," Omega averred.

"Oh, thank Maker," Teknon breathed.

"Now," Echo continued, offering a smile, "there's some very important paperwork Meg and I are here to witness."

"Right this way, then," a relieved Teknon said, turning and leading the way.

* * *

The official signing of membership paperwork in the Pan-Galactic Coalition was quick and easy. Omega and Echo both initialled it as duly-authorized witnesses, and Teknon's administrative assistants promptly transmitted it to Aleancë, the capitol world of the Coalition.

"Now what?" Omega wondered. "And where's Doron today?"

"Oh, he was not required at the signing, so he opted to remain home and set things in order, after many weeks away," Teknon said with a smile. "He said the medicinal herb beds were in much need of weeding! And the dust was nearly a finger's width deep over all his books. But he will be here soon. There will be a banquet in honor of the signing, you see—I did mention that yesterday, did I not? I hope so—and he will be in attendance. We do hope you will be able to join us as well, as honored guests. But if you need to depart, we must not keep you."

"No, no," Echo demurred. "Part of the reason we're here is to help establish diplomatic relations, so that you've got one person with whom you're already familiar, and another that you at least know by reputation,

42

to help things along.”

“Right,” Omega said, smiling back. “We’d be honored to stay and celebrate with you. I think it’s something that deserves celebrating!”

“What she said,” Echo agreed. “And then we’ll probably take the rest of the day exploring Edeptis City and getting more familiar with your culture. Then we’ll spend the night, and leave tomorrow morning. If that suits you, Minister Teknon.”

“I think it would be delightful,” Teknon agreed. “I...hope you will not mind if I provide someone to function as your guide in your explorations, and do not accompany you myself. I had rather planned to go home and...rest...after the banquet...”

“Entirely understandable,” Omega murmured, keeping a straight face with an effort. “Doron told us that the, um, celebrations, would run quite late last night, and be, uh, VERY...energetic.”

Teknon raised what passed for an Edeptan eyebrow, and Omega promptly slapped on her most innocuous expression. The Edeptan snorted, and suddenly he, Echo, and Omega were all laughing.

“I...I suppose...that is one way...to put it,” Teknon agreed through his laughter. “I commence to think I am getting a bit too old for that sort of thing any more, however.”

* * *

A fresh-faced Doron—possibly the only native, adult inhabitant of the city who was in such condition—joined them for the signatory banquet, then volunteered to show Alpha One about for the afternoon. Teknon, realizing that the three had become friends during Doron’s time on Earth, approved the plan, and retired to his own home, as the three set out to explore Edeptis City together.

“And then I should like it if you will come to my home for dinner,” Doron invited. “I harvested my gardens this morning, and visited the market for the rest, so it will all be wonderfully fresh and delicious. Besides, I wish to return some of the hospitality shown me on Earth! And...it will give us a chance to say our proper goodbyes, away from curious eyes.”

Echo and Omega exchanged looks.

“We’d love to,” Omega agreed with a gentle smile.

* * *

Edeptis City was a lovely place, full of well-manicured parks and gardens, with quaint little shops and stalls. It was quiet in the aftermath of the previous night's festivities, and the Agents found themselves among the only patrons of the various storekeepers. The afternoon and evening were enjoyable, Doron's dinner meal more than lived up to expectations, and even Echo found he was reluctant to leave Doron at its end.

But eventually Alpha One found themselves back in the *Trojan Horse* late that night, with little in the way of further business to attend on Edeptis.

Chapter 3

The silver saucer lifted smoothly off the red field of Edeptis at the hands of its experienced pilot the next morning.

The scarlet-skinned denizens of the planet on the far side of the Milky Way Galaxy cheered and held up hands in a complicated farewell salute as the spacecraft rose off the ground, headed up through the pink-tinged atmosphere.

Through the saucer's cockpit window, two black-clad figures could be seen within. The figure with the braided silver crown waved enthusiastically in response; the tall, dark-haired being held up one hand momentarily, then occupied himself with their ascent.

* * *

As the pink sky deepened to burgundy and finally to black, and the ship headed out of the system, the attractive occupant of the co-pilot seat sighed softly.

"Echo...do you ever get used to that?" Omega asked her partner in wonder, eyes glued to the view before her.

"Get used to what?" the veteran Agent looked up from the helm long enough to glance at her. She smiled, rueful, but never looked away from the view.

"Well, I guess that answers my question..."

Echo grinned ever so slightly.

"No, Meg, you never get used to going exo. No matter how many times. No matter what planet. Not really. Even when you think I'm not payin' any attention to it, I am. Just between us, it's probably my favorite part of a space flight, I guess."

"Yeah," Omega responded, still unable to tear her eyes away from the sight of the star field outside the window. "It's... I..."

* * *

She choked slightly, and Echo glanced at her in concern. The wide blue eyes shone as if lit from within as they gazed into deep space, and Echo watched for a long moment, then considerately dimmed the interior lighting so that it didn't compete with the full glory of the star field.

After all, he decided, *with Doron along, I'm sure she kept a lotta this corked up for the trip outbound...except for that one late-night dance, I sup-pose. And I haven't seen anything else on the video monitors, so she bottled it all up after that. I'll give her some time to get emotional over it, here, for a bit. She's earned it, after all these years.*

"Ohhh..." she sighed then. "I'm finally...I..."

"You made it 'out here,' Meg," Echo said gently. "The co-opted NASA astronaut is finally in space. And spanning the galaxy, no less."

* * *

"Yes. Do...do you know how long I've waited...what this means to me..." Omega whispered. She felt a gentle hand grasp her shoulder, and eventually she tore her gaze away from the stars long enough to glance into a pair of golden-brown eyes.

Echo said nothing, but he had let his expression soften a bit; there was a hint of a smile in the dark eyes, and Omega knew he did understand and was pleased for her. *More,* she suddenly realized, *he planned this! He probably set it up with Fox so that Alpha One would get this assignment, as an excuse to get me out here and show me the ropes! I mean, they could easily have handed it over to the Diplomacy department, and that's prob-ably where it OUGHT to have gone...but it didn't. Because he wanted it for ME as a...a gift. Yeah, that's it. This is his thank-you gift of sorts to me for... everything, I guess. Wahoo!* She flashed him a delighted, grateful smile, and the corners of his mouth curved upward somewhat.

"I feel like a kid in a candy store!" she declared. "Echo, can I...can we...oh, this is gonna sound silly..."

"What?"

"I've been waiting the whole trip, until it was just us, to ask this! Don't laugh, but...can we kill the artificial gravity for a few minutes?"

"Mm... I don't see why not. Just take it slow, baby. Losing your lunch in zero-g wouldn't be much fun. For either of us."

"Oh, yeah. I know about 'space adaptation syndrome'..."

"Is that what NASA calls it?"

"Yeah."

"Okay, Meg, get ready, 'cause here goes..." Echo keyed a sequence on the helm panel, and Omega felt herself float up against the seat straps. She smiled again, eager, and unbuckled the five-point harness, then pushed gently upward, drifting free. Echo swiveled the pilot's seat around, and

46

folded his arms as he watched his partner maneuver herself into the center of the open flight deck.

"Woop," she exclaimed, as her forward momentum slowed, "there's a trick to this!"

* * *

Echo chuckled as Omega, stranded in midair, flailed around and tried to figure out how to resume her motion through the cabin.

"Hang on, Meg," Echo said, unstrapping and pushing off the deck. "I'm on my way." His trajectory took him into her at an oblique angle, and he caught her in his arms and carried her along with him, up toward the overhead panel. "Reach out and get ready to stop us, baby, otherwise we'll slam into the overhead," Echo instructed. "Use your arms like shock absorbers."

Omega got them stopped successfully without hitting the ceiling, and Echo told her, "It's not a trick, so much as it is learning to judge how hard you need to push to get where you want to go. Push too easy, you get stranded—"

"Just found that out the hard way," she muttered, and he grinned.

"—Push too hard, you smack into something. Watch." Leaving her on the overhead panel, Echo pushed off, aiming for the doorway leading back into the rest of the ship. He floated gracefully, calmly, across the cabin, catching the door frame in both hands as he drifted through the open archway, then he turned and moved into a 'standing' position. Wedging his feet against the inside of the door frame to hold himself in place, Echo held out his hands in invitation. "C'mon, Meg. Aim for me, and give it a fairly good kick. I'll catch you if you misjudge."

"Oookay. We have liftoff," Omega said, gamely shoving hard off the deckhead. She moved across the flight deck toward Echo at a reasonable speed, and he caught her as she neared.

"Much better," he told her. "Grab the bulkhead." He pointed to one of the handholds positioned here and there, for just such times as this, when the artificial gravity was off—whether intentionally or not. Omega held the grip in one hand and the edge of the doorway in the other, as Echo continued, "This one's more advanced. Watch me." He allowed himself to drift slightly forward, then kicked off the wall, headed back to the pilot's seat. Just before reaching the chair, he tucked, somersaulted and twisted around almost like a high-diver, then relaxed and reached back behind him to catch the chair's arms, pulling himself down as he settled gently into it. "There. Your turn."

"You want me to do that?!"

"Yep. Just like in the gym, Meg, only slower."

"What if I accidentally kick the helm controls?"

"You won't. I won't let you." Echo got up and maneuvered between the seat and the console, bracing himself. "Okay. The controls now have a meat shield named Echo. Ready?"

"Yeah. Here I come," Omega said, kicking off the door frame. She sailed smoothly across the cabin toward the pilot's seat.

"Now go into your tuck. Flip...and twist at the waist...that's it," Echo instructed, and Omega obeyed. "Now come out into a sitting position..." He reached out and put his hands lightly on her waist, guiding her the last couple of feet down into the chair. "There. Good, Meg. Training you is a piece of cake. You always catch on fast."

"You know why, don'tcha?" A grinning Omega looked over her shoulder at her partner. Echo cocked his head to one side, inviting her to elaborate. "Have you ever noticed how I can always find you in a crowd, even from a distance, even when you're disguised?" she continued.

"Yeah...but what does that have to do with how fast you pick up on something?"

"It's the same reason behind both."

"Which is?" a curious Echo asked.

"I study how you move."

"Move?!" Echo reiterated, startled. "How *I* move??"

* * *

"Yeah. When you're trying to teach me a new move, Echo, you nearly always demonstrate it first, just like you did a minute ago. So I watch really close and try to analyze what you're doing in real-time, during your demonstration. Then I try to duplicate it as near as I can," Omega explained. "In the process, I've learned to recognize you by your body movements."

"So...is that also how you can almost read my mind in a fight?" Echo asked, patently intrigued.

"Mm...partly, I guess. What's your excuse?" she grinned.

"For what?"

"Reading my mind in a fight."

"Who says I'm not?" he deadpanned, and she rolled her eyes, then stuck out her tongue. Echo raised an eyebrow at her cheek.

* * *

"Okay. Just for that, let's see how well you do on your own, then." Feeling mischievous, Echo grinned. "I want you to start right where you are, move over into the co-pilot's seat, then back to the port navigation station—you can sit in the chair there, or not. From there, go straight across the flight deck to the starboard bulkhead, then back up to the center of the deckhead, and return to the pilot's seat. Throw in three somersaults—your discretion. And here, let me define 'somersault' as a rotation about one or more axes, not necessarily the strict tumbling definition."

"Oh boy," Omega muttered, lost in thought and apparently, per Echo's judgement, reviewing the 'course' in her mind.

"Relax," Echo said quietly, sobering. "Otherwise, you'll get uptight and ricochet all around the cabin. We're supposed to be havin' fun with the training, here." Omega grinned at the 'ricochet' imagery, and Echo knew his remark had had the desired effect. She nodded then with a sly smile.

"All right, Echo, watch this!"

"Good thing we don't have any beer, then," he deadpanned again, and Omega stuck her tongue out at him again, adding a raspberry for good measure.

Omega pushed off almost straight up, flipping upside-down to plant her feet against the overhead, then shoving lightly off and repeating the maneuver to settle momentarily in her own chair. A strong push against the seat's base sent her soaring past Echo toward the navigation console, pirouetting slowly as she went.

"Roll axis," Echo noted. "That's one."

Echo sat back down in the co-pilot's seat and strapped in, grinning in patent enjoyment as he watched his partner improvising.

* * *

Omega lightly contacted the wall above the nav console with her hands, letting her body crumple slowly against the bulkhead. As soon as her feet contacted the bulkhead, she kicked off powerfully, headed across the flight deck, body straight, arms extended outward to the side as she spun three times end-over-end.

"Pitch," Echo observed. "That's two."

Timing it perfectly, Omega let her feet rotate around just as she reached the far bulkhead, and she stood on the wall for a split-second. Then Omega flexed at the ankle and knee, twisting slightly as she did so...and seconds later, she was spread-eagled and spinning across the cabin.

"Whoa, flat spin yaw," Echo said, raising an impressed eyebrow. "Three. Nice job."

Moments after, she knelt upside-down on the overhead in the center of the deck.

Grinning down at her companion, a mischievous Omega proceeded to 'crawl' across the overhead until she was directly above the pilot seat. Then she did a slow, carefully-controlled handstand on the ceiling, and pushed off lightly with her fingertips, 'seating' herself in mid-air and crossing her legs as she drifted softly down into the chair. As soon as her posterior touched the seat, Omega grabbed the seat arms to halt her momentum, then folded her arms and turned her head, looking at Echo, expectant.

Echo met Omega's gaze with a straight face, but she caught the twinkle in his eye as he turned back to the helm, and she smiled, pleased.

"All right, Meg," he said, "we've escorted Doron home to Edeptis, done all the required diplomatic stuff, and we're well out of the Edeptan system. The rest of this trip is all yours, Ms. Assistant Division Chief. We got two full Division weeks for the entire trip, and only a couple days gone. So by the time we get home a little over a week and a half from now, you'll be a certified Division One spacecraft pilot. Strap back in, so I can turn the grav back on, and get ready for your first full-up lesson in warp navigation."

* * *

The ex-astronaut with the doctorate in astrophysics caught on as rapidly to warp navigation as she did to weightless 'navigation.' After a quick review of technique, her partner set her several brief courses to calculate and program, and checked them carefully when she was finished. Echo found Omega's calculations to be flawlessly executed, as he had expected. Consequently, using her programmed courses, it didn't take them long to skip about, all over that galactic quadrant.

"Okay, Meg, so far so good. Pick our next stop. However far you want to go, so long as we stay inside our galaxy. It would take way the hell longer than we've got time, to try to go outside it."

"It's possible to go outside it?" she asked in surprise.

"Well, yeah," Echo pointed out. "There's nothing to stop us, as such. The science and tech don't change. It's just that, once you get past the little satellite galaxies close in, the distances become so great that it takes an awful long time...like, months to years, depending."

"Ooo."

"Yeah."

"All right. Mm, lemme think...oh! Wanna do an actual first contact? You made comm contact with the Ganotians on your way to get Doron."

"No, we'd better not. I know for a fact that, before we left, Fox was working on setting up a first contact through the Diplomacy department. Sugar was heading up the team. As it was, this mission—or, well, the 'returning Doron to his homeworld' part—was gonna go to them, too, but I snagged it for us. I thought Doron would appreciate it, for one thing; and I knew you'd have a blast, for another. Then we found out that the Edeptans expressly WANTED you an' me to come, so as far as Fox was concerned, it was a done deal."

"Aw," Omega murmured, offering a grateful smile, and Echo felt his cheeks heat.

"Um, yeah," he admitted. "Besides, Fox and I talked it over, and... Well, okay, I'll 'fess up. Grabbing that mission for Alpha One was my way of saying thanks for...for everything you did during that whole Cortian mess, Meg. That said, I still had to convince Fox, an' sentimental thank-yous weren't gonna cut it—even if he DID agree with me—so I pointed out that, as the newly-appointed assistant chief of Alpha Line, it only made sense to do this, and get you as much experience and as many certifications as possible, while we had a good chance and plenty of time to do it." He shrugged. "See, I understand that whole 'I'm not ready for this' thing we talked about the other day, you and me. 'Cause I was there myself, once upon a time. So by the time we're done with this, you'll be as ready as I can help you be, at least for anything to do with spaceflight."

* * *

"Oh..." she murmured, all the while thinking, *I knew it! I knew it! That's so sweet!* But she hid the full extent of warmth it produced, allowing him instead to see only the happy gratitude. He smiled at her expression, then continued.

"Yeah. So I pitched it as, 'We'll return Doron, and help expedite any paperwork for PGLEIA membership, and then I'll take Meg on a marathon training session. When we get back, she'll be certified in anything to do with a spacecraft that I'm able to do.' And Fox went for it without hesitation. For that matter, Pulgey approved of the idea, too, not that he had any real need to provide input. But I think it made Fox feel better about accepting the proposal; he wanted to, but didn't want to appear partial or something."

"All right; I can see that."

"At any rate, we want this to go well, which is one reason I was so worried about diplomacy on Edeptis," Echo explained, earnest. "So we do NOT want to interfere with Sugar's handling of the Ganotian thing, or show up unexpectedly, or anything like that—not after co-opting the other mission that was going to Diplomacy. Just...no. We don't want to risk screwing it up for him, or pissing him off."

* * *

"Oh. Okay, good point, and I'm all right with that. Sugar's definitely a friend, and he really helped us out on the whole Cortian thing, so...yeah. Um, he didn't get, like, upset or mad or anything, that we were taking Doron home...?" Omega wondered, forehead scrunching in worry.

"Nah. I actually went to him, one on one, before I approached Fox with it. I explained the whole thing, including how much you wanted to get into space, and how much Alpha Line needed you to have the experience. And Sugar said it was a good plan, and to go forward to Fox with it, especially since Doron knew us—it made more sense for us to do it, in the circumstances. And that was before we got the input from Edeptis, which pretty much clinched it."

"All right. That's all cool, then. So 'most anything BUT the Ganotians, huh?"

"Right."

"Okay. Let me think a minute," Omega said, brow furrowed. Suddenly her eyes lit up and she smiled. "Oh yeah!"

"What?"

"Does it have to be a planet?" she asked.

"No, I suppose not..." Echo cocked his head to one side, curious.

"How 'bout lettin' me get up close and personal with the Orion Nebula? Or, well, the entire molecular cloud complex, really...but kinda focused on the Great Nebula."

"Hm. Yeah, it oughta make for a good postcard. 'Dear Romeo and India: Nice trip. This is the view out the window of our room. Wish you were here. Omega and Echo.'"

Echo was rewarded by a peal of laughter, then Omega caught her breath, and Echo grinned. Before she could ask, he answered. "Yes, I can get a picture using the sensors. But I'm not gonna send Romeo and India a postcard."

"Aw. Okay." Omega grinned in reply. "I guess I can live with that. Actually, I wanted to blow it up, frame it, and hang it in my living area. I thought it might make an interesting counterpoint to the Orion Nebula photo I made with my telescope, that's hangin' in your living area next door..."

"Ooo. You're right, it would. We can do that. But it won't be as easy a navigational calculation as the stuff I assigned you."

"What do you mean?"

"You got a pretty big volume of space there for your target destination, so you'll need to figure out where in that volume you actually want to end up. And if you want a photo of the nebula, you'll need to consider field of view, angle, and perspective, when you select that point to end up." He looked at her, and cocked his eyebrow. "Think you can handle that yet?"

Omega scrunched up her face, considering.

"Yeah, I think I can," she decided after a few moments. "A lot of that should be just basic trigonometry, so it ought not to be too hard. I'll give it a shot, I think. As long as you're willing to answer questions, or help me if I get stuck."

"That goes without saying, baby. This is a training session, not an exam or something. The certification exam comes later, though, and I will be giving one, so just remember that. Okay, work out where you wanna end up, pull your coordinates for that locus, and start calculating," Echo ordered.

"Ooookeydoke. Let's see here..." Omega bent back over the pilot's console terminal and began work, as Echo watched over her shoulder. Given all of the parameters she had to consider, it took longer than her other exercise calculations, because she had to work out angles, multiple-vector resultants, and the like. But her scientific and mathematic background stood her in good stead, and in short enough order, she had finished—without having to ask for help—and glanced up at Echo, questioning. He nodded approval.

"You're a natural at this. Go ahead and download it to the navigation computer." Echo sat down in the co-pilot's chair and strapped in. "Okay. Ready when you are."

"All right...aaaand 'Engage'!" Omega said, initiating the navcomp. As the spacecraft jumped into warp, she turned to Echo and grinned. "I've been dying to use that..."

Echo rolled his eyes.

"I'll just bet you have," he muttered, then snorted.

* * *

The saucer dropped out of Alcubierre warp a couple of tens of light years away from the core of the nebula proper, entering station-keeping mode. This distance was far enough to enable the diffuse cloud to be readily seen, its colors and details brightly lit by the Trapezium cluster of very hot, very young stars at its core. Yet the tiny-by-comparison spacecraft was still quite thoroughly embedded in the far larger Orion Molecular Cloud Complex—a titanic star-forming cloud of gas and dust that was several hundred light years in diameter, and which also included, among numerous others, the Horsehead and Flame Nebulae as part of its overall volume. From end to end and side to side, the cloud complex stretched the entire length and width of the constellation as seen from Earth. And the *Trojan Horse* currently nestled in its midst.

The pilot of the *Trojan Horse* looked up and gasped, sapphire-blue eyes wide.

"Ohhh...Echo...look at it...it's beautiful...!"

Echo divided his attention between the glowing gas cloud outside the window, and the rapt face beside him. "Mm-hmm. Yes, it IS beautiful," he murmured, without specifying. "I take it you'd like to stay here for a while?"

"It...it'd be nice. I'd kind of like to explore it, you know, run a sensor scan and stuff. I know the Coalition Sciences people probably already have tons of data, but..."

"But you want to find out for yourself."

"Yeah." Omega gave him a sheepish grin. He nodded and offered a slight smile in return.

"That works," Echo said, glancing at his watch. "And before you ask: No, it's not a stupid suggestion. Since it's a star-forming region, and the cloud complex is really huge, there's always new discoveries being made around here, so I'm sure the other scientists aren't going to mind a brief, informal survey by a colleague who happened to be in the area. We need to stay away from the Trapezium Cluster at the heart, though. You know it's got a damn big black hole in there, right?"

"Oh, that's been confirmed? I knew it was suspected, just on the basis of the dynamics of the cluster," Omega noted. "Some o' those stars are flyin' every which way."

"Well, it's not in the open science literature on Earth, but yeah, it's a known navigational hazard for the nebula region," Echo verified. "Galactic astronav folks mapped it out, like, decades ago, I guess. Maybe centuries. Way before there was ever a Division One Agency, at any rate. Not to mention, most of the main stars of the cluster are putting out some serious hard UV and x-ray radiation. So we'll want to keep our distance to avoid being fried. This ship is good, but its equipment's not nearly hard-core enough for THAT kinda exploration."

"Yeah, I knew that." Omega nodded affirmation. "That's why I picked HERE to park and sightsee."

"Okay, that's good. But it's getting late, and I dunno about you, but I'm tired..."

"Yeah, I hate to admit it, but I am."

"No shame in that, baby; we've been busy today. All right. Tell you what—I'll set up the sensors to get your picture, then we can program 'em to take your data, and let it run all night, while we snooze. Watch what I'm doing, now." His fingers danced over the console for a few seconds as she watched closely, then he hit a button. "There goes the start of the picture scan. Did you get how I did that?"

"Yeah. You set the field of view, the depth, the rate of scan..."

"Right. Good eye. Now, what kind of data do you want, Meg?"

* * *

A little while later, the image was done; the data take was well under way, the digital autopilot was station-keeping, the alerts and alarms were set...and Omega was still sitting at the console looking out. Echo laid a hand on her shoulder as he stood.

"Time to get some sleep, Meg."

She glanced up, startled.

"Oh. Sorry, Echo. I was...out there." She pointed at the main viewport. Echo nodded once, unsurprised.

"All right. I'm bedding down in the port sleep station, like I did when Doron was aboard. No sense in moving our luggage around at this point."

"Not that we've got much. One bag each."

"Yeah, but I got my shaving kit stuff all set an' spread out in the head, already."

"Okay. No argument, just sayin'. I'll take the starboard side when I go to bed, then."

"Meg..." Echo paused until he had her full attention. "Don't stay up all night, baby. It hasn't been that long since the Cortian slavers tried to... fry you under their ion drive," he said quietly.

"Yeah. But you took care of 'em."

"Taking care of YOU is what I'm trying to do now. It's only been a couple-few weeks, Meg. And we had a damn busy day today as it was. The medics are good, and Doron's procedures are great, but don't overdo it, okay?"

"Okay. Good night, Echo."

"G'night, Meg."

Echo headed out of the flight deck. Behind him, Omega returned her attention to the celestial view.

* * *

A couple of hours later, Echo woke and saw a shaft of light coming in around the edge of the sleep station door. He glanced at the wall chronometer.

"Aw, hell, Meg." Slightly irritated, he crawled out of his bunk and into his trousers—having stuffed the annoying pajama pants into the very bottom of his duffel bag after arriving at Edeptis—then he headed for the flight deck. He stopped in its doorway.

Omega had evidently prepared for bed as she had promised, but hadn't been able to resist one last look at the nebula before retiring, for her hair was unbraided and loose, spilling about her shoulders, and she was wrapped in a pajama top and her new favorite robe—a black jacquard silk concoction discreetly trimmed with lace and acquired shortly after Christmas, a late-delivered holiday gift from Fox and Zebra.

But the figure slumped in the pilot's seat was sound asleep, a happy smile on the relaxed face.

Echo moved over to the helm and stood for a moment, hands on hips, looking down with a tolerant—perhaps even affectionate—smile at the beautiful woman bathed in the soft multicolored light filtering through the cockpit window.

Hm, he thought to himself, and quickly checked the security video for the flight deck.

But it gave no indication that Omega had done anything other than it appeared: prepared for bed, come back out for one last look, stayed too long, and fallen asleep in the chair. *Though,* he decided, *I'd bet my entire next paycheck that she's DREAMING about dancing through all that.* He cast a swift, appreciative glance of his own out the main port, at the glorious cloud of gas and dust visible there.

Then he slipped his arms under her, picked her up and carried her into the starboard sleeping berth. A moment later Echo emerged, quietly closed the door, and entered the port sleep station, dimming the cabin lights as he went.

* * *

But the relatively insignificant incident had affected him, nevertheless. Putting Omega to bed before returning to his own bunk had stirred the feelings that Echo was trying hard to control, in order to be able to properly train her to be as competent an interstellar pilot as she was at everything else she did. Echo was a consummate professional, tough and resourceful, but the fact remained that, over the holidays some months earlier, he had suddenly realized he had fallen in love with his partner. When she nearly died saving his life only a few weeks previous, he had discovered just how deep that love ran.

And, after putting Omega to bed, he found his senses full of her, his mind dwelling on her scent, the feel of her in his arms, the silver gleam of the silken hair.

So as had become usual for him in recent months, Echo fell asleep thinking of his partner.

And as usual, thinking became dreaming.

* * *

They were strolling through Central Park, hand in hand, chatting about whatever came to mind, taking welcome time off at the end of another successful mission, when a giant, iridescent green slug appeared in front of them, flanked by easily a dozen giant canaries and rainbow lorikeets, all in body armor. The avians promptly drew down on Alpha One, taking them captive. Echo was tightly bound hand and foot, immobile; but the creatures had a different intent for his partner. He watched, helpless, as Omega floated into the air, some five feet off the ground, her body frozen in place by the telepathic gastropoid.

"Echo, help me!" she cried. "I can't move! Echo!"

"Hang on, baby," he called, struggling against his bonds. "I'm coming!"

"Hurry!"

"Doin' the best I can!"

Just then, one of the giant canaries stepped forward, a flamethrower strapped to its back, the nozzle in hand, and aimed it at Omega.

"NO!" Echo cried.

"Ace! ACE! HELP ME! I CAN'T MOVE! Echo! No! NOOO!"

"STOP IT!" Echo yelled. "What do you want from us?!"

"Death," came the answer from more than two dozen throats and minds. The Cortian pressed the trigger. A jet of flame shot from the nozzle and engulfed the woman he loved, igniting her very skin.

Omega began to scream.

With Echo's voice.

* * *

Echo startled awake in his bunk, sitting bolt upright, his nude body drenched in a cold sweat, his heart pounding. The sound of his own voice crying out in horror died in his ears, and he was abruptly thankful for sound-dampening technology aboard the Division One vessels.

Shit, he thought, dismayed, as he switched on the light. *Here I go with the nightmares again. I already talked to Eta about this. He said I just needed time to learn to cope with the memories, and told me how. But I could sure use some uninterrupted sleep. His techniques might actually work better, then.*

He sat for a few minutes, schooling his pulse and respiration back to something approximating normal levels, and trying to put the memory of his partner's burning body out of his mind. The fact that he'd seen it happen in real life, not so very long ago, made it difficult.

Well, hell, he decided. *I'll just slip into the next berth and check on her. She won't mind, and it'll make me feel better...not to mention seeing her, healthy and whole, will help erase the memories a little. At least for now.*

Echo rose and, rather than taking long enough to don his trousers, simply wrapped his own robe about his naked form before he slipped out of the compartment, headed across the passageway to the other berth compartment.

* * *

I better not turn on any lights, Echo thought, as he entered the compartment where his partner and companion slept. *I don't wanna actually wake her up. I just need it to register on my subconscious that she really is okay.* He paused, giving his still-sleepy eyes a chance to adjust to the low light levels; each berth compartment had the equivalent of a soft orange nightlight, which provided just enough illumination to navigate the area without running into anything, and which had been designed to produce light in wavelengths that would not unduly disturb humanoid sleep patterns.

There she is, Echo thought, spotting the platinum blonde head resting quietly on a pillow on the bottom right-hand bunk, where he had placed her only a few hours before. He tiptoed over on cold, bare feet to stand beside her bunk and look down at her, allowing his gaze to take in everything: the long, almost-white blonde hair, which she had taken out of its customary braid in order to sleep more comfortably, and which now spilled across the pillow like spun silver, gleaming softly in the low light; briefly he remembered the feel of it against his bare chest when he had carried her off to bed. The sculpted planes of her cheekbones; the strong, firm line of her jaw; the pert little nose, all branded themselves on his memory in that moment. Closed eyelids fanned long, pale lashes across the tops of her cheeks.

Her athletic, curvaceous body curled in a loose fetal position beneath the covers, on her side, facing him; one hand was tucked between her cheek and the pillow, childlike. Briefly, he recalled what that body felt like in his arms—as he carried her unconscious form, as he figure-skated with her, as he danced with her. What it felt like under his hands as he massaged taut muscles, loosening her body after injury.

Damn. She is so beautiful, floated through his mind, and suddenly he was thankful the Arcturan ambassador had verified she WASN'T an actual telepath. *At least not yet,* he amended. *Who knows what that magnificent brain of hers will do in the future, though? But maybe by then, I'll have figured out how to get her attention, the way I want it. And hopefully, she'll want it, too.*

Without thinking, he reached out and brushed a stray wisp of hair from her face.

* * *

At the whisper-light touch, Omega woke in her bunk, promptly coming to the realization that someone was in the compartment, standing over her, looking at her. She grunted in surprise, then recognized the faint silhouette.

"Echo? Is that you, hon, or am I dreaming?"

"Yeah, it's me. Did I wake you?"

"Um, I dunno. I jus' realized somebody was watching me, an' I guess it woke me up."

"I'm sorry..."

"'S all right. I'm a little confused, though, 'cause the last thing I remember is the flight deck, an' lookin' at the nebula..."

"That would be because you fell asleep out there, and I had to get up and carry you back to your bunk."

"Oh. Sorry."

"It's all right. I kinda expected it, to tell the truth."

"Everything okay?"

"...Yeah, I guess so."

Omega pushed into a seated position and studied her partner's body language; it was still too dark in the room for her to see his face very well, at least until she woke up more, and he had thoughtfully NOT turned on the compartment light and thereby blinded her. He stood close to her bunk, not quite leaning over her, but his upper body was definitely bowed toward her, the shoulders slightly rounded, as if he were subconsciously sheltering her from something. Suddenly she understood.

"You dreamed about it again, didn't you?" she asked shrewdly. "The Cortian thing."

Echo sighed, then sat down on the edge of the bunk opposite her. The aisle between bunks was not wide, so he was still near enough to touch. *And,* she considered, *he seems to want it that way, right now.*

"...Yeah," he finally admitted. "I, uh...I kinda had to..." he shrugged, "come see that you were okay." He hesitated. "That doesn't upset you, does it? I know it's stupid..."

"Nah. I get it. And it's not stupid at all. Truth to tell, I've had a couple nightmares of my own, since that whole mess went down. Dreams where I didn't get there in time or something, and I got to watch YOU get killed." Omega threw the covers back and swung her bare feet off the bed, pressing her tiptoes against the cold deck as she tugged her pajama top into place, to avoid inadvertently flashing her partner.

"You too?"

"Oh, hell yeah, Ace."

"But...it wouldn't be as strong an image for you, would it...?"

"The hell you say!" Omega exclaimed. "Remember, the visions were real enough to touch, Echo. And completely realistic. Would you like for me to describe it?" she offered, crisp. "I can, you know. I can tell you how your body blistered, the skin cracking and peeling, the smell of roasting flesh, the—"

"Enough." Echo held up a hand, averting his face. "It's too soon after the damn dream for that kinda detail, baby. I believe you. But..."

"But what?"

"Well, it's just...you've never come looking for me in the middle of the night. At least, not that I know about."

"No," Omega sighed. "I've thought about it a few times—really wanted to, at least twice, but..." It was her turn to shrug.

"But...?"

"Well, while you've had to take care of ME a couple times after various missions, you were kinda more, um, independent after YOU got shot Christmas Eve," Omega pointed out. "Yeah, I looked out for you an' junk, but you never gave me permission to come into your bedroom to check on you...and you were really specific, when I came into the Agency, about how not even partners were allowed in bedrooms unless permission was given..."

"Oh. Well, uh," he began, and Omega could have sworn Echo's shadowed face darkened, likely flushing, "you, um, know why, right?"

"I kinda figured you slept in the buff, Ace," Omega pointed out. "But it isn't like I haven't seen naked guys before. Astronaut corps and stuff, ya know. When you're putting on a spaghetti suit to do EVA training, ya tend to show some skin."

"Whoa. Did YOU...?"

"Um," this time Omega felt her own face heat with a blush, "not if I could help it. They had special rooms for those of us who wanted it, and I generally wanted it. But I still ended up getting some pretty detailed looks at several of the, ah, more unreserved male astronauts. Couple of the females, too, for that matter."

"Oh. Yeah, I guess so."

* * *

Shit, I didn't think about that, Echo thought in consternation. *And astronauts are the pick of the litter, and stay in hella good shape.* He stifled a sigh. *Oh well.*

"...You're not gonna, are you?" she asked then, seeming somewhat discouraged.

"Huh? Gonna what?" Echo asked, confused at the dichotomy between his thoughts and her question.

"Give me permission."

"Meg! Baby, you assumed correctly about my, uh, sleepwear, or rather, lack thereof. I'm not, I mean, if you come in and I've, I dunno, kicked off the covers or something..."

"If I did, and you had, I'd simply spread 'em back over you, Ace," Omega said with an audible sigh. "I swear to you, I wouldn't melt, and I wouldn't break—and neither would you—and I sure wouldn't take advantage of the situation, if that's what you're worried about."

"NO! I know you wouldn't! It isn't that..." Echo broke off. *It's that, if I wake up and you're standing right there, I got no way in hell to hide how I feel about you,* he thought, realizing her feelings had been hurt by what seemed to her like a rejection. *But how can I explain it to you without giving away that very thing?*

"What is it, then?"

"Look, Meg," Echo tried, "I get that you've seen your colleagues naked before. But I'm not...I'm not like that. I don't..."

"Oh!" Omega said, sitting up straighter, and seeming a bit surprised.

"You'd be embarrassed?"

"Oh, HELL yeah."

"But..." Even in the semi-darkness he could see her scrunch her forehead in puzzlement. "Why?"

"Why what?"

"Why would you be embarrassed? I mean, look, Ace, between the gym and running around our quarters in our off hours, and, well, having to staunch blood from bullet wounds and alien beastie gouges and crap like that, I've already seen a good bit of you," Omega pointed out. "And as far as I can see, you got NOTHING to be embarrassed about."

"Huh?"

"You're built, hon. Most people consider astronauts the cream of the crop, but every one that I've seen in the altogether would probably turn green with envy if he got a look at you without your shirt."

"Well...minus the battle scars, maybe..."

Omega shrugged.

"None of 'em are disfiguring, Echo. And they're not very prominent at all, really. YOU see 'em, but the rest of us, not so much. I understand where you're coming from, though, 'cause I was scared when they brought me outta the regen tank, that...well, I figured everything was working, and I felt okay, but I didn't know what I LOOKED like. So I get it. But you need to know something. See, you may think of 'em as scars, but some of us look at 'em and see your trophies. They mean you WON. You fought like hell, and you came out on top. You're still standing, you're still working, healthy, in one piece, doing your job. At the top of the Agency, no less. To be honest, most of the time, I don't even notice 'em—there's really not that much TO notice. But when I do, that's what I think. I think, 'That's my partner, Mr. Badass, and that right there's the mark of how tough he is'...and I feel proud of you. And proud that I'm your partner."

"Oh..." He studied her face, which was open and straightforward... and, it suddenly registered on him, proud. *She means it. Damn. She really means it.*

"Yeah, I do mean it," she declared, having evidently managed to read his expression in the dim light. "I don't think you have anything to be ashamed of or embarrassed over, if I—or anybody else—were to get a look at you without any clothes."

"...Okay, if you say so," he allowed.

"I say so." She grinned at him.

"But there IS still something that I'd be embarrassed over, if you walked in and...you know."

"I can't imagine what."

"Aw, Meg, don't make me have to spell it out for you."

"Hey, I'm not the one who wandered in here, ya know," she teased. "I was sound asleep until you came in. You should be glad I'm conversing coherently."

They both laughed, and it eased the tension Echo felt, just a little bit. He decided to try to give her a hint as to the cause of his discomfort. *And if she figures out it might be more personal than my generic explanation, well,* he considered, *maybe her reaction will tell me if I got a snowball's chance on Mercury with her.*

"Look, baby," he began, "one of your degrees is in biology, right?"

"Yeah. So?"

"How much do you know about, um, what happens to men—I mean physiologically—when they're asleep and, uh, dreaming?"

"Wha— oh! You mean, um, the guy bits?"

Echo smeared his hand down his face, not sure whether to laugh or groan. "Yeah, baby, that's what I mean. And guys do dream about that shit, an' we do react as if it was really happening. So if you come in, and I'm havin' a particularly, well, let's just say a really GOOD dream, it could get damn embarrassing, damn fast. Especially if I happen to wake up with you leaning over me, like you just did with me." *Never mind that I'd almost certainly be dreaming about YOU,* he added mentally—but did not say aloud. *And then to wake up and find you there...that could get complicated in a hurry.*

"Oh..."

"What?"

"Well, I guess I can see it," she admitted. "I just thought..."

* * *

I thought it was because you just flat didn't want me there, she finished her sentence mentally. *I couldn't blame you for that, all things considered. And probably part of your reluctance, especially given what you just spelled out, is the ooky-factor of waking up and finding your very own personal, genetically-tinkered, telepathically-programmed assassin stand-ing right there. Gotta make you think, 'Is she here to kill me this time?' at least for a second.*

"Aw. C'mon, Meg," Echo reproached her, gazing directly at her face, and she grasped that she'd let too much of her emotions show in her expression, and he'd deduced the rest. "It's got nothing to do with that whole Slug shit. You should know that by now."

"Doesn't it?" Omega murmured, stifling a sigh. "If you say so, Ace."

"I do say so. As somebody recently told me." He stood. "Look, it's late and I didn't mean to wake you up. Lemme go back to my berth and let you get back to sleep. You're okay, and I'm far enough out from the dream now to probably sleep like a log once I go back to bed."

"...Okay," Omega answered, stuffing the feeling of rejection into a corner of her mind. *I guess it was time to divert my attention,* she decided.

Abruptly Echo stepped toward her, reached down, and caught her chin in his fingers, gently tilting her head back to coax her to look up at him.

"All right, look," he said, studying her face in the dim lighting. "I'll think about it, and if I can figure out how to make it work, you'll get that invitation. If it's half as much of a relief for you as it was for me just now, I'll do my best."

"You could always wear pajamas."

"Actually, no, I can't. I've tried wearing pajamas, or at least sleep pants, a couple times since you became my partner, for the sake of propriety an' junk. 'Cause, see, X-ray didn't give a rat's ass, and was as apt to run around our quarters buck-naked as I am—as I WAS—and Romeo was even worse!"

"Whoa," Omega muttered, as she instantly pictured three strapping, handsome men of different ages, stark naked, wandering around their joint quarters.

* * *

"Aw, c'mon, now," Echo grumbled, hearing the remark. "Quit that."

"Quit what?"

"Your eyes just got bigger than they were when you were staring at the nebula outside. Quit picturing the lot of us in...you know." Echo studied her face as it flushed. *I suppose that's promising,* he decided. *It isn't like she ever knew X-ray, and I know she's not interested in Romeo. Maybe I*

65

shouldn't be tellin' her to quit imagining ME like that.

"Um, sorry," Omega apologized, dropping her gaze. "I just...hadn't thought about it before, and it kinda..."

"Yeah, I know. I painted a mental picture for you. Sorry about that. Or, well, let's just say that as long as you're not drooling too badly, I can put up with it, I guess." He gave her a wicked grin as she shot a startled glance at him; she flushed even deeper and glanced away, into shadow...but not before he saw the slightly shy but wholly mischievous half-grin that curved her lips. *Yesss!* he thought, before continuing aloud. "That's better. Anyway, like I was sayin', I've tried wearing some sorta pajamas. But the things just chafe the hell outta me. They get wedged in the most damn inconvenient places, and I feel like I'm all tied up. I flat don't sleep. Or if I do, it's only for an hour or two at a go, until things get all twisted up again."

"Even silk?"

"Even silk."

"What about plain ol' boxers? There's not so much material there to get all twisted up."

He raised a thoughtful eyebrow.

"Now that...might work," he decided. "Gimme time to think about it and try a few things once we get home, and I'll let you know."

* * *

"Okay. Thanks, Echo."

"You're welcome, Meg. Just realize something for me, okay?"

"What's that?"

"It isn't you. It's about me trying to be a gentleman FOR you."

"Oh." That put matters in a completely different light, and Omega offered him a tentative smile. "All right, Ace. I'll remember that."

"G'night, baby."

"G'night, hon."

And Echo vanished through the compartment door.

Much to the relief of both members of Alpha One, the rest of the sleep period was quiet and uninterrupted.

* * *

"Okay, Meg," Echo told his partner the next day, "I sent your picture and data back to Headquarters. They'll download it to your computer account, and it'll be waiting when we get back. You can look at it in the ship's

66

computer later today if you want to. But right now, it's time for another lesson." He sighed. "Dammit," he muttered under his breath.

"Oh? What's that?" Omega asked, curious.

"Come on with me," Echo said, heading aft with something of a resigned air and motioning Omega to follow. They entered the aft deck and Echo opened a locker, pointing to its contents. "Here you go, Meg. This one's yours. Fox has 'em custom-made for each agent. I assume you already know how to put on a spaghetti suit?"

"EVA?!" she exclaimed.

"Of course. If something breaks, you need to know how to go out and fix it." Echo watched with amusement as Omega tried valiantly to restrain her exuberance. "I'll wait outside. You go ahead, strip down, and put on the life support undergarment. It's a little different from NASA's, but it's pretty obvious how, so I shouldn't need to help you. If I do, let me know and I'll see what I can do, without embarrassing both of us too bad. Yell when you're done. It really takes at least two to get the pressure suit on, especially the first time." As the door closed behind him, he heard a muffled whoop of joy, and he grinned, then settled back against the wall of the passageway to wait.

"Echo!" he heard after a few minutes. "Ready for the pressure suit."

"Okay," he responded immediately, coming back into the aft compartment, where he studiously avoided staring at the shapely figure in the skintight mesh, lest he become too distracted. "Take the upper half of the outer suit and use the hook-and-loop strips to fasten it to the bulkhead over there. Good. Now let's get the bottom half on you..."

* * *

"You ready, Meg?" Omega heard over the headset in her 'Snoopy hat' as she stood in the airlock. She turned and looked at the white-suited, helmeted figure beside her as she adjusted the small backpack that held life support and maneuvering units.

"Echo...I've prepared for this my whole life. How much readier do I need to be?" she asked, voice soft, unaware that her eyes were shining like jewels. He nodded in understanding, and got down to business.

"Tether latch?" He clipped his suit tether to an airlock anchor.

"Tether latch..." Omega imitated his action.

"Cycling airlock."

"Copy. Cycling airlock..." Omega responded, as Echo hit the control. The hatch behind them closed, the pressure dropped to as near zero as the airlock's pumps could manage—which was awfully close, all in all—and the outer airlock hatch opened.

* * *

The pair stepped to the edge of the deck, and a fair-skinned face fairly glowed, the blue eyes shining brilliantly. Echo waited patiently, silently, for a moment, in order for the wave of excitement that he knew was flooding his partner to subside; then he held out a gauntleted right hand, open, palm up.

"Ready for egress?"

"Ready for egress," Omega replied, and laid her left hand in Echo's. He promptly wrapped his fingers firmly around hers.

"Just take one step and push off, Meg. I've gotcha," he said, encouraging. "On three. One...two...three."

* * *

Two space-suited figures stepped forward and floated out from the saucer's hatch, tethers unreeling behind them. The taller of the two, in solid white, turned to check his partner, who had wide, distinguishing black stripes circling sleeves and thighs.

"Well?" Then Echo chuckled. "Slow down, Meg, you're gonna pull a neck muscle."

"No, no, no!" She grinned, still twisting her head about in every direction. "Gotta see it all, right now!"

"Comfortable?"

"Uh-huh..." she replied absently.

"No disorientation?" Echo verified, ignoring the lack of comm protocol in the circumstances. *Because, for just these moments,* he understood, *she's overwhelmed. And it's just me. I'll let it slide.*

"Well, it feels a little funny in the pit of my stomach if I look down past my feet," she observed, doing exactly that.

"That's normal. You'll get used to it in a little while."

"Okay."

"Meg, I'm gonna let go of you now."

"Ohhh...why does this feel like the time Romeo taught me to ice skate?" Omega said, shooting him a rueful grin.

"Look at it like this—you can't fall down, this time." Echo grinned.

Omega snorted in amusement, then sobered.

"I know, but..." She tried to shrug in the spacesuit; it came out as an awkward shifting of her shoulders and arms. "I guess it depends on your definition. I...don't wanna screw up, Ace. Not on an EVA. It's a good way for somebody to end up dead, and I know it."

"You scared? I won't let go if you don't want me to."

"No...no, it's okay. You're right. It's time to solo."

"Attagirl. Here you go." Echo released her hand, and Omega drifted a few feet away. "Now use the backpack controls at your wrist to come back to me. Light touch. That's it," Echo encouraged as Omega gingerly maneuvered herself back to the white figure with the black 'E' inscribed on its left breast. "Okay, now turn, head straight out from the ship about twenty yards, and return upside-down."

Omega followed instructions, moving about twenty yards away from Echo, then he saw her stop and begin station-keeping with her back to him.

"Meg? Everything okay? Meg??" Echo maneuvered out to his partner to check on her, and found her just floating, totally overwhelmed by the unobstructed view of the nebula. "Meg?" Echo asked softly.

Her mouth opened, but nothing came out; her eyes welled with tears.

"Meg, don't cry," Echo cautioned. "That's not a good plan in a spacesuit in zero-gee. Come on, let's turn around and go back to the ship."

"It's...it's like I'm...in it..."

"You are. Well, in the edge of it, anyway. And definitely in the middle of the cloud complex overall. Now, let's finish your EVA training, and then you can dangle at the end of the tether for a while and just look."

"...O-okay. Let's see—um, upside-down, headed back, you said. If I pitch one-eighty, that oughta do it." Using the backpack jet controls on her left wrist, Omega slowly, reluctantly, spun forward about an axis of rotation through her hipbones, until she faced away from the nebula. Echo used his own controls to turn around at the same time. Just then, a shocked—and delighted—gasp escaped Omega as the galactic core became visible to her left, off the starboard side of the hull of their spacecraft. The corners of Echo's lips turned up a bit in affectionate response, as he realized what had happened.

"Good. You chose the simplest maneuver," Echo approved, verbally ignoring the loud gasp. "How could you have done it otherwise?"

"Um...uh. Uh, yeah," she murmured; he grasped that she was rapidly gathering her briefly-scattered wits, and waited patiently. "Yaw and roll of one hundred eighty degrees each."

"Right. Now let's head back."

* * *

As the Alpha One team moved slowly back toward their ship, Omega looked up at her partner from her—relatively—inverted position. "Wow."

"Wow what?"

"I always knew you were a pretty tall man, Echo, but from down here you look like a pro basketball player."

* * *

"Perspective. Football, actually. But not pro." Echo was dismissive. "I'm tall enough to play basketball, but I liked football better."

"Football?"

"Yeah. I played in school. I was on the offensive line."

"Were you good?"

"Pretty decent, I guess. Our team was, and some of us as individual players were, ranked in the state. Well, the team was number one in the state in our division."

"'Some of us players' included you, I'd bet."

"Um, yeah; it did."

"What rank? And what position?"

"By the time I was a senior, my main position was blind-side tackle," Echo told her. "We had two quarterbacks, one a southpaw an' one not, so which side I played depended on which quarterback was in for that game. But I also played tight end sometimes. Coach said I had good hands. And I was fast, with these long legs. Damn, that was a long time ago." He shook his head inside his helmet.

"Nuh-uh. That ain't past-tense, Ace," she informed him. "You still ARE fast, damn fast! And having seen what you can do with weapons in hand, I believe every word your coach said. You didn't say what your state ranking was, though."

"Oh. I was number 2 in the state as a tackle. Coach wanted 'em to rank me as a tight end, too, 'cause he figured I'd be top dog in that position, but if I remember right, there was some kinda rule against it. And we didn't get to choose which, because I was initially listed as a tackle, and then Coach added tight end, and...anyway. They picked what they considered my primary position and went with it. I had a football scholarship to college," he admitted, "but then the First Contact happened, and...well, life kinda turned upside-down there, for a while."

Omega paused for a split-second, evidently in respect for his losses, before responding.

"You...all right?"

"Huh? Oh. Yeah, I'm fine. Like I said, it was a long time ago."

"Okay. Hm. You know, I like football. Used to play touch football with some of my cousins, even."

"Really? That's cool. But knowing you, somehow I'm not surprised. Cousins, huh? Where are they now, then? You've said you don't really have any family left, 'cept for that one distant cousin..."

"Oh," Omega said, her voice flat. Echo hid a wince.

"I shouldn't have asked that one, huh?"

"No," she sighed. "It's okay. I just...that was a bad year. It was back when I was a sophomore in high school, and Huntsville is in what's called Dixie Alley, second only to Tornado Alley itself for number of tornadoes per year, some of 'em really big and strong—only you can't see 'em comin' too much because of the terrain and the trees. And my cousins—Mom was an only child, so they were all on Dad's side—my cousins were mostly all from this one little town a little ways outside Huntsville—just a wide spot in the road, really. Three houses, all right next to each other, 'cause family. And that spring, there was a LOT of rough weather..."

"Aw shit," Echo murmured, suddenly understanding. "I get that picture. Wow. You've been to more funerals before you were thirty than some elderly folks I've known, baby."

"...I know." She paused. "At least no aliens had anything to do with THAT one. Unless you're gonna tell me that gastropoids have weather-control technology, or telekinetic powers strong enough."

"Nope. To either one. And, while I know a couple of alien races who do weather control tech, none of 'em can gin up a tornado. Might be able to bust one—emphasis on might—but not make one. Let alone control it. So no worries there. Let's go back to talkin' football," he offered, looking to divert her mind from painful memories. "Oh, and you can flip right-side up now."

"I...can get behind that idea." Omega nodded, and offered him a somewhat wobbly, but nevertheless grateful smile. They paused in their progress back toward the *Trojan Horse* long enough for Omega to right herself; it was entirely possible to do so while continuing the translation maneuver, but Echo didn't want to risk her getting motion-sick on her very first spacewalk.

"So okay," he continued their sports discussion. "You're pretty familiar with the game, if you've played touch football that much."

"Yeah. I think I coulda played full-on with 'em, but the adults didn't want us to. Said it'd be more like rugby than football, especially without all the pads an' junk."

"Well, they were right about that. Y'all coulda got hurt pretty bad, tryin' to play it full-contact without the gear."

"Prob'ly so, but it sure was fun. We'll have to go see a game sometime, you an' me, Ace."

"Okay, it's a date. Sounds like a really good way to spend an afternoon or evening, though I guess we'll have to wait until this fall to do it. What sports did you play in school?" Echo asked.

"Me?" Omega said, raising her eyebrows. "Mm, I actually wasn't much into playing team sports in school, although I did play a little softball. First baseman. Tennis, racquetball. Ran track one year. Blew out a knee. I was on crutches for a while. Same year as the tornado. Like I said, bad year." She sighed.

"You've got a bum knee? I've never seen you have trouble with it."

"No; the doctors said they'd never seen anything like it. A torn meniscus normally doesn't heal too well on its own. 'Course, now you and I know why. Human genetics don't allow for that kind of healing, but alien genetics do."

"At least, when it's been combined with human," Echo amended, and Omega attempted another shrug inside the spacesuit, this time with a bit more success as she learned how to manipulate it.

"Whatever."

Echo glanced at her in concern, then said, "Okay, Meg, let's do a couple more maneuvers, then we'll try some work with the toolkit..."

* * *

A knock came on the doorframe of Fox's office, and he looked up from his interminable paperwork. Alpha Two stood there.

"You rang, boss-man?" Romeo said, offering an infectious grin.

"And we answered," India added.

"Come on in, you two," Fox said, waving them in with a smile. "It seems I have some mail for you both."

"Huh?" both members of Alpha Two said at once, surprised.

"Some mail for you got delivered to me, and I thought I'd better ensure you saw it," Fox reiterated with a smirk. He hit several keys on his desk's virtual keypad, and one of the big wall screens lit up with a spectacular image of gas and dust clouds, brilliantly illumined by the forming stars within.

"Oh, hey, wow, India, look!" Romeo exclaimed, pointing. "Ain't that th' same astronomy whatsis picture that Meg took with 'er telescope, an' Echo got framed on 'is wall?"

"Yeah, it is," India agreed. "What's it called, again?"

"The Orion Nebula," Fox filled in. "There's a message that came with the image."

He hit another series of keystrokes, and contrasting text popped up in the bottom of the image.

Dear Romeo and India:

Nice trip. This is the view out the window of our room. Wish you were here.

~Omega and Echo

"Gee, I wonder what those two are doing," India said, snickering.

"Well, I'd lay money there's really two messages there," Romeo said with a grin.

"Oh? What, and from who?" Fox wondered. "Because I got the same 'postcard.'"

"Th' picture's from Meg," Romeo decided, "though I bet Echo helped her get it, maybe even did it himself, if she don't know th' equipment yet. But it 'uz her idea to send it back to us."

"Keep going," India said.

"Th' writing's from Echo, 'cause he prob'ly told Meg he'd do it—or not," he grinned, "actually prob'ly not, knowin' him, an' then went an' did it anyway; but his tongue is so deep in his cheek, it's pokin' a hole through."

"Knowing the two of them, I think you nailed it," Fox declared with a matching grin.

"Me, too," India agreed.

All three burst out laughing.

* * *

With training finished, a highly-satisfied Echo hung back near the air-lock and let his partner have a little time to herself at the end of her tether. He contented himself with watching silently as her stiff, straight posture slowly relaxed, adopting the weightless-neutral position, spread-eagling slightly and bending at knees, elbows, and hips. One hand extended, fingers spread, as if to touch the glowing colors of the nebula.

Without realizing it, Echo also relaxed into a similar position, a slight smile gracing his handsome, chiseled features as he watched his partner, the woman who was so dear to him, living the dream she had had for so very many years. Somewhere inside was a deep, heartfelt warmth borne of gratitude for being privileged to be her companion and teacher in those moments—the one person in the universe present at the fulfilment of that dream, able to watch and enjoy her responses.

And this, right here, right now, he fully realized, *exceeds her adult dreams by a huge margin, because NASA doesn't yet have interstellar flight capability; hell, they're still workin' on manned solar system. So the dream I'm gettin' to see fulfilled, right this instant, right in front of me, is the big one, the one she had as a little girl, before she got taught the meaning of the word, 'can't.' She's up close and personal with her very favorite astronomical object—damn, she's sittin' in it! There aren't too many people in the galaxy, let alone on Earth, lucky enough to bear witness to a thing like that.*

After several moments, his own gaze followed hers out, into the depths of the gigantic nebula, and he, too, lost himself in a silent contemplation of its beauty.

After a while, Echo glanced at the suit chronometer in the visor's heads-up display, raised an eyebrow, looked again, then sighed noiselessly. He hit the control panel on the back of his wrist and used his backpack maneuvering system to make his way to his partner. Once beside her, he looked at the blissful face, then followed the blue gaze outward once more, into the enigmatic depths of the gas cloud.

* * *

"It's gorgeous, isn't it?" he murmured then. "So beautiful."

"Yes...and mysterious." Omega paused, then offered a quotation. "'The most beautiful thing we can experience is the mysterious. It is the source of all true art and all science. He to whom this emotion is a stranger, who can no longer pause to wonder, and stand rapt in awe, is as good as dead.' Albert Einstein." She shook her head inside her helmet. "Nobody's ever claimed I was dead. Not where this is concerned."

"No." Echo paused, then added, "Nor in any other way I can think of."

"You either."

"No, I guess not."

They floated side by side, silent for long minutes, simply looking.

"Thank you." Echo's tone was low, but contained a profound gratitude.

"For what?" Omega asked, startled.

* * *

"X-ray, my first partner, often made a point of reminding me to stop and...just look. You know, the whole 'stop and smell the roses' thing? But... you show me how." Echo let his quiet voice reflect the thoughtfulness of his musings. *Meg is as necessary to my...to the partnership...* He broke off and mentally shook his head. *No, Echo, be honest with yourself—she's as important to ME as X-ray was, maybe more,* he mused. *They both make me stop and think.*

"How do I do that?" she asked, watching him, puzzled.

"By being you, mostly. That blasted omnipresent curiosity, wonder, and enthusiasm." He met her eyes and grinned to take any unintended sting out of the teasing remark, then sobered. "You're a damn good partner, Meg. And a...a damn good friend."

Omega smiled, a pleased, almost shy expression, and the male Agent felt warmth suffuse his being. But before his reaction could give him away, Echo abruptly became all business again.

"I hate to do it, Meg, but—"

"It's time to go in, isn't it?" she realized, disappointment obvious.

"Yes. Past time for it, actually, baby."

"Okay. I guess you're glad." She sighed. They began maneuvering back to the ship.

"What makes you say that?"

"I thought you hated EVAs." She glanced at him meaningfully, and he knew she had heard and understood his earlier curse, on the flight deck that morning.

"Well," Echo hedged. "There are EVAs, and then there are spacewalks from hell. This one was in the former category."

"Good. I'm...really glad you didn't hate doing this with me, Ace. Because this was...it was..." Omega was at a loss for words.

"It was special. I know. That's why it was in the former category. Begin ingress."

"Beginning ingress," Omega replied, as they entered the hatch together and cycled the airlock closed.

* * *

"We were out there that long?!" Omega exclaimed when she saw the helm chronometer.

"Yep," Echo answered, grinning. "All day."

"No wonder I'm so tired and hungry..."

"Uh-huh; me too. We missed half our meals for the day, and never noticed until now. And spacewalks aren't exactly light on energy expenditure to begin with. Let's go down into the galley and fix some dinner, and make it a big one. Then I'm for bed pretty soon after. Working in pressure suits for that many hours is quite a workout."

"Sounds like a plan."

"And, Meg?"

"Yeah, Echo?"

"Try not to fall asleep at the helm tonight, okay?"

"Oh..."

Chapter 4

The next day, Omega began looking over her newly-obtained data, trying to decide what to check out first; Echo wanted her to get a taste of system, and even planetary, exploration in addition to everything else, and this was as good a location to scout as any. There would be plenty of relatively new systems to study, and that made for lots of exploratory training opportunities. Consequently, they had sectioned off the area into a three-dimensional grid—each section of which was a cube—and Omega was studying them, one after another, looking for anything new or anomalous.

She had been studying the sensor data for some little time, while Echo alternated between reading the novel he'd brought along and surreptitiously watching his partner, a hobby he'd developed in recent weeks, as he tried to learn to read her even better. The fact that he secretly enjoyed looking at her didn't hurt in the least.

So he saw when she scowled, chewed on her lip, then stared off into space, thinking. Finally, she glanced over at him. He pretended to have been reading.

"Ace?"

"Mm?"

"Am I bothering you?"

"No, why?"

"Could you come look at something, then? I'm not quite sure what to make of it. I mean, I THINK I do, but it might just be wishful thinking. I'd like you to tell me if I'm all wet or not."

"Sure, baby," Echo agreed. He laid aside the book, rose, and moved to stand behind her chair at the navcomp station, studying the data over her shoulder. "What's up?"

"Look at this. It's a planet."

Echo stood beside her and studied the readouts for a moment.

"Yep, you got a planet. Did you check the—"

"Yeah, I did. Look here."

Trying to hide her excitement, Omega entered some commands, and the display toggled to the navigational charts and maps. Echo studied those a bit longer, then leaned forward and put both arms around his partner to key in some adjustments to the display settings. He knit his brows, considering the result, then toggled back to the sensor data. Another quick flip between the displays served to confirm his suspicions.

"Yeah, baby, I see it. And you're not all wet. That planet isn't on the charts. You've discovered a new world. Maybe a whole new system."

"Cool," Omega said with a huge grin, no longer trying to hide her excitement. Echo gave her a grin of his own.

"All right. That means we're initiating PGLEIA new-planet protocols," he told her.

"Which are?"

"We get to go check it out. After sending a standard notification to PGLEIA HQ and Division One HQ." He hit a few more keystrokes, bringing up a form. "There. Fill in the blanks and send it, then take your seat in the pilot's chair."

"Roger that," Omega replied, focusing on the form.

* * *

From low orbit—which Omega rather neatly executed all on her own—they did a more detailed survey of the planetary surface. There were several large continents, surrounded by plentiful oceans; sensors indicated said oceans were comprised largely of saline water, and the continents were heavily forested in shades that ranged from deep teal through bright blue and into purple and violet shades. But as Omega told Echo, considering the central star was a blue-white spectral type A, with peak intensity in the blue part of the spectrum, that was hardly surprising. Canyons, mountain ranges and the odd volcano, visible from orbit, spoke to active tectonics—this was emphatically a living planet in every sense, not a dead world.

"I'm not seeing anything showing on the sensors but plant life, Echo," Omega noted then. "The readings are kinda weird on some of that, though."

"Yeah, I'm seein' it too. I wonder..."

"Well, it looks safe, anyway. At least according to the sensors." Omega shrugged. "Ready to set down and have a good look around?"

"I'm not sure if it's THAT safe, Meg," Echo warned his partner. "We're gonna take this nice and slow. Make sure to follow all the unknown-planet protocols. You've studied 'em, right?"

"Oh, yeah."

"Good. I want this by the book, and then some."

"Um, okay, if you say so, Ace," Omega responded, puzzled. "So... blasters, just in case there's something the sensors aren't picking up?"

"BOTH blasters. For both of us. AND our Winchester & Teslas," Echo decided. "And maybe some tachyon splitter rifles, to boot."

"Aw, now, Ace, that's just overkill."

"I don't think so, Meg. Trust me on this. This ain't my first rodeo, baby."

"Good point. Okay."

* * *

Much of the newly-discovered world's land masses were heavily forested, some of which was almost jungle-like. But with coaching from Echo, Omega managed to find a suitable clearing, not too far off a coastal shoreline, and land the *Trojan Horse.*

"That wasn't half bad," Echo encouraged. Omega made a face.

"It was kinda bumpy on the set-down," she noted.

"That was your very first landing, Meg," Echo pointed out. "If all you had was a few bumps, you did damn good. You know how the old adage goes— 'Any landing you can walk away from—'"

"'—Is a good one,'" she finished.

"Right. Leave the running lights on."

"Oh? How come?"

"Because that's a thick forest out there, almost a jungle, and it'll help us spot the ship from a distance."

"Oh." She obeyed, setting the craft into a landed stand-by mode. "I still don't understand why we didn't just land on the beach. It's only about a klick thataway, and it was nice and broad and flat." She waved her hand in the general direction of the shoreline.

"With no idea how deep the sand was, or how high the tides come? Remember, there's two big moons."

"Oh. Well, yeah, okay. I really need to get my head outta the Earth paradigm, I guess. Damn, I got a lot to learn about this stuff."

"Patience, baby; that's normal for first-timers, and I completely expected it. That's why we're training you on all of it. And don't sweat it. You're getting there, fast, and doing really good. And don't be afraid of looking stupid—because you don't—or hesitant to ask questions, because you won't know if you don't ask. I want you to LEARN on this trip, not get wrapped around the axle about looking stupid, merely because you've never experienced it before. Just trust me to guide you through it, okay? 'Cause I will."

"Okay, Ace."

"Now, you verified the air?"

"Yeah. Breathable, nothing toxic, high enough pressure. Interesting ratio of oxygen to carbon dioxide, but considering the level of plant life, and with little to nothing in the way of animals, it's about what I'd expect, speaking in terms of the biology."

"Good. Let's grab some rifles from the armory stowage, and go have a look around."

"I'd rather just use my blasters..."

"What do you mean?"

"Well, it takes both hands to use the rifle, and it's longer and less maneuverable than blasters," Omega explained. "I mean, they're even longer than a standard bullet-type rifle on Earth. I CAN use one, and will, if you insist. But I feel more...um, what's the word...versatile, I guess, with both blasters in hand." She mimicked spinning left and firing, then spinning right and firing, before remaining in place and firing left, then right, in rapid sequence. Echo raised an eyebrow.

"But they aren't as powerful as the rifles, and they don't have the range," he pointed out. "And the rifles' power supply lasts longer without charging."

"Yeah, but if I can get off better than twice the number of shots with the blaster in a given time, what difference does it make?" she asked. "Dead is dead, ya know? And surely we're not gonna be out so long we run our BLASTERS down." She shrugged. "It's okay. You have a reason for wanting to use the tachyon-splitter rifles, so let's go with those. But unless there's living rocks out there—which we didn't see signs of, on the sensor data—the blasters are gonna go through the plant life like the proverbial hot knife an' butter."

Dammit. I hate it when she makes a point like that. But rookie, she sure ain't, so I need to trust HER gut, too. Echo drew a deep breath and sighed. "I expect I'm gonna regret this, but...okay, we'll go with just the blasters."

"And Winchester an' Teslas," she noted, patting the small of his back.

"That'll do...for now," Echo decided.

* * *

As they stood at the hatch looking out at the blue-tinged jungle, Echo turned to Omega.

"All right. You've never done this sort of thing before, but I have, a couple times at least. So I'm gonna take the point for now, until we see just what we're getting into."

"Why are you so worried, Ace? There's no animal life here," Omega wondered.

"You're not a Doc Smith fan, are you?" Echo asked with some dark amusement.

"Um, no, the books are outta print, so...well, I've read a couple of the Lensman books, but..." Omega shrugged. "They're hard to get my hands on. Why?"

"Oh, if you were, you'd probably recognize the situation, is all. Remind me to loan you my copies when we get home. Look, Meg, it's like this—just because it's all plant life doesn't mean there's nothing intelligent, or that there's no predators. Remember Preeg, the little Dendroid kid?"

"Yeah—oh. The Dendroids were sentient, and mobile...and they were plant-based."

"Right. And to a limited extent, they're omnivores. And the larger, um, well, I guess technically they're herbivores, but hey—PREDATORS, I guess we'll call 'em, on the Dendroids' homeworld are big and strong and mean. And even Earth has carnivorous plants—several different species. And some of those move. Pitcher plants don't, I'll grant you, but Venus flytraps, sundews..."

"True. Yeah, okay. I get it now, Ace. Just because it's all plants doesn't mean there's NOT something out there that would like us for lunch."

"Exactly. Good. I figured it was just a matter of shifting your paradigms."

"Yeah, pretty much. You'd think, since I was an astronaut, I'd already be thinking like that, but frankly, we were always thinking more in terms of finding bacteria and stuff."

"No problem, and I understand. Follow my lead now, and we should be fine."

"Right behind you."

He hit the button to cycle the airlock, and brought up both of his blasters.

Beside him, Omega drew and hefted one of hers as well.

They stepped out of the hatch.

* * *

Echo led the way out, easing down the ramp to the ground as he looked around, studying the terrain and foliage, looking for anything that seemed 'off' to him. Both blasters were drawn and in ready position.

Behind him, Omega chose to wield only one blaster, holding it in a firm isosceles grip, pointed obliquely at the ground, ready to raise at an instant's notice. She released it with one hand long enough to click the spacecraft's remote, closing the hatch behind them.

"Good plan, and glad to see you thought of it without my prompting," Echo murmured without looking back, hearing the beep, followed by the soft whir of the hatch cycling closed. "That way, nothing can get curious and go looking inside.

"Right," Omega agreed. "Which way you wanna head?"

"Mm," Echo considered, looking around, "let's go this way. We'll have a look at that beach from ground level, and probably get a decent idea of whether or not it would be a better landing site than where we are."

"And if it is, do we come back and move?"

"Maybe. We can talk about it, anyway. It might be easier for you to land and take off from that beach. I know you were worried about a gust of wind blowing you into the trees."

"Oh, HELL yes."

"Okay, let's go. Keep your eyes peeled every which way for threats, as well as new discoveries."

"Copy that."

They set out.

* * *

"Ooo. Nice beach," Omega decided, as they stepped out into the greenish-gray sand and looked across the surf. The system's white-hot sun beat down overhead, and Echo turned to glance at his partner. "What?" she asked, seeing his scrutiny.

"You put on your sunscreen before we left the ship, didn't you?" he asked.

"Yeah, why— oh, I get it. A blue-white star of spectral type A2 V will fry my behind in about two minutes, right?"

"Yeah. And I'd really rather not have you badly sunburned. I mean, the atmosphere will attenuate some of it, but still." Echo stared at her hair. "Lean down and let me see the top of your head."

Omega bent.

"Good. No hair parts or any scalp showing," he observed.

"No, I thought about that, and re-did my hair to avoid it. And I put that special heavy-duty sunblock on my ears and nose, too, on top of the regular sunscreen. I even put sunscreen on the backs of my hands and my neck."

"And the rest of you is pretty covered up. Okay, we should be good."

"What about you?"

"Remember when I hit the head just before we landed?"

"Yup?"

"I put it on then. I may be half-Apache, but I can still sunburn. Especially under a different kind of star."

As they walked, Omega kicked at the sand.

"Looks like it's firm enough. Hard to tell how deep, but it's pretty packed."

"Yeah, it is. I'm still not sure I'm keen on setting a multi-ton spacecraft on it, though. If it's got a high interstitial water content, we could have a mess." He waved a hand at the ocean before them.

"Well, good point, I guess. I'm still trying to figure out what it's made out of. It's gray-green, which makes me think marble-type, but too dark, and too hard and sharp for a limestone or calcite, which latter is what most marble is, anyway. But it isn't quite a lava sand, like on Hawaii. I'm wondering if it's a feldspar or the like, maybe with a pyroxene or serpentine in it, to give it that green tint."

"Look over there," Echo pointed into the distance, in a direction roughly local magnetic north from their position, the beach running approximately north-south in that area. "Some sort of reddish rock outcrops, embedded in all the greenish-gray stuff. What do you make of that?"

"Ooo." Omega paused, shaded her hands, and stared in the direction Echo pointed. Then she turned in a slow circle, surveying the terrain. "Oh, there we go," she said, pointing inland. "Mountain range, and look waaaay on off that way—see the itty-bitty plume over that peak?"

"Uh-oh," Echo murmured, following her directions. "This is a volcanic area."

"Yeah. So we probably ARE on a lava-based sand of some sort, and those red boulders are likely a slightly different chemistry lava flow outcropping. Be prepared for the ground to move a little from time to time. And no, you were right—we probably don't need to move the ship down here after all, or the beach could liquefy. Never mind tsunami potential." She turned in the opposite direction, aiming generally south. "Let's go over here. I see a clearing up ahead, where the jungle looks to go away, and I wanna see what we can make of it."

"Works for me," Echo decided. "Just watch your step. You never know when there's gonna be something under the sand that wants you for a snack."

"And you know this how?"

"How do you think?"

"Ew!"

* * *

Behind Alpha One, several of the red rock outcrops began to stir. One rolled over and into a more upright position. Something approximating eyes rose up on short blue-purple stems and popped open.

Abruptly what had appeared to be limp, blue-green seaweed strands draped across the boulder rose up and began waving in the air. A creaking, clacking sound came from the top of the creature. Within seconds the rest of the 'boulders' had moved into the same vertical position, multiple eyestalks swiveling to look after the humans moving down the beach. As they grew more active, their color intensified and deepened, becoming more plum-hued than the brick red they had appeared only moments before.

More clacking was followed by soft ripping sounds, as thick root-like appendages were pulled from the firm-packed sand.

Minutes later, at least a dozen of the creatures crept down the beach in Alpha One's wake...

...Stalking.

* * *

"Wow, look at this," Omega exclaimed, looking inland from the edge of the beach. "Whole different ecosystem, here."

"What do you suppose happened?" Echo wondered. "I mean, I see all the trees an' junk laid down and half-rotted, and... What the hell are those things, anyway?" He waved his hand at the towering organisms.

"Giant fungi of some sort," Omega determined, eyeing the tree-like, cornflower-blue growths; the stems were the size of large tree trunks, and the caps were narrow, irregular, and deeply pitted. This or that fungus had the occasional mottled patch of raisin- or Prussian-blue-toned spots on its cap. "I think Earth used to have some of those. At least, that's what I remember seeing in my studies on the fossil record. Well, not these identical ones, but similar. These are way big, though...how tall would you say that one is? Twenty, twenty-five feet?"

"Mm, yeah, that looks about right. They sorta remind me of Earth 'shrooms, but I can't recall which kind..."

Omega shrugged.

"Some species of morel, maybe?"

"Yeah, that's what I'm thinking of! Morels. I wonder if these are good eating, too. NO. Do NOT try one." Echo shot her a stern glance. "I know you, Ms. Curiosity Killed the Cat."

Omega just grinned.

"Okay baby, you're the scientist, here. So what do you think happened to wipe out such a huge part of the jungle?" Echo continued.

Omega pursed her lips, considering.

"I'm betting something like a hurricane made landfall here, a few local years back," she decided, "and maybe spun off multiple tornadoes or something. Or maybe just an exceptionally strong waterspout. It flattened the jungle in this swath, so the fungi grabbed the opportunity and moved in."

"Well, there's sure enough of 'em," Echo noted. "Look, they're all over the hillside, there."

"Not that it's very hilly," Omega observed. "We're probably on the edge of the flood plain of that river we saw from the air. Wanna go have a look at the big 'shrooms?"

"Sure. This area is more open than the jungle was. We ought to be able to see anything coming, pretty easily."

"Let's go, then."

"Right beside you, baby."

* * *

As they entered the area of devastation, Echo glanced around and made a decision.

"C'mere, Meg, and lemme show you how to do something," Echo said, getting out his cell phone as he headed toward his partner.

"What's that, Ace?" Omega wondered, moving to his side. He held his phone where she could readily see the display.

"Remember that old TV show you love, where the science officer carries around that gadget that reads off sensor shit about the stuff around 'em?"

"Yeah? Oh, don't TELL me..." Omega's sapphire eyes were wide with delight.

"Well, not quite," Echo said with a grin. "It isn't nearly as fancy, and it can't do nearly as much. But this app here," he tapped the icon, opening it, "serves kinda the same purpose. It'll give you basic passive sensor readings, off whatever you point the camera lens at. So we'll get back with at least some data on the stuff down here."

"That's...cool," Omega decided, getting out her own phone and trying it. "I wondered what that app was for! I also wondered why you insisted we bring our phones, since we weren't gonna split up or anything. And there sure as hell isn't any SIGNAL around here!" she chuckled.

"Well, splitting up can happen accidentally anyway," Echo pointed out. "You KNOW that."

"Yeah, but the line-of-sight signal is pretty limited on these things, just on account of the battery," she pointed out. "Especially in all that jungle."

"Fair enough, but a little is still better than nothing. On a big expedition, though, they bring along a commsat or three and put 'em in temporary orbits around the planet being explored, so that the exploration teams can stay in contact, not that it helps us here. But yeah, this thing is a lot more than a regular cell phone. It just looks like one, for the sake of camouflage back on Earth."

"Yeah, I figured THAT stuff out a long time back. But I still didn't know it could do all THIS. Awright, lemme have a look at these giant mushrooms. Oh, and keep an eye out for a big caterpillar smoking a hookah."

Echo snorted.

"Just don't go nibbling 'em," he advised again. "No telling what they'd do. Getting bigger or smaller is the least of my worries."

"No shit."

* * *

Back at the beach, the pack of strange creatures made surprisingly good time down the packed sand, scuttling stealthily but rapidly on their dark, brownish-wine-colored root-legs. Whenever either member of Alpha One glanced around, however, they promptly flung themselves to the ground and burrowed down, resuming the appearance of boulders half-buried in the sand.

By the time Alpha One disappeared among the gigantic mushrooms, headed up along what looked to be a drainage ravine, the stalking pack had reached the edge of the debris field. Eye-stalks swiveled about, and a soft chittering rose from the group. A human might have thought they sounded... concerned.

Abruptly they tightened their formation, staying within leaf's-reach of each other...

...And entered the debris field together.

Following Alpha One.

* * *

Having ascertained before landing that the newly-discovered planet had a magnetic field, determined its orientation, and programmed it into their system, Echo checked the compass app on his phone, verifying their orientation and direction of motion. Then he and Omega pressed onward, deeper into the mushroom field, exploring the area and attempting to determine the reason for the slightly odd readings they were obtaining from the various plant and fungal growths.

But after several hours of such meandering exploration, Echo's belly let out a loud growl, and Omega's answered in kind.

"Hah," Omega said, laughing, as she paused in scanning one of the largest of the fungi, "the dinosaur guts are telling us it's mealtime, I suppose. After missing most of our meals yesterday while on EVA, I guess we ought to eat, today."

"Yeah, and I didn't even bring a protein bar with me," Echo noted. "Did you?"

"Nope. Frankly, I didn't think we'd be out here this long."

"Me neither. Well, let's head back to the ship and grab a bite to eat," Echo decided. "We can always resume exploring after we eat first lunch. And maybe bring along something for second lunch, and eat it while we're out. I'm not seeing anything of any real concern..."

"Yeah, that sounds good, Ace," Omega agreed, turning around. "Huh."

"What?"

"I thought we came from this direction..." She pointed.

"Yeah, we did, we—" Echo turned and looked. "What the hell...?"

"Didn't we follow that little ravine up the hill, and come around that big dead log, there?"

"We did," Echo vowed, "I swear we did. I know, 'cause I remember thinking that dead trunk was about the size of a sequoia trunk, back on Earth. But there weren't any of those giant mushrooms there, then...were there?"

"Not that I recall," Omega confirmed. "They— whuh?" She spun to her right.

"What is it, Meg?" Echo wondered, shading his eyes from the bright alien sun and studying the downhill slope.

"I thought I saw..." She broke off and shook her head. "Something moved, Ace. I saw it out of the corner of my eye."

"What was it?"

"You aren't gonna believe me."

"Try me."

"I think I saw a mushroom move. Like, quiver, kinda."

"Yeah, that makes sense," Echo decided. "Because I've been identifying little details of the route we took to this point, so I know we DID come up, right by that log. And the ONLY explanation is that the mushrooms shifted position behind us."

"You mean...they're ambulatory?"

"Yeah, that or they grow REALLY damn fast. But I'd say so. In fa— uh-oh."

Omega and Echo exchanged a long look. After a moment Omega scrunched her face.

"I need to turn around and look at the one I was studying just now, don't I...?" She jerked her thumb back over her shoulder.

Echo nodded, and without another word, they both turned.

The twenty-foot-tall fungus, which roughly resembled a huge black-foot morel with a stem easily a foot and a half or better in diameter—and which had been a good ten feet from Omega—now towered over her, mere inches from her body. Echo leaped backward, bouncing off another and falling between two more before tumbling into a clearing.

But to his dismay, Omega remained somewhere in the middle of what was now a tight cluster of the fungi.

"Echo! ACE!" he heard her cry. "ACE! GET ME OUT! Ow! That HURTS! They're covering me up, Ace! No, dammit! NO! LET ME G— mmph! Mmph! MMMM!"

Silence fell...except for a disturbing shuffling sound, as the giant mushrooms quivered around his partner's body.

Horrified, Echo yanked his blaster, aiming it at the cluster—and then stopped.

Meg is in there someplace, he realized, *and if the blaster beam is the hot knife through butter that we both think it will be for these things, I'll cut her in two, too. How the hell...?*

Abruptly the experienced Agent threw himself to the ground, choked the beam down to as small a diameter as it would go...and fired, slicing through the dirt inches below the surface. This sheared through the subsurface stem and severed the mushrooms from their mycelium; seconds later, they quivered in death throes and began falling away, eventually disgorging his partner, who staggered and almost fell. He leaped up and ran to her, grabbing her and steadying her, without ever holstering his blaster.

"You okay, baby? You're not hurt, are you?"

"N-no, I, I'm okay, Ace," she panted. "It was gettin' hard to breathe in there fast, though. I'm glad you didn't take long to kill the damn things."

"You look kinda...I dunno," he said, surveying her while keeping an eye on the other fungi in the area; they were starting to move toward the pair of Agents, easing into a circle about them. "All...mottled. Like something was trying to digest you, I guess."

"It was," Omega admitted, "an' it didn't feel great, but I don't think I'm hurt. My skin might be kinda sensitive for a while, though. Let's get outta here before they get us fenced in. The ravine we came up is over there." She pointed.

"No, that'll take too long," Echo disagreed. "We're nearly half a mile from the beach. It gives these things too much of a chance to outmaneuver us. Look, to our right, over here. We're not far from the edge of the jungle—maybe a couple hundred yards at most. I vote we head straight into it from here. And mow down any of these damn infernal things that get in our way."

"That works," Omega said, shoving her cell phone into its appropriate pocket and unholstering both blasters. "I sure wished I had my blaster in hand instead of my phone when they tried to nom me, though I dunno how well firing it while INSIDE the damn thing would have worked."

"Yeah, that mighta cooked you right along with it," Echo agreed, "an' I dunno about you, but I had enough of that scenario already."

"Yeah. C'mon, let's go."

They headed for the edge of the rainforest at a trot, shooting at any mushrooms that got in the way.

* * *

Just up from the beach, the dark-purple creatures with the blue-green frond 'arms' and root-like 'legs' moved through the fungus field with experienced dexterity, using them as cover while never remaining in one place long enough to be engulfed, themselves.

One of the creatures used the thorny part of an arm frond to grasp a section of a nearby fungus stem, ripping a large chunk right out of the body of the mushroom, which quivered in what appeared to be a pain response and shuffled away. The purplish being casually dropped it into an orifice on top of its rounded body—which lacked an obvious head—and within seconds, a soft, mushy, grinding sound came from the orifice, as thorny protuberances made short work of the hunk of mushroom. Once the snack had been consumed, it made a pleased whirring sound and followed its mates up the hill in the wake of Alpha One.

Just then, a hollow, hooting noise came from the front of the pack, and they all paused. Multiple eye stalks—some had only two, most had three or more—swiveled to look uphill and to the right.

The two humans could just be made out, running across the gentle slope of the hillside, dodging around giant fungi, who were attempting to cut them off and herd them into a cluster. From time to time a bright light shone from one of the humans' appendages, and whenever that happened, one or more mushrooms fell over, the stem cut completely through.

A series of three loud hoots came from the creature in the lead, and suddenly the entire pack started running.

Straight for the forest's edge, and Alpha One.

* * *

"Did you hear that?" Omega asked, measuring her words so that she could continue to run at her partner's side.

"That hoot-owl sound? Yeah, I heard it," Echo confirmed. "Dunno what it was. I can't think it's good, though."

"Me neither. I just hope it isn't anything else we have to contend with."

They reached the edge of the storm's devastation, running under the blue trees for a good fifty feet, which distance had been Omega's considered opinion on the likely extent of the mycelium—the joint root-complex of the mushroom field—per Echo's urgent inquiry. Then they paused to allow Omega to finish catching her breath after nearly being eaten.

"I sure would like to lean up against one of these tree-things," she said, still sucking air, "but after that little adventure, I'm not gonna risk it."

"Poke it with a stick and see if it moves or anything," Echo recommended.

Omega found a fallen branch and, after ascertaining there were no mushrooms growing on it, she turned and poked the nearest tree very gently. When it showed no sign of reacting, she tried a little harder, then harder still. Finally she hauled off and whacked it hard, baseball-bat style, but it remained inert and unmoving, even as the dead branch shattered against it.

Meanwhile, Echo moved a little closer to the edge of the forest, looking back into the cleared area to try to identify the owl-like sound they had heard. He put one hand to his forehead, shielding his eyes from the bright sunlight, and surveyed the old tornado track, looking for anything that might have made the sounds they had heard. Abruptly he gaped, dropping his hand to his side, as his jaw went slack.

"Oh damn! Baby, drop everything and let's haul ass!" he exclaimed, spinning toward her, just as she leaned against the tree trunk. "We got a big pack of...SOMEthing...hot on our trail! There's more of 'em than I wanna try to shoot down, and we need to get outta here fast!"

"Huh?" Omega said, glancing at him and in the process, seeing the creatures which had been stalking them, now charging toward Alpha One's position behind him. When a small clump of mushrooms tried to block one group of the creatures, the creatures simply attacked the mushrooms, chewing through them in seconds. "Oh shit! You were RIGHT, we SHOULDA brought the rifles, dammit!"

The human Agents turned and ran, aiming for the direction they estimated the *Trojan Horse* to be.

* * *

The pair ducked and dodged trees and vines and undergrowth in the strange jungle, heading back in the direction of the *Trojan Horse*, concentrating on outdistancing the creatures pursuing them. Abruptly an odd screech came from in front and to the left side, and Alpha One skidded to a halt: Another pack of the bizarre predators had answered the hooting calls of the first, flanking the humans, and springing up just past a thick hedge of fleshy succulent plants shaded a light periwinkle—a pale blue-purple—nearly waist-high, and vaguely resembling Venus flytraps, only far, far larger. A single purple spike, like a horn, rose from each clump of the giant flytrap foliage, and the large 'traps' were open, but the pair could make out little else in the dense jungle undergrowth and perpetual gloom.

But before Omega and Echo could react, the round purple predators charged through the hedge—and died, as the hedge came to life, its thick purple leaves grabbing up the invaders and pulling them, screaming, down into a large central orifice, located in the center of each clump of foliage near the large horn-like structure, which abruptly sprouted what looked to the humans vaguely like an eye. Mere moments after each predator disappeared into the orifice, reddish-purple fluids spurted several feet into the air.

"Oh shit," Omega breathed, horrified. "The life forms on this planet are insane!"

"And lethal," Echo agreed. "C'mon, baby—this way! We'll have to try to dodge around 'em—that first group is right on our heels!"

"Damn, we SO shoulda brought the tachyon-splitter rifles!"

"You read my mind!"

"I swear, I'll never disagree on a planetfall tactic again, Ace!"

"Good! Let's go!"

They turned to the right, dodging around the animated hedge, and resumed running for the ship.

* * *

"It's a good thing we can run faster than they can. What the hell are they?! They look like...giant BEETS!" Omega wondered as they sprinted. "Giant, feral beta vulgaris!"

"Well, they appear to be intelligent," Echo said, dodging a root that snaked out in front of him, shooting it with his blaster, then stopping for a moment to look for the ship, "so they're sapient. They seem to run in packs, like wolves, and it sure looks like they're intent on eating us..."

"Right. I think they got some sort of mouth-thing on the top, among those blue-green leaf-fronds, with..." Omega paused, turned, and craned her neck to try to get a better look, leaning one arm against the nearest tree... after first making sure it was the same species she had whacked without response, previously.

"LOOK OUT, MEG!" Echo shouted, as one of the creatures, hidden behind the tree on which his partner leaned, leaped out at her. His blasters already in hand, he leveled one and fired.

An earthy, slightly sweet odor filled the air, overlain with an acrid, burnt-sugar smell, as the creature fell dead with a scorched, sizzling hole through its middle, bubbling a thin, purplish-red 'blood,' and Echo grabbed his partner's hand and jerked her away. The other creatures, farther back and unnerved by the sudden and unexpected death of one of their number by the bright lights the strange tall creatures could produce, paused, eye-stalks gaping in uncertain surprise.

"Let's go!" he declared, and they resumed their sprint for the ship. "THAT should have given you a good look."

"Damn, did it ever!" Omega exclaimed with a shiver. "Yeah, they got kind of thorn-like teeth in a mouth up where the stem should be. The leaves around it were acting sorta like the arms on an octopus, reaching out and wanting to pull stuff toward the mouth."

"And that bastard was obviously after YOU for lunch."

"Right, so carnivorous."

"Yeah, and you nailed it—they look like four-foot-tall giant beets, running on their 'roots'..."

"Okay, so? What do you make of 'em?"

"It looks like your everyday bunch of sapient dire beets to me, baby."

Omega snorted, but kept running.

"All right, sapient dire beets it is," she agreed. "And they run in packs."

"Bunches. Beets come in bunches."

"Oh-kaaaaay. If you say so." Omega shook her head, then looked around. "Echo, shouldn't we have reached the ship by now?"

"Yeah, we should. That's...not good. And I haven't been able to spot it, either."

"Did we go the wrong way?"

"Probably. I'm betting we got turned around when we entered the woods at a run, from a different location than we left it, with these things chattering and howling on our heels. Not to mention ducking around giant 'shrooms an' tree trunks an' cannibal hedgerows an' shit. Cover me, best you can." He stopped again, and Omega halted beside him, both blasters up, trying to look in all directions at once.

"Whatcha doin'?" she wondered, as he pulled his smart phone again and activated the locator app, running a search for the ship's beacon.

"Tryin' to find our ship."

"You don't s'pose those things can climb, do you?" she asked, glancing at the space over their heads, and surveying it with a skeptical eye.

"Dunno. I wouldn't think so; I don't see any appendages suited to climb WITH. Do you? You're the one with the biology degree," he offered somewhat absently, not bothering to look up to check.

"No, I agree with you."

"Okay. Watch overhead, just in case."

"I'm tryin' to. But I was as much wondering if we should take to the trees and pull a Tarzan, as anything."

"Well, it's an idea," Echo said, still studying the display on his phone screen with intensity. Then he hit a button; in the distance to their left, several loud honks sounded. "There we go. Yeah, we angled off the route a bit, there. It's over this way, about a third of a klick." He pointed toward the sound.

"You wanna try climbing up?"

"Might be worth it. Provided there's nothing else up THERE." Echo moved to the nearest tree. "C'mon, baby, and hurry. Lemme give you a leg up into the tree, before they get brave enough to try again, in spite of our guns."

* * *

They managed to scramble up into the lower limbs of the tree—which, to Omega, looked more like some sort of ancient fern, or perhaps a branching variant of a cycad, than any of the trees to which she was accustomed, its deep-teal-shaded leaves notwithstanding—before the dire beets could figure out what they were doing. And sure enough, the dire beets clustered around the base of the tree...but did not attempt to climb it. Instead, they hooted, growled, and flung detritus in frustration.

"So, okay, we wanna make like Tarzan, right?" Omega wondered, reaching for a navy-toned vine-like tendril, its tapering tip shading to eggplant and amethyst.

"NO! Don't touch it yet!" Echo exclaimed, flinging out a warning hand. "Grab a stick and poke—"

But it was too late. The inch-thick tendril curled about Omega's wrist with all the strength of a carbon-fiber cable. Instantly several dozen other tendrils of similar size rose into the air and began waving about, searching for their prey—Omega.

"Ahh!" she cried, trying to jerk away, but held fast. "Dammit! Why can't I get my head around it!? All the plants on this damn planet are out to eat us!"

"Hold on, baby!" Echo cried, glancing behind, below, and above himself as he drew a blaster again. A swift twist of the control mechanism choked it back down to a fine beam, and a flick of the wrist as he fired sliced the beam through the tendrils like a scythe through wheat. The vine quivered as if in pain, and a hissing sound, like many leaves rubbing together, rose from somewhere nearby. The dismembered tendril around Omega's arm went limp. She jerked it off her wrist and flung it away, and the severed pieces fell to the forest floor below, where the bunch of sapient dire beets promptly dived on them in a feeding frenzy. The sounds of snapping and gnashing floated up to them, along with an odd kind of gurgling, growling noise.

Echo grabbed Omega's hand and dragged her to the far side of the tree, where there were no vines, and rather than trying to leap to the nearest tree, they jumped to the ground behind the bunch of dire beets.

They hit the ground running, Echo keeping one eye on his cell phone display to ensure they were headed for the *Trojan Horse*.

* * *

But the dire beets finished their appetizer all too quickly, and soon the hunt was on once more.

"I think they're getting faster," Echo observed as the pair ran.

"You noticed that, too, huh?"

"Yeah, and I'm not happy about it."

"Me nei— Aw damn!"

"What?" Echo panted.

"There's another hedge of those blasted giant purple flytrap things, between us an' the ship!" Omega pointed.

"Yeah, I see 'em," Echo noted. "It's only about six or eight feet across. Don't slow up, Meg. Maneuver Alpha-One-B-twenty-seven. Up and over."

"Ace, won't that leave you...?"

"Don't worry about me. I'm taller, with longer legs. I wanna get you over those things, and then I'll get myself over. With any luck, it'll cut off our pursuers; I can't tell how long the hedge is, can you?"

"No, but it's gotta be pretty long, 'cause I don't see a way to run around it."

"Okay, we're gonna have to time this right," Echo said, as they rapidly approached the large plants, whose purplish-blue leaf-traps were waving lightly, even though there was no breeze, there in the depths of the jungle-like forest. "Get ready to put on a burst of speed. In three...two...one...GO!"

Omega and Echo both accelerated, and as he passed close by her with his longer stride, Echo reached out and grabbed his partner by the shoulder and the rear waistband of her trousers, just before twisting hard from the waist. Seconds later, his momentum had added to hers, and she was airborne, flying through the air well above the reach of any of the giant flytrap plants. She hit the ground on the far side, tucked and rolled, coming up in a kneeling position, both blasters out.

Unfortunately, the move, while effective in clearing Omega over the obstacle, slowed Echo by a significant amount. He dug in, accelerating forward again, and leaping at the last possible instant, attempting to combine altitude with distance in his jump.

It wasn't as successful as he'd hoped.

Sensing the air movement produced by Echo's passage above it, one of the flytraps shot upward, snagging his right foot in a vise-like grip. Before he could even react, the relatively short but incredibly strong frond acted as a rope and halted his forward momentum, transferring it into a rotational motion instead. Echo slammed into the ground face-first, mere feet from the base of the plant, and lay there for a moment, stunned. Instantly the lone eye on the purple horn opened, surveying the area and fixating on

Echo's prone form.

* * *

"ACE! Damn!" Omega cried, as the plant started withdrawing the trap holding Echo's foot, pulling him back toward its central orifice—which, from Omega's perspective, appeared easily large enough to take Echo's entire body in one or two bites. "NO you don't, you sonuvabitch!"

She leveled her right blaster at the plant, ensuring that her aim was well over Echo's body, and yelled, "Echo! Stay down!" A grunt was his only reply, but it told her he was conscious and understood, so she opened fire on the heart of the giant flytrap.

A high-pitched, quavering wail rose from somewhere in the middle of the plant; all its fronds shot up into the air, trembling as if in intense pain. The eye instantly closed, the entire horn retreating deep into the foliage. The trap clutching Echo's foot released to join the other fronds. Then the entire lot collapsed to the ground, limp and wilting. A faint wisp of smoke rose from the blackened center of the clump of foliage.

Omega ran to her partner's side, and helped Echo roll over and sit up.

"You okay, Ace?" Omega wondered, examining him quickly, then brushing the dirt off his face.

"Yeah," he gasped. "Jus' got th' wind knocked outta me. Gimme a second."

"Ooh. You may or may not end up with a couple o' black eyes, there, Ace," Omega observed, gingerly palpating his cheekbones, then his nose. "That hurt?"

"No more than anything else at the moment."

"Open your mouth. Lemme check your teeth."

Echo obeyed.

"No, you're good. We—"

She was interrupted by a hooting ululation from the other side of the lethal hedgerow. They both looked up, to see the entire bunch of sapient dire beets advancing...on the now-dead giant flytrap. The ones in the lead took the opportunity for an additional snack; the dead flytrap was rapidly being devoured.

Which meant that within minutes, there would be no obstacle at all between them and Alpha One.

"Aw shit," Omega grumbled, realizing. "I gave 'em a way through."

97

"And kept me from being lunch," Echo said, scrambling to his feet. "C'mon. Let's go before THEY have us for lunch."

Alpha One turned in the direction of their ship, and ran.

* * *

"Damn, Ace, these little bastards are FAST," Omega said, spinning and shooting at the nearest one, before turning back toward the *Trojan Horse*.

"Yeah, and they're—SHIT! Meg, all halt! Turn and face 'em, weapons out! And watch your six! They're trying to flank us again! I got the right side; you keep an eye on the left."

"Oh boy," Omega murmured, obeying instructions. The bunch of sapient dire beets had formed a semicircle, centered on Alpha One; those on the ends were attempting to sneak between the Agents and their spacecraft, which was at last in view, though some hundred yards or more off. "Aw, hell—you're right." She drew both blasters again; Echo already had his in hand, having put the cell phone away when he caught a glimpse of the *Trojan Horse*'s running lights through the foliage. "What do we do now?"

"Hang on, and be ready to open 'er up. I expect 'em to—"

Just then, the center of the semicircle charged, shrieking and chittering with their thorn-teeth.

"FIRE!" Echo shouted. "Open fire, Meg! And keep shooting until they back off!"

The air filled with the high-pitched whine of four blasters on continuous discharge. This was underscored by the angry snarls and dying shrieks of the dire beets. After fully two and a half minutes, the remaining bunch of beets backed off.

"There's more of 'em than there were," Omega decided, easing off the triggers, but not lowering her weapons. "There were only maybe fifteen or twenty originally, out in the mushroom field. But there's at least that many dead on the ground, now. And several times that, spread out through the trees, trying to outflank us."

"And—" Echo spun to his right and fired, swinging the blaster like a machine gun. Three beets went down. "They're gonna manage it, if we're not damn careful."

Omega twisted and followed suit; two more dropped to their left.

But the line had managed to move closer.

"Damn," Echo breathed. "That ain't good."

"Nope," Omega agreed. She saw a movement out of the corner of her eye, and spun to fire again. Another beet dropped dead, a neat hole singed through its center.

But each time the Agents turned to fire, the semicircle eased ever closer to the beleaguered pair of Agents. Soon they were close enough that, each time Alpha One's blasters found a target, the purplish-red juices spurting from the wound splattered the two. And the power cell indicator lights on all four blasters had turned yellow; the next lowest level was orange. If they turned red, Alpha One had only moments before their primary weapons died, and they would be forced to resort to their Winchester & Teslas, which were not meant for full-combat situations.

"They're working together," Echo observed of the dire beets. "Willing to sacrifice a few of their number, in order to take us down."

"Do you suppose they're pissed off that we've killed some of 'em? Okay, a lot of 'em?"

"Given that they never made ANY friendly overtures, and by my observations, they've been hunting us since before we even noticed 'em, I really don't care, baby. It's them or us," Echo noted, "and I don't intend it should be us. Our back is to the ship; just keep easing that way. And don't let 'em get between us and the ship, or it's all over."

"Right. Damn, Echo, I never thought my salad would be the one trying to eat ME..."

And with that, the bunch of beets attacked, en masse. Alpha One opened up with all four blasters, and just kept firing. Beet 'blood' splattered the forest in the vegetarian carnage.

"Ugh. I never could stand beets. Good shot! That's it, Meg. Just keep shooting, baby. Pretend you're making borscht."

"My ancestry's SCOTTISH, Echo, not Russian! I dunno HOW to make borscht!"

"Don't tell Fox, then; he loves the stuff. And don't sweat it. You've got a great start, Meg. Keep shooting."

"Damn! How many o' these things ARE there, anyway?!"

"They're only your garden-variety sapient dire beet, baby. They come in bunches."

"This is a damn big bunch, then! There must be around a hundred of 'em by now!"

"Just keep making borscht, like I told you."

"Stop with the borscht, already! We're startin' to look like the aftermath of a gang bang, dammit, and neither of us is even HURT yet! Well, except for your eyes, which are already turnin' black."

"Uh-huh. Let's keep it that way. And yeah, I'm really glad I won't be around when Laundry gets THESE Suits. I think even my shorts are purple, at this point."

"Ew! T.M.I., Echo!"

"Sorry, baby, but it's the truth. Shoot and angle for the ship, shoot and angle for the ship. That's it. Just keep going."

"Aaaand my right blaster's power indicator just turned orange..."

"Mine too. Ignore it. Just keep going."

* * *

At last they made it to the hatch; the power indicator for each Agent's principal blaster had begun to blink red as they set foot on the ramp, and would cease functioning momentarily. Echo covered them, keeping the dire beets well back from the gangway by means of some serious gun-fu, while Omega hit the remote to open the hatch, darted inside the airlock and prepped the hatch armor, so that all Echo had to do was slap his hand on the emergency button, and the whole thing would slam shut, locking the dire beets outside. Then she ran for the flight deck—checking for stray dire beets and any other carnivorous foliage as she went, just in case some sort of spore or the like had managed to get in earlier, before they sealed the ship—as Echo darted into the airlock and hit the emergency button. A loud *CLANG!* sounded as the hatch slammed shut and the armor closed over it.

"Let's get outta here, baby!" Echo said, holstering his blasters as he entered the flight deck. Omega was already strapped into the pilot's seat and initiating the liftoff procedure. "Where are we headed?"

"Up, right now," Omega replied, curt. "We'll worry about our next destination once we get away from these damn things."

"Fair enough." Banging came from the lower hull, and Echo frowned. "I think I'm glad these things can't jump too high. Let alone climb."

"Hell, yeah. Should we check the hull integrity before we go exo?"

"Nah. It isn't like they have weapons," Echo pointed out. "And while those excuses for teeth would do a number on us, they're not going to faze the gamma-titano-chromasteel alloy hull. But running an interior scan-and-sterilization would probably be a good plan right now."

"All right. Siddown and strap in, then. I'm lifting off in about three seconds," she warned, entering the sequence that began the procedure to locate and identify any undesired alien life forms—even spores—aboard the vessel and destroy it, even as she finished launch prep. Echo plopped into the co-pilot's seat and grabbed the restraint harness; one second later, he was tightly strapped in.

"All right, baby. I'm ready when you are."

"Okay, stand by; I'm about to lift off." She grabbed the stick. Abruptly Omega stopped the launch prep. "No, I'm not."

"Huh? What? We're not lifting off? Why not?"

"Because I know what it feels like to be under the drive when a ship takes off," Omega murmured, and Echo felt himself pale. "Vicious little veggies or not, I'm not gonna do that to 'em. Borscht, when they're attacking us, is one thing. Roasted beets, when we're safe inside our can, is another."

"Oh. Um. Yeah, good point. I'm okay with that. They can't get to us as long as we stay in here anyhow, so if we wait long enough, they should get bored and go away."

"Right."

"Gimme your blasters and I'll go swap out the power units real quick, then plug in the old ones to charge. While I'm doin' that, you close the cockpit windows so they can't see movement, turn off the running lights, and let's kick back for a bit and see what happens."

Omega did just that, then pulled up the external sensor view, and together they watched as the dire beets banged around and postured outside the ship.

* * *

It took the better part of an hour, but by ones and twos, the dire beets finally realized that their hoped-for prey was holed up in a nutshell they couldn't crack, and wandered away, resuming the hunt elsewhere. Half an hour after that, the *Trojan Horse* was alone in the clearing.

Five minutes later, the *Trojan Horse* was ascending serenely through the cloudy atmosphere into the relatively young planetary system hidden within the nebula.

* * *

"Wow. I'm glad to get outta THAT," Omega decided once they'd made exo, then she looked down at herself. "Geez, what a mess. Now I get your comment about purple shorts."

"Yeah. Wanna lay money on your underthings bein' purple, too?"

"Er, no, I don't think so," Omega decided, peeling the sticky, sodden front of her once-white shirt off her skin. "I expect you'd win that one, no contest. I'm thinkin' I'm gonna need steel wool just to get my skin back to its normal color."

"Me too. Good thing we got multiple showers onboard." He glanced at her. "On second thought, you'd better not scrub quite THAT hard, Meg. Looks like the fungal digestive juices might have sensitized your skin a little, like you thought."

"Oh. Okay. What, I got some blotchy places?"

"Other than the beet juice?" Echo snorted. "Yeah, there's a couple of pale patches under the purple shit, right here," he waved a finger over her right cheek, then her left, "and some reddened areas over here. I think I'm glad they only developed to digest plant material, and not animal tissues. Otherwise, you might be in a lot more trouble."

"Yeah, I've been thinking about that," Omega said. "And I'm puzzled. I mean, I get why some Earth-based plants are carnivorous—they often grow in areas that are nutrient-poor, so they consume insects and small animals to make up for that lack. But...they don't move around, not like these! And these...THINK." She shook her head. "Does Division One University have some, like, exobiology courses?"

"Sure. Why?"

"'Cause I think I'm gonna take some when we get back. I'm not understanding this."

"Not understanding what?"

"The whole predatory, ambulatory carnivores thing. Or maybe that's herbivores; I dunno." Omega shrugged. "I mean, okay, you got the people-trap plants, and the vines, and all. But they just grab whatever happens by. Then you got the fungi, that seem to go looking for the most likely places to find nutrients of ANY sort, but they still sorta just grab whatever goes by. Only they work together to do it...which makes a certain sense, I guess, because they probably all share a mycelium," she pondered. "And it probably acts like a hive mind, a group nervous system, so they all work together 'cause they're really part of one organism..."

"Now you're starting to get it, I think," Echo decided.

"But it's the whole sapient dire beets thing I really don't understand," Omega protested. "What do they need to go running around predating for?"

"Oh, well, I might be able to explain that, at least a little," Echo considered. "See, one of my Diplomacy professors was a Dendroid, back when, and Professor Gurmeenos and I had some after-class conversations over beer about how the Dendroids probably developed. Dendroids are omnivores, but there's archaeological evidence that they were once hunter-gatherers. Carnivores," he pointed out, "mostly. Well, in as much as you can call one plant that eats another plant 'carnivorous,' I guess. Their dendrologists—kinda the equivalent of an anthropologist—think that the trick is the development of a sentient brain. Once the Dendroids started to think, then they had to have significantly increased nutrition, in the form of both calories and nutrients, to sustain that brain. And to do that, they had to be able to move around and hunt."

"So...you're saying that, at least for plants, the mobility comes secondary to the ability to think and plan?"

"Yeah, to a point, anyway. That was what Gurmeenos thought, though. I gather it sorta came in fits and spurts, you know, a burst of brain growth, a shot of mobility, leading to more brain growth, to more mobility, and it just...snowballed. Not sayin' it has anything to do with Earth animals, let alone humans, but that's how they think it worked on the Dendroid homeworld. I could see something like that maybe being in effect on this planet we just cleared from, too. Anyway, let's go get..." he stood, and there was a sticky, ripping sound as the synthetic material of the co-pilot's seat stuck to his clothing—which was in turn stuck to his body—and peeled loose, "...cleaned up. Ieech. That felt...nasty."

"Yeah. And we probably need to wipe down these seats with a wet cloth, too. Maybe some of the console, even."

"Ugh. Good idea. And then," Echo's stomach growled, "we grab first lunch."

"Finally," Omega agreed, glancing at the console chronometer. "Considering it's already past time for second lunch."

"Yeah. So. Where you wanna go next?"

"I'm not sure," Omega decided. "I'm thinkin' we should just head for the next block in our grid."

"That works," Echo agreed, untying his gummy necktie and stripping it from the collar of his ruined shirt with some difficulty. "We probably need to get outta the system and put 'er into station-keeping for a little bit, though. The quicker we get to the beet juice stains, the easier it'll be to get it off our skins." He gave her a once-over. "And your hair. You got a big purple splotch."

"Oh, great. Good point. Stand by one, then." Omega brought the spacecraft to a halt and began establishing a safe station-keeping mode.

"Co-pilot standing by. Literally." He grinned, pleased at the notion that she was, in fact, officially piloting, as he stood in the center of the deck and watched her work. *Damn, my girl—my partner,* he caught himself, *is smart as a whip.* Suddenly an image of Chase came to mind, and he hid the wince. *Shit. Dammit, that's gotta stop. Just...stop. It's supposed to be over with. Besides, she's dead. It isn't like I could make up with her, even if I wanted to.*

Moments later, the *Trojan Horse* was station-keeping between nascent systems in the nebula, with various alerts and alarms set, and Omega unstrapped and stood, likewise peeling herself off the seat with a grimace. Together they headed aft, stripping out of ruined outer garments as they went.

"What on earth do we do with this mess?" Omega wondered, holding an armful of soggy, badly-stained neckties, jackets, shoes, socks, and other assorted items. Both Agents still wore their trousers and shirts, but those were plastered to their bodies with beet juice, which was starting to dry.

"Dump 'em in a pile, for now." Echo pointed at the deck in a corner. "I dunno 'bout you, but I'll need to go through my pockets and see what equipment can be salvaged, not to mention getting my warp pockets outta the jacket. I'm hoping nothing's messed up TOO bad."

"Yeah, me too."

"Then I'm thinking we just flash-burn the lot, and jettison the ash," Echo concluded. "I doubt even offworld launderers are gonna get this shit out. I mean, we can take it to 'em when we get back, but damn. And we don't need any spores that adhered to 'em starting to grow, before we can get home. So I think we should go with a scorched-Suit policy!" He chuckled. "Then we run another ship decontamination, just to make sure."

"Okay," Omega said, heading for the port shower bay. "Works for me."

"Hey, Meg?" Echo called after her. She paused and turned back.

"Yeah, Ace?"

"While you're in the shower, you might wanna think about something..."

"What's that?"

"Well, the planet was YOUR discovery, so you get to name it. Be thinking what you wanna call it—planet, system, lifeforms, and all—and when we're both dressed and back on the flight deck, we'll enter the data, location, an' shit, along with your code name, and send it to Division One Headquarters. Fox will forward it to the Council, and all the astrocartographers will be scrambling to add your new system to their maps. Oh, and congratulations. You discovered something new—something big—on your very first offworld mission."

"Cool," Omega said with a grin. "Thanks."

* * *

Considerably later, Alpha One met back up on the flight deck. Omega's pale blonde hair was a bit mottled in places, with odd, pale berry-pink-colored patches here and there, and Echo had a spray of similar color across his ear and neck that he hadn't quite been able to scrub away—at least, not without making the skin raw—but otherwise they were, more or less, back to normal.

"That's better," Echo decided.

"Ain't that the truth," Omega agreed. "My fingers were startin' to stick together. Damn, Ace, the drain looked like that scene from *Psycho*, through at least the first half of my shower!"

"Tell me about it," Echo averred. "An' yeah, my shorts were purple."

"So were mine. Bra, too."

A mental image of a certain lace-and-satin bra, stained a deep wine shade, flashed into Echo's mind's eye. Brown eyes abruptly went wide. He blinked, and it was immediately followed by an image of his partner, clad only in said bra and panties, splotched and stained with beet juice, and this time the flight deck seemed to brighten, as his eyes dilated. *Whoa baby,* was his immediate thought, which was then closely followed by, *Well, shit. Watch it, Echo, before you put your foot in it. 'Nother topic, 'nother topic...*

aha.

"Um, so you got a name for the planet yet?" he asked.

"Yeah." Omega shot him an amused glance, and he realized he probably had not fooled her.

Damn, he thought, hiding the chagrin. *Well, but she isn't upset, at least. That's a good thing…and a good sign, I think. Besides, turn about's fair play. I painted a mental image for her the other night; I guess it was her turn. Huh. I…wonder if it was deliberate.*

"Okay, then," he said aloud, heading for the navigation station. "I think—"

"Damn, Ace, you're limping! What's wrong?" Omega asked, concerned.

"Eh, nothing too serious," he demurred. "I think I got a pulled muscle, or maybe a little sprain in my leg, where that damn flytrap plant—or people-trap, or whatever we're gonna call it—grabbed my foot. Tibialis anterior, judging by the location. Acute shin splints, basically. My foot's a little bruised, too. I'd never have guessed the thing was that strong." Echo shrugged. "It's a good thing we didn't wait any longer to strip and clean up, either. Those traps had some sort of digestive acid or something in 'em. It was starting to eat through my shoe. Probably wouldn't have done my foot any good, if it got all the way through the leather."

"You gonna be okay? Should I maybe have a look at it, or run the medscanner over it, or something?"

"Nah, I'll be fine. Don't sweat it. I'll pop some analgesics to reduce any inflammation once we finally get some lunch in us, and I might ice it later or something. When we get ready for bed, you can wave the medscanner at it, and maybe help me ice it. I think I saw a little bottle of Rejuvic in the medical kit. You can swab my face, shin, and foot, and I can swab those digestive-juice patches on your face and hands, just before we go to bed."

"Okay. You're sure you're all right?"

"I'm sure. If it goes to bothering me, I'll let you have a look-see then and there, but for now, let's plan the rest of the day."

"Okeydoke. We need to report the planetary data, and determine what grid block we're gonna explore next."

"Yup. I guess we need to name the various indigenous life forms we discovered, too. I found some bits and pieces of that people-trap plant stuck to my sock and junk," he noted. "I scanned it and made sure it was well and truly dead—even dug out the medscanner and set it for Dendroid, just to be sure—then I put it in a special quarantine-type sample container and stuck it in stowage. We can turn it over to Biology when we get home, and they can study it."

"Oh, great idea," Omega said, silver-blonde eyebrows shooting up. "I found some pieces of that vine in my jacket sleeve, you know, tendrils. Lemme go get it and you can show me how to do all that, and we'll add it in with the trapper-thing sample. An' I guess we can always wring out our shirts to get some dire beet 'blood' for a sample. Assuming it's not too dried out yet."

"Okay, go get it and we'll do that while we work some stuff out."

"Like what?" Omega pawed through the pile of sticky clothing until she came up with the dead plant matter, while Echo fished out his cell phone, then dug around in stowage, producing a medscanner as well as a small airtight container.

"Names. Here, lemme see."

"Oh, yeah, good point," she said, handing him the bits of vine. "Well, we got the sapient dire beets...that would render scientifically as *Bete dirus sapiens*..."

"Yup."

"Let's call the fungi *Exomorchella giganticae carnivora*..." Omega decided. "They sorta looked like giant morels, anyway, like you said. And the trap-things that almost got you..." She broke off and snorted, then snickered.

"All right. Let's hear it," Echo said, longsuffering. He rolled his eyes.

"How 'bout *Aphroditus gigantopopulus carnivora*? Or we could call it *Gigantopurpura cibicida depopulis*..."

It was Echo's turn to snort. Loudly.

"Well, it DID have purple traps, blue-purple leaves, one horn and one eye per plant, and it was a people-eater after a fashion—a would-be one, at least—but it couldn't fly, thank God. Okay, that'll work. The exobiologists will roll their eyes, but they'll go with it. And those vines?"

"How about *Exoliana edmundspencerica*?"

A lone bark of laughter escaped Echo.

"I didn't know you'd read that Madagascar story." He moved over to the navigation console, pulled up the appropriate forms on the display, and began entering the names, while Omega closed the stowage compartment.

"Yeah, well, I saw you reading it a couple weeks ago and got intrigued," she told him. "In this instance, it fits."

"Yeah, it does. Okay, we got the life form names..."

"Almost everything's 'carnivora,' though."

"But everything WAS carnivore! Well, except the trees. What do we call those?"

"Mm. Cycadaceae orionis?"

"I like it. And don't worry about the 'carnivora' thing, Meg. It's cool; it happens like that sometimes."

"See, though, when we're not there, they really aren't carnivores at all. They're plants that eat other plants. They're— oh! When you were telling me about the Dendroid homeworld, you called 'em predators! What's the Latin for predator?"

"Um, lessee..." Echo pondered for a moment, finally coming up with, "I think it's just praedator—'predator,' but with the 'ae' dipthong."

"Okay, what about, uh, what was it...? Aha! What about 'Exomorchella giganticae praedatoria,' and 'Aphroditus gigantopopulus praedatoria?'"

"Oh! I like the mushroom one! But I think I like your 'purple people-eater' name better than the 'giant Venus people-trap,'" Echo decided, making the necessary corrections on the electronic form. "Okay, got 'em. Now we'll use the navigation console to get the exact location of the planet and its star; the astronav comp can extrapolate the planet's orbit." He finally sat down at the console, allowing room for Omega to lean over him, watching and learning how to do it herself, the next time she had occasion to do so. A whiff of her perfume reached his nose, and he smiled to himself, an absent expression as he continued to work.

Moments later, Echo had all of the information sketched out in the electronic new-planet form. He looked up.

"You see how I did all that?"

"Yeah, I got it."

"So you can do it yourself next time?"

"I think so. Might want you lookin' over my shoulder at first."

"I can do that. Okay, all I need now is the system name and the planet's name," he told her.

"All right." Omega leaned forward and tapped the screen. "The star—and the star system name—is Betanin."

Echo keyed in the name, then hit <enter>. The cursor tabbed to the next field.

"Got it. And the planet's name?" he asked.

Omega grinned wickedly.

"Borscht," she replied.

Echo's jaw dropped, and he collapsed on the console, laughing.

* * *

Once due samples had been taken from their Suits and properly and safely stowed in the quarantined stowage, Alpha One did indeed flash-incinerate the sticky remains of their Suits, ejecting the ash overboard into space. Then they cleaned the pilot and co-pilot seats, delicately mopped up the control panel, ran another decontamination of the *Trojan Horse*, and started surveying the next section of their three-dimensional grid.

Echo did in fact let Omega tend his leg that night; he had minor swelling and bruising to the foot, ankle, and shin area, but nothing that appeared to be serious to either of the two Agents. He iced the entire thing with several chemical cold packs wrapped about the leg and foot, then they swabbed each other's various boo-boos with Rejuvic—including Echo's forehead, nose and cheekbones; both eyes were notably black—perforce using up the entire tiny vial of that potent liquid medication. Omega then carefully strapped Echo's ankle, ensuring it would be supported if it were, in fact, sprained. Echo popped an analgesic, and they went to bed.

By the next day, his face was back to normal, and other than some residual tenderness, the leg no longer bothered him.

Chapter 5

Gradually they worked their way through the next three grid blocks in the succeeding days. Omega found two more systems, the first containing three planets, the second only one. But none of them were developed enough to have life, and the last one didn't even have a central star...at least, not one that had ignited yet.

Echo watched, pleased and proud, as Omega grew more and more skilled with the search for new systems, and the explorations thereof. They even set down briefly on one of the planets in the three-world system, despite the fact that the atmosphere was less than hospitable and the gravity a lot higher than Earth's, in order to give her some basic experience in planetside EVA while wearing their spacesuits.

At the end of the second day out from the discovery of Borscht, Echo had decided that, on the following day, they would try something a little different, a little riskier: They would venture closer to the Trapezium Cluster, so that Omega could experience celestial navigation near a black hole.

"Not real close," he told her, "because this ship isn't outfitted with the necessary shielding against all that hard rad. But close enough so that you start getting some of the spacetime distortion, and have to compensate for it in your navigation."

"Ooo," Omega said, considering the matter. "That sounds...right up my alley."

"Yeah, I thought so, too," Echo agreed. "So. You up for it?"

"You bet, Ace!"

"All right, then. It's late, and you've had a very long, successful day of planet-hunting. Ready for bed?"

"Um, I guess so."

"That was...not as enthusiastic as I expected it to be. Wait. You want to sit out here and look at it some more, don't you?"

"Well, maybe a few more minutes. Just, you know, down time, not planet-hunting or anything. Kick back and enjoy the view, ya know what I mean?"

"Yeah, I get it. Feel like company, while you do?"

"If it's you? Always, Ace."

She smiled at him, and he smiled back, feeling something inside warm at her immediate, unquestioning acceptance of his companionship.

So they put the *Trojan Horse* into their standard nighttime station-keeping mode, complete with alarms and alerts set, then settled back in the pilot and co-pilot seats, slouching comfortably with a bedtime snack—of cookies and milk, no less—in hand, nibbling and staring outward into the nebula. Privately, Echo wished they had some of Omega's homemade cookies instead of prepackaged, but they weren't half-bad, even so. They finished their snack, and continued to sit in silence, staring outward at the undimmed beauty of the nebula.

"This is just glorious," Omega murmured then.

"Uh-huh," was all Echo replied. She turned toward him.

"You mean that, Ace?"

"Yeah, baby, I do. I'm not..." Echo broke off, looking for words. "I read a lot, so you'd think I could do better than that, I guess. Plus, there's the linguistics degrees. But I'm not a poet, and I don't often talk a lot about what I'm thinking or feeling...you, of all people, know that."

"But I usually know what you're thinking or feeling, anyway."

"Yeah, you do. Because we're a lot alike, and you 'get' me. And that's a good thing, generally."

"Yup." She nodded. "I hear a 'but' comin'."

"Not a 'but,' exactly. Only...well, I guess what I'm trying to say is, just 'cause I may not gush about something, don't make the mistake of thinking I can't appreciate its beauty. I got eyes in my head," Echo said, "and a pretty good sense of aesthetics, I think. But I'm..."

"A man of few words, and very private," Omega finished for him. "I know. I understand that, and it isn't a BAD thing at all, Echo. In fact, I appreciate it. Because among other things it means, when I'm sitting here looking at this, and I'm totally awed by it, my partner is maintaining a respectful silence, which ALLOWS me to be awed by it. Rather than having to deal with an ongoing babble of words, which...with something like this..." she swept a hand out, over the console, from one side of the main viewport to the other, "...is completely inadequate anyway."

"Exactly."

"I scored big time, when I got you for a partner, Ace."

"That's funny, baby. I was thinking the same thing about you." Echo glanced at his wrist chronometer, then sighed. "About time to call it a day."

"Aw! Just five more minutes?" she pleaded. Echo raised an eyebrow.

"Two."

"Four!"

"Three."

"Done!"

They laughed.

* * *

The alarms dragged each of them from a deep sleep, and they met in the corridor, both still trying to get decently covered. Omega flung the black robe over her pajama top as Echo struggled with a recalcitrant zipper, stuck partway on his trousers in his haste. Bare skin showed in the gap, and he had not had time to grab a shirt.

"Oh, the hell with it," he muttered, releasing the zipper's pull tab and glancing up at his partner, annoyance—and a certain amount of embarrassment—on his face.

"Don't worry about it, Echo," Omega tossed over her shoulder, already headed for the flight deck, Echo right behind. "You're covered."

"Barely," he grumbled.

"You're decent, and it sounds like we've got more important things to worry about. I'm not gonna notice if, uh, if something, you know...slips."

"Good, 'cause the damn thing just might."

* * *

Red lights flashed all over the control consoles when they reached the flight deck. "Aw, shit!" Echo exclaimed, after one good visual scan. "Meg, pull up the sensor readouts—fast."

"On it." She dropped into the co-pilot's seat and reached for the controls. "What's wrong?"

"Offhand, it looks to me like we've been fired on."

"Fired on?!"

"Yeah. I don't see 'em at the moment—"

"You're saying we're tumbleweed, Ace."

"Yeah, that's exactly what I'm saying. So we need to find 'em with the sensors."

"Okay...wait, I got 'em! Range, one thousand klicks; azimuth, one-six-seven; altitude, minus thirty-two. They're behind us, and a little bit below. Uh-oh..."

"What?"

"Echo, take a look at this..."

Echo bent over Omega's shoulder, looking at the readout under her fingertip, and swore.

"Dammit. It's Cortian."

* * *

"...It's worth a try, Echo," Omega told him, as they brainstormed quickly. "Just let me do it."

"...Okay, Meg," Echo said, grudging. "Go ahead and give it a shot."

Omega keyed the broadcast switch.

"PGLEIA *Trojan Horse* to unidentified vessel. We are on a peaceful training mission. Why have you fired upon us?"

"*Trojan Horse*, this is the Cortian vessel *Pindar*. Your subterfuge is useless. We are aware that the Alpha One team of malefactors from the illegitimate, so-called Pan-Galactic Division One Agency crews this vessel, and that you criminally caused the destruction of our flagship *Trindak* approximately thirty Earth days ago. We are here as a police action. Surrender or prepare to be destroyed."

Echo leaned over and pushed Omega's hand off the comm switch. "This is Agent Echo. My partner had no part in the battle which destroyed the *Trindak*. Let her go, and I'll surrender."

"NO, Echo!" Omega cried.

"That is unacceptable," came the reply. "Communiqués from *Trindak* before its destruction indicate your partner was heavily involved in the illegal altercation which resulted in its being driven from Earth, and which ultimately led to *Trindak*'s final battle. In any event, you are both prime acquisitions and should make excellent breeding stock."

The two Agents looked at each other in something akin to horror.

"They think of us as animals," Omega whispered, then her blue eyes blazed. "Echo—I've been a lab rat once before. Not again. Not EVER again." Omega grabbed for the force field controls, bringing up the protective field and maximizing it. Then she buckled in and booted the targeting computer. "Strap in, Echo. Fly this bird like you've never flown before, Ace. These damn asshole sons of bitches are about to become part of the nebula on their way to the bottom level of hell, the shit-bag bastards."

113

Echo stared at his partner in shock for a moment. He heard the stream of harsh epithets from the normally-smiling lips, saw the cold, hard, merciless expression in the sapphire gaze, and wondered. *Whoa. I have NEVER heard her curse like that before. Meg, what the hell happened to you? What exactly did my old enemy do to you...? TELL me, baby; don't keep it bottled up like this.*

"Echo! Break right, Ace! They've got a target lock! NOW!!"

Echo dropped into the pilot's seat and grabbed the controls, slamming their craft into a hard starboard translation maneuver, just as the green Cortian ray weapons sliced through their previous location.

In response, Omega's skilled fingers flitted over the weapons console, and purple beams lanced from the *Trojan Horse*. They struck the much larger *Pindar* in several places, and little puffs of atmosphere exited before the alien ship's self-repair systems kicked in.

"Good shot," Echo remarked, as he put their ship into a hard loop, dogfight-style. The *Trojan Horse*'s frame screamed in protest, the inertial dampeners struggling to keep up, but everything held as it was designed to do. "Here's another one for you, right up their...engines."

"Got it," Omega replied, curt, setting up and triggering another firing sequence. This time, when the purple beams lanced into the Cortian ship, a series of small explosions raced outward from the contact point. "Looks like we're in good shape so far, Ace."

"So far," Echo answered in a noncommittal tone, watching the larger enemy slave ship intently as they passed it by. "They just kicked it into high gear. Hang on."

The *Pindar* turned to follow the Division One saucer as it shot by on its follow-through. Echo executed a series of evasive maneuvers, plunging into the heart of the cloud complex—the very densest of the gas and dust clouds that comprised the star-forming region—for cover as green beams peppered space around them. The artificial gravity of the *Trojan Horse* strove to compensate as he bobbed and weaved their craft.

"Umph," Omega grunted as she bounced hard in her seat, five-point harness digging painfully into her shoulders, which were only protected by a layer of thin cotton and another, even thinner, layer of silk. "Nice job, Ace," she said, voice and expression ferocious. "They won't lay a finger on us, with you at the helm."

Echo ignored the comment for the moment, busy avoiding the deadly beams.

"Coming around for another pass, Meg. Be ready."

"I'll make it a strafing run..." She released the shoulder straps, rubbing her bruised right shoulder—which was still a bit tender after being gnawed on by a giant fungus; the digestive juices had soaked into her clothing, as it turned out, and it had taken too long to get back to the ship and strip—as she reached for the weapons controls. The trans-warp boson cannons fired at her command, and this time Alpha One saw hull panels cartwheel away from the slaver ship. A lone bipedal body floated out of the opening thus created, carried by a jet of escaping atmosphere, and the pair watched in silence as it flailed frantically for several moments before becoming still.

Both Agents sighed softly then. *That's sure not how I'd want to go,* Echo thought, *and if we'd been closer, I'd have tried to take it prisoner, just to save its life. But we were too far away to do anything. And the Cortian captain didn't even seem to try.*

"Echo," Omega said then, voice more subdued than before, "sensors are showing they've sustained serious damage. Do you want to give 'em a chance to back down?"

Good. That did the trick. I've got my Meg back again, Echo thought, showing no reaction, but reaching for the comm. *The bloodthirsty version is gone. Can't say as I blame her, though. I felt that way myself about the* Trindak *when they toasted her.* He keyed the mike.

"*Trojan Horse* to *Pindar*. Our sensors show you have sustained heavy damage. Do you wish to break off the engagement?"

The only answer was a barrage of green rays which Echo swiftly dodged.

"Okay, Meg," he growled, "enough of this shit. Take 'em out."

"With pleasure."

Echo brought the *Trojan Horse* in for a close pass as Omega targeted the areas already damaged on the alien spacecraft.

"Firing...now." The tachyonic boson beams lanced outward at Omega's behest, digging deep into the wounds of the *Pindar*, and abruptly a blinding white flare erupted from the damaged vessel. "Whoa—looks like I hit a sore spot..."

"Shit—she's going!" Echo exclaimed, watching the Cortian vessel seem to detonate. He kicked the *Trojan Horse* into a hard, right-angle maneuver at maximum thrust, headed away from the *Pindar*, calling, "Hold on tight, Meg! Shields at max?"

"Affirm!" she responded. "Shields at one-oh-two and undamaged."

"Sensors aft," Echo barked.

"Sensors aft. Virtual heads-up?"

"Do it."

A 3-D tactical display of the sensor readings materialized in front of Echo, at Omega's command. It showed a dense wave of shrapnel and debris rapidly advancing on their saucer, propelled in part by the explosively expanding atmosphere released from the large Cortian spacecraft...as well as the fulminantly-vaporized components of part of that craft. Echo wedged his legs between the seat and the console, bracing himself in lieu of the straps he'd never had a chance to don.

"Too close!" he exclaimed. "Meg, we're gonna get—"

A severe impact rocked the vessel, and Echo fought to stay seated as intense pain shot through one shin—the same one the giant flytrap had injured on Borscht. Wrestling with the stick, he called to his partner.

"DAMN! We took a hit to the entire prop system! Meg, bring me up a navigation display! I need to see what's out there in this glowing pea soup!" He continued to fight the unresponsive controls, as a massive shadow gradually formed in the cloud ahead of them. "Meg, I need that—" Echo glanced at his partner. "Oh, hell," he whispered. "Baby?"

Omega was slumped across the co-pilot's panel, unconscious, a sticky red liquid trickling down the console's surface from a gash in her scalp.

Echo got off a mayday on the interstellar comm just before atmospheric entry. Then he tried desperately to re-establish enough maneuvering capability to soften their landing.

Unfortunately, it wasn't enough.

* * *

"Uuuunnh..." Omega slowly raised her throbbing head from the console. "Ohhh...wha' happen'...?" As memory returned, she snapped upright, then clutched her head. "Ooo—don't do that!" she told herself, and—slowly—raised her head to look out the tilted cockpit window. "What —?!"

Outside the ship, a desolate moonscape appeared, boulder-strewn, shrouded in a thick, greenish-gray miasma. Unfortunately, she saw it twice:

her vision was double, likely as a result of the head wound.

"This...is not good..." she whispered. "Echo...?"

Omega glanced over at the empty pilot's seat; it was then that she realized the spacecraft rested on a slight incline. An unconscious Echo lay crumpled under the navigation console on the port bulkhead, downslope.

"ECHO!!" Omega released the remaining three straps of her harness and lunged forward. Immediately, she staggered and fell, head pounding. She put one hand to her temple; it came away blood-covered. "Aw, crud," she grumbled, and began crawling toward her unconscious partner.

An alarm sounded, and Omega stopped, torn.

"Uh-oh. That's the master alarm. Ace, I'm sorry, partner, but you're gonna have to wait..." With an effort, Omega clawed her way back into the co-pilot's chair. She squinted hard in order to bring the double images as closely into focus as she could. "Oh, no," she murmured when she saw the readouts. She punched off the audio alert.

"What's...what's wrong?" The groggy voice came from behind.

"Echo?" Omega glanced back. "We've got a...a hull breach and a slow leak. Outside atmosphere's only about nine-point-five PSI, composition carbon monoxide, carbon dioxide, chlorine, hydrochloric acid..." She spoke hesitantly, speech slurred, occasionally stumbling over the words.

"Venus-like, in other words."

"Yes, except for the pressure, which is a good bit lower. If we don't stop the leak, we'll start suffering from hypoxia. Then when the pressure is equalized to outside, the poisonous planetary gases will start coming in. And that'll be it."

"All right. Do we have enough systems up to show us where the leak is?" Echo asked, voice unusually rough.

"Not exactly. It looks to be somewhere in the aft compartments, down below, I think. C'mon, let's go see if we can find it."

"Meg...I can't." It was almost—but not quite—a groan.

* * *

"What?? Why not?" A momentary flash of fear crossed Omega's face. Echo saw it, and he closed his eyes for a second, in mental as well as physical pain, before responding.

"Both legs are busted, and I think my left wrist is sprained—"

"Echo!" Omega turned toward him, wearing a look of shocked horror and concern.

"—You're gonna have to do this on your own, honey. I'm...sorry."

Omega drew a deep breath, then stood and took a single step toward the door, but staggered and fell, landing hard on her hands and knees with a soft exclamation.

"Meg?!"

"I'm...I'm all right, Echo." She struggled back to her feet, only to stumble and fall again. This time one hand slid out from under her, and her chest smacked into the deck. She lay for a moment, the wind knocked out of her, gasping.

"Meg...look at me."

Omega got to her hands and knees, and slowly raised her head to look at Echo. As he studied her, seeing the blood-smeared cheek, the unfocused gaze and dilated, uneven pupils, Echo drew his brows together in intense concern.

"Damn! Meg, it looks like you've got a severe concussion, and a nasty scalp laceration."

"I know. I got double vision, too..." She crawled to the doorway and used it to stand, then disappeared from Echo's view as she made her way into the bowels of the ship, clutching to the handholds on the bulkheads.

* * *

In the aft compartment, Omega leaned against the interior partition and carefully scrutinized the exterior bulkheads in the dim emergency lighting, but saw no sign of a leak. She made her way with some difficulty down to the lower deck, which held the galley, then to the engine room on the lowest deck.

"Nothing here, either, at least that I can see," she muttered, crawling back up the small stair.

"Echo," she said, stumbling onto the flight deck, hanging to the wall holds with white knuckles, "this isn't gonna work. I can't just eyeball it and tell where the leak is." She sat down beside Echo and started examining him. "Yep, both legs are broken, Ace. And this...aw, damn."

"What?"

"I think that people-eater trap thing back on Borscht did more damage than we figured, Echo," Omega told him, easing light fingers over the broken limb, sketching out the damage. "The break looks to be right here, under the residual bruising where that thing grabbed you and messed up your leg."

"Well...crap," Echo said, somewhat blank. "Meaning I probably had some stress fractures or something from that little run-in...which the crash then did a number on."

"Right. And it's not just your wrist, either. Looks like your shoulder's dislocated."

"Meg, worry about me later. Your first priority is that leak."

"I know, Echo, but I gotta think. Which isn't too easy right now with this ostrich egg on my head. Meantime, I can at least make you a little more comfortable. Let's get that shoulder back in place. Here." Omega scooted up close to his back, pulled him into her chest, and carefully manipulated Echo's arm into position, as he tried not to wince. "Ready? On three. One... two...three."

"Mmph." His grunt of suppressed pain was accompanied by a faint, hollow popping sound as the shoulder slid back into its proper position.

"There. Now let's straighten you out a bit." Omega crawled about, easing Echo out of his crumpled position, then quickly sprawled across his chest, holding him in place as the spacecraft shifted abruptly, settling into the impact site and leveling out. "Oh, blast an' damn it! Echo, waitaminit!" Omega scurried as fast as she could to the helm, where she scanned a section of the console that Echo recognized as the propulsion system controls.

"Good call, Meg. How's it look?"

"Well, no worries here, at any rate. Best I can see—which I admit isn't great right now—our prop can't blow, because it isn't there anymore. We're not getting off the planet under our own steam, that's for certain. I knew the engine room didn't look right."

"It's a wonder we didn't crack open like an egg, then. Chances are, that's where our hull breach is."

"Yeah, probably, but I dunno exactly where." Omega thought for a moment. "Mm. I sure wish we had a cigarette lighter."

"I do."

"What?! But...okay, I knew you smoked at one time, but I thought you quit, like, ages ago. Like, way before you and I ever met."

"You're right; I did. All told, I smoked less than a year—prob'ly less than six months—way back when I was in my late teens. What, maybe...

nineteen? Yeah, that sounds about right. To tell the truth—and I'd only ever admit this to you, and maybe Fox—it was all about tryin' to look like a big, badass agent. I didn't like the cigs at all; I always had this stale aftertaste in my mouth like I'd been lickin' an ashtray. One of the other Originals smoked, see, and I thought it looked cool. I never did figure out what he did about the aftertaste...or even if he GOT that, 'cause I was still soggy behind the ears and too embarrassed to ask. I finally got tired of the disgusting mouth, which made everything I ate taste bad, or at least off, so I quit. But the lighters have proved useful more than once, so I try to keep one on me."

"Good. On two counts," Omega smiled. "And you're plenty badass anyway. You don't need anything to prove it. So can I borrow it? The lighter, I mean?"

"Sure." Echo reached for his left pocket. "Uunnh. Shit." He grimaced, holding his left shoulder.

"What's wrong?"

"I can't reach it," he replied in pained annoyance. "I've either torn the rotator cuff, or I'm just too damn stiff to move. Come and get it. It's in my left pants pocket."

"Hooh-kay..." Omega stumbled over and knelt beside her partner, uncomfortable with what she was about to do, and trying to figure out how to offer an apology in advance, just in case things accidentally got more intimate than she intended. "Uh...it's not like exploring your pants pocket is, um, exactly something I do every day..."

"Well, not while I'm in 'em, at least." Echo grinned slightly, apparently trying to tease her and lighten her mood. Omega offered him a wry smile as reward, and he nodded once, seeming pleased. "Well, dive in," he told her, waving his good hand at his trousers. So she gingerly fished in his trousers pocket, and eventually brought out the lighter...along with a multi-tool, pocket knife, lip balm, and several other small odds and ends Echo was apparently wont to keep in his pockets.

"There it is," she said, picking it out of the handful of items. "Wait, rather than putting all this back, do you wanna put some of this stuff in the other pocket, so you can get to it?"

"Nah...well, wait. Gimme the lip balm, the multi-tool, an' the knife, an' I'll stick it over here, yeah."

Omega put the requested items in his right hand before returning the rest to his left pocket as he squirreled the others into his right pocket. Then she held up the lighter, checking to determine the fuel level.

"What are you gonna do with it?" a curious Echo asked, watching.

"I'm gonna try to find the leak."

"How?"

"The flame will flicker a lot in whichever compartment the leak is in. Then, if I can come up with some paper or cardboard, I can set it smoldering and trace the smoke to the leak," Omega elaborated.

"Ooo, nice idea. I've got a paperback on my bunk. Grab it and rip the cover off," Echo volunteered. "I think I left it on my pillow, or thereabouts."

"I hate to rip up your book like that."

"It's okay. It's battered to hell an' back anyway; the back cover is already about half torn loose. I picked it up a couple weeks ago for a quarter, down at the used book store, just because I wanted to re-read it. I can get another copy."

"Oh, all right then. While I track down the leak, figure out something for me."

"What?"

"How I fix it once I've found it."

* * *

Omega leaned up against the doorframe in the aft EVA prep compartment, held Echo's cigarette lighter at arm's length, and ignited it, holding it steady with both hands, though in her condition, it was an effort.

The tip of the flame drifted slowly back toward the corridor, away from the aft compartment.

* * *

Down in the galley, a similar phenomenon occurred; she followed it out and down to the hatchway into the engine room. There, the cigarette lighter's flame danced a merry jig.

"Makes sense," Omega muttered. "Lowest deck. Engine room. Losin' the prop probably weakened it structurally. Then the impact likely cracked the hull. Echo's right; we're lucky we didn't split wide open. We'd both be dead now, if we had."

Omega pulled the book cover out of the pocket of her robe and glanced at it, then chuckled. It was *Robinson Crusoe*.

"Well, I guess that's appropriate. I wonder which of us is Friday. No,

121

on second thought, I expect that'd be me." She lit the corner of the cover, waited until it caught well, then waved it about until the open flames were extinguished, and only a few tiny glowing coals were in evidence. She watched carefully as a thin wisp of smoke rose into the cabin air and floated aft.

Crawling slowly, Omega followed the drifting plume of smoke until it contacted the bulkhead at a seam. Licking her fingers, she ran them along the seam until she felt the cool airflow. Then she traced out the extent of the ruptured seam with the wet-finger method, pulled a marker out of her robe pocket, and outlined the leak.

* * *

Having disposed of the destroyed book cover in the galley sink, and run water over it to ensure it was extinguished, Omega made her way with some difficulty back onto the flight deck. As soon as she entered the compartment, she addressed her partner.

"Okeydoke, Echo, I found it. It's downstairs in the engine room, all right, on the aft side...assuming a saucer has a side, I guess. Or a fore an' aft, rather. I figure the impact probably sent a shock wave back through the hull, bulging it out in the back, and it popped the seam, by the look. It was already weakened from the external units of the propulsion system getting ripped out, so it probably was easier to bust it open than it might have been, otherwise."

"Mmh. That makes sense."

"Yeah. Now..." she put her hand to her head and sighed in pain, "now I gotta fix it."

"Well, I've come up...with a low-tech way...and a high-tech way," Echo said, his voice slow and thick. Omega sat down on the deck beside him and laid one hand on his bare shoulder; it was cold, and she realized he was going into shock. She slipped off her robe and laid it over him, tucking it around him. It wasn't bulky, but it was silk, which was an excellent insulator. "What...are you doing?" he asked, surprised.

"Checking on you. You're in shock, Ace. As soon as I plug this leak, I promise I'm gonna see to you." She winced as pain stabbed her temple. "What's the low-tech?"

"A sheet of Irikian polymer...and übertape."

"Mm...what's the biggest piece of polymer we've got on board?"

"Oh, 'bout fifteen inches square, prob'ly..." Echo slurred the words slightly.

"Hm. I dunno," Omega said, considering. "Like I said, a seal popped between plates. The rupture is a good two feet long, at least; maybe a little more. I suppose I could try overlapping a couple of sheets with tape, on th' diagonal. What's the high-tech?"

"Blaster...on a low setting...used as a welder. But you'll haveta go...on EVA...to do it. Gotta be...done outside."

"Okay. I'm gonna try the polymer first." Omega got up, using the bulkhead to steady herself, holding to the regularly-spaced handholds, and started for the storage lockers on the middle deck.

* * *

Down in the engine room, Omega carefully joined two pieces of the tough alien plastic with the super-strong gray tape used by the Division One agents. *You can tell there's more men than women agents in the equipment development department, at least for now,* Omega thought with amused affection as she worked; *we've even got our own special kinda duct tape.* She laid her creation over the burst seam, and air pressure immediately pushed it tight against the leak. Omega outlined the polymer with more tape, then ran moistened fingers around the edges.

"No airflow—at least for the time being. I just don't know how long it'll hold against that battery acid out there. But it'll do for now, and Echo needs taking care of."

Omega detoured by the medical station to get equipment and supplies, then slowly worked her way back to the flight deck.

* * *

There, she found that Echo was badly chilled and in a semiconscious stupor. She knelt beside her partner and, digging surgical scissors from the ship's medical kit, cut Echo's trouser legs open to the thigh, checking for compound fractures.

"Good," she murmured, relieved. "Ace? Are you with me, hon?"

No answer. Omega pulled an osmosive micropore syringe from the sophisticated medical kit, filled it with painkiller, and administered it directly into Echo's near thigh. Then she cautiously set his legs—one shin was snapped, and the other thigh was broken, apparently from where he braced himself in lieu of seat straps—and splinted them with the equipment from the kit. Omega put a wrist brace on the sprained joint, and a stabilizer on Echo's damaged shoulder, slipping his arm into a sling to help support it. Then she fished special fasteners from the kit and closed up his trouser legs, to provide some additional warmth, while still allowing for ready access to the injured limbs.

Next, she crawled aft, into the sleeping quarters, and proceeded to drag all of the bedclothes she could get her hands on out to the flight deck, where she formed a crude nest of pillows, sheets, and blankets.

"All right, Ace, in you go," Omega said, working the unconscious man into the pallet with great difficulty, given how many of his limbs she had to avoid using for leverage. "Umph. There. Hope you don't mind sleeping on the floor. If I could stand up by myself, I could maybe get you into a bunk. But as it is, this'll have to do." She took the remaining covers and spread them over her insensate partner, tucking them around him very gently, allowing a hint of the deep affection she felt for him to come through in her touch, since it could not embarrass him in his current state. "There we are, honey. Now you oughta be good to go for a while."

Omega crawled over to the helm and pulled herself up into the pilot seat. "Now let's see here...good. The leak's stopped. Air sc-scrubbers okay...for now. Blast it. I thought it was getting colder in here! With the warp system gone, we don't have enough power for the thermal con-conditioners. Nnh...I'm gonna kill the guy with the jackhammer if he doesn't lay off my head. Okay...battery power only, then. Switching over life support. It's still gonna get cold in here... Oh, check the automated mayday... good..." Omega's head drooped. "Mmmh... Ah'm so tired...but Ah....Ah need to get...get mah Suit on...move some food an' water up here...check Echo again..."

Omega slid out of the chair and crawled over to Echo's cocoon, picked up a medical scanner, and ran it over the still form of her partner. She had just wits enough to register that the scanner's readouts were within acceptable limits before she slumped to the cold deck.

* * *

When Omega regained consciousness, she was warm. A gentle, almost tender, touch at her battered right temple could have caused pain, but didn't. She lay quietly as her head was bandaged comfortably, then she sighed.

"Guy wi' th' jackhammer mus' be takin' a coffee break," she murmured groggily. "'Bout damn time."

"Meg?" Echo's voice came from a distance. "Wake up, Meg. I need to check you out."

"Nuh-uh...sleep...so tired..."

"No, baby. Wake up. Wake up for me, now. Come on, honey, wake up."

With a groan, Omega opened her eyes until they were scant slits, and tried unsuccessfully to focus on the face that leaned over her.

* * *

Echo checked the pupils of her eyes: they were still dilated and unequal. *Shit,* he thought, worried, *if Meg's got a skull fracture, there's not a damn thing I can do. I can't even walk.*

"Meg...do you know where you are?" Echo asked, carefully hiding his concern as her eyes slid closed again.

"Uh-huh." A woozy Omega nodded slowly against the pillow Echo had put under her head, then winced. "Ship...crashed. Echo banged up. Fixed leak...sorta. Fixed Echo...sorta. Bed on deck. Scrubbers. Life support. Heaters on batteries...mayday."

"Good girl." Echo blinked at the enumeration. "Wow. You've been busy."

"'Zat you, Ace?" She still sounded sleepy, and Echo noted that, except for allowing him to check her pupils for concussion, she had yet to truly open her eyes.

"Yeah, baby, it's me."

"You aw'right?"

"I'm...okay, under the circumstances. Thanks."

"Sorry it...took s' long..."

"Threat to life takes priority over busted legs. You did exactly what you should have done."

"Oh!" Suddenly Omega was wide awake, and sat up with a start. "Ooo," she moaned, her upper body doing a kind of slow precession as her head spun. Both hands went to her head.

Echo had managed to prop himself up with pillows, and now he took his partner's shoulder with his good hand, restraining her.

"Easy, baby. Slow down, there. You've got a...a concussion. You need

125

to lie down and rest for a bit. Only don't go back to sleep for a little while."

* * *

"If I lie down," Omega responded, doing her best to be reasonable and logical, "who's gonna bring the food and water up from the galley? Who's gonna watch the ship readouts?"

"Dammit, Meg..." Echo began, and paused. "I hate it when we're both right." He sighed. "All right. One trip, and one only. Grab as much as you can carry."

Omega nodded, wincing at the motion, and crawled out of the nest which Echo had somehow managed to make for her out of his own.

"I'll be back as soon as I can," she murmured, easing to her feet with the help of the nearby wall, before making her slow way along that wall to the door.

* * *

A little while later, Omega returned, crawling across the deck in black trousers and white untucked shirt sans necktie or jacket, dragging a bag of supplies, including nonperishable food items and bottled juice and water, in one hand. Over one shoulder she had slung an undershirt and white dress shirt for Echo.

"Here," she handed the garments to him. "You need more clothes. It's gettin' cold in here. Um...I swiped one of your under-shirts. Downstairs is gettin' pretty cold. And my Suit jacket won't let me crawl too well—at least, not up and down stairs—so I really needed an extra layer. I, uh, I hope you don't mind..."

"No, that's fine."

"Here's munchies, tools, and general stuff I thought might be useful." She put the bag down within Echo's easy reach. "Oh, I threw your paperback in there, too, in case you wanted to read. Now I'm gonna go check our status." Echo watched as Omega crawled to the helm and painfully pulled herself up and into one of the chairs. "Ow. Where's zero-g when it'd actually be useful? I could sure use some knee pads, too," she muttered, and commenced studying the readouts. Abruptly her brow furrowed. "Uh-oh. Um...Echo?"

"Yeah? What's wrong?" he asked, seeing her frown.

"I...can't read it..." Omega whispered.

* * *

126

"This is a nice fix we're in, Ace," Omega chuckled shakily from her seat on the deck beside Echo's makeshift bed. "The man of action can hardly move, and the woman of intellect can barely think."

"So it's not merely a case of being unable to focus your eyes?" Echo asked.

"That's a big part of it, but yeah. I look at the readouts, and can't pull my wits together enough to figure out what they mean. And...I think it's getting worse." She stared down at her fidgeting hands. "Echo, I...I don't know what to do."

A strong male hand rubbed across Omega's taut shoulders, soothing, and she looked up at her partner.

"It's okay, Meg," Echo said, voice soft. "You're doing fine. Everything's gonna be all right. We'll just have to shift gears a little bit. Can you focus well enough to call off the instrument readings to me?"

"I think so. Oh! You can't get to 'em to see, but you'll know what they mean. I CAN get to 'em, but can't figure out what they mean..."

"Right. So you sit at the helm and call off the values to me, I interpret 'em, figure out what needs doing, and tell you how to do it."

"Okay! That'll work!"

"All right then, partner, let's get to it. We'll lick this, you and me, together."

* * *

Once they were done checking statuses, with Omega calling out values and Echo verifying them, he made her lie back down.

"It's okay, Meg. The ship's status is acceptable. You need to lie down before you fall down."

"I'm fine, Echo. It's just a bump on the head."

*I hope...*he thought. "How are your ears?"

"My ears?"

"Yeah. Any congestion or drainage? Stopped up?"

"No, not that I've noticed."

"Okay." Echo considered the matter. *A concussion victim isn't supposed to go to sleep for the first few hours,* he realized. *But she already has. Though I'm not completely sure if she fell asleep or flat passed out. And we're past the end point for that by now, anyway, according to the chronometer on the helm.* He sighed. *It can't hurt any worse, I guess. And I can tell she's worn out, just by looking at her.* "Come and lie down, then."

"All right," Omega sighed. "If you insist."

"I do."

Omega slid out of the seat, crawled back over to the little bedroll Echo had created for her out of his own, and wormed her way under the blankets, sighing as her aching head sank into the pillow. Echo took one look at her position and immediately decided, *Uh-oh. That won't do at all.*

"Face me."

"What?" Omega murmured.

"Roll over onto your left side and face me, Meg. Try not to put weight on that head wound," Echo told her.

"Uh. Okay, I get it." She acquiesced, then studied him for a moment. "What's the deal with your shirt?"

"Oh," Echo said, glancing down at the open shirt and his exposed chest. "I couldn't get the t-shirt on with this bum shoulder. And the dress shirt won't button over the shoulder brace anyway, let alone getting the sling off and it on. So I just slipped it on to cover my arms and back."

"Hm. What if I slit the shoulder seam?"

"Don't worry about it, Meg. You bundled me up pretty good here; I won't get cold for now. Get some rest." Echo picked up the paperback Omega had brought him, and resumed where he'd left off.

* * *

After about half an hour, Omega stirred restlessly, and Echo glanced up from his book.

"You still awake?" he asked her.

"Yeah. And likely to be." She looked up at him with tired eyes.

"Head hurt?"

"It's not too bad lying down," Omega hedged. "It's just...it's so quiet...I mean, no engines, most of the ship sounds are gone, 'cause what makes 'em isn't running—isn't even THERE anymore—and...and...so I keep...thinking."

Echo watched her for a moment, realizing what she was thinking about.

"Anything I can do? Rock you to sleep?" he teased, trying to ease her tension. Omega chuckled.

"No, but you're close. Read to me?"

"Read to you?"

"Yeah."

"I'm afraid I don't have any Dr. Seuss, Meg," Echo teased again.

"No," Omega said, sounding sheepish, "but you've got a good reading voice. I realized that when you read to me in the regeneration pod after...after the Cortians cooked me. And I usually read in bed to unwind, anyway."

"But you can't read for yourself right now."

"No."

"So you want me to read you to sleep?"

"Uh—never mind, Echo. Forget it. When you say it out loud like that, it sounds pretty stupid. Go on back to your book, an' I'm sorry I interrupted you. Good night." Omega settled back into the pillow and closed her eyes in obvious determination.

Echo studied the quiet form, noting the tight ball her body made under the blankets, the stiff jaw, the faint crease between the silver brows. He flipped to the front of the book.

"'I was born in the year 1632, in the city of York, of a good family, though not of that country, my father being a foreigner of Bremen who settled first at Hull. He got a good estate by merchandise...'"

Chapter 6

"Meg? Wake up. C'mon, sleepyhead. It's important." Echo shook his partner gently but insistently. "Wake up."

"Wha'?" Unfocused blue eyes blinked up at him. "Whassup?"

"It's going to storm." Echo pointed at the ominous greenish-gray clouds, striated with streaks of dirty yellow, gathering outside the cockpit window.

"Oh? Rain. Tha's nice..." The blue eyes fluttered closed.

"Meg," Echo said, shaking her again, "THIS rain is hydrochloric acid."

There was a pause, then Omega abruptly sat bolt upright.

"Oh damn! Will the ship take it??" She held her throbbing head in her hands as Echo answered.

"Yeah, the hull will, but the cockpit window won't, not for long. You need to close the blast shutters."

"Okay..." Omega made her way across the deck as rapidly as she could, and climbed into the co-pilot's chair. "Uh. Where..."

"Panel delta-one-one."

"Um..."

"Oh, sorry. I forgot for a sec." Echo sat up as straight as he could, frowning at the discomfort in his legs, and leaned over to get a good view. "Top of the console. Now left...left...left...little more...now down two. No, the other one. That's it."

Omega followed his directions, then flipped the switch, and the shutters closed slowly over the window—just as a tremendous lightning bolt illuminated the cabin.

"Shit!" Echo said with a grin, blinking. "Helluva big popgun."

* * *

Omega heard the grin in his voice, but didn't respond; she was too busy trying to orient herself as the thunderclap shook the spacecraft.

"Echo..." she moaned, sliding out of the chair to the deck, where she lay prone, "I...I think I'm...gonna be...sick..."

"Damn. What happened?"

"That lightning...it blinded me. My eyes are SO messed up, anyway.

Now the window's closed...the cabin's so dim...only emergency lights. Dizzy...ugh..."

* * *

"Just a minute, Meg," Echo said, rummaging in the medical kit and grabbing a bottle of water from their food store. "Hang on. Lie real still and try not to get sick, okay?"

He tied the bottle in his shirttail and dropped a hypo in his shirt pocket, then flipped the covers back and began dragging himself painfully across the deck toward his stricken partner, using only his right arm.

* * *

Omega looked up at the sound of cloth abrading against the deck.

"No, Ace. Don't..."

"Hold still," he reiterated, panting. "I'm okay. I'm using my good arm. It's just that that's ALL I got to use, an' I'm tryin' to keep my legs from moving much, so it's wearing me out."

"Okay. Be careful."

"Always." When Echo reached her, he handed Omega the water bottle and gasped, "Here. Roll up your sleeve and...then drink this. Real slow. Try to sip it, if you can." Echo administered the hypo as Omega sipped the cool water. "There," he sighed, easing himself to the deck. "That oughta help the nausea and dizziness."

The two Agents sprawled on the cold floor of the flight deck in the semi-darkness, panting quietly in pain as the storm raged outside. Eventually Omega raised her head, tentative and testing.

"Wow. Good. It stays put."

"What?" Echo asked, opening his eyes.

"My head. It finally quit makin' like ocean waves; that stuff you gave me worked really good. Okay, let's get you back to bed. Mm, this is gonna be tricky. I can't pull your left arm, an' I don't wanna risk the right one. Oh, I know. Roll onto your back," Omega told Echo, and he complied.

She stood slowly and carefully, helped him sit up, then grabbed the waistband of his trousers, hooking her fingers through the belt loops; he hadn't had time to finish fastening the stuck zipper on his trousers earlier, let alone thread a belt through them, though Omega noticed that the fly was now fully zipped, hiding Echo's lower abdomen once more. It had been properly closed at some point, likely while she slept...though she hated to think how much pain it must have cost him, with his sprained wrist and bum shoulder, in his effort to be a gentleman for her.

"All right, I think this is gonna work. Now lean back against my arms," she told him. "There. Good. Try to relax and not move around a lot. I'm gonna drag you back over to the blankets."

"Won't you fall, Meg?"

"Not if we go ahead and do it right now. Whatever you gave me is working awful damn good. I'm serious. This is the best I've felt since we crashed. I can almost even see straight."

With some considerable effort, Omega got Echo bundled back up and resting comfortably, coaxing him to take pain medication and eat a little bit; she fully understood that his earlier effort to reach her would not have exhausted him so badly had he not also been combatting severe pain. He refused to admit it, even when she confronted him directly...but he did consent to take the pain medication with relatively little resistance, which told her all she needed to know.

And they both realized the fact that they had experienced two consecutive days of multiple missed meals in the last week was not helping matters. Their normal reserves were low to begin with, and it had left them mildly weaker than normal. Their usual routines would not have caused a problem, but this situation was anything but routine. Factor in their severe and, in Echo's case, extensive injuries, and it was telling on them—the pair were running down far faster than they otherwise might.

After a while, as the storm outside quieted, Echo's head drooped, and he drifted into a much-needed sleep. Omega nodded to herself, satisfied, then stood and cautiously wobbled over to the helm and studied it. One red light blinked insistently at her.

"Aw, hell. Not again..." she said softly.

* * *

Omega held the cigarette lighter in the doorway of the dark engine room. The flame danced and flickered. Using it as a light source, she stumbled over to the outer bulkhead and examined the polymer patch over the burst seam. It had melted along the entire length of the hull rupture.

'Meg...this rain is hydrochloric acid,' Echo had said.

She grabbed a nearby object—it happened to be a maintenance manual for the engines that were no longer there—and flung it across the cabin

132

with some considerable force. It hit the far bulkhead and slid down it to the deck.

"Aw, dammit to hell," an overwrought Omega said, with feeling.

* * *

When Echo woke up several hours later with a sensation that something had awakened him, Omega was nowhere to be seen.

"Meg?" he murmured groggily. "You there?"

"Hi, Echo," Omega's voice came clearly to him. "If you look on my pillow, I've put out your pain medication, a bottle of O.J., and something that'll haveta do for breakfast. Sorry it can't be scrambled eggs and bacon, but nothing in the galley is really workin' right now."

Echo glanced to his right, and picked up the juice bottle and the pre-packaged meal—it was country-fried steak, with mashed potatoes and gravy, and whole-kernel corn—but he ignored the medication.

"Echo—take the medicine."

He blinked, scanned the empty room, popped open the juice, sipped it, then turned to the meal.

"ECHO."

"What?!" Echo was annoyed.

"I'm gonna bug you until you take it, Ace. I need your help, and I need you free of pain so you'll be as clear-headed as possible—'cause I'm not."

"Where the hell are you, anyway?"

A hollow knock sounded from the vicinity of the helm. Echo followed the direction of the sound, searching for its source, and realized the blast shutters had been opened by a couple of feet. A black-striped, space-suited figure waved from the other side of the cockpit window. Echo abruptly sat up straight, ignoring the pain of shoulder and leg.

"Shit! Meg, what the hell are you doing out there?! Get in here now, dammit!"

"No can do, Ace. We got a leak again. The storm ate clean through the Irikian poly-polymer stuff like paper in a bonfire. I've got a blaster—" the white figure held up the weapon, "and I'm gonna try to weld the leak closed before the air out here eats through my suit. Now are you gonna help me or not?"

Without another moment's hesitation, Echo scooped up the capsules, popped them in his mouth, and knocked back the juice. Only then did he realize that he was wearing his 'Snoopy hat,' the comm cowl from his own spacesuit, when the tiny microphone got in the way of taking the medication; somehow, Omega had slipped the cowl on him in his sleep, without ever waking him up.

"Thanks, Ace," Omega said quietly. "Now tell me what setting to put this blaster on."

"Power level two, with a particle acceleration multiplier of four. Choke the beam all the way down."

"Uhh...two, then four...choke it...all right, it's there," Omega remarked, adjusting the weapon. "Have you ever done this before?"

"Yeah, a couple times. X-ray showed me how, years ago. And I think Fox taught him. It's...a long story. I'll tell you later."

"Okay, good. I'm headed back now. Got any tips for me?" The white figure disappeared from Echo's field of view, headed around the curve of the saucer.

"First off, is there any chance at all that I can get a visual on you?" Echo asked.

"I don't think so, Ace. I checked on that first thing. Our rear sensors got creamed by the Cortian stuff that hit us. And this ship doesn't have the hovering holovid thingies...not that I think one a' those would survive this pea soup out here anyway. Sorry."

"Oh well. It was worth a try. Have you ever welded anything?" Echo asked. Tense, he stared out the cockpit window at the bleak landscape of the alien world as he listened, intent.

"Yeah, back on the farm, years ago as a teenager," Omega responded. "I helped Dad fix a broken tractor hitch, an' some other stuff like that. I was pretty decent at it. It's been a while, but I know what I'm doin' with an arc-welder."

"Okay, great. Your solar visor will work all right for a welding mask, so make sure you put that down before you start to work. And with those degrees of yours, I'm sure you know that, while some of the atmospheric gases here would be considered flammable on Earth, without any source of oxygen, you've got nothing to worry about. In fact, the carbon monoxide and dioxide would tend to quench any flames. But you might get a little flaring right around the cracked seam, if any oxygen gets through from inside, so be careful. It's gonna be pretty much like a regular weld, just without a welding rod. Take it slow enough to get a good bead, but not so slow that you burn through. It'll be hard to melt the alloy, so be patient."

"Copy that. I patched the, uh, the polymer before I suited up, so you shouldn't get any...um, toxic stuff comin' in while I do this. Or at least, not much. And having the oxygen flare things up oughta be moot, too."

"Good. And when you come back inside, make sure you run the airlock through a venting and blow-off cycle, in case any of those same gases have adsorbed on your spacesuit. It shouldn't, but it never hurts to be thorough. There'll be a button right next to the standard airlock cycle button for that, and it'll be labeled, if you can read it. If you can't, it's to the left of the cycle button, same size, and blue instead of red."

"Oh, got it. All right, I'm here and I'm in position. Here we go."

"Be really careful, Meg. Like I said, it shouldn't spark with the blaster, but you never know. And our spacesuits are good, but they'll still burn through if something hot enough hits 'em. Try not to stay out there too long, either; I'm not sure how long the suit'll hold against the acidic air."

"Okay. So far so good, Echo. The metal is melting nice and smooth, it just takes a while, like you said. I've got a good puddle of melt here, and I'm starting the bead now."

"Good."

* * *

Outside, Omega had the gold helmet visor down, thanks mostly to Echo's reminder, and lay on her stomach on the cold ground—she knew it was cold, because she could feel it leaching the heat from her suit—wielding the blaster with caution. It was slow going due to the metallurgical properties of the space-faring alloy, as well as the location of the leak, practically underneath the saucer. And it took all of her impaired concentration to accomplish the difficult task.

"Meg? How's it going?" Echo's voice filtered to her ears.

"It's going all right, Echo. Got about...mmm...say six inches of bead, so far."

"Ah, okay. So you're 'bout a quarter of the way? You said the rupture was about two feet long, right?"

"Uh...yeah, an' yeah." She eased the beam of the blaster along the split seam, manipulating it delicately so as not only to melt the metal of the hull, but to nudge the melt this way or that, filling the breach.

"How are you feeling?"

"Okay, I suppose. I took another round of that stuff you gave me, just before I suited up. Boy, did that take a while, all by myself. I thought I'd never get the bottom of the damn pressure suit on, especially with the compression-garment part. Anyway, I'm flat on my belly, so if I get loopy, at least I don't have too far to fall," she deadpanned, and was rewarded by a faint chuckle. "I just wish my Snoopy hat was a little looser." She winced despite herself.

"Is it hurting that goose egg?" Echo's voice asked in sympathy.

"Dinosaur egg feels more like it, at this point," Omega remarked. "Felt like I was trying to fit two heads into one hat, putting it on."

"Ow."

"Uh-huh."

"How far along are you now?" Echo asked.

"Mmm...nearly a foot. Not quite halfway."

"Can you go any faster?" Echo pressed.

"Not and be sure I've got an...an airtight weld. Relax, Ace; hush, and let me do this."

* * *

Inside the spacecraft, an apprehensive Echo watched the threatening gray-green clouds re-forming, ominous on the indistinct horizon. *Meg, hurry up, baby,* he thought, worried. *That pressure suit won't last a minute in a hellstorm like that. Damn, it's building by the second.*

"Meg?" Echo began dragging himself torturously toward the helm.

"'Bout a foot and a half, Echo."

"Meg—" He reached the co-pilot seat.

"As fast as I can, Echo." A pause. "What's up? It's not like Joe Cool to be so antsy."

"Let's just say...April showers aren't as pleasant...around here as... they are back home," Echo panted as he wrestled his way up into the chair, with his legs, shoulder and wrist screaming in pain the entire time.

"...Huh? —Oh shit!"

"Hurry up, Meg," Echo urged, eyes glued to the window. "The storm's building fast now."

"Haangg ooon...juussst a little mooorre..."

"Come on! It's almost on top of us!" Echo hit the blast shutter switch.

"One mooore—there!" A pause. "Oh, boy..."

"RUN, Meg!"

"I'm—unh!—running as fast as—ahh!"

Echo saw the first drops fall as the shutters met.

"Meg! Where are you?!" he called.

"Airlo— aaah! Aaah! Close! Close! Oh! Oh! Cycle! Vent an' blow! Ahh! Hurry, hurry!"

"MEG!" Echo swiveled the chair to look down the dim passageway toward the ship's aft. Nothing was visible.

"Aah! Aah! Get it off, get it off, get it off!"

"Meg, answer me!!"

"Didn't—didn't quite make it...huh..."

Oh, shit. "How bad?"

"Not...not real bad. Echo, I'm headed for the shower—!"

"I'll get the medikit ready."

No answer was forthcoming, but as Echo yanked off the comm cowl, he heard running feet in the depths of the ship. Sliding his splinted legs out straight in front of him, Echo lowered himself to the deck in an agonizing triceps-press type of move, left arm and both legs protesting vehemently the whole way. The sound of flowing liquid drifted from the corridor— Omega had evidently not bothered closing any doors behind her—as Echo dragged himself across the cabin as fast as he could, making a beeline for the medikit beside the pallet beds on the deck. He stiffened in horror as Omega cried out.

"OoOOoooo! It's COLD!!"

Echo stopped, sinking to the deck in relief, laughing.

* * *

Some time later, Omega stumbled into the flight deck, wrapped only in her black silk robe, which she had retrieved from Echo earlier, once she'd gotten him bundled in his pallet on the deck. Wordlessly, she sat down beside Echo on the blankets, turned her back to him, and slipped the robe off her shoulders, exposing her bare upper back. Echo's eyes narrowed in sympathetic pain as he saw the acid burns in the dim light, and he hissed softly.

"...Please...?" It was all she had to say, and more than she needed to say. Echo immediately began treating the burns on his partner's shoulders

137

and upper back while the storm raged outside. As he worked, Echo talked to take Omega's mind off the pain.

"Did you get the welding done?" he asked casually.

"Yeah, I did."

"Is it a good weld?"

"According to your cigarette lighter, it is. Oooh."

"Sorry." Echo froze at the gasp of pain, then continued treating the burn, but made his touch as light and gentle as he knew how to make it.

"It's okay, hon. It's not your fault. My shoulders just got eaten half off." Omega was matter-of-fact. She started to shrug, then apparently thought better of it, freezing with her shoulders in an odd, not-quite-lifted position, before easing them back down to a normal posture.

"What's it like out there?" he followed up, keeping his partner occupied.

"It's kinda...weird out there."

"What do you mean?"

"It's almost like you're swimming to go anywhere, the air is so...so thick. And looking through it, well, it...kind of acts like...a lens, I guess. I could sorta see AROUND stuff, if you get me..." Omega tried to explain.

"That'd be the different refractive indices of the gases in the atmosphere, I suppose. Did you get dizzy?"

"Not too much," she answered, then admitted, "but I tried to pay attention to what I was doing and not look around a whole lot."

"There. Shoulders feel better now?" Echo asked, finishing with a cool, numbing spray bandage.

"Yeah, a lot. Thanks," Omega said, pulling the robe back up around her throat and shivering, chilled in the cold cabin air.

"Is anywhere else burned?" Echo eyed her in concern.

"Well..." She turned around and held out her hands. Her soft blue eyes were glazed with pain.

"Aw, damn, Meg," Echo whispered, staring at the raw, bleeding fingertips.

"I had to get the suit off, Echo," she murmured. "The acid was eating right through it. What's left of it is still in the, um, airlock. Same thing with the blaster. I hated to lose that blaster. It's the one we con-confiscated from Tango in Antarctica, on our first real mission as Alpha One. Kinda my first trophy, I guess you could say. An' I suppose Fox will have to have another spacesuit made for me..."

"Why don't you lie down and rest while I doctor on these?" Echo suggested quietly.

"Okay," a passive Omega responded, curling up on her left side and holding her hands stiffly in front of her.

Shocked at her immediate obedience when normally she would have insisted on weathering it out, Echo stared at her for a long moment. Then he reached out, gently taking one of her poor, wounded hands in his and treating it.

No argument? he wondered, worried. *No toughing through it? Shit. She must be wiped out.* He laid her left hand down and started on her right, repeating his ministrations. *Dammit, where's Fox with a rescue team? We could really use some help about now. Or at least a medic. I wish we'd brought Alpha Two along. Then again, we might only have twice the number of people bashed up, if we had.*

"There," he said softly, finished with the application of the topical medications. "How's that?"

"Better. Thanks. Can you, um, bandage 'em?"

"Sure." Echo reached for the dressings. "Why?"

"'Cause I need to, uh, be able to use my hands."

"You need to rest."

"So do you," Omega responded. "And we will as soon as we check the...um, statuses."

"That makes me think," Echo said as he bandaged. "If you can't read the panel now, how did you know about the leak?"

"Same little blinky red light that showed the leak before." Omega caught herself, then shook her head sadly against the pillow. "'Little blinky lights.' Damn it. I never thought I'd ever fit the dumb blonde image." She watched as Echo completed the bandages. "Um, Ace?"

"Hm?"

"Is my head...messed up bad?"

Echo looked away, making a business of packing the equipment back in the medical bag so he wouldn't have to look at her. He made his reply as casual and unassuming as he could. "I don't know, Meg."

"Can you check me with the scan-thing?"

"I did, while you were asleep," Echo admitted, still refusing to meet her eyes.

"Yeah? What did it say?"

Finally, unable to put off a direct response any longer, he looked at her, meeting the cerulean gaze.

"Meg, I'm not a doctor," Echo said, voice very quiet. "I've got advanced field medical training, like you, but...the med scan was...the complexity...well, India could probably have interpreted it..."

"So you really don't know? You're not just sayin' that to avoid tellin' me?"

"No. I really don't know."

"Okay, let's check the stupid lights, so we can rest," she sighed, sitting up. Omega stood, staggered, and fell. "Ow. Wow, that stuff musta wore off already. There wasn't much to begin with, and I used the last of it to get suited up and do the welding."

"Well, shit. When we get back, we need to tell Ship's Supplies to start packing a LOT more meds in the onboard medikits." Echo shook his head. "Sample sizes won't cut it, not for an Alpha Line team. If we only had some more Rejuvic, it would sure help. I could get those acid burns of yours healed up in a couple days, max. Maybe overnight."

"Yeah, I know. So here we go again." Once more, Omega was forced to resort to crawling painfully on hands and knees to the controls, where with an effort, she hoisted herself into a chair and studied the console, brow furrowed. "Okay, the blinky red light is out."

"Good. The pressure has stabilized, and the leak is corked." Echo leaned back against the pillows, trying to hide his own pain.

* * *

But Omega's sharp ears heard a somewhat strained note in his familiar voice, and she glanced back quickly, in time to see a momentary grimace cross his face. She frowned, then turned swiftly back to the console as Echo looked up.

"I've got a different red light, Echo."

"Where?"

"Um..." Omega tried to figure out how to tell him; finally, she gave up and simply pointed. "Here."

* * *

Echo noted Omega's rapidly increasing incoherence, and his eyes grew troubled.

"Meg, have you eaten?"

"Before I went on...before I went outside. You were still asleep."

"Okay. It was worth a shot." Echo sighed, eyes still narrowed in worry. "What does the readout beside the warning light say?"

Omega blinked, and squinted. Stopped and rubbed her fists into her eyes. Blinked again. "Batt...batt..."

"Battery."

"L...low. Numbers are...oh...oh...nine."

"Damn. We're losin' the batteries. How's the interstellar mayday?"

"Uh. Yeah, that's over here. Green light. Oh...nine...seven."

"Good. What's the Mission Elapsed Time?"

"Four-four-oh...an' three-six." Unconsciously, Omega brushed a hand across her eyes, then rubbed her temple.

Echo saw the gestures, and realized they meant that her head hurt, and her vision was blurred. *Not good,* he thought. *SO not good.*

"Four hundred forty and a half hours, give or take," he told her instead. "A little more than five Agency days before Fox expects us home. Damn. Hm..."

"What is it?"

"Lemme think at you, Meg," Echo mused, staring up at the shadowy deckhead above him. "We're in the middle of what you call an emission nebula, which is astronomer-ese for 'a big cloud of ionized gas.'"

"Uh-huh..." Her eyes were blank, uncomprehending. Echo noticed out of the corner of his eye, but he pretended not to see.

Damn it to hell, he thought, deeply pained. *And that's her own principal field of study.* He mentally shook his head, now intensely worried, and continued his previous train of thought.

"And ionized gas can interfere with communications."

"Um...yeah." Omega frowned with the effort of concentrating.

"So we can't count on the Division One installations hearing our S.O.S. Not from this distance. Not at our current power levels."

"No...I, um, I guess not..." Omega was subdued. She put a bandaged hand to her head.

"On the other hand," Echo continued, "one Cortian ship has already caught up to us; that's why we're in this fix. There's gotta be more around—probably close by. The *Pindar* was certain to have backup. An S.O.S. is as good as an 'X marks the spot' to them."

"Yeah, I suppose so."

Echo shifted in discomfort.

"Kill the mayday, Meg."

"But..."

"Put us on short-range, and see if you can set it up for proximity response. It'll draw less power, that way. If I need to come over there and help, I will, 'cause what I want is to tie it into the sensors, so that it'll only react to a PGLEIA-configured spacecraft. Fox will come looking in about five days at most—maybe sooner, since we'll have stopped checking in regularly. In the meantime, we need to concentrate everything we've got on hiding and staying alive. Bump down the heat a little, too."

* * *

Omega thought hard, studying the console, then flipped a few switches with bandaged, freshly-burned fingers, wincing at the contact pain. She scanned the console, then hit several more switches and adjusted a sliding toggle. After another survey of the console, she adjusted additional settings.

"Um, Echo?"

"Yeah, baby?"

"I got everything done except the special prox-proxim-ity sensor thing. I've never had to do that, and you've never shown me how. Is it this...?" She pointed at a section of the panel.

"Yeah, that's it. Lessee, enter the mayday code, toggle to the sensor suite setting, then enter code 'PGLEIA 010101.' That oughta do it."

"Echo...how is Fox gonna find us?" she wondered, as she obeyed his orders. "We're a really little needle in an awful big haystack. We could be anywhere, on a...tr-trainin' mission like this." The battery warning light shut off as the power draw dropped substantially; Omega slid back onto the floor and crawled over to Echo.

"We sent him your Orion Nebula 'postcard,' remember?" Echo grinned. "Not to mention the reports of the new planet discoveries. The nebula is the first place he'll start."

"Oh. Yeah, that's a good point. It's still a pretty damn big haystack, though. The whole big cloud thing an' all." Omega pulled the covers off

Echo and reached for his near leg.

"What the hell do you think you're doing?"

"Checkin' your legs, Echo. You're hurtin'—don't try to pretend you're not—and you've been movin' around way too much. Maybe you messed up the...messed up the...these things." She started removing the splint on his right shin. As she slipped it off carefully, Echo groaned despite himself.

"Ooo! Oh no! Oh, Echo, hon, you messed it up all right. Oooh. It's a...a com-...it's poking through," Omega said, wincing for him.

"Well, shit," he grumbled, paling a bit as he got a good look at the open wound, the bloody, sharp tip of a broken bone protruding. "I knew it felt awfully damn raw. I guess it's a good thing there's no major blood vessels right there, or I'd be in deep kimchee by now. If not outrightly dead."

"Yeah, Ace, an' I'd be in trouble," Omega noted, "'cause I dunno if I can get outta this situation without your ex-exper..."

"Experience?"

"That. Yeah." She used the emergency hand sterilizer found in the medikit to ensure she wouldn't contaminate the open wound, then dug around in the medical bag and got out a pair of sterile gloves and the antipathogenics. "Lean back," she ordered him, donning the gloves. "This isn't gonna be fun for you or me."

He complied, and she swabbed the open wound down, bone and all, to help prevent infection. Echo stiffened fractionally, and his jaw tightened substantially as he paled, but he gave no other reaction. Omega glanced sharply at him, then handed him the medical bag.

"Here. Pick out something to help it not hurt. I gotta fix this."

Without protest, Echo pulled out the strongest painkiller in the kit, and loaded the minimum dose into another osmosive micropore syringe. Omega took it from him and pumped it calmly into his thigh. Within moments, Echo relaxed as it took effect.

"That's better," she decided, and resumed work on his leg.

"Question?" he asked quietly as his partner studied the compound fracture preparatory to re-setting it.

"What?"

"You welded the leak fine, and you're treating me almost as well, I think, as India could in these conditions. But you can't handle the helm..."

"I can't think of the right words, and I can't see too good. And I can't...

can't think hard. But I don't have to think like...like that...to do this." She pointed at his leg. "I sorta...just see what to do. Then I do it."

"Aha. Higher-order, abstract, verbal." Echo nodded. "That's what's impaired. And you're still learning the helm. That makes sense."

"Ready, Echo?"

"Yeah." Echo steeled himself. Omega commenced the process of re-setting the leg. Echo arched in excruciating pain, and a gasping cry escaped him despite his best efforts.

* * *

Omega glanced at his white face, then stopped what she was doing and pulled out most of the pillows propping him up, easing him into a prone position.

"There. Lay down. Don't you go konkin' out on me," she told him, stern.

Omega got the painkiller and gave Echo a larger dose. When it took effect, and she saw his body relax again, she resumed her task. Within minutes this time, the bones were in place, the open wound was cleaned and bandaged, and the splint was back on Echo's leg.

Omega pumped a syringe of antibiotic into Echo's right thigh, then moved to his left thigh; it was in better shape, and she merely adjusted the splint, ensuring it wasn't too tight. Then she gently bundled up her partner in the chilly cabin, surreptitiously and affectionately tucking him in, almost like a child. He gave her a slight, weary smile then, and she realized he knew what she had done...and appreciated it.

"Okay, Ace, all done," she told him in a soft voice. "Go to sleep, hon."

* * *

The lethargic man nodded, the soporific effect of the painkillers taking strong effect by this time. Echo closed his eyes and was almost instantly sound asleep.

Omega sat watching him for long minutes, the soft blue eyes caring and sad. Then she crawled slowly out of the room.

* * *

She came back some time later, once again dressed in her own Suit trousers and one of Echo's dress shirts—rather larger than her own, the better to avoid chafing acid-burned shoulders—carrying something.

She quickly tucked the mysterious object under her pillow, re-formed her own little nest of bedclothes, curled up inside it, and fell into an exhausted sleep.

* * *

Many hours later, when Echo awoke, he found Omega already wide awake and propped up with pillows in the semi-darkness near him. She held a leather-bound book open on her lap, fingering it thoughtfully.

"What have you got there?" a groggy Echo murmured, struggling to clear his brain of the dopey feeling produced by the powerful pain medication.

"Hm? Oh, this is Daddy's Bible," she said, looking up. "I always take it with me. But I dunno how it got here. I didn't know I was coming on this trip, so I didn't pack anything. You and Fox really surprised me!" She smiled.

"Good!" Echo grinned, gradually becoming more coherent. "Although it's...not turning out exactly according to plan. Anyway, I packed everything for you, Meg. I've always seen it in your gear when we go on an extended assignment. So when I snuck into your quarters to pack your bag while you handled the prep for the Alpha Line departure ceremony—not to mention taking Pulgey to watch you observe with your telescope—I grabbed it and threw it in your duffel bag."

"Aha! NOW I get it! Is that how my fav'rit' new robe got here, too?" she asked, grinning at him.

"The black silk one? Yep."

"Thanks. You did a good job packin' ev'rything."

"Did I forget anything?"

"No." Omega thought for a moment, then her cheeks turned a faint shade of pink. "I didn't know you knew that much about my...per-personal stuff."

"Does it bother you?" Echo asked, watching her reaction. "That I know so much about you, that I can do that?"

"I don't know," she answered honestly. "I think I'm a little em-em-barrassed."

"Don't you think you could do the same for me, by now?" Echo asked. "We've been partners—well, if you count the training, too—for pretty close on a year."

Omega mused thoughtfully for a moment.

145

"Mm...well, you know, I think I could, at that," she decided. "But you travel a lot lighter."

"You don't travel very heavily. I grabbed your toiletry kit, your dad's Bible, your robe, a men's pajama shirt, and your underthings," Echo enumerated, and then watched as Omega blushed at the completeness of the list. He didn't tell her that he found said underthings sexy as hell, and had had to work hard to keep his mind on his business. *Not that they're especially fancy,* he considered. *Meg's practical, after all. But they're still pretty.* His attention returned to her face, which was still red. "Aw. C'mon, Meg, we're partners. Don't go getting embarrassed on me over a little thing like bras and panties. Emphasis on little," he ribbed her, trying to get her to relax about the matter. She pursed her lips in response, drawing a deep, uncomfortable breath, so he tried again. "As you pointed out about digging in my pockets, it wasn't like you were in 'em at the time," Echo continued to tease her, and this time she smiled slightly. "There we go. That's better. So—turn about is fair play, and all that. What would you grab for me?"

"Oh, well, lemme think," Omega murmured, her face returning to its normal hue. "Fox would have Supplies stow your Suits onboard, like he did mine, so I don't gotta worry about those things. I guess I'd grab your shaving kit outta your bathroom, and um, some underwear—"

"What kind?" Echo decided to try. *And her reaction should tell me a lot,* he thought.

"Huh?"

"I've got a range of shorts in my wardrobe, depending on what I'm gonna be doing," he pointed out. "Boxers, briefs, bikinis..."

"Oh," she murmured, cheeks turning pink. "I...didn't know that. I never had occasion to, um, root around in your underwear drawer." She thought for a moment. "I think I'd get mostly boxers, then throw in some briefs an' bikinis just in case."

Echo blinked in surprise.

"That's...right," he admitted, "but, um, how did you figure that out?"

His partner gave him an impish grin.

"No V.P.L.," she told him.

"Huh? What the hell is...?"

"It's a girl thing, I guess. It means 'Visible Panty Lines.' Your trousers an' jeans always fit you smoothly, and there's never any, uh, like, elastic lines or wrinkles or anything like that. So I'm figuring silk, or maybe silk knit, boxers."

Echo felt his face heat. *Damn. She's actually looked at my ass enough to know that, an' to figure out what kinda shorts I wear. But does she like...?* He shot her a puzzled glance.

"Yeah, they look good on ya," she responded to that look, mischievous grin deepening. "An' I take it, I got your choice right?"

"Uh, um, yeah," Echo confirmed, scrambling for words, as the heat in his face deepened. *Shit,* he thought, blinking in bemusement. *I think that means she likes my ass. At least, I hope it means she likes my ass.*

"An' yeah, you got a cute butt," she answered his expression, smirk nearly ear to ear by this time. His face felt supernova-hot at that point. He waved a hand to tell her to continue, uncertain exactly what to say in reply, and somewhat afraid to even attempt it. "Oh, okay. So lemme see, where was I...?" she responded, still smirking.

"Shaving kit, shorts..." His voice sounded slightly strained to his own ears; he hoped she didn't notice. *Well, hell. Judging by the slight raising of her eyebrows and pursing of her lips, she did. Damnation. Whatever happened to 'calm, cool, collected Echo, the unflappable Agent'?*

"Oh yeah," she continued. "Your shaving kit, shorts...your pocket knife, cigarette lighter—but no cigarettes," she smiled, "a couple o' good books—"

"From where?" Echo interrupted. The heat in his face was finally fading, to his relief.

"What?"

"How would you know what I was currently reading?" he prompted.

"That's easy. I'd check your bedside table and the end of the coffee table next to your recliner, or maybe the end table between the recliner an' the couch."

"Very good!" He nodded, pleased. "Anything else?"

"Mm—I might grab your multi, um, multi-tool. If you weren't already carrying it, that is. Which also goes for the knife an' lighter, I guess. I figure you'd have your blaster, brain, um, brain bleacher," she forced out the words, "and goggle-glasses on you, too, knowing you. So I think that's it."

"Great job!" Echo nodded again, in intense satisfaction and approval...as well as no little bit of secret delight at how well she knew him and observed his habits. "You'd have it right. Every bit."

"Good. Let me know if you ever need help packin', next time." Omega grinned, then sobered. "Anyway," she said, glancing back down at the Bible in her hands, "Thanks. For packing this, I mean."

They were quiet for a long moment, as Omega ran her bandaged fingertips across the open page. The movement, Echo decided, was almost like a caress, revealing her deep feeling for the words contained therein. *But,* he recognized, *what she's NOT doing...is reading it.*

"You can't read it, can you?" Echo asked then, verifying his suspicions.

"...No." She sighed.

"Do you want me to get the flashlight and read from it for you?"

"No, that's okay. I don't have to be able to read it now to r'member what it says."

"We'll have to make sure the rescue team grabs it when they pick us up. I'd hate for you to lose it," Echo said considerately, nodding.

Omega hesitated, then replied simply, "...Yes."

"They'll be here soon, Meg." Echo glanced at her sharply, noting the hesitation.

"I know, Echo."

"You haven't given up, have you, baby?"

"No."

"Good."

"But, Echo?"

"Hm?"

"What's gonna be left of...of my head...when they do get here?"

"What...do you mean?" Echo stared at Omega in shock, trying to hide the frisson of fear that shook his frame. *Oh damn. She's more aware of her condition than I thought. Than I'd hoped.* He mentally shook his head. *I shoulda known, though. According to Zebra, she's one of the most... AWARE...humans that's ever lived, so it stands to reason she'd know. But maybe I can talk her into the notion that it isn't serious, so she won't worry. Maybe it ISN'T serious. But it's a long shot, given the symptoms.*

* * *

"C'mon. You know eezackly what I mean, Ace," Omega chastised him. "Quit tryin' to hide it from me, 'cause it won't work. Do you think I don't know what's happenin' to me? What I was, and what I could do,

148

only a few days ago, and now...I can't even read the damn control panels." Omega leaned into the pillows and stared up into the darkness. "Echo...this is something I've wondered about a lot lately...do you think I've still got a...a soul?"

Pained brown eyes narrowed.

"You know what I believe, Meg," Echo replied then.

"I know. Same as me, pretty much. That's why I asked."

"What do you mean, 'still'?"

"Well, I'm not...I'm not...oh, dammit, what's the WORD?!"

* * *

"Describe it," Echo said, trying to help his frustrated partner.

"Person from home."

"Agent?"

"No, the whole place. The big place."

"The city? The planet?" Echo guessed.

"That's it! Pla-net." The Ph.D. astrophysicist stumbled over the word.

"Terran."

"No—the other one."

"Human?"

"Yeah! That's the one. Human. I'm not human anymore, Echo, and I'm not from any other...planet. I'm just kind of a...a made-up person."

"Artificial," Echo supplied, more and more agonized as he listened to his once-brilliant partner struggling merely to communicate. "But you're not, Meg."

"Sure I am, Echo. I got all that...other-planet...stuff stuck onto my... my..."

"Genes."

"Yeah. That makes me something that isn't like any real person, any-where else, so I just wonder..." she patted the heirloom Bible in her hands. "Does this ap-app-...work for me anymore? I don't think God would forget me," Omega said, with a childlike trust and simplicity that threatened to wrench Echo's guts out. "I just don't know what He wants me to do any more. 'Specially now. Echo, I don't wanna be like this." Omega bowed her head, then looked up at him, tear-filled blue eyes meeting tormented brown ones. Abruptly Omega handed the Bible to Echo. "Here. I want you to have it."

149

"Why?" Echo asked in a low voice, not sure he wanted to hear the answer. He took the book of Scripture slowly.

"'Cause I'm not goin' home, Echo."

He felt the blood drain from his face, and the cabin spun momentarily.

"Meg—do you know something you're not telling me?"

"You mean, do I kinda...know...I'm dying? No. The other way. I know I'm not. That's what scares me."

"Then why—"

"'Cause I de-decided."

* * *

Echo's eyes widened in surprise and puzzlement, and Omega, realizing he didn't understand, continued.

"Look, it's like this, Ace. I'll stay here and help you 'til I know Fox is close. Then I'll go away. I don't want Fox, and Romeo and India, to see me like this..."

"Where will you go?" Echo whispered, seeming stunned. She gestured.

"Outside."

"But your spacesuit's trashed."

"I know." She shrugged. "I don't want it."

* * *

"But you'll—" Echo broke off abruptly as Omega's intent dawned on him. "Meg, don't! The medics can straighten you out!"

"Echo, I'm broken."

"So am I." Echo pointed to his legs, desperate to make her understand.

Omega crawled over to sit close beside her partner, looking down at his legs and running bandaged hands gently along them, almost caressing.

"You're easy to fix, hon. I'm not. I still know that much. They don't even know how my head works in the first place, 'specially after that whole mess with th' slavers. Yeah, I know they got the regen pod thing, but they gotta know what to put in it before it'll fix a person. An' they don't know about this. Not even Doron knew about this. What if they can't fix me?" She raised her head and gazed steadily at him, waiting for his response.

Echo had no response to give; he looked away, glancing around the spacecraft's cabin, distraught and uncertain what to do.

"I...I...you..." he tried, but no other words came.

* * *

"I'll tell you," Omega answered her own question. "I won't be able to do...stuff...with you any more, Echo. No more flying around the stars. No more floating in the pretty colored clouds. No more playing with numbers. No more neat strange people from other stars. Just a little, white room with people who feel sorry for me looking in a window all the time, and getting poked and prodded every day for as long as I live. A...lab rat." She shook her head. "No. Never again."

"I won't let you go, Meg." A determined Echo set his jaw stubbornly, watching her with something that looked to her a lot like sincere, intense affection deep in the dark eyes. She bit her lip, suddenly realizing that this was going to hurt him, probably badly; but she was out of options she considered acceptable.

"You can't stop me, Echo." Omega laid her hand on one of the leg splints, her meaning plain. Then she pushed the Bible, which Echo still clutched unconsciously, up against his chest. "Promise me you'll think about me once in a while?"

Echo gazed at her blankly, face very pale as he whispered, "Yes."

"Good." Omega gently brushed his hair back with gauze-wrapped fingers, then began crawling toward the passageway. Echo jerked upright.

"Meg?! You're not—"

"No. Fox isn't here yet. I told you; I won't leave you alone," she reminded him, glancing over her shoulder. "I'm gonna go try to find some more blankets for us to use. It's gettin' colder in here. Anyway, I...I jus' need to be by myself for a while..." She let her suddenly-wobbly voice trail off.

* * *

Omega left the flight deck, headed deeper into the bowels of the derelict spacecraft...alone.

A distraught Echo slumped down into the pillows, Omega's family Bible held close against his chest, and stared upward into the darkness.

For the first time in his life, Echo knew what it was to fear the future.

Chapter 7

"Any word yet?" Romeo asked India, as he came into the Alpha Line briefing room.

"No, there isn't," India admitted. "They're nearly a whole day late reporting in."

"That's not like 'em," Romeo noted.

"Nope." India bit her lip. "Well, they could have just gotten busy..."

"BOTH of 'em? You KNOW Echo's a stickler f'r shit like that."

"Yeah. And Meg might as well be his twin, when it comes to that sort of thing."

"Yup." Romeo turned, walking over to the door overlooking the Core, and staring out, deep in thought. He shoved his hands deep into his trousers pockets and stood there, mulling the situation. India came to his side.

"You're worried."

"Yeah, I am. Maybe Meg done rubbed off on me or somethin', but I got a bad feeling about this."

"Should we go to Fox?"

"An' tell 'im what? Alpha One is late checkin' in? If they're explorin' a planet an' aren't back t' th' ship yet, 'cause Meg found somethin' she wanted t' check out, then there's a perfectly logical reason," Romeo pointed out. "An' you know, this bein' a trainin' mission, Echo gonna indulge her curiosity as much as he can, if f'r no other reason than 'cause it's another learnin' opportunity. Never mind he gets a kick outta watching her do that kinda shit."

"True..." India shrugged. "And they've already discovered...what? Three new systems? Half a dozen new planets?"

"Yeah, thereabouts."

"So...what do we do?"

Romeo turned back to her.

"We wait," he said.

* * *

A good six or more hours later, Omega returned, dragging the last of the bunk bedclothes—having scavenged all of the half-dozen bunks in each berth by this time—and some emergency blankets from stowage. Her face was tearstained and sleep-creased, as if she had cried herself to sleep, but Echo chose not to mention it. Omega wordlessly spread the blankets on top of the nest already on the deck, then made her way to the helm and hoisted herself into a chair with an obvious effort.

"How's it look, Meg?" Echo asked, voice quiet.

"Nothing blinking," she said.

"Well, that's good. What does the clock say?"

"Um..." Omega studied for a moment, squinting. "F-four-eight-four... one-three."

"What?! How'd it get to be that time?!" Echo sat up, startled.

"I was gone a while. And you slept a long time, Echo."

"Maybe. But..."

"The ane- anesth-...the stuff to make you not hurt..."

"Oh. Yeah, I guess that makes sense." Echo nodded and leaned back against the pillows. "How 'bout the batteries?"

"Um...oh, oh, five."

"All right; it's gonna be a close one," Echo remarked. "Meg, bump the heaters down some more. Right-hand panel...up...a little more...right there."

Omega moved her hand to the indicated place, and reduced the thermal conditioners.

"It's gonna get cold."

"Yeah. But we shouldn't freeze, if we bundle up good. And we've gotta make the power last until Fox gets here, so he can pick up our emergency beacon."

"Anything else?" Omega asked.

"Yeah—the emergency beacon."

"Little green light."

"Steady or blinking?"

"Steady."

"Anything on the sensors?" Echo asked.

"Uh...no. Everything is just zeroes," Omega said.

"Okay," Echo responded. "No Cortians."

"No Fox, either."

"No..." *Can you dread being rescued?* Echo wondered, watching his partner and brooding. *Is it really a rescue then?* After a bit, Echo realized that Omega was curiously, almost absently, punching buttons on the console, in what seemed to be a deliberate sequence. He sat up unobtrusively, stuffing every pillow within reach behind his back, and watched silently. A glow shimmered into existence as a screen lit up on the console, casting a soft, low, multicolored illumination on Omega's face.

"Ohhh," she sighed, a smile lighting her expression as she gazed at the screen. Then she looked around at him. "Your picture's good, Echo," she said.

"What picture?"

"The one you made for me of the...the pretty clouds."

"Is that what you're looking at?"

"Uh-huh," Omega replied, smiling at him. Her eyes grew distant and dreamy, and Echo somehow knew that she was remembering their spacewalk. "It looks just like it did during the EVA..." she murmured. Echo blinked.

"During the what?" he asked casually.

"The EVA."

"What's that stand for?"

"Extra-vehic—" Omega snapped back to the present, eyes wide.

"Go ahead. Finish it."

"I...I can't, now." Omega frowned with the effort of concentrating. Echo patted the blankets beside him.

"Come over here. But power off that screen first."

A preoccupied Omega automatically hit a few switches, and the screen went dark, the computer returning to low-power standby mode. Echo watched, eyebrow raised in curious consideration; then, as she started to slide to the deck, he said, "No. Try to walk. Take it slow."

Omega stood gradually, holding the chair; stayed still for a bit. Released the chair. Stepped forward...

Stumbled. Caught herself; took another step. And another. And another. Her brows were knit in intense effort.

When she reached the nest, Omega sank to the decking, obviously fearful of falling on top of her already severely injured partner, and crawled to his side.

"Sit," Echo invited, patting the blankets beside him with his right hand. Wordlessly, Omega turned and sat where he indicated. Echo put an arm around Omega's shoulders from behind, and pulled her back against his good shoulder, flipping the covers over her to keep her warm. Her eyes closed momentarily and her lips curved upward in a slight smile, as she leaned against him, pushing him deeper into the pile of pillows.

"Relax, Meg," Echo murmured into her ear. "Quit worrying. Everything's gonna be fine. Let your mind wander for a change, and just rest. I know you're cold; I can feel it, like this—your arms are like ice. Close your eyes, snuggle into me, and get warm," he commanded, voice quiet, slipping loose arms around her waist from behind—as best he could, with the bad shoulder—to keep her close, hoping it would encourage her to relax. *She's already slept some,* he realized, *and it apparently helped. Along with venting some emotions, judging by the tearstains. Maybe if I can get her to unwind a little—'cause she's tighter than piano wire, right now—it'll help even more.*

After a minute or two, he felt her tired, battered body sag lightly against his as she obeyed. Her head started to loll forward, and he caught it in his hand and eased it back until it rested comfortably on his shoulder, her cheek tucked into the side of his neck.

"There we go," he murmured, soothing. "That's good, baby. Nice an' comfortable an' warm. Feels good, huh? Us all warm an' cozy?"

"Yeah..."

"Good. Shh, now. Let everything go. I'm right here, and I gotcha."

She sighed, a soft sound, continuing to relax. Echo waited, patient, as he felt her breathing slow, becoming shallow and regular.

When another few minutes had passed, Echo breathed in her ear, "Remember our spacewalk?"

"Mm-hmm." By the sound of her, Echo decided she was half-asleep.

"Tell me all about it. I want to know what you thought, what you felt. Everything."

"It was...beautiful," Omega murmured dreamily, as Echo listened, intent on her words. "Overwhelming. The nebula had...so many colors. Huge...delicate filaments of gas...proto-stellar objects...HII emission regions...never mind the Trapezium Cluster and the black hole...I could barely breathe, I was so excited...to finally be there, after so long dreaming of it..."

Intensely relieved, Echo let his own head drop into the pillows, eyes closed, smiling at the return of his partner's normal intellect. He opened his eyes, looked up, deep into the darkness, and nodded in thanks.

"Now, Meg...tell me about the sensor data on the nebula."

"I haven't seen it all yet, Echo."

"Well, but what do you expect to see?"

"Mm..." her voice was still faraway, soft, "elemental composition mostly hydrogen, some helium, and a few others, like lithium and oxygen. Maybe a few chemical compounds, fairly simple. You know what I mean. Carbon monoxide, formaldehyde. Hydrogen chloride. Hm. Similar to the atmosphere outside, actually," the scientist mused. "Which makes sense, when you think about it. The protoplanet condensed out of the nebula, after all."

"Keep going," Echo said, as she paused. "I'm listening."

"Well," Omega instinctively turned her head further toward him, eyes still closed, "a lotta ionization, of course. Evidence of ongoing star formation—that's what the Orion Nebula is, you know, a stellar obstetrics ward... the whole Orion cloud complex is, basically..."

"I'm still listening." With an effort, Echo put the fingers of his bad hand under Omega's chin, relying on the sling and splints to support his arm, and gently turned her head toward him even more. She twisted her body around in the curve of his right arm, automatically following Echo's hand, and continued.

"We're probably in a protostellar system now. That's why it's so cold—no sun, at least not yet, 'cause fusion probably hasn't initiated yet— and why the atmosphere is so—"

"Open your eyes and look at me."

Without thinking about it, Omega opened her eyes and gazed into Echo's. "—Pri-mor...di...al..." She caught her breath. They reclined in each other's arms for a long moment, frozen, simply staring at each other. Then Echo smiled, triumphant.

"You were saying, baby...?"

"...That...that the planetary atmosphere hasn't had time to...mature, I guess you could say. This stellar system is still being 'born'. It'll take volcanic outgassing, and the eventual development of algaes and such to modify the atmosphere..."

The wide, startled blue eyes suddenly glowed with understanding, and Echo grinned. He pulled her head back down to his shoulder momentarily as he hugged her, fondly riffling the bloodstained white-blonde hair with one hand, careful to avoid the gauze wrapping it, then released her.

"Welcome back, Doctor," he said, and Omega flopped backward onto the pillows and blankets, laughing in relief.

* * *

"Whoa, Meg, slow down!" Echo cautioned. "You've still got a big lump on your head."

"I know, Echo, but we can see our breath in here. If I can just figure out..." Omega studied the console with intensity.

"Meg, give it a rest," Echo said, waving a hand. "Trust me. There's no more power to pull. What's left of the battery has to be saved for the sensors and S.O.S. beacon."

"All right," she sighed. "Do you want me to see if I can get you into a bunk in one of the sleep stations? You'd probably be more comfortable. Not to mention warmer. You'd be up off the deck, at least."

"No, I think I should stay here," Echo decided, after a couple of moments to consider the matter. "We're not out of the woods yet, even if you are better, and we might need to put our heads together for something. And you aren't as familiar with the ship's systems as I am."

"That's true. Okay, if you're sure."

"I'm sure."

"Maybe...maybe I can drag one of the bunk mattresses in here?" she wondered. "It'd provide additional insulation from the deck, and be cushier than the deck, to boot."

"NO. Ease up, Meg. If I have to, I'll pull rank and make it an order. Those things are fastened down, they're hard to detach, and you aren't so much recovered that I want to risk your heaving one of the damn things around and messing yourself up again. Now come over here and get under the covers before you freeze," Echo commanded. "You're ten shades of blue."

"Brrr!" Omega grinned, jumping up and practically diving into the cocoon of blankets, "make that eleven."

"Trying for twelve?" Echo grinned in return. "Did you set the audio on the proximity alarm?"

"Yeah. And cranked the volume to be loud enough to wake us up, if we happen to have dozed off. If anything at all comes close to planet-fall, we'll know it."

"Good," Echo said, satisfied. "In that case..." He ducked his head, pulling the blankets up and completely disappearing from sight.

Omega looked across the twilit wilderness of blankets and thermal covers at the lump that was her companion.

"Good idea," she muttered, and vanished beneath her own covers.

The flight deck of the derelict *Trojan Horse* fell silent, except for the soft muffled breathing of two battered, exhausted Division One Agents as they fell asleep.

* * *

Some little time later, after a solid and restful nap, a now-awake Echo lay, thoughtful beneath the tent of blankets, musing. After a bit, he pulled the blankets back and sat up, looking across the deck at the small mound of covers that was Omega. He watched the slow rise and fall of the blankets that marked her respiration, and nodded to himself. *Still asleep. Good. She needs it, bad. I won't bother her, then.*

He pulled the medical kit into his lap, scrabbled in it, and brought out the spare medscanner and its repair toolkit. Then he dragged the bag of supplies over, and extracted more tools.

"Hm. Wonder if she put—" Echo dug around in the bag and pulled out an extra proto-cyclotron blaster from the onboard armory, a pocket spectral analyzer, and a spare brain bleacher, as well as an extra pair of goggle-glasses, all from the onboard equipment stowage. "Damn," Echo muttered, shooting a grin at the sleeping lump of blankets, "you're a helluva partner, Meg. All the spare parts I could ask for, and then some. And that, with your noggin messed up."

Echo put on the goggle-glasses for the sake of safety before he carefully disassembled the brain bleacher, sorting its components into two piles. Then he tossed the glasses to one side and repeated the process on the blaster and analyzer.

"That oughta do it," he remarked softly with satisfaction. "Now, let's see..." Echo picked up the medscanner and removed the cover. Then he studied it for a moment. "Mm. There we go." He selected a part from one of the piles beside him, and began attaching it to the medscanner.

After a while, one end of the medscanner started to resemble an electronic hedgehog. Echo continued to work quietly as Omega slept.

* * *

Omega awoke, cold, stiff, and in darkness, as someone shook her.

"Meg, wake up." Echo's voice was muffled. "Wake up, baby. C'mon, Meg. I hate like hell to wake you up, but I need you to do something for me. And it's better if we go ahead and get it done, rather than wait and risk it."

Sleepy and confused, she muttered, "Wha? Where—?"

The covers over her vanished, revealing Echo's concerned face in the gloom.

"You okay down there?"

Omega blinked a couple of times.

"Yeah, I'm fine," she finally allowed. "I just forgot where I was for a bit. I was dreaming."

* * *

"Oh. Sorry 'bout that. What about?" Echo made conversation, giving his partner a chance to orient herself and wake up properly.

"Huh?" A groggy Omega sat up, still a little woozy from deep sleep.

"What were you dreaming about?"

"Oh, uh, well...I uh, I don't remember now," she hedged, sticking her fists into her eyes and rubbing them like a child even as her cheeks turned faintly pink. Simultaneously, she stretched luxuriously from head to foot, instinctively arching her back. The overall effect was very un-childlike.

"Uh-huh." Echo watched with a smile, not entirely secretly enjoying the view; but after several moments, the smile faded. "Meg?" There was an oddly wistful quality in the inflection. "Who were you...? I mean, did...?" He broke off. *No,* he thought. *No matter how much I want to. Now is NOT the time for THAT discussion.*

"What?" Omega pulled her hands out of her face and looked up.

"...Never mind." Echo studied her for a moment. "You awake now?"

"More or less. Whatcha need?"

"Legs," Echo said succinctly, with some little irritation. "But since they aren't working, I want you to drag me over to the helm." He waved the medscanner, now bristling with nonstandard appendages. His pockets were crammed with tools—both shirt and pants pockets, stuffed nigh to splitting seams. "I need to hook something up."

* * *

Without further question, Omega stood, took Echo's right hand in both of hers, and obligingly pulled him to the pilot console.

"What on earth did you do to that thing?" she finally asked, and nodded toward the medscanner.

"Oh, I've just been tinkering with it a little bit. I had an idea. Right here," Echo said, and Omega stopped between the pilot and co-pilot seats.

"That's not the only one we got, is it?" she asked, concerned.

"Oh no; there's always at least two in the onboard kits. It's for redundancy, you know, like what NASA does. In case one gets lost or busted. This is the spare. The one we been using is still in the kit."

"Oh, ok."

"Now help me get this panel off, will you?" He emptied his pockets into a neat little pile of tools on the deck, right next to the base of the console.

"Okay," Omega responded, stretching out on the deck next to her tool-wielding partner. "I'll get this side." She pulled her trusty old Swiss army knife from a pocket and set to work.

A few minutes later, the panel underneath the console was lying to one side, the flashlight had been folded into its lantern mode, and most of Echo's upper body was inside the console, as he lay on his back and worked. Omega handed him tools as he needed them.

"Echo—what are you doing?"

"Mm...let's just call it a little precaution."

"Against what?"

"Undesirables."

Omega raised an eyebrow. Finally, her curiosity got the better of her.

"Hold still," she muttered, put one hand on the floor on either side of Echo's chest, and ducked her head into the opening. Then she surveyed the flashlight-illumined console guts. Echo paused and lowered his arms to give Omega room in the confined space. "Mm..." was the only sound she made as her eyes traced the circuitry Echo worked to modify.

* * *

"Well?" Echo asked, smiling to himself at her characteristic inquisitiveness.

"Well...I see where you're hooking it in. And I see the general principle of what you've hooked in. At least, I think I do. My head still hurts a bit," she made excuse. "But I have to admit, I don't see why."

"I hope you won't have to," Echo said, resuming work. "But since you're in here, hold this—" he took her right hand and wrapped it around the kluged medscanner, "while I get it connected in."

"All right, hang on a minute," Omega said, shifting her weight onto her left arm. "Can you scoot over a bit? I'm doing a sustained, one-armed push-up here, and I can't hold it forever."

"Yeah, hang—" Echo winced, as pain shot through his lower limbs from his attempt to move aside. "Maybe not."

"Why?"

"Legs," Echo said tersely.

"Oh. Okay."

"I'll hurry." He resumed attaching the medscanner.

* * *

Echo concentrated on the connections, intent on getting the scanner hooked in just so, to ensure it functioned properly when he was done, else it would be useless. After several minutes, he felt his partner nudge his right side.

"Hold still, Meg," Echo said absently, focusing on his task. "I've gotta get a good junction here or it won't work."

"Sorry..."

Echo worked for a few more minutes, making one delicate connection after another.

"Can you hold it a little higher, Meg? Keep it still."

"I'll try..." The medscanner inched upward.

"That's good."

"Okay."

After another couple of moments, Echo noticed a movement out of the corner of his eye, and turned his head to look. The muscles in Omega's left arm were trembling violently. His eyes shot to her face, which was intent on the medscanner; her lower lip was caught between her teeth, and beads of sweat stood out on her pale forehead and upper lip. But the medscanner stayed rock-steady.

"Oh, damn, Meg!" Echo exclaimed, dropping his tools and taking the medscanner from her grasp. With a gasp of relief, Omega dropped her right hand to the floor and shifted her weight onto it, letting her head droop forward. "Why didn't you say something, baby?!"

161

"You were busy."

"Then why didn't you just lie down?"

"I tried to. You told me to hold still."

"Aw, shit. I was concentrating..."

"I know. There's not really room beside you anyway."

"You could've just rested against my chest."

"You're banged up enough already, Ace. I didn't wanna squosh you."

"You're not exactly a circus fat lady, Meg." Echo raised an amused eyebrow. "I don't think I'm in any danger. Of being 'squoshed,' that is."

Omega shrugged.

"All right, my arm's rested. Let's go at it again," she said.

"Wait," Echo interjected. "Hold out your hand and show me."

Omega extended her right hand; it was steady. Echo frowned.

"Nice try, but I'm more observant than THAT. The left one."

Omega slowly extended her left hand; it shook noticeably.

"Arm's rested, huh?" Echo drawled.

"I'll manage," Omega said. "Besides, can you get it hooked up at this point with just your own two hands?"

"No," Echo admitted, pondering options. "Especially considering that I've really only got about one and a half, what with the shoulder and wrist messed up."

"Exactly. So let's get to it."

"No, wait. Let me think a second."

"...Okay."

"Oh...mm...yeah, I suppose that might work..."

"You sound a little doubtful. What is it?"

Echo considered his partner for a long moment.

* * *

"Meg, you trust me. And we're...close." It was a question couched as a statement. Omega blinked, surprised that he had to ask.

"Of course, Echo. That goes without saying. You're..." she shrugged, "probably the closest friend I've got. Maybe that I've ever had."

And she just admitted it to me, directly, for the first time, he thought, warm affection filling him.

The smile was only visible in the dark eyes as Echo said quietly, "Okay then, pal, roll over on your back. I want you right here." He patted his chest.

* * *

Omega complied as best she could in the confined space, resting her upper back on his belly, and Echo cautiously released the medscanner, allowing it to dangle for a few moments, unattended. Then he hooked his elbows under her arms, avoiding the acid burns, and pulled up, favoring his left shoulder, sliding her onto his chest. When she realized what he was doing, she raised her head to position her feet and help push herself into place.

"Watch it!!" Echo exclaimed, catching her forehead with one hand just before it hit the top of the opening. "You're just getting over one concussion, Meg. Let's not go through that again."

"Sorry. I was trying not to stomp on your busted legs."

"'Preciate that a lot, but let's not do it at the expense of your noggin. Bend your knees and put one foot on either side of my legs. Good. Now push with your legs, lift your butt a little, and slide up until your head's under my chin."

"How's this?" Omega asked, sliding carefully across his chest.

"Hang on a minute." Echo adjusted the position of his bum shoulder. "Okay, that's good. Can you reach the gadget from there?"

Omega extended both hands and pushed the jury-rigged gizmo into place with ease.

"Will that do?"

"There we go. Perfect." Echo fished his tools off the deck beside him and resumed work, his long arms easily wrapping around and past his partner, whose torso now rested on his chest and belly; he could feel her body relax, just a little, into his, and he smiled slightly. *And that was the very first time she's told ME that I was her best bud, ever,* he reiterated to himself, before adding aloud, "Now you can help me, but it also gives you a chance to rest. I'm betting those back, chest and arm muscles are burnin' like hell by now."

"I feel like I been pumpin' a barbell, yeah."

* * *

"I think it's a little warmer this way, too, actually. We get to share body heat," he decided.

"Yeah, it is, a lot. I was wondering how you were managing to do such detailed work," Omega admitted. "My hands are almost numb. It must be

163

near thirty degrees in here. Fahrenheit," she added with a grin, anticipating Echo by the feel of his inhalation beneath her.

He chuckled.

* * *

"Well, thirty Celsius wouldn't be too bad about now," he remarked.

"No. That'd be...let's see...about 86 degrees Fahrenheit. Ooo."

"Yeah. Let's talk Fox into sending us somewhere that temperature when we get home. I think we've more than earned it." Echo silently noted the nearly effortless mental calculation, smiling inwardly, even as an intense sensation of relief swept through him. *My baby's gonna be all right,* he thought, elated. *She's comin' home with me after all.*

* * *

"You're the department chief, Ace. I'm just trying to remember which drawer my bikini's in." Omega couldn't see her intrigued partner's eyes light behind her at mention of the swimwear.

"Yeah, but you're my assistant chief now. I expect some help," Echo replied.

"Okay. Let's decide where we want him to send us first, though."

"Fair enough," Echo said, continuing to work. "Just a few more connections to go, Meg. Let's see...someplace hot. And I guess it needs sunshine and a beach, if you're packing a bikini."

"I might look a little out of place otherwise," she deadpanned. "I'd suggest Canaveral National Seashore, but they have a tendency to recognize former astronauts around there."

"Hell, no. If we're gonna do this, let's pull out all the stops," Echo said. "If you want to stay Earth-based, let's shoot for Bali, Fiji or Tahiti. If you're still willing to go off-planet after all this, I'll take you to Zeta Aurigae Four."

"Hm. I'm thinking rather hedonistic here. That's a new side of you, Ace! I like it! Zeta Aurigae Four?" Omega smiled over her shoulder at Echo. Echo raised his eyebrows at her; Omega wondered if she only imagined a certain suggestiveness in the expression.

"Beats the hell out of freezing our asses off here, don't you think, baby?" he pointed out. "Haven't you heard of Zeta Aurigae Four?"

"No, I can't say as I have. And it wasn't mentioned in any of my studies, or the case histories I worked on, when I was training. At least, not by that name, I guess.”

“Ah, okay. Well, one of its nicknames is ‘Eden’. That should tell you a lot.”

“Ooo. Yeah, it does. You ever been there?”

“Once.”

“Aha,” Omega responded, knowing. “Who was the lucky...‘companion’?” she asked, glancing up and grinning, making her own expression deliberately suggestive, to see if she could evoke a response.

“X-ray,” Echo said flatly, and they both laughed.

“Sounds like a story there to me,” Omega said, and Echo grinned.

“Yeah. Let me get this last connection, then we can get bundled back up, and I’ll tell you.”

“Deal.”

* * *

“...So anyway, this green-skinned bombshell comes up to X-ray, flings her arms around him, and puts a tongue-lock on him, just as Fox comes through the door,” Echo told Omega as they lay wrapped and buried in all the blankets—and approximations of blankets, as well as any other loose thermal insulation—that could be found, anywhere on the spacecraft.

Omega sprawled on her belly, chin pillowed on folded arms, legs stretched out behind her; Echo was lying on his right side, head propped up on his right elbow. They were side by side, and close enough together to share body heat, though not quite touching; the spacecraft’s cabin was nastily cold by this point. The flashlight, still in lantern mode, sitting nearby provided enough illumination for them to see each other; Omega had earlier made a comment that all they were lacking was a stack of comic books, and Echo had laughed before launching into his story.

“Oh, no—what timing,” Omega exclaimed then, following her partner’s story closely. “What did X-ray do?”

“Well, X-ray turned more shades of red than I’ve ever seen a human turn before or since, but he was stuck—after all, this was no less than the premier’s daughter, and he couldn’t afford to offend her. Fox very calmly walks directly up to them and just stands there. Now, from where I am, I can see X-ray’s face, and when he saw Fox...well, I think if he could have jumped into a black hole at that point, he’d have cheerfully done it. But Fox taps 'em both on the shoulder, as calm as if he was just asking to cut in on a dance, and as soon as the premier's daughter lets X-ray go, Fox grabs her, dips her, and plants one on her that lasts a full five minutes. I mean, we're talkin' tonsil-hockey, here."

"Whaaat?!" Omega cried, a shocked, delighted grin on her face. "Fox?! Our Fox??"

"Yep."

"What did Zebra think?!"

"They weren't an item at that point," Echo pointed out. "In fact, I don't think she'd even been recruited yet, if I remember right. This was years back, baby...um, at least a decade? Maybe a little over...lemme think..." He estimated briefly, wagging fingers in an absent fashion as he mentally calculated; then, slipping into hints of his native Texan dialect, concluded, "Musta been about sixteen years back, I think. So...no Zebra, Fox lookin' AND feelin' my current age at most, and X-ray in his, oh, early to mid-forties, I reckon. Fox wasn't the Director yet, but he WAS head of the Diplomacy department, an' he'd already been named Director Oboe's successor..."

"Oh, okay, I get it," Omega got out around giggles. "So Fox was feelin' spry an' sexy, but poor X-ray was prob'ly feelin' every bit of his age, never mind getting caught! Well, what did the premier's DAUGHTER think, then??"

"Not a damn thing. Turns out that, in their culture, swapping spit like that—I mean literally; it was a chemical thing—was the equivalent of a handshake. Fox was just being polite. But I thought X-ray was gonna have a coronary."

"Oh, that is a beaut! A royal one!" Omega wiped tears from her eyes, she was laughing so hard. "And just what were you doing through all this, Ace?"

"Whaddaya think Ah was doin'?" Echo grinned, as his native Texan accent emerged in full. "Ah was sittin' over in the corner, the rookie agent kid watchin' the whole damn thing, laughin' fit to bust behind mah hands, and tryin' not to stomp the floor, or beat mah hands on the chair, or, or... whatever, 'cause Ah was laughing so hard. 'Bout like you just were."

"Ah'll bet you were," Omega teased, letting her own Southern dialect out to play, then she cocked her head to one side. "Did anybody see ya laughing?"

"Oh, hell yeah. There wasn't anything Ah could duck behind to hide or nothin'. So X-ray an' Fox both saw it. It just made X-ray turn an extra couple shades o' red."

"And Fox?"

"You know that twinkle he gets in his eyes when he gets the joke, but because of his position, he can't show it?"

"Ah-haha!" Omega chortled. "So he totally got it...and played along?"

"Hell, yeah!"

Omega rolled on her back and spent the next couple of minutes doubled up with howling laughter, rocking back and forth, as Echo grinned.

"You know, I would love to have met X-ray," she finally got out, lips still twitching.

"Yeah," Echo said thoughtfully, sobering slightly. "I think you two would have liked each other."

"You miss him?" Omega, seeing his reaction, gentled her voice.

"I...think about him from time to time." Echo glanced away.

"He was a good bit older than you."

"Yeah. He was my mentor, and my trainer. He was already pushing forty at the time of the First Contact, though—he was older, back then, than I am now. As young as I was when we first teamed up, X-ray was... somewhere between an older brother and a father figure, I guess. Closer to father figure, but...not quite. Dad hadn't been dead that long, you see. I really looked up to him at first; he had all the answers, you know? Then, as I got a little maturity and experience under my belt, I started relating to him more..." Echo shrugged. "More on an even level, if you get me. Less mentor and protégé, and more...two male friends, comrades in arms, I guess."

"Best buddies, for sure."

"Oh, yeah." The dark eyes smiled fondly in reminiscence. Omega studied those eyes as they stared through her into the past, then it was her turn to glance away. She sighed almost inaudibly. Almost.

* * *

The brown eyes blinked at the sound, returning to the present, and Echo saw his partner's bleak, tired, pale face, and read its downcast expression.

"Meg? You okay?" he asked, deeply concerned at her sudden shift in mood.

"Yeah, Echo, I'm fine. Still got a little headache. No big wup. I'll be all right."

"That's not all of it."

"You know me...too well." Omega raised a rueful eyebrow. "But it's not a big deal."

"C'mon, Meg. Out with it."

"Oh, Echo, it's just stupid. Let it go."

"Not if it's bothering you. Spill it."

"I guess I'm...kind of envious of you and X-ray," she confessed. "I've never had that kind of relationship with anyone."

"I thought you had," Echo said quietly, pained at her remark, dropping his gaze to stare down at the blanket-swathed deck.

"I...don't understand. With who?"

"Me."

* * *

They were silent for a long moment. Omega watched Echo's averted face closely.

"But...but X-ray..." she tried.

"Is gone, Meg. He died—he sacrificed himself so the rest of us could take down Kenny." Echo shrugged, seeming suddenly weary and discouraged. "Just another one of Slug's efforts to get back at me."

"Kenny was the brother of the dude you were chasing the night you and I met, right?"

"Right; Cartman was Kenny's litter-mate. The way Fox and I got it figured, X-ray died during what was actually Slug's first attempt to bring you across my path...or vice versa, depending on how you want to view it." He shrugged. "I guess he didn't quite figure on X-ray being willing to bite it in order to stop Kenny. Not that any of the rest of us expected it, either, dammit. If I'd known what he had planned, I'd have found a way to stop him. That's one of my biggest regrets, I guess. But as a result, we took out the Teludal before he had a chance to run, like Cartman did." Echo sighed. "So...yeah. Thanks to Slug, I lost my partner and my best bud in one go."

"Ace?"

"Mm?"

"Are you...okay? I mean, with X-ray being gone..."

"Yeah. I am, now," Echo averred, quiet. "It's been a couple-three years, by this point. It still hurts if I think about it, you know, kinda like how you hurt if you think about your folks, but..."

"Yeah. You learn to deal, to get on with life."

"Exactly, baby. And I have. I've moved on. Got a new partner an' everything."

He threw her a slight grin, and she returned it. Then they were quiet again.

"Does this mean..." Omega wondered after several moments, knitting silver brows in consideration, still watching her partner and pondering if she should ask her next question, "that there's, um...maybe I shouldn't ask this." She broke off, shook her head and looked away, changing her mind.

"Ask what?"

"Nothing. Never mind."

"C'mon, Meg. Don't pull this on me. At least finish your question."

"I...look, Echo, I don't wanna hurt you, and it might. Just let it go."

"I'm not gonna let it go, and you're not gonna hurt me. Finish already."

"Okay, you asked for it," she sighed. "Does this mean there's maybe a...a vacancy in the, the 'best buddy' department?"

Echo looked up, meeting her eyes. There was an odd, intense expression in the golden-brown gaze.

"Now that you mention it, there might be," he told her. "Do you know any potential applicants?"

"Mmmmaybe." Her heart leaped. *If I can't have the kinda relationship with Echo that I'd like to have, this would be great instead,* she thought, hopeful. *At least we could be close. ClosER, even.*

"Well, then. Care to hear the requirements?" he asked.

"Sure!"

"Lemme think for a sec..." Echo paused in thought. "Okay. It has to be somebody I can always count on. Somebody I trust...with my life. Gotta be good to have at my back in a fight, literally and figuratively. Somebody who gets a kick out of my jokes. Likes the same things I do. We have to work really well together. Practically—sometimes literally—read each other's minds. Partner preferred. Brains, blonde hair, and blue eyes a definite plus." He lightly ruffled her hair, careful not to bump the lump on her head, and they both grinned. "You wouldn't happen to know a qualified party who'd like the job, would you?"

"I might," Omega replied with a smile. "I just might."

* * *

After hours of talk, both small and deep, Echo had insisted his partner take something for the residual headache. In turn, Omega had administered a dose of painkiller to ease the intense discomfort of Echo's legs; then, ignoring her own burned fingers, she had carefully massaged and lightly stretched his stiff, injured shoulder.

"You're good, baby," Echo murmured, letting her do as she would to his shoulder as the pain in it eased.

"Thanks, hon," Omega replied, continuing to work. "I know the anatomy an' junk, and I can sorta feel where the knots and bumps are. Then I just...work on 'em until the lumps ease up. Does that feel better?"

"Yeah, it does. Don't stop...unless your fingers are hurting."

"I won't, and I'm fine. Besides, it's kinda helping me pay you back for all the times you've worked out my oopsies in recent months. Especially a certain ice skating incident." She leaned over his shoulder so he could see her grin, and he returned it, then sobered, thinking.

"I'm guessing, since you'd never had a massage before joining the Agency, that you aren't certified as a therapist yourself, huh?"

"No."

"You should get the training and certification sometime."

Omega stopped, her hands frozen on his shoulder. Her eyes widened in mild horror.

"What? Am I doin' something wrong? Does it hurt?" she almost babbled.

"Huh?"

"You, um. You said I needed training, so...I figured..."

"Oh! No, no, baby, I didn't mean it like that at ALL. I guess I didn't make the train of thought clear," Echo said, feeling sheepish. "What I should have said was that you've got natural talent at this. You're really good, and you could only get better with training."

"Oh. Okay, I see," Omega replied in relief. "Yeah, I guess that might be a good idea. I doubt I'd be using it on anybody but you, but the more skill I have with stuff like that, the more I can help you, if something happens. Or," she added, seeming thoughtful, even as she resumed working on his shoulder, "just being able to do for you like you do for me, and work out the stiffness an' junk from our day-to-day missions."

Echo mentally envisioned Omega working on his nude body as he lay on a massage table, deciding her idea had merit...just before something seemed to go wrong with his diaphragm. His breath caught in his chest, and suddenly he couldn't seem to suck it in fast enough. With an effort the likes of which no one else would ever know, he managed to drag his suddenly-rapid, nearly panting respiration down into a more normal rhythm.

"You okay, Ace? You almost gasped, just now."

"Uh, yeah, I'm...I'm fine," he said. *Well, I AM fine; it isn't a lie,* he told himself. *And I can't tell her that she just revved my engines, not until I find out if she'd be offended by the idea...or welcome it.*

"Then what's wrong?"

"Um. Sore spot in there, I think." *THAT is sure no lie, either,* he thought. *Damn, I messed myself up this time.*

"Oh. Do I need to find it and try to work it out, or is it one that would be better left alone?"

"I'm not sure yet. Go back over that last area, just use a lighter touch."

"Okay. But once we find it, you might have to tell me what to do to help it. After all, you're the one with the massage certification, at least for now."

"I can do that..."

* * *

By the time Omega was finished with her ministrations to his various wounded body parts, a relaxed, deeply grateful Echo was half-asleep in their makeshift tent of blankets.

Omega curled up within close arm's reach in case Echo needed something, clicked off the flashlight, and the two battered companions got some much-needed rest.

Chapter 8

But about five hours later, the Alpha One team was rudely awakened from a sound sleep by the proximity alarm. Blankets flew everywhere as the two Agents practically exploded upward into sitting positions, and seconds later, Omega was in the co-pilot's seat.

"What have we got, Meg?" Echo asked.

"Looks like we got a ship on approach, Ace, about...um, say a million klicks out yet."

"Fox?"

"I can't tell that yet. We don't have enough power to boost the sensors that much."

"All right. Kill the audio before I kill it. 'Cause I'll do it the permanent way."

"Roger that," she grinned, shutting off the alarm. "Okay, it's almost in range...seven hundred an' fifty thousand kilometers and closing...hm. It looks like it's in a search pattern..."

"That's a good sign."

"Yeah. Six hundred thousand...uh-oh..."

"'Uh-oh'?" Echo tensed automatically, slipping his right hand into his trouser pocket.

"Oh shit! Echo—it's CORTIAN! What do I do?! We don't have enough power for heat, much less shields or weapons!"

"Meg, kill everything except the proximity sensor—everything! Fast! Then get over here and help me curl up my legs."

Omega stabbed buttons rapidly with painful, white-wrapped fingers, darkening the console, then ran to her partner. Echo rolled onto his right side, and Omega helped him curl his body into a loose fetal position. He held up the corner of the covers.

"Now get under here. Hurry."

She wormed under the blankets with him, tugging them over their heads, and Echo wrapped his arms around her waist from behind, pulling her in as close to his chest as he could get her, then fitting his torso to hers.

"What are you doing?!" she asked, astonished by his seeming presumption.

"Ssh. Hold still, or we're dead," Echo whispered in Omega's ear. "I'm not sure how far the field extends."

"Field? What field?"

"Yeah, field. The gizmo we wired into the sensors? It's a cobbled-together version of the sensor scrambler R&D was trying out on the *Tour de Force*. It centers the field on this." Omega felt Echo's hands move slightly at her waist, then a small metal plate—that had once been part of a brain bleacher's guts—poked her lightly in the stomach. "It won't extend very far; we just don't have enough juice—I'm running it off a spare blaster power pack. And it isn't quite as sophisticated. But if we stay inside it, don't make too much noise or vibration, and the rest of the ship is basically a dead hulk, it'll look like we didn't survive the crash."

"So I need to scootch in as close to you as I can get. And stay curled up small."

"That's the idea, yeah."

Omega inched even closer, easing herself carefully into the curve of her partner's body, being especially wary of his damaged legs.

"There. How's that?" she whispered.

"We'll know it's okay if they don't fire. Or land."

"Copy that. It's a lot warmer, too."

"Yeah, it is, actually. I didn't think about that. It's a nice side effect," Echo admitted.

"Uh-huh. You know, this lends a whole new meaning to the term, 'close friends', I guess," she joked.

"Yep. Are you okay?"

"...Yeah. Why?" Omega was suddenly guarded.

"Your heart's pounding like a jackrabbit's."

* * *

Omega was silent. The blue eyes, could Echo have seen them, were momentarily defenseless.

"Meg? What's up?" Echo pressed.

"Uh...I was...just...thinking."

"About—?"

* * *

"About..." she paused, brainstorming rapidly for a likely subject— other than the real reason for her reaction, which was Echo's arms around her, his body pressed against hers—then got sidetracked by the result. "Echo, what if they send down a search party to check out our crash?"

"We've got blasters and Winchester & Teslas." Echo's voice was grim, matter-of-fact. "Not to mention the tachyon-splitter rifles."

"Okay. There should be a spare blaster in the supply bag."

"Not any more," Echo replied. "I cannibalized it to make this." He waved the field remote slightly. Omega nodded slowly.

* * *

"Echo?"

"What?"

"I won't be taken." Omega's voice was low, decided. Echo's arms tightened around her in understanding.

"Neither will I."

"Together?"

"If it comes to that."

After a few moments, Omega whispered again. "This is gonna drive me crazy, lying here blind and deaf."

* * *

"Oh. Sorry. We're not. Can you see well enough to read this?" Echo held the scrambling field remote in front of her chest, and Omega realized it still had parts of the brain bleacher and medscanner display screens attached, now merged into one unit. But it had been heavily modified; it now depicted a scaled graphic—the Alpha One team's location, and a moving blip.

"Oh! I see it. Yeah, they're still there."

"How far off are they?"

"Um...oh, okay, I see how to read it, I think. Does the scale change?"

"Yeah, depending on how close they are. It should shift scale automatically."

"Okay. Looks like they're in synchronous orbit around this planetesimal now, maybe a couple thousand klicks out."

"Checking us out, then. Hold real still." After a minute, Echo poked her lightly in the belly. "Hey! Quit holding your breath. You'll pass out. I said hold still. I didn't say don't breathe."

"Oh," Omega gasped, "I was, wasn't I?"

"Meg?"

"Hm?"

"You feel so...strongly...about this. What happened to you when you were a...'lab rat'?" Echo asked, his voice soft.

* * *

Echo felt Omega's entire body stiffen at the question.

"Not now, Echo."

"Why not? We're not going anywhere. Besides, I thought we were..." he pulled her even nearer briefly, in an approximation of an affectionate hug, trying to lighten her mood, "'close friends,' you and me. Especially after you applied for the 'best buddy' position."

"I'll...tell you someday. I promise."

"Close...but not close enough, huh?" Echo grew very quiet, feeling rejected. "I'll shut up, then. Sorry."

"No, Echo, don't, please. It's not that at all. I will tell you eventually, I swear I will. It's just...look, have you really talked to anybody about watching the Cortians turn me into a...a lump of charcoal? I know you got the counseling, but I mean, like, the details?"

"No." Echo winced at the memory.

"Why not?"

"It's not something I...prefer to think about."

"Then why do you expect me to make casual conversation about my treatment by an alien version of Joseph Mengele?"

"Mengele?!" Echo froze in shock. "Meg—Slug tortured you??"

He felt her curl into a tighter ball.

"I was genetically 'enhanced'—both physically and mentally—I was programmed, and I was brainwashed, Echo. All I...okay, look. For right now, let's just say that the word 'vivisection' applied, that Slug wasn't unduly concerned with my comfort—he didn't believe in any kind of anesthesia—and let it go until some other time to discuss details, all right?"

"WHAT?! Oh, shit, Meg..." he breathed. A horrified Echo rested his forehead against his partner's hair for a brief instant, his arms clasping her tightly against himself in a fierce embrace as he instinctively tried to wrap his body around hers to protect it. "Damn. All so Slug could get revenge on me. Aw, honey. I...I can't— I don't—"

"Sssh," Omega whispered, looking down at the remote in Echo's hand. "Open your hand up, Ace. You've got it balled around the whatsit and I can't read it. Something just changed."

Startled, Echo uncurled his fingers from the hard fist he'd made at his partner's revelation, and Omega studied the display.

"Oh, crap," she whispered.

"What?"

"Echo—be thinking about the best place to do our Alamo routine, hon. A small object just detached from the larger spacecraft..."

* * *

"Hold on, Meg!" Echo said moments later, clamping his struggling partner against him as hard as he could. "Stay still, baby. They haven't called our bluff yet. They're just nosing around. If it's an unmanned probe, they won't catch us. We can fool it. Stay cool. Trust me."

"But the weapons cache is in the aft—"

"I know that. But we don't need 'em yet," Echo said sharply, and Omega quieted.

"Okay. I-I'm...sorry, Echo. I'm...I'm knee-jerking." Her voice was low and husky. "Really, really bad."

"I know, and I get it now, baby," Echo murmured then. "You have good reason. But I...I won't let them take you, Meg. I swear to you on everything I hold dear. If...if I have to do it myself, I won't let 'em get you." *It'll rip my guts out to do it,* he thought, swallowing hard, *but since I'll be eating my own gun in the next moment, I won't have to deal with it too long.*

Omega relaxed noticeably.

"All right," she replied, voice still husky. "And...and if it comes to that, I'll...do the same, if you want me to."

"Yeah. Okay, deal."

"Thanks."

"Ditto."

Echo cautiously eased his grip on Omega, and she lay, still and unmoving, beside him.

"I'm not going anywhere now," she told him. "I swear."

"That's my girl. Status?" Echo raised the remote slightly so she could see it.

"Hm," Omega said, studying the display.

"'Hm' what?"

"I...don't know what the hell it's doing..."

176

"Well, it's not like the display is real sophisticated. I didn't have a helluva lot to work with. Let me see..." Echo tilted his head to peer over Omega's shoulder at the softly-lit display, trying not to move the remote's position any more than he could help, while not bumping her acid burns. "Oh, I know why you don't understand it. You haven't ever seen this tactic before. This is a good sign. Look, see how the range display is oscillating?"

"Yeah?"

"That's an automated probe in a search mode. It'll gradually come closer, move over us, and go on. If we stay put and stay calm, we can fool it."

"We're gonna be here for hours."

"Probably." Echo studied her. "Meg, I know you find this situation... disturbing, uncomfortable, physically and mentally—"

* * *

"Got that right," she breathed, glancing down at the strong arms, firm around her, and wishing she dared relax into them. Echo didn't hear the remark.

"—And I know you're really tense about our situation. But you need to loosen up, baby. Everything's under control, I swear it is. This thing woke us in the middle of our sleep period. Do you think you can maybe get some more sleep?"

"Sleep?! Echo, you have gotta be kidding me."

"No, I'm not. Look, Meg, you're so tense right now, every muscle you've got is contracted. Never mind the fact that you're all banged up. You're wearing yourself out."

"How do you know that?"

"Meg," Echo responded, exasperated, "you're stiff as a board." Abruptly, he poked a fingertip into her belly; she jumped, but he was right—her abdominal muscles were rock-hard. A quaking began, deep in the muscle, and spread until the core of her body trembled, despite her best efforts. "See what I mean?" Echo said, pulling her back against his body. "Relax."

"Yeah, okay; I'll try. But I still don't see how I can sleep." Omega tried to wrap her arms around her middle to quell the trembling, but Echo's were already there, and he tightened them in what was apparently an effort to help her calm herself. Omega withdrew her own arms quickly.

"I thought you trusted me," Echo replied, voice soft.

"What on earth does that have to do with my not being able to sleep?"

"Do you really think I'm gonna let anything happen to you while you're asleep? You wouldn't let anything happen to me."

"...True."

"What does the readout say?" he asked.

"Mm. The thing's still searching. It's a little closer. But not much."

"So we're gonna be here a while, like you said. Try to get some rest, even if you can't sleep. I'll keep an eye on the Cortians for a couple of hours, then we can trade off. I swear, once you fall asleep, I'll wake you if anything happens."

"You have to," Omega said, settling down and trying to relax.

"Why is that?" Echo asked, puzzled.

"I'm your legs right now."

* * *

"Good point. Okay, Legs, get some sleep," Echo deadpanned. "You're in good hands—literally." He dared to let one hand rub her belly very gently, in soft circular motions.

"Huh," Omega said through a yawn, seeming to settle at the contact, her body loosening in his arms, "in the shape we're in, we make about one good Agent between us."

"Well, we're doing a little better than that. Now that your concussion's better, we make about one good TWO-HEADED Agent between us." Echo grinned, feeling Omega's sleepy giggle and pleased to discover that, not only did she NOT take offense at the light abdominal massage, it appeared to help her calm. *Which,* he concluded privately as he continued the motion, *also indicates she probably likes it. Good. A relaxation tactic for me to use on her in the future.* "And while I'm thinkin' about it," he added, "how are the acid burns?"

"Mm? Oh," she responded, already half-asleep, "doin' okay, considerin'. Bandages on m' hands...help a lot." Omega yawned again, then murmured absently, "But mah back an' shoulders are so sore...even th' shirt hurts. Good thing Ah borrowed a couple o' y'r shirts. Can't...wear...anything else..." And with that, she was asleep, snuggled warm against his body.

What the hell...? he thought, shocked. *That explains...the soft...on top of my forearms...she's...there isn't...she hasn't got...her bra isn't...oh, man...*

A startled Echo was left holding his partner, watching over her in the darkness.

* * *

Omega slept quietly in Echo's arms, her breathing slow and steady. With each inhalation, two soft, warm mounds brushed Echo's forearms, skin separated from skin only by a double thickness of lightweight broadcloth—her shirt, and his shirtsleeve.

I guess it stands to reason, he decided, watching his partner, the woman he loved, sleep soundly, trusting him to guard her. *Her shoulders weren't in horrible shape, thanks in part to the helmet deflecting the rain, but the acid burns were serious enough to hurt, all right. Hell, a shoulder holster might even be painful. Especially with the weight. So I can't see wearing a bra on top of that at all, with all the straps an' elastic an' shit. I know I sure as hell wouldn't, in her position.*

The problem is, now I know it, Echo considered, rueful. *And that way lies definite temptation. Which I gotta resist like hell; best buddies we now are, lovers we aren't. And I'm still tryin' to figure out if she'd even be open to the idea.* Then another thought struck him. *Damn. Am I putting pressure on the burns, holding her like this?*

He pulled his head back far enough to study her shoulders in the scant reflected light from the remote's display, trying to remember the extent of her burns, when he had treated them.

No, I think I'm good, as long as I don't do something like tucking my face into her shoulder as I doze off, or something. That might be kinda uncomfortable for her. But she DID seem to like it when I rubbed her stomach. It was about as relaxing to her as a sleeping pill, it looked like to me. So that's a good sign. And something I really probably ought to remember for future reference.

And damn, but does she have a beautiful body. She doesn't NEED the bra; I couldn't even tell she wasn't wearing one, by, um, by the shape of things through the shirt. But it probably feels better to, uh, support stuff, Echo decided, *whenever we're running or fighting or crap like that. Kinda like a guy's jockstrap for some activities, I guess. Only prettier. A lot prettier.*

He glanced over her shoulder again, being careful not to bump it with his chin, to look at the remote display. After her revelations regarding her abduction and modification, now he fully understood her secret fears of capture—even though she had only sketched the barest imagery for him; his own imagination, coupled with knowledge of the criminal responsible, readily filled in the details. It bothered him intensely that she had suffered so at the hands of his old foe...and all so that said foe could taunt him, could use his closeness to his partner as a means to attack. And Echo had been entirely sincere in his promise to ensure she could not be taken...even if it meant shooting her point-blank himself, before taking his own life.

But if we keep still, and this thing works, he thought, *it won't come to that. Please God, don't let it come to that.*

He drew a deep breath, put the disturbing thoughts out of his mind with an effort, and focused on watching the blip that depicted the drone as it oscillated through its search pattern. In the back of his mind, and with conscious self-permission, he let the sensations of Omega's slow, steady breathing, and the warmth of her body, soothe his own tensions.

* * *

Omega stood on the dune overlooking the silver beach, scanning the horizon. A warm breeze caressed her skin; the loose tassels hanging from the knots of her black string bikini brushed against her thighs as the air stirred them. Overhead, the bright blue sun spilled heat over the tropical terrain, as she looked about for one of their number who had gone missing.

"Meg?" a familiar voice called behind her. "C'mere a minute, would ya, baby? I got somebody I need you to meet before we head out on this."

Omega turned toward her Suit-clad partner, who stood there with an older man, also dressed in a Suit.

"Wow, son, are you really gonna let her go on this mission dressed in that?" the other man asked Echo.

"Why not? It's black, so it's not like she's 'outta uniform,'" Echo said with a chuckle. "And it looks damn good on her. Especially with those hol-sters strapped over it. Major badass, there."

"What you said. I ain't arguin' aesthetics, here, Echo. But if one 'a those strings breaks at the wrong time, it'll be a damn sight more serious than a simple distraction," the other man said.

"Aw, hush," Echo grumbled, moving to Omega's side and checking out the type of knots holding the bikini in place. "Lemme see those strings

here, baby. Gotta make certain of the structural integrity, ya know. Nobody gets to see THAT...but me." He tugged gently on the snugly-tied straps, then nodded, satisfied. *"See? I TOLD you,"* he said to the other man, who laughed.

"Made ya look," he said, still chuckling.

"Dammit, X-ray, behave, just for once," Echo demanded. *"You'd think I was the senior Agent, not you."* He turned to Omega. *"Meg, this is my first partner, X-ray. He's gonna help us find Fox. X-ray, this is my life partner, Omega."*

"Hi, X-ray," Omega said with a smile, offering a hand. *"I've heard a lot about you. Pleased to finally meet you."*

"The feeling's mutual, young lady, and so have I," X-ray agreed, taking her hand. But instead of shaking it, he bowed over it in a courtly fashion, mimicking kissing it.

"Hey, now, cut that out," Echo fussed. *"She's MINE, not yours, buddy."*

"I know. I just like seeing you with your shorts all in a wad," X-ray told the younger man with another laugh. He cut a mischievous glance at Omega, who merely rolled her eyes, producing another bark of laughter from him.

"Do we know what happened to Fox?" Omega asked.

"Well, yes and no," Echo admitted. *"Do you remember that green-skinned chick, the daughter of the premier?"*

"Yeah?"

"Seems she decided he was her type, so she kidnapped him an' ran off with him," Echo explained. *"Zebra is pitching an unholy fit, and Pulgey Entiyti isn't that happy, either..."*

"Though for entirely different reasons," X-ray remarked with a grin. *"Fox is, after all, the Director these days."*

"Yeah, I'd expect so," Omega agreed. *"I wouldn't be too happy either, if somebody ran off with this guy."* She took Echo's arm. *"I mean, because of both reasons, really."*

"I'll bet," X-ray said, shooting Echo a wicked grin. *"One thing I'll say, you got good taste, son."*

"Um, I think I'm the one with the good taste, X-ray," Omega murmured. *"After all, he's not actually...interested...like that."*

"The hell you say," X-ray said, raising a skeptical eyebrow. "Well, I suppose you'll find out soon enough. Echo, you're the department chief; what say we get this Fox hunt under way?"

Omega groaned, then laughed. Echo rolled his eyes.

"All right, c'mon you two, let's go," he said.

"What about Alpha Two?" Omega wondered, as she and X-ray turned to follow Echo across the dunes toward a flowering forest in the near distance.

"They'll be meeting up with us later, baby. C'mon. I got a lead as to where she took him, an' you'll be wanting that bikini pretty soon..."

* * *

"Mmmph." Omega stirred at last, and made an uninhibited, full-body stretch in her partner's arms as she awoke.

"Damn it, Meg, hold still," an urgent Echo hissed. "The probe's right on top of us."

Omega immediately pulled in tight with a soft little exclamation as she came fully awake.

"Ooo, shit! Sorry. Did I goof?" she breathed. Echo glanced over her shoulder at the remote unit, watching it for long moments.

"No, I don't think so. It hasn't altered its search pattern," he finally decided. He laid the palm of one hand flat against her belly. "Yep, I thought so. Why'd you get hot all of a sudden?" he murmured, curious.

"Um...'cause I think I just beat X-ray's record."

"...X-ray's record?"

"For most shades of red a person can turn..."

"Oh, that," Echo chuckled softly. "Why?"

"Uh...well, I...I'm not used to...to waking up...uh..."

"Oh. It threw you off to wake up with me curled up right here with you?"

"Yeah. Um. Just a little bit."

"Does it make you uncomfortable?"

"Depends on how you define it, I guess." She shrugged against his arms. "Do I mind? I suppose not. I trust you. We're..." Echo heard the smile, "'close friends.'"

"Actually, I've decided to accept your application," he told her. "So you can now officially use the term, 'best buddies.'"

"Aw! Okay. Thanks, Ace."

"I think the thanks is mine, baby. Now, you were saying you didn't mind...except I heard an implied 'but' in there."

"Oh. Yeah. So yeah, I don't mind, 'cause I trust my, um, my best buddy. BUT...am I accustomed to it? Big fat 'no'. Am I...embarrassed? That also depends. Did I...um, do anything while I was asleep to...?"

"Huh? What do you mean?"

* * *

"Um, well...uh, like...remember when you were tellin' me why you didn't invite me into your bedroom to check on you, last Christmas when you got shot?" Omega tried, not entirely sure how to get the notion across without embarrassing both of them. *Maybe if I reference that, sorta oblique and all, he'll get the message without me having to say any more,* she decided.

"Nooo...oh, wait, yeah, the other night, after the nightmare," Echo recalled. "You mean the whole 'guy bits' stuff, right?"

"Uh, yeah." *Whew. He got it.*

"So you were havin' a really good dream, huh?"

"Kinda, yeah. So I just...was wondering if..."

"But..." Echo broke off, seeming uncertain, then tried again. "It isn't like women have it all hangin' out there to see..."

Omega barely stifled a snort at what was obviously an unintentional double entendre on Echo's part, and then she felt his body grow warmer as he realized what he'd said and flushed, himself.

"I'll grant you that," she agreed. "But...there's still, er, signs, ya know."

"Well, yeah..."

"So...that's what I'm askin', Ace..."

"Okay. Um. Well, I didn't pick up on anything at the time, so probably not, but lessee, lemme think. Huh. No, not that I noticed, at all. I thought you slept like a rock, as you like to put it. You barely moved. Don't worry about it, Meg," Echo tried to set her at ease. "Even if you did, it's not a big deal."

"Mm," Omega responded, noncommittal.

"So did you...sleep well?"

"Like a rock," she reiterated, feeling sheepish. "Warm and cozy. You,

183

uh, well, you make a terrific heater, Ace."

"Well...good. Glad I'm useful for something. Especially when I'm this bunged up." Echo grinned. "So you were, uh, dreaming, huh?"

"Yeah, as a matter of fact. And it was a nice one."

"Hold that thought." Echo gestured with the remote. "What's it say?"

Omega studied the gadget's readout. "It's finally moving away. But still taking its time. Looks like you'll be able to take a nap, too."

"That works." Echo shifted slightly with a soft grunt of pain. "Now. Tell me about this nice dream of yours. If you can, that is, without...well, you know."

"What time is it?" she asked casually.

"The last dose of painkiller has worn off, if that's what you're asking, and I know it is. I'm fine."

"And I can't get to the medical kit anyway," Omega sighed in intense regret. "I really wish I'd thought to grab the thing when I dove in here with you, after the Cortians showed. I was...too agitated. I'm really sorry about that, Ace."

"Eh. 20/20 hindsight and all that. I don't blame you, and I'm not dyin'. Now tell me about this dream. Or can you talk about it?"

"Yeah, I can talk about it. It wasn't, um, like THAT."

"All right. So tell me."

"Okay. I dreamed about Zeta Aurigae Four."

"Hmm," Echo replied. "Were you there?"

"Uh-huh."

"Was I there?"

"Uh-huh."

"Separately or together?"

"Together. We were on a mission. It was pretty funny, actually."

"How so?"

"We were there to find Fox. Some green-skinned babe had kidnapped him for her mate, an' Zebra was twelve kinds of pissed about it. X-ray was helping us."

"Oh, really? Did we find Fox?"

"Yeah," Omega chuckled, "but he wasn't too thrilled about it."

"I'll just bet," Echo grinned. "What was X-ray like in your dream?"

"Oh, I'd say...eighteen, maybe as much as twenty years older 'n you.

Not as tall, but not short, either; I'd say right around six feet. Very distinguished-looking, sorta like a college professor, almost. Steel-gray hair, clean shaven, kinda blue-gray eyes. Sharp as a tack. He joked around a bunch, too. I thought he had a great sense of humor. You and he bantered, a whole lot. But if somebody ticked him off, or threatened one of us—watch out."

To her surprise, Omega felt Echo stiffen.

"Go on," he murmured quietly.

"Ace? Is everything—?"

"Fine. Go on."

"Well, the three of us had an absolute blast together. You and X-ray really got off on one-liners, and I thought X-ray would tease me half to death."

"Why?"

"'Cause, for some strange reason, instead of my black Suit, I was wearing a black string bikini, and X-ray kept wantin' to make a bet with you on how long it'd be before...uh, well, before one of the strings broke in a fight. You didn't seem too keen on that idea; every time X-ray said something, you'd come check the suit's 'structural integrity'. I wasn't sure whether to be flattered or insulted."

* * *

A slight sputter that might have been amusement escaped Echo despite himself, then he sobered.

"So tell me what Zeta Aurigae Four was like in your dream."

"Mmm..." Omega purred, and Echo raised his eyebrows at the suggestiveness of the sound. "Warm and tropical. I was glad to be in that bikini. I think I'd have been way too hot in a Suit, even if it was summer-weight. I didn't see how you guys could stay so cool in the Suits. Lush foliage in shades of blue and green. Huge flowers in every color you could imagine. A light-blue sun. Silver beaches. Two moons..."

As she went on with her description, Echo grew more and more dumbfounded. Finally he reacted.

"Meg," he interrupted in a strained voice, "I don't know what the hell that was, but it was no dream."

"What do you mean?" Omega asked, sounding confused.

"That's exactly what Eden looks like, right down to the color of the star. And I couldn't have painted a better picture of X-ray myself. I didn't tell you those details in my story. Have you ever seen pictures of X-ray, or of me with him?"

"No, I never have," Omega averred. "Not even a group shot, at least to know who I was lookin' at. I know that sorta stuff is classified and all, and other than just curiosity about your first partner, I never had a real—you know, legitimate—reason to see 'em, so I never tried..."

"That's...even more interesting."

"Aw shit. Echo...do you think I'm getting inside your head again, like I did after the Cortians burned me?" Omega's voice was barely audible.

"I don't know, Meg. If you did, I didn't sense anything this time. And you weren't in a coma, just asleep."

"Yeah. But I got this nasty klonk on the head, too."

* * *

"True. Well, there's only one way to find out." Echo shifted, getting as comfortable as he could, then Omega felt him lean slightly against her back, his body going slack. "C'mon in. I'm ready when you are."

"You mean...try to establish a telepathic link?"

"Yup."

"I'd...rather not, Echo."

"Why?"

"I feel like I'm invading you. Violating you. Among other things."

"That's because that's pretty much the main kind of experience you've had with telepathy, Meg. Well, except for Zz'r'p, I guess. But it doesn't have to be like that. It's all right; I'm okay with it. You have my full permission. Encouragement, even. Now give it a shot, baby." Echo was reassuring.

"I...are you sure?"

"I'm sure."

"All right. Here goes."

* * *

Omega gave a precautionary glance at the remote first, and nodded, satisfied, even as Echo looked over her shoulder to check the same thing: The probe was still moving steadily away.

Then Echo felt Omega's body slowly relax and go limp, sagging against him as it had while she slept. Completely trusting her, willing to

186

risk discovery of his feelings in the circumstances—because she'd be able to sense his honorable intent, without doubt, and it would negate the need to maintain a defense—Echo dropped his psychic walls and opened up to his partner as best he knew how.

Meg? You there? he called.

Distantly, he thought he heard, *Echo?*

Meg! I hear you, I think! Echo felt an unexpected twinge of pain insinuate itself into his head just above his right temple—the very area Omega had struck and injured during the crash. *Damn, hon', this is hurting you,* he realized. *I didn't think about that. Stop. We'll try again later.* Echo pulled back and opened his eyes.

"Meg?"

His partner lay still against him, unmoving.

"Meg?" Echo shook her gently. "Meg, come on back." She didn't react. His gut clenched tight. "Baby? Uh-oh. Don't do this to me, now..."

When she still failed to respond, he shook her again, a little harder. With a start, Omega opened her eyes. Echo stifled a sigh of titanic relief.

"Uhn. Owtch." Omega's hands went to her temples. "Ohh. Did anybody get the registration number on that tank? I think it's using my head for a hood ornament..."

"Are you okay?" Echo queried, concerned. "I didn't stop to consider that it might hurt."

"Neither...did I," Omega said slowly. "I'm...I'm okay."

"You sure?"

"Yeah."

"Oh, damn, Meg, I just noticed!" Echo exclaimed, horrified at the comprehension. "You've been resting all this time on your right side..."

"So?"

"You've been lying on your head wound. That's exactly what you don't need to be doing."

"Well, we can't turn over now. I'm fine. Kick back and get some sleep. It's your turn," a matter-of-fact Omega told Echo.

"You sure?"

"Sure. Give me the, um...the gizmo. Whatever the hell we're callin' it."

"Gizmo works. All right. Here." Echo handed her the remote, then extended his arms past her torso and tucked in his chilled hands, one on either side of her belly. "Mm. That's nice an' warm. Good night, baby."

"G' night, Ace."

* * *

Echo settled down behind Omega, and she heard his breathing gradually slow, settling into a steady rhythm, until she knew he was asleep. But his body never completely relaxed, and from time to time, he stirred in a restless fashion. When he tried to adjust his legs, then grunted in his sleep, her suspicions were confirmed.

"It hurts pretty bad, doesn't it, Ace?" Omega whispered to the unusually-vulnerable form wrapped around her. A sleeping Echo didn't answer, but then, Omega hadn't expected him to. Glancing down at the remote, she sighed. "The damn stupid medikit's only a few feet away, but it might as well be at home, for all the good it does us right now," she grumbled, then grew thoughtful. "I wonder...I picked up a few things, when he invited me in..."

Suddenly she broke off the thought, distracted by another that had occurred to her.

"He invited me in. He...INVITED me in. Into his HEAD. That's...way more intimate than, than inviting me to come check on his injuries while he's in bed or something. That's...that's serious trust. Of his inmost secrets. With ME. Trust...OF me. He really, really meant it—I really am his best friend now, and he let me right in." She wrapped her arms around his and hugged them for a moment, wanting to return that trust and affection, even if he wouldn't know it. She shook her head, feeling a warmth, a rush of love and caring, flood her being.

Omega waited a few minutes for it to subside, then tried to regather her scattered plan and her wits.

"Okay, so lemme see. I spotted a couple places while I was in there. So...I think maybe..." A flash of pain crossed her face, and she rubbed at the now-ragged gauze around her head, thinking hard. "There...and...there? Or maybe...maybe I better not. I might not—"

Just then, Echo tried to shift his legs again, then groaned softly in his sleep.

"Uh. Yeah, no. That does it," Omega told herself, determined. "I'm givin' it a try. No matter what." She closed her eyes; her jaws clenched against the throbbing in her head. After a moment, Omega extended her left hand back over her shoulder, careful not to inadvertently punch Echo in the doing, as she couldn't tell for sure exactly where his head was, though she felt his warm breath feathering through her hair. The bandaged fingers lightly brushed Echo's face; she frowned, and withdrew the hand. Omega peeled the gauze away, exposing the raw, acid-burned fingertips, then she reached back again. With a wince of pain at the contact this time, Omega ran gentle fingers over Echo's temple, exploring, almost caressing, all while noting the hot, feverish feel of his skin...before closing her eyes.

After a few moments of this contact, Echo relaxed completely with a sigh, his body slumping cozily against her, and sank deeper into sleep. Omega held the pose for a few seconds longer, then drew her hand back, opened her eyes, and looked down at the remote. Tears welled in the blue eyes, and Omega watched the Cortian probe on the display in silence for a long time.

Echo slept comfortably for several hours.

* * *

Alpha One was off duty, clad in comfortable jeans and t-shirts, strolling through a lovely meadow on Zeta Aurigae Four. The skies were clear, save for a couple of fluffy white clouds to the west; soft breezes caressed their skin.

Echo found a patch of cool shade beneath a copse of flowering trees, the sweet, slightly spicy perfume of their blossoms scenting the air, and put down the picnic basket, even as Omega spread a blanket on the grass. They sat down side by side, and Omega pulled out their meal—fully loaded submarine sandwiches, chips, and a bottle of wine with a couple of small plastic goblets. A single, long-stemmed rose in a bud vase completed the decoration. Echo raised an eyebrow, and glanced at his life partner, who smiled back.

"In honor of our first Valentine's Day," she told him, and he nodded in understanding.

It didn't take long for the food to disappear, and the pair sat close together, sipping from their wine glasses. When they were empty, Echo took Omega's with his own, and put them aside, then pulled her into his arms, tasting the residue of the red wine in her mouth as he kissed her.

Soon he eased her to the blanket, his body covering hers as he deep-

ened the kiss. She sighed in something that sounded very like contentment, and he raised his head, gazing down into twin sapphires, though he wondered for a brief moment how sapphires could smile like that.

"Are you okay with this?" he asked.

"Yeah, I'm happy," she told him. "I love you."

Echo's chest threatened to burst with the tsunami of happiness that flooded it at her declaration.

"I love you, too," he breathed. "Now?"

"Now..."

* * *

As Omega lay, quietly watching the remote's display, her partner wrapped around her body and sleeping soundly, she heard him murmur something unintelligible, then shift his torso slightly. She glanced over her shoulder to verify that he was indeed asleep and not trying to talk to her, then returned her attention to the display.

Moments later, Echo murmured something again, adjusted his arms around her waist, then tucked his face into her hair at the back of her head. She smiled to herself.

Somebody's dreamin', she thought with affection. *Hope it's a good one. At least he's not hurtin' now.* She sighed, a despondent sound. *If that's what it takes, that's what it takes.*

She rubbed her temple again and settled back down, trying to relax into his warm body and stop the worried litany that kept running through her mind. *I got a partner with two really busted legs, a dislocated shoulder, an' a sprained wrist; I got a doozy of a klonk on my head, and some nasty acid burns; we got a dyin' spaceship, slavers overhead lookin' for any signs we're NOT dead, an' no idea when...or even if...rescue is gonna show. I mean, how is Fox gonna find us? We're a really little needle in an awful damn big haystack. And because we've had to make ourselves look dead so the Cortians can't find us, that means we've made ourselves pretty much invisible to Fox, too. An' I'm too new to this space stuff to really have any bright ideas—hell, NASA was still working on the solar system! Not that I'm that good brainstormin' with the dino egg on my head anyway; DAMN, my head hurts!*

This...doesn't look good for Alpha One. She rubbed her head again. *I guess...if it comes to us dyin' here, alone together, I'm gonna 'fess up to him and tell him how I feel. At least he'll know that he'll die next to somebody who loves him, somebody who'd do anything for him. Including giving him up, if I had to...if he didn't want what I've got. And I can't think he would. Maybe I should keep my mouth shut, after all. He doesn't need that squick factor, I suppose.*

About then, it entered Omega's consciousness that her partner's body had changed conformation in some fashion. She frowned, temporarily puzzled, then pressed her torso back against his in an effort to determine what was going on, since she couldn't turn around and look for fear of exposing herself outside the cloaking field. Abruptly she became aware of the difference...and what it implied.

Oh wow, she thought in surprise, *Ace is havin' a really DAMN good dream! This sorta thing must be exactly why he didn't want me just waltzin' in an' out of his bedroom, I guess. I bet he's dreamin' about...about Chase.*

She found the concept disturbing on a fundamental level; lying in her sleeping partner's arms and considering confessing her love for him, all while he dreamed—in what was obviously an intimate fashion—of another woman, was troubling and seemed to her like a sort of violation of his being. The feeling was heightened by the fact that she would have given a body part to be the woman about whom he was dreaming.

So she tried to wriggle out of his embrace, intending to get just far enough away to break the physical contact without moving so far away that she exited the cloaking field, just in case the Cortian vessel was watching in addition to the searching drone.

But as soon as she tried to move away, his arms tightened, locking down around her and keeping her pinned against his body.

"Nuh-uh. C'me back 'ere, you," he slurred under his breath. "No' lettin' you go. Mm."

"Ace?" she murmured. "You awake, hon?"

Echo gave no answer, and Omega concluded that he was soundly asleep. More, judging from the way his body reacted to her efforts to extricate herself, she was afraid that if she pushed the matter, he might end up causing more damage to his legs...a matter about which she was already worried. His skin had felt warm earlier; it was starting to feel downright hot to her touch.

We don't need that hole in his leg where the bone came through gettin' infected. But if he's feverish, that explains the dreams and everything, she decided. *Well, we're both dressed, and other than, uh, what's goin' on with him 'down south,' he's not actually moving much at all. And what's goin' on is a normal bodily thing. So I guess I'll just lay here an'...*

She broke off her train of thought. The temptation was strong to fantasize about what he was dreaming.

But that's not fair to either of us, she concluded. *He's still grievin' Chase, and all it's gonna do for me is get my hopes up, when I already know he's not interested.* She sighed silently. *His expression at the Christmas party, when I tried to catch him under the mistletoe along with the others, was proof enough of that. I can't imagine him bein' interested anyway. What guy with any sense is gonna be interested in a kluged-together...creature... intended to be his killer? An' Echo's got good sense and smarts aplenty, so forget that. I guess I'll just lay here and watch the probe drone on the display, and wait for him to wake up.*

So she settled back into the position she had had, against his torso. This resulted in Echo emitting a soft, contented sigh that tickled her ear, and leaning into her body. Omega gave a mental shrug, and tried hard to focus on the remote display, watching as the drone finally ceased search operations and returned to its mother ship.

Shortly thereafter, and seeming—to Omega's thought—reluctant to take the action, the Cortian vessel broke orbit and departed. She let out a long, quiet breath of released tension, realizing that, at least on this level, they were safe for the time, and their subterfuge had worked. A sleeping Echo still wasn't letting go, though, so she tried to relax and get some more rest, herself. In the circumstances, however, sleep for her was unlikely, and she knew it—the situation with Echo was too uncomfortable to her mind. *Let alone the notion that that Cortian ship is probably still out there watching, just out of range of our under-powered sensors,* she thought.

But she also knew from experience that the body could still take rest without ever going to sleep. And if she could manage to quiet her thoughts, even her mind could rest. But that last proved to be the sticking point, as it turned out. Too restless to manage it, Omega finally simply forced herself to lie still, so as not to wake her partner before he finished his sleep.

So it was a considerable relief when, about an hour later, Echo started to stir, and gave evidence of waking soon.

This is gonna get interesting, she decided, nibbling at her lower lip in concern. *The 'guy bits' are still pretty active down there. I hope it doesn't embarrass him too much. I guess I better pretend I didn't notice, and not say anything...unless he does, I s'pose. I'd try to fake being asleep, for his sake, but he knows me too well; I don't think he'd buy it.*

* * *

Oh shit, Echo thought, his entire body stiffening in chagrin as he came to full consciousness and became aware of the sensations in his groin. *I went and did exactly what I didn't want to happen. This is precisely why I've hesitated to give Meg the invitation she wants, to come check on me at night in my bedroom. Damn, that was some dream. And now I'm awake... and here she is, and I'm holding her close. I just wish...oh well. I guess I better hope she's been too occupied to notice. I won't say anything unless she does. After all, she's got that degree in biology; she knows how this stuff works.*

* * *

When he awoke, Omega felt him freeze for an instant.

"Yup, now I know how it feels," he breathed, one hand releasing her waist to rake through his hair. Unfortunately, that hand happened to be his left, with its injured wrist and shoulder, so he grunted—she assumed because a spasm of pain shot through it—and let it drop back to her side. Finally he addressed her directly. "Uhn. So. Good morning, or something. Whatever the hell time it is."

"G' mornin', Ace. Have a good sleep?"

"Yeah, pretty good, I guess, Meg. What's, uh, what's happening with the Cortian drone?"

"They're all gone."

"Gone?"

"Uh-huh. I'd 'a moved so you could have more room, but you weren't lettin' go, an' I didn't want to wake you."

Echo slowly released her at that, and Omega rolled over to face him, clicking on the flashlight. "How do you feel?" she asked then.

"Pretty damn good, actually. This is the least pain I've been in since the crash."

"Good." Omega nodded.

"How are you doing?" Echo asked.

"...Okay."

"All right." Echo began pulling the blankets back. "We need to reset the proximity alert to look for Fox."

Omega's eyes widened in horror.

"Oh, no," she mouthed silently. Echo rolled onto his back, then sat up, pushing aside the blankets, and Omega slowly followed suit.

"Well, come on, Meg," he said, when she continued to sit beside him. "Get a move on."

"Echo, I...I don't think I can." She looked down, studying the emergency blanket that lay across her.

"Why not?" he glanced at her, puzzled, curiosity obviously engaged.

'Um...while you were asleep...you hurt, and...and since I couldn't get to the kit, I tried going into your head again, and I managed to find the right place, and...and I made it stop hurting, so you could sleep better. Are...are you mad?"

A hesitant, worried Omega glanced up at her partner with considerable uncertainty at the admission. Echo tilted his head slightly, looking at his partner with dark eyes that were warm with caring gratitude.

"Thank you," he said softly. "Your head must be splitting, Meg."

"Well, um...do you think maybe you could wrap this back up for me?" she asked, holding out her left hand, and diverting his attention in the process.

"Sure," Echo said, reaching for the kit. "Why did you take it off?"

"I needed to touch you to make your legs stop hurting," Omega said simply.

"Oh—I get it. Direct contact," he remarked, applying ointment to the sensitive wound with a gentle touch, before re-bandaging her hand.

"Yeah."

* * *

"Okay, all done. Want something for your head?" Echo said, replacing the bandaging supplies in the kit and rummaging for analgesics.

"I...don't think you've got anything in there that'll fix my head, Echo," Omega said in a low voice.

Echo's head snapped up at her phrasing; he turned to see a listless Omega staring down at her hands.

"Meg—you didn't...you're not..." he stammered, horrified. She nodded. "Oh, damn—NO!"

"Echo," Omega said earnestly, watching him, "you hurt. You couldn't even sleep good. I had to do something. It was killin' me, hearing you groan in your sleep. I took a...took a...a chance," the word finally came to her. "I didn't know if it would even work, and I didn't know for sure it would do this to me. But I HAD to try."

"Are you still doing it? Blocking my pain?"

"I don't know. I think so. It still doesn't hurt, right?"

"Stop it, Meg!" a fierce Echo ordered. "NOW!"

Omega flinched away.

"I'm sorry," she whispered, childlike, her eyes filling with tears. "I'm so sorry. I didn't mean to, to in-invade your, your pri-vacy. I tried not to! I only went to the place I saw that the pain was, I swear! I just...wanted you to feel better."

Echo froze, realizing that, in her condition, she had misunderstood; then he pulled himself over to her with his good arm.

"Shh now, hush. Hush, baby. I'm not angry, Meg," he murmured, touching the bandage at her temple with gentle fingertips. "I'm grateful. More than you know. But you need to stop, now, before you hurt yourself more. I'd rather endure some pain and discomfort, than see you injured... again...because of me."

Omega searched Echo's eyes in the dim emergency lighting, apparently looking for and seeing his earnestness, then she said, "Okay, I'll try. Hold still." She put out her right hand, then huffed in exasperation.

"What is it?"

"Bandages." She began tugging at them in frustration. "Bandages everywhere. I'm so sick of bandages!"

"Whoa, wait a minute, there. Hold on. Here, lemme get it. We need to re-do this one anyway. It's getting kinda ragged." Echo carefully removed the gauze on her right hand. "There. Try that."

Omega rested her fingertips against the side of Echo's face, and he chuckled despite the seriousness of the situation.

"What?" she wondered.

"The way Romeo's always teasing us about having a mind link like that TV show, if he could see us now, we'd never hear the end of it." He grinned.

"Shush, you," Omega said, snickering. "It's hard enough for me to think without you making me laugh."

"Sorry." Echo watched as his partner—*no,* he corrected himself, *my... closest friend, and...and more, if I can manage it*—closed her eyes and concentrated as well as she could. A frown creased her face, and Echo gradually became aware of a deep warmth beneath the poor burned fingertips. At the same time, Echo also became aware of the pain in his legs, and he stirred restlessly.

"There," Omega said, opening her eyes. "Is it hurting again?"

"...No. I'm fine."

"Don't lie to me, Ace. I know you better than that. 'Sides, nice way to treat your best buddy," Omega remonstrated with him.

"I wasn't lying," Echo protested. "I was—"

"Trying to make us both feel better," she finished.

"Well...yeah."

"Look at me, Echo," she demanded, voice firm. At that adjuration, he met her eyes. "Do you hurt, or not? I have to know, so I'll know if I stopped, like you wanted."

"Let's just say I know I've got two busted legs again."

"Okay. Grab the kit and let's get some painkiller in you."

"That can wait, Meg. You sound a little more like your normal self, now that you're not tending to me, blocking my pain."

"Yeah. For now, I guess. But...not completely," Omega answered with a shrug. "I...can tell."

"Damn it. I knew you didn't need to lie on that bump, all that time." Echo sighed.

"I guess I need to try the controls now?"

"Yeah."

Omega clambered into the co-pilot seat and studied the controls. "Let's see," she mused, scanning the various panels. "Watch what I'm doing, Echo."

"I am." Echo leaned forward.

"This...and this." She flipped a couple of switches with her left hand. "That's what I remember."

"Good. That's right," Echo told her. "Any warning lights?"

"Nope. Everything's green."

"Sensors?"

"Zeroes. Nobody here but us chickens."

"Okay. Get back under here before you freeze. Temperature's gotta be around twenty by now."

"You got it," Omega replied. "Grab the kit and let's take care of your legs."

"And your fingers," Echo reminded her.

* * *

As Echo re-bandaged Omega's fingers, she got an odd look on her face. "What's wrong?" he asked her.

"Do you feel okay, Ace?"

"Damn, Meg," Echo responded, allowing nothing but deadpan sarcasm in his tone, "if you define 'okay' as two broken legs, a sprained wrist, a bum shoulder, and chilled-to-the-bone freezing, not to mention an alien manhunt going on somewhere overhead, I'm just fine."

Omega pulled a face.

"No, I mean...oh, here." She pressed her palm to Echo's forehead, then his cheek. "Yeah, I was afraid of that while you were sleeping. You're awfully hot, Ace. I think you've got a fever."

"Huh. Then that's probably part of what's causing the chills," he observed. "What do you think it's from? Being generally beat up?"

"I've got a sneakin' idea, an' I don't like it very much..." she murmured, as her forehead creased with worry. "Lemme check that shin of yours."

Echo watched as Omega carefully slipped off the splint and removed the bandage on the compound fracture.

"Shit," he muttered when they got a look at the festering wound. "That explains it."

"Yeah," Omega agreed. "You got a rip-roaring good infection going on here, Ace. Let's see what we can do. I'm gonna have to pack it. And shoot you fulla anti-buggum stuff. AND get that fever down."

"Okay," Echo sighed. "I'll get the stuff ready for you." He tugged the medical bag close and studied its contents. "Okay, Meg, here's a good full-spectrum galactic antipathogenic; it oughta take care of whatever bug I've managed to get in there. Shoot me up." He handed her a syringe and bottle, and Omega skillfully filled the syringe, administering it high on Echo's thigh, cutting his trouser leg open a little farther to give her access.

"All right. Now we need to clean this out." Omega glanced around. "Hand me a bottle of water."

"I dunno if this'll work, Meg." Echo handed her a container. "The stuff is slush. It's damn cold in here."

"Hmm..." Omega paused in thought, then unexpectedly dropped the bottle down her shirt front, where it nestled between her breasts. "Aaah! Ooo, that's cold," she gasped, as a shocked Echo looked askance. "Well, at least it'll melt," she grinned in response to his glance. "Now, get me some packing ready, and make sure it's soaked with the same stuff we just shot you full of."

"On it."

"And hand me a painkiller."

"You hurting?" Echo shot a swift, concerned glance at her.

"No, silly," she grinned. "Well, yeah, I am, but it's for you, not me. If you think cleaning this out is gonna feel good, think again. And pop something to bring your fever down while you're at it, okay?"

* * *

A short time later, Echo was thoroughly "drugged up," as Omega put it; the water had melted, and the packing was prepared. Omega made certain Echo was lying flat, spread a disposable medical towel under his calf to absorb any contaminated fluids, then set to work.

"Okay, Ace," Omega began talking to the drowsy man, trying to keep his attention away from what she was doing. "Think we got a snowball's chance on this planet of talking Fox into sending us to Eden?" Meanwhile, she worked continuously with water, swab, and gauze, flushing the open wound as best she could, tending Echo with infinite care.

"Mmh. Good question." Echo slurred the words slightly under the influence of the alien narcotic. "I dunno. But if we put our heads together, and you pour on that Southern charm, I'd say we've got a pretty damn good chance." He grinned.

"Why, that is just so kind o' yew to say, Rhett," Omega teased, letting the Southern dialect flow like warm molasses as she started packing the wound. "Ah just know that we'll manage Fox real well, sugah."

"Damn, Meg." Echo chuckled to himself. "Is there a man on the planet you can't wrap around your little finger? Earth, I mean, not this one."

198

Omega suddenly sobered. *Yeah, and I'm lookin' at one,* she thought... but did not say.

"One or two," she answered quietly instead. Echo, still thoroughly medicated, missed her subdued response.

"How's the leg coming?" he asked.

"Coming right along," Omega replied, glad for the change of subject. "I got it cleaned out the best I can with what I got, the packing is in, and I'm bandaging you back up right now. There. Now let's get the splint back on...easy... No, hon, hold still and let me do it," she told him, as a groggy Echo tried to help. "You might accidentally twist your leg or something, and then we'd have a real mess on our hands. Okay, that's got it. All patched up, Ace."

"Thanks, Meg..." Echo murmured, sounding—and looking—very sleepy.

"Hey, I'm just takin' care o' my best friend," Omega said softly, rubbing his knee with gentle affection. She finished the gesture with a light pat. "Now quit fightin' the medicine and go on back to sleep, Echo."

"No argument there..." he replied, and Echo was asleep.

Chapter 9

In the ensuing hours, Omega found herself waging an all-out war against the infection that had attacked Echo's body. Her partner and companion, semiconscious—often unconscious—from a high fever, tossed restlessly in their blanket tent. Omega confiscated the t-shirt that Echo had been unable to get over his shoulder, and used it, along with almost all of the slushy drinking water, to sponge him down and keep his fever manageable.

"C'mon, Ace," she murmured, injecting still another dose of antibiotic into his thigh. "Work with me here. I'm NOT gonna lose this fight. I'm not gonna lose YOU. And I'm not gonna let YOU lose this LEG. Even if they can manage to regenerate the thing, you'll still be out of it for weeks— maybe months, if they gotta re-teach you to use it."

Omega removed the splint and began the delicate process of changing out the packing in the infected wound.

"Oh, wow. Mm. That's not good," she observed to herself, seeing the bloody pus that contaminated the packing. "I really hope I was able to get to this in time."

Carefully, she disposed of the contaminated packing, prepared more packing, and just as carefully inserted it into the injury. Then she re-splinted the leg and added an analgesic to the medical cocktail circulating in Echo's bloodstream, to bring down his fever while fighting the infection from that front.

"X-ray..." Echo murmured then, tossing his head. "X-ray, I'm sorry, pal. I'm so sorry..."

"Echo? X-ray's not here, hon," Omega told him in a soft tone, sponging him down. "It's Meg. Everything's all right, Echo. Just relax. Just relax, Ace. We got this."

"I'm sorry, ol' buddy," a delirious Echo reiterated. "I'm not replacing you..."

Omega blinked in surprise, and stopped for a moment, listening.

"...Nobody's ever gonna replace you, pal..."

Omega bowed her head, a bleak look appearing in the blue eyes as a nearly-unbearable sense of rejection swept through her being. *So much for that 'best buddy' position,* she decided, stifling a sigh of pain. *I guess he was just tryin' to build up my confidence in us as a team, or something.* Then she resumed sponging Echo down.

"...But nobody will ever replace Meg, either," Echo continued. "C'mon, lemme introduce you to her. You'll like her. A lot. We'll make a helluva team, all three of us. Us three? We'll find Fox in no time. And if I get Romeo and India too, lemme tell ya, we got the damn Cortians' whole freakin' planet licked..."

Echo's current partner smiled, her eyes welling with unaccustomed tears for a brief moment as she worked. Relief and affection washed through her, erasing the memory of rejection from moments before.

"Yeah, Ace," she told him, "we do make a helluva team...all of us. But especially...you an' me."

* * *

As time went on, a feverish, unconscious Echo sank ever deeper into a nightmarish blend of dream and hallucination, commandeering certain all-too-recent experiences as abundant fodder. He tossed and turned restlessly, kicking and struggling, trying to fight off the vivid imagery, unaware that his partner was trying desperately to hold his legs still, so he would not wound them even further.

* * *

Standing in the back door of their joint quarters, Echo held Omega close, kissing her deeply, as he felt their minds slip into a comfortable connection, sharing thought, emotion and sensation; dimly he felt gratitude toward the Deltiri ambassador, Zz'r'p, for teaching her how to establish and maintain such a link. Soon, he planned to sweep her into his arms and carry her to the bedroom, there to complete the union in a more...physical... fashion. A sensation of decided approval came back to him from his partner, and he grinned to himself.

But suddenly yellow-plumed aliens surrounded them, firing projectile weapons before retreating, running into their spacecraft. Echo was only mildly shocked to find that Alpha One was no longer in their quarters, but in a spacecraft hangar; more, his partner gasped in sudden shock and pain as her shattered leg buckled beneath her. He crushed Omega tight against his body to keep her upright.

"Run, Echo!" she told him, breath coming in sharp pants of pain. "Get out of here, while you can!"

"Not without you!" he declared, and attempted to lift her into his arms.

But for some reason, neither his arms nor legs would function. It was as if he were in slow motion, barely able to move, unable to lift Omega, unable to run...even as he heard the alien craft's interplanetary ion engines come online.

"No!" he cried.

"Ace, RUN!" Omega screamed.

"NO!" he shouted back.

And the engines ignited.

So did Alpha One. He could only watch as the body of the woman he loved became a living torch, feeling her searing agony as well as his own, through their mental link.

Despite himself, Echo screamed.

* * *

Abruptly, Echo's activity ramped up dramatically, from restless, spasmodic motion to outright writhing and beating against the deck. Grunts and moans escaped his lips, and he panted hard, as if in deep pain.

Omega threw herself across Echo's fevered body, flinging her arms out in a valiant effort to try to hold his legs still, as he began to thrash about in his delirium, crying out and calling her name. It didn't take anything close to her normal intellect to understand that the fever dreams had induced a flashback, probably with some sort of nasty little twist, dredged from his subconscious.

Most likely, he's mixin' me burnin' with him gettin' telepathically caught in my own flashback, she decided, biting her lip. *Damn, Ace. I never meant for that to happen. Wish I coulda stopped it faster, for your sake. 'Specially at the moment,* she realized. *But hey. Maybe I can get you t' use th' brain bleacher now, to forget all that shit. If we can manage t' live, an' get home from this mess, that is. WHOA! Hold still!*

"ACE!" she called. "Echo? It's Meg, it's Omega. Can you hear me, hon? It's okay, everything's okay, but you need to be still! You're gonna make things worse with these busted legs!"

"Meg!" the sick man cried, voice weak, as he thrashed again, almost convulsing beneath her. "MEG! GET YOURSELF OUT! I'm burning! I'm burning—no! YOU'RE burning!! Ahhh!"

"Oh, dear God, help me! I gotta stop this somehow," Omega groaned, grabbing for his legs, shifting her position, trying to find any combination of moves that would hold his much larger frame still and steady, lest one compound fracture become two, and the infection she fought so diligently should work its way deeper into his body. As matters currently stood, his leg was at definite risk. But if the infection got into his bloodstream, chances were, he would die despite Omega's best efforts. "Ace! It's me! It's Meg! Honey, listen to me, you gotta listen to me! I'm okay! You're okay—but you won't be, if you don't HOLD STILL!"

Finally, unable to stop his banging about in any other way, Omega quickly sat up, grabbed the medikit, and scrabbled through it, searching hastily for any kind of sedative.

At long last—at least, it seemed long to her, though it was only a few seconds—she came up with a pre-loaded syringe of nobrikazin, a powerful galactic pharmaceutical of some repute. It was one, she knew, that India kept handy in her personal field medikit, and had once told her all about it, even explaining how and when to dose with it.

"An' this is sure one 'a those situations," she determined, expression grim. "Here we go, Ace! It's lights-out time."

Adjusting the syringe's settings based on his size and weight, she shot a full dose into Echo's shoulder. Then she threw herself across him once more, holding him down with all the strength she had.

* * *

Echo heard Omega screaming his name as she burned alive, but there was nothing he could do; he, too, was on fire, and their mental link shared the torture between them, heightening it horribly. He grabbed for her, trying to throw her out of the range of the firing engine, but could only watch in horror as his hands disintegrated into ash before he could grasp her.

He let out a howl of anguish, as much from the realization that Omega was going to die with him as at the pain, and together they collapsed to the hangar deck, two bodies at the center of a hellish inferno that they could not escape.

At last, oblivion took him.

* * *

Echo let out one last weak, tortured howl, then his body slumped and grew still. Omega grabbed the remaining medscanner and ran it over his quiet form, checking his vitals.

"Thank God," she breathed, relieved by the respite. "That did the trick. Wow. Maybe I better try to keep him under for a bit, until I can get this fever down to levels I can handle better."

She sat back and sighed, resting for a few moments and trying to catch her breath; she had been badly frightened by that little incident. But after a couple of minutes to recover her own composure, she reached for his legs in some concern.

"Okay, Ace," she told the unconscious man, "now I gotta check to see what kinda damage you did..."

* * *

For a wonder, Omega's splint and bandage job had held fast, keeping Echo's broken legs in position despite his kicking and flailing. She checked to verify that both legs were still properly set; after a few moments she decided that they needed a bit of adjusting, though nothing too serious. She eased them back into the correct conformation, then doctored the open wound in his leg from the compound fracture, cleaning it gently and re-administering the antibiotic medications, before packing and bandaging it and slipping the splints back into position.

Then, to ensure his comfort, she used the special fasteners in the adjunct to the medikit, and loosely fastened his trousers legs closed, keeping him warm, before flipping the bedclothes back over his body.

Then she leaned back against the nearest console, picked up a partly-used bottle of water, and sipped on it, as she watched her partner and tried to rest, herself.

* * *

Omega kept one eye on her partner and one eye on her wrist chronometer as she inventoried the medikit, looking for sedatives and narcotics to keep Echo in a more relaxed state.

Unfortunately, she had already used much of it in her efforts to tend Echo's more serious wounds.

"There's only one more full dose of the no-nobrik-azin, at least for Echo's weight and height," she murmured, searching, "an' not much of anything else. And I might need all of that for taking care of the wound." She looked up and focused her attention on Echo, then glanced at her wrist chronometer again. "Mm. That should keep him out for another couple hours. But if he isn't settled by then, I dunno WHAT I'm gonna do."

She raked a bandaged hand across her head, dislodging the gauze wrapped around her goose egg just a bit. Then she settled down to watch Echo, burrowing under as many covers as she could, while she tried to devise some sort of plan to keep him in one piece and alive, until Fox and the rest of Division One could arrive...

...If they ever did.

* * *

Sure enough, as the nobrikazin started wearing off, Echo grew restless again. His body became increasingly active, moans escaping him, and a distressed Omega sucked in a deep breath, pressing the heel of one hand to her forehead.

It wasn't just her worry about the additional damage he could cause to his legs that disturbed her; it was also her partner's groans. Echo tended toward stoicism, and did not readily admit to pain, let alone vocalize it. Hearing sounds of pain issuing from his throat was troubling in the extreme.

"This ain't gonna cut it," she decided then, as he began to squirm and then to writhe once more. "All on account 'a me gettin' toasted, too. No, I gotta stop this, some kinda way. And I think I know how. But I gotta not mess myself up any worse than I already am. I gotta be able to think enough to work out how to take the best care of him I can, or he's not gonna make it."

Omega crawled out of her mound of blankets and over to Echo's side. She studied him carefully, then leaned close.

"Ace? It's me. It's Omega," she breathed in his ear; it had not escaped her notice earlier that her cries for him to settle had seemed to feed into whatever nightmare scenario his frenzied, feverish mind was conjuring. "Can you hear me?"

"Mmh," he groaned, turning his head toward her briefly, before tossing about once more.

"Okay, you can hear me. Are you conscious, hon? Can you work with me, here?"

That request failed to elicit a response, and she huffed briefly, thinking fast.

"All right, I gotta do this the hard way," she grumbled. "He ain't gonna like it, but I don't got a lotta choices at th' moment. I don't have near

205

enough medicine left in the kit to do it otherwise." She studied his head and body; he hadn't started bashing about like he had earlier...not yet, anyway. And Omega intended to prevent that at all costs.

"I can't take these off," she considered, looking down at her fingers, "because he's not awake to re-do 'em, I can't bandage my own hands, and I need to protect my fingers from getting the infection in the raw burns when I'm taking care of him. So...let's try it THIS way."

Omega laid the heels of her hands against her partner's temples, making the contact as light as she could, then closed her eyes and began to breathe slowly, deeply, and regularly. When her body had relaxed as much as it was going to do given the situation, she reached out mentally, being careful not to invade his private thoughts, looking for the right places in his mind...

...And Echo settled, his body calming even as his mind quieted. He sighed, and relaxed into the makeshift pallet on which he lay.

Omega sat back, letting her hands drop away from his face, with a sigh of her own. A sharp, stabbing pain shot through her temples, and she clutched at her head, stifling the cry that nearly escaped her.

"Oh, this is gonna be hard," she whispered. "Ace, hurry an' get better, 'cause if you don't, I'm gonna be awful broken before I get you outta this." She let out another sigh. "Okay, honey, it's time to change th' packin's again."

She reached for the splint on his shin.

* * *

"...Have they checked in yet?" India asked her partner, who was temporarily seated at the Alpha Line chief's desk, reviewing paperwork in Echo's absence.

"No," Romeo replied, frowning. He sat back in the desk chair with a sigh, and looked up at her. "Not a word f'r a couple days now. I mean, we got th' notifications of th' planetary system discoveries...an' then, nuthin'. I'm startin' t' get real worried. It ain't like them—either of 'em."

"You told Fox?"

"Been puttin' it in th' daily status reports, but he hasn't said anything—leastways, not yet. I wanted t' talk t' you 'bout whether or not I need t' go forward to 'im an' request a straight-up meeting to find out if somethin' done gone wrong."

"I'd say yes, honey. And soon."

"You'll come with?"

"Oh HELL yes."

"Consider it done, then," Romeo said, reaching for his cell phone.

* * *

"Over two Division days?" Fox verified, startled. "We've gotten nothing from them since that third system discovery report?"

"Right, Fox," Romeo declared, as India nodded. "Well over. Not even any basic check-ins. It ain't like 'em, and I'm gettin' damn concerned. I had it in th' status reports, but I talked t' India, and we figured I should elevate it to you, just in case you hadn't seen it."

"All right," Fox said with a worried frown. "No, I hadn't seen it, I'm afraid—I've been busy following the Ganotian negotiations, and assumed Alpha One, being on just a training mission at this point, could take care of itself pretty well. You were right to elevate it to my attention—it isn't like either of 'em not to at least do a daily check-in of SOME sort, usually a couple times a day if they can. And on a training mission, they ought to be able to do so, fairly readily. Keep me posted."

"Wilco, Fox."

"Meanwhile, unless you've objections, I think I'm going to put out a request to the other Divisions, and see if anyone has seen 'em. Maybe there's been equipment problems, and they had to put in somewhere for repairs or something."

"Sounds like a plan to me, boss-man," Romeo murmured.

"Yeah, no objections here," India agreed.

"Good. They're due home in a couple days' time; if we can't locate them by then, and if they don't return on time, we'll move on it. If we discover there's something wrong, we'll move immediately. So if you hear ANYthing, either way, let me know at once."

"Roger that, Fox," Romeo agreed.

"Fox, is there a reason we don't move NOW?" India wondered.

"Yes, India, there is. If Alpha One has fallen into a situation other than the training mission they started on, they may have gone under cover. If we then proceed to barge in on things, it could blow that cover and put them in greater danger." Fox paused. "Remember, Echo is a highly experienced field agent. And Omega is his protégé and partner, and the only real difference between them is her lesser experience, which he's working hard to fill in. And she's as determined as he is on that."

"Oh. Okay, I get it."

"Let me add," Fox said, earnest, holding up his hands and gesturing to emphasize his words, "that that is NO negative reflection on Alpha Two at all. But India, you've specified that you aren't interested in the chain of command, you just want to be the department medic. That's a GOOD thing; we need one in Alpha Line. Romeo, you're a fair bit younger...but you're number 3 in the department, right behind those two. And they, and I, KNOW that, and we are all working to ensure you have the same kind of mentoring and training. You both understand this, correct?"

"Oh yes, Fox, that was never in question," India murmured.

"That," Romeo averred. "I get it, an' I'm fine with it. Meg's the assistant chief NOW, so she needs th' trainin' as fast as Echo c'n get it to her, an' she's got th' head on 'er shoulders to take it all in. Me, I got some maturin' to do to make the best leader I c'n be, an' I know it. It's all good."

"Good."

"But damn, Fox, this headin' up th' department while they're gone ain't easy."

"You're doing fine, son," Fox murmured. "If I didn't think you could do it, I'd never have agreed to it."

"You sure?"

"Positive." Fox met his eyes, ensuring the young man saw the confidence there. "Now, go let the rest of Alpha Line know, and let's get as many eyes and ears across the galaxy as we can...looking out for our missing family members."

"Right," Romeo agreed, vehement. "'Cause they ain't just th' bosses. Not t' us."

"C'mon, honey, let's go," India murmured, taking Romeo's arm. "We got some serious work to do."

"Don't I know it."

* * *

"...So yes, Pul, it looks like they've gone missing," Fox explained to the dragon face on the viewscreen. As soon as Alpha Two had left, he had closed the door, opaqued the bay window, and placed the call to the current Interim Chairbeing of the Ennead, Pulgey Entiyti, former employer of one 'deceased' Franz Levy, and oldest and dearest friend of the man Levy became. "And I just can't think that's good, so soon after recent events."

"Mm. You make an excellent point, Franz," Entiyti murmured. "And it is not like them; I know Echo well enough to know better, and quickly came to realize during my recent visit, Omega very much resembles him in such matters."

"Exactly. So..."

"You are worried. As you should be. I will put out word, and I will certainly notify the galaxy-wide PGLEIA agencies, and we will look for our missing family members."

"Thanks, Pul. I knew you'd help."

"Always, my friend. Whenever and however I can."

* * *

Hour after hour Omega tended her partner, unceasing, until the infection was reduced and Echo's fever dropped. When at last he fell into a quiet sleep, his fever-flushed skin slowly reverting to its normal color, Omega finally allowed herself a moment of repose...at least marginally. It was only then that she permitted herself to notice the splitting headache once more.

"Awright, I gotta do something 'bout this broken head. Ace seems t' have settled, an' I need ta get outta his head an' hope my head gets back t' normal when I do. So lessee here..."

Once again, she put the heels of her hands on either side of his face, lightly pressing against Echo's temples. She closed her eyes, reached out, and mentally disengaged herself from Echo as best she knew how, considering she was functioning with very little training and a whole lot of sheer instinct.

Just then, he grunted in his sleep and tried to shift his legs in a restless fashion, and she knew she had managed to disengage. She eased her hands away from his face, and simply sat watching him for long minutes, making sure he was not going to lapse back into hallucinatory flashbacks.

When fully five minutes had passed, and Echo showed no signs of mental or emotional distress, Omega sighed in relief. She had noticed a kind of lifting of pressure, of strain, in her own head at the cessation of the mental link, and her head had eased somewhat, even as her ability to think clearly improved. But the headache was not fully gone, and just then, it made itself known with another stabbing pain in the injured temple.

"Mmh. Ow. I oughta take something for that, I guess. Lemme see... what have we got?" Omega pawed through the medical bag. She came up empty. "Or maybe not. Damn. I musta used it all to bring Echo's fever down. Oh well. I've dealt with it this long; I can go a while longer, I guess. It's gotta stop eventually. At least it's not as bad as it was."

She turned out the flashlight and laid down nearby, glad to stretch out for a few moments; her back hurt almost as much as her head, after many hours of bending over her partner's prone form. A minute later, she was sound asleep.

* * *

"Echo! Aw, blast an' damn!" Omega sat bolt upright with a start. "I fell asleep! I gotta check on 'im!"

"Ease up, Meg," a familiar, if weak, voice came from the darkness nearby. "I'm okay. I feel like shit, but I'm all right."

* * *

The flashlight clicked on, and Echo saw a tired, drained Omega bending over him, helping him sit up. Then she grabbed the medscanner, lying nearby, and ran it over his torso.

"Oh, good. Your fever's down almost to normal, Ace. Do you think maybe you can sip on some fruit juice?" Omega asked him. "You're probably dehydrated."

"Isn't it all frozen?" Echo asked.

"No," Omega said with a grin. "I used the containers as ice packs on you, while you were feverish."

"Heh. That works. Okay, give me some, then."

"Here." Omega opened a bottle of orange juice, then helped him hold it, and a thirsty Echo drank it down as fast as he could. "Easy, easy there, Ace! Don't make yourself sick."

"I'm not. Tastes good."

After he had soaked up some fluids, Echo looked up at his partner, watching as she checked on his leg. "I take it I was out for a while?"

"Uh-huh."

"Fever talk?"

"A little." She shrugged, but didn't look at him. "Nothing...important." She grimaced. "Well...I think you might have had a flashback. A pretty bad one. But other than that, nah."

Echo nodded thoughtfully, watching her as she focused on his leg. "I... think I may remember a little of that. Yeah, it...was bad."

"Think you might consider lettin' us brain-bleach out some of the details, now?"

"YOU still can't forget."

"No. But..." she shrugged. "Since Zz'r'p uncovered it, I can't forget the stuff Slug did, either. By rights, I guess I should be crazy by now. But I'm not. The way I figure it, he probably did something to prevent that, too."

The pair were silent for a time, as Omega worked on Echo's leg.

"Were you up and tending me the whole time?" he finally asked.

"Pretty much." Omega was dismissive.

"How's the head?"

"It hurts. Nothing new there. Here we go. This leg is in MUCH better shape, Echo," Omega said, replacing the splint.

"Have you taken anything?"

"Taken who-what, now?" Omega asked absently, filling a hypo with more antipathogen.

"Something for your head."

"Oh. No." The medication went into Echo's thigh.

"Okay, then. Let's fix that, right now," Echo muttered to himself, drawing the medical kit into his lap with some effort and scrabbling in it.

* * *

Omega watched patiently, waiting for him to discover what she already had. After a couple of minutes, he glanced up at her in surprise and concern. "What the hell happened to all the analgesics?!"

"Infection and fever happened to 'em," she replied, succinct.

"You used 'em all on me?!"

"Yeah."

He scrabbled again, eyes widening further.

"The painkillers? The sedatives?"

"Flashbacks an' shit. I was trying everything I could think of to keep you calm, so you didn't do the same thing to THAT leg," she pointed at the broken femur, "that you did to THIS one. Let alone making this one worse." She pointed at the shin with the compound fracture. "You were kickin' and fightin' fit to kill something."

"But, Meg, your head—"

211

"Echo, a headache isn't in the same ballpark as a high fever, let alone a raging infection like you had. You even started hallucinating and...well, you weren't convulsing, exactly, but it wasn't far off. You were flopping all over the deck and fighting like crazy! I tried every position I could think of, to hold you down and keep you still, and I couldn't do it. I had to knock you out completely just to keep you from injuring yourself worse! And your fever went sky-high, and I couldn't get that damn infection knocked out! I thought for a bit there that...that I might lose you." She broke off and swallowed. "It's okay. Trust me, I've...dealt with a lot worse things than a headache." She took the empty juice bottle and disposed of it in a nearby trash bag from stowage, one that she had fetched some time earlier for the purpose. "How are you feeling now, Ace?"

"Better. Why don't you get some rest?" Echo suggested. "You were up for—how long?—tending me."

"Um...'bout a day an' a half, I think."

"Earth day?"

"No—Agency. Like, the whole thing. Night an' day."

"What?! You're pullin' my leg."

"Nope. You've been out for a while now. Besides, the shape your legs are in at the moment? No way I'm pullin' on one." She shot him a mischievous glance, then gnawed her lip for a second. "Well, maybe to set it, I guess. But you better behave, so I don't have to set it a third-an'-a-half time."

"Aw. Hell, Meg."

"Hey, Ace, what are best buddies for?" A tired Omega offered a gentle smile. "I think I will take a proper nap now, though, if you don't mind—on one condition."

"What's that?"

"You promise to wake me up if you need anything."

"I'll wake you if anything comes up." Echo nodded.

Omega folded her arms and glared at him.

"What?" Echo asked, blinking in startlement at her reaction.

"That wasn't what I said. I said, 'Wake me if you NEED ANYTHING,' not, 'if anything comes up'. Get with it, Ace."

"Meg, I'm fine."

"Uh-huh," Omega replied, unconvinced. "Let's see you move twelve inches to the right."

"Okay." With some effort, Echo rolled onto his right side and tried to drag himself toward his partner. Within seconds, he had broken into a cold sweat, but had hardly moved. "Damn," he panted, "what the hell?"

"Echo, hon, listen to me—you've been very, very sick," Omega said, keeping her voice soft and gentle as she explained. "Believe me; you were out of it and have NO idea. You're too weak to do much at all right now. So promise me you'll wake me up if you need anything."

"I guess I don't have much choice," he sighed.

"You have a choice. I'll just stay awake." She commenced rearranging her side of their blanket fort's sleeping pallet, so that she wouldn't fall asleep too readily.

"NO! No, baby, get some sleep! I can tell you're worn out, just by looking at you. The circles under your eyes are so dark, you almost look like you took a two by four to the face. I'll wake you if I need ANYTHING, I swear," Echo finally agreed. "But..."

"But what?"

"As tired as you are, is it okay if I wait until I actually do NEED... whatever, before I wake you up?" he wondered.

"As opposed to what?" She eyed him, skeptical.

"As opposed to, say, 'I got the munchies, I'll wake Meg so she can hand me something to eat.' I'm talking, I wait until my stomach actually declares it's empty and is growling about it, and THEN I wake you."

"Oh. All right, I get it, and yeah, that'll work. And...I appreciate the consideration, hon. Oh, speaking of consumables—here, drink on this." Omega handed him another juice container. "When you've finished that, put this in you." She gave him the last prepackaged meal...without telling him. "I need you strong enough to sit up and help me when Fox gets here."

"Fair enough, Legs," Echo grinned, accepting the comestibles.

"Okay. Um, the, uh, the urinal is on the other side of you, just in case. Should be within reach for you."

"What?" Echo's voice was flat, and his pale face flushed a bit.

"The portable urinal thing is lying beside you, right there." Omega pointed. "I had it handy in case we, uh, you needed it. So now we need to get you rehydrated, and needing it will be the first good sign I have that you got enough fluids in you."

"No, wait just a damn minute, here. I was out for over a whole Division day?"

"Yeah."

"So..." He ran a hand through his hair, standing it on end. "Did I...? I mean, did you have to...?"

"Oh!" Omega said, feeling her own cheeks heat as she finally grasped what he was asking. "No, I couldn't get any fluids into you much, and as high as your temperature got, I expect you were all but flash-evaporating what was in you. You never, um, I didn't have to, uh, you know...it didn't get used."

"Aha. Which," Echo said, nodding as his face went back to its normal color, "is how you KNOW I'm dehydrated."

"Exactly."

"All right. But...you were prepared to." It was a declaration, made to sound vaguely like a question. Omega met his eyes, her gaze straightforward and clear.

"Echo, when you're hurt, when you're sick, when it's just us, and nobody to help me take care of you...yes. Of course, I was prepared to do it," she told him. "It's all PART OF taking care of you. I understand you're reserved, and that it would embarrass you, 'cause I'm the same way. But in this situation, there were way more important things for me to deal with than modesty—like keeping you alive and going. Partner, best buddy, family...you're all of those things to me, Ace. So yes. I will do whatever is necessary to see you come out of this alive, and as healthy as I can manage, given whatever I got to work with."

Echo bit his lip, nodding to himself, as he dropped his gaze.

"Okay," he said, apparently taking her statements at face value. But she could see the slight smile in the brown eyes, and grasped that he was pleased at her response. "This all the juice bottles an' junk, sitting here?" He pointed at a stack of plastic bottles of various hues.

"Yeah, that's them."

"I'll work on tucking a few of those in me, after I get done eating, then. No sense letting all your hard work go to waste by letting myself get in worse shape."

"Good. Thanks, Ace."

"Just promise me one thing."

"What's that?"

His face reddened again.

"Uh, well, when you wake up, try NOT to catch me takin' a leak or something."

"Promise," she chuckled. "Privacy is privacy, even for best buds. Good night, Echo."

"Sleep well, Meg."

And Echo sipped his drink as he watched his companion drop into a deep, exhausted sleep, close beside him.

* * *

Romeo, India at his side, stood at the head of the Alpha Line briefing room in front of the giant Division One and Alpha Line logos, addressing all fourteen remaining teams of that department. He had, very deliberately, grabbed one of the classroom-style desks and turned it around to face the rest of the room, rather than use one of the plush, ergonomic desk chairs provided for the departmental chief and assistant chief. Those were, he considered, reserved for Alpha One, and he was not about to usurp them, hence the rank-and-file desk. But at India's private suggestion before the meeting, he rose to his feet to address the department.

"...So I need a couple volunteer teams," Romeo said to the assembled Alpha Line as he finished briefing them on the situation. "If you're a certified pilot, so much the better, but if you're not, that's okay, 'cause Fox has already promised to provide pilots if needed."

* * *

Concerned, Monkey glanced at Kako, his new partner; together they now formed Alpha Eight. Since finding himself inadvertently caught in a seditious conspiracy—instigated by an alien who had murdered, then replicated and impersonated, his previous partner—Monkey had done an about-face: After accusing Alpha One of disloyalty and treason only to have them request a second chance for him and his fellows when the deception came to light, he had come to a serious appreciation of the pair who led the department in which he now served probation.

This, in turn, quickly led to a deep loyalty to Alpha One, as he saw firsthand the fairness and honor with which they strove to operate. He was, consequently, thankful that it was the alien shapeshifter who had fired the weapon that had nearly killed Echo, and not himself, during that ill-fated adventure.

* * *

Kako, an agent from the Moscow Office who had applied and been accepted into Alpha Line right after his first partner had retired, had only become Monkey's new partner in the last few weeks, but the pair got along like bread and jam from the first. So when Kako saw that look from his partner, he knew what it meant, and he fully approved—the recent altercation with the Cortians at the Chicago Spaceport had shown him just how worthy of respect the leaders of Alpha Line were. He raised an eyebrow and nodded slightly, then they stood together.

"Alpha Eight wolunteers," Kako declared in his soft Russian accent.

"Alpha Four here," Easy said, rising with his partner.

"Alpha Six," Nuts added. He and Jack stood. This was followed by team after Alpha Line team, rising to their feet to volunteer.

"Alpha Twelve!"

"Alpha Ten!"

"Aw, hell, Romeo," Uniform, of Alpha Five, said. "You might as well have asked for a standing ovation or something. This is Echo and Omega we're talkin' about here. Every last damn Alpha Line team'll volunteer to go find 'em and bring 'em home. Count us all in."

A general murmur of approval at the statement went around the large briefing room.

"Okay, that's good," Romeo decided, waving them back to their seats, "an' we might end up needin' all of ya before this is over with, 'cause I'm gettin' a bad feeling about it. But for now, I saw Eight, Four, and Six first on their feet. So you three teams are the search parties. Alpha One's last known locus was the Orion Nebula..."

"Ouch. As Omega would say, that's an awful little needle in a damn big haystack," Monkey murmured.

"Yeah. But Fox has small, fast saucers ready for ya t' use, an' we gridded off the nebula, so we already have an efficient search pattern worked out—all you have t' do is follow it. And like I said, if you need a pilot, we got those, too." Romeo looked around the room. "Y'all good with this? Okay. I want those three teams to stay here; the rest of you, go get clear of anything else you're lined up t' be doin', and remain on standby alert. Alpha Line dismissed."

* * *

"So what's the scoop?" Monkey asked, when all but the volunteers had departed.

"I already gave y'all the run-down," Romeo said, getting out the search grid map.

"Yeah, but we're talkin' the stuff you didn't say," Golf replied. "You know, what you and Fox think has happened to Omega and Echo."

"It's all on the QT, Romeo," Easy murmured. "It won't go any farther. But if we're gonna do an effective search for 'em, we need to know what we ought to keep an eye out for."

"They're right, honey," India murmured.

"Okay," Romeo acquiesced, but grudgingly. "After they took Doron home, Alpha One 'uz gonna do a training run f'r Meg. She been dyin' t' get into space anyway, astronaut an' all. So Echo had plans to do it up right—piloting an' celestial navigation, spacewalks, deep space emergency repair, three-dimensional grid search, planetary survey an' exploration, th' whole ball o' wax. Way I understood it from Fox, Echo wanted t' make sure she was ready f'r anything, bein' th' new assistant chief."

"Sounds like Echo," Nuts averred.

"And like something Omega would love doing," Monkey agreed.

"Right," Romeo said, nodding. "But based on one a' their planet-side reports, they already done run into some damn nasty shit on one planet—man-eatin' plants an' such. Fox is worried they ran into somethin' that 'uz more than one team could handle."

The others pondered that for a moment.

"Well, it's possible," Jack decided. "Kinda hard to imagine of those two, but yeah."

Kako scrutinized their interim leader.

"Zat is not vhat vorries you, though, is it, Romeo?" he asked.

"Not so much, no," Romeo confessed.

"What is it, then?" Monkey pressed.

"Well, 'member how, when Echo made th' emergency run t' fetch Doron t' begin with? How th' Cortians tried t' sneak up on 'im an' grab 'im in th' wormhole?"

"Yeah?"

"It ain't like that 'uz the only Cortian ship out there, guys," Romeo pointed out. "There's a whole damn planet full of em."

The others fell silent, gaping at him in horror.

"Aw, damn," Monkey whispered, shocked. "You think..."

"Maybe," Romeo said, holding up a restraining hand. "On top o' all that, Fox dug in an' found out that the PGLEIA station at Eta Orionis reported one lone mayday call, just a fragment that cut off all of a sudden...apparently comin' from somewhere in th' nebula, a couple days back. Along about th' time Alpha One stopped reportin' in. They sent a reply, but got nuthin'." Romeo paused, then pulled a face. "They ain't a big station, mostly equipped for dry-dock work, so they couldn't send out a search team. An' somehow, the whole incident missed gettin' reported all the way up th' chain to Fox. We think they concluded it 'uz an accidental call." He shook his head. "Like I said, small station, small staff. Not experienced in search an' rescue."

"Damn, damn, damn," Jack grumbled.

"But they have offered to be a staging area for any searches we attempt, since they're relatively close, and between Earth and the nebula," India added.

"Exactly," Romeo confirmed. "It's all some stuff for us t' keep in our hip pockets, anyway. Just...watch your six out there. That's all I'm sayin', here." Romeo turned to Echo's desk. "Now, let's go over this grid search, an' break it up between y'all..."

* * *

"...You know, Ace, I'll say it one more time: All we need is a stack of comic books under here, and I'd feel about eight years old again." Omega grinned at her partner.

They were relatively comfortably ensconced—considering—in their flashlight-illuminated nest of blankets, swapping stories and jokes to pass the time until they were rescued. Echo was recovering slowly from his infection.

"Yeah, I guess so," Echo chuckled. "Okay, Legs, your turn for a story."

"Oh, then let me think. Aha, I got one. This one's a story from when I was working Shuttle payload ops out of Huntsville. On one mission I worked, I was sitting across from the Data Management Coordinator, or DMC, who was next to TV-Operations. One of the human experiments flown was LBNP—"

218

"What? LBN...?"

"Oh, sorry. It's an acronym. Lower Body Negative Pressure, LBNP, was an experiment to see if they could pull the blood and fluids down from the torso into the legs. You know how in extended microgravity the fluid redistributes itself and all? They were looking for ways to normalize the body for long-duration space travel, since NASA doesn't have artificial gravity, and the body is used to the blood and fluids pooling in the feet and legs. But without gravity it tends to redistribute uniformly throughout the body, and that causes problems ranging from mild sinusitis to inner ear problems, vertigo, and more—I'm sure you're familiar with THAT syndrome. So anyhow, the experiment required the subject to get into what looked like a short sleeping bag. Then they sucked part of the air out of the bag, which was sealed at the waist, creating a negative pressure on the butt, legs, and feet. Mild suction, basically."

"Okay, I see."

"Right. We were in LOS and the PAO—"

"Whoa, whoa. Define acronyms for me as you go, baby. I'm not as familiar with NASA terminology as you are; if it doesn't overlap this job, I'm probably unfamiliar with it."

"Oops! It's so ingrained in me, after so many years, I forget I'm doin' it," she apologized. "Be patient with me; it's been so long that I may have to think a minute to remember what the acronym stands for. All right, lessee. LOS is loss of signal; the bird was out of range of the comm satellites, so we couldn't communicate with 'em. And PAO is the Public Affairs Office, which as usual was bugging us about needing more cabin video. Which is kinda hard to do when you don't have any comm signal for downlinking the video."

"Okay, I've got the picture."

"So as soon as we came back 'over the hill' into range of the satellite, we had the Crew Interface Coordinator, or CIC, which is payload operations' version of CapCom, request permission to 'come into the cabin' with a live camera feed. Standard procedure; the cameras are already mounted around the cabin in the places we want 'em to be, for good video angles. All that needs to happen is to go live with 'em—but it's the equivalent of a non-crew member entering the cabin, in terms of privacy, so they refer to it as 'coming in.' We heard CIC voice the request, and DMC—uh, the Data

Management Coordinator—as well as TV-Ops, AND me, all of us heard a crew member give the okay. So TV-Ops asked INCO at JSC—er, Johnson, you know, Mission Control in Houston—to activate the cabin camera. We go live with the cabin video—goin' out through the NASA television cable feed to God an' everybody—and see two mission specialists an' a payload specialist huddled around the LBNP bag, and Lars Jorgensen, the guy who was supposed to get inside it, with his back to the camera. Only, about 30 seconds in, Lars suddenly drops his pants! The CIC freaks out, and DMC and TV-Ops step on each other's comm, yelling frantically at INCO—uh, Integrated Communications Officer, I think it was; he was the guy in charge of the communications team at Johnson—to kill the feed. I swear, it took well over a minute to get INCO to respond!" Omega laughed. "I think he stayed off the comm loops on purpose."

"Aw damn!" Echo chortled, slapping the pallet beneath him with his good hand. "So...what? America got a great big full moon, courtesy of NASA?!"

"Well, not quite," Omega grinned. "Thing is, see, Lars had on boxers under his flight uniform pants, which tend to balloon out in microgravity anyway, so there really was no full moon flash, and not a view of anything except legs, really...but nobody stopped long enough to check! They just started scramblin' to kill the feed! And at the splashdown party at Marshall afterwards, Lars laughed fit to kill about the whole thing."

"HA! But it sent a panic through no less than TWO control centers?"

"Exactly!" Omega giggled. "Remember Uncle Lar? Back at YuleCon, at Christmas?"

"Your old pal? I sure do."

"Well, he and I later found a little boy doll at a local novelty store that would drop its pants when you squeezed a bulb...and we presented it to Andy, the TV-Ops guy on duty when all that went down. His colleague John got hold of it and stuck it in the public viewing window behind his console position in the control center. Stayed there for about one full shift, I think, before the Payload Ops Director saw it and ordered it either gone or destroyed..."

"I bet," Echo chuckled. "So which was it?"

"To be honest," she said with a grin, shaking her head and shrugging, "I really don't know. But I'd bet on gone. Those guys always had a great sense of humor, and it's probably sitting on somebody's desk at home, to this day."

"But what about you?"

"Whaddaya mean?"

"All the stories you've told so far are about other people. Things that you SAW, sure, but you weren't involved in 'em. I just want you to tell me some stories about YOU, Meg. A decade in the space program has gotta make for some good ones."

"Nah, not really," Omega demurred. "I played it pretty straight-laced. Took it real seriously. Maybe too seriously, thinking back on it."

"Oh, come on, Meg," Echo pressed. "You mean to tell me nothing funny ever happened to you? I'm not buyin' it."

"Well..." she hedged sheepishly, "there was the practical joke war in the Astronaut Office while I was qualifying..."

"Uh-huh," Echo grinned in anticipation. "Now we're goin'. Let's have it."

"I suppose I started it." Omega smiled, reminiscent. "See, I discovered early on that, if you applied pressure to the outside of the office doors juuusst so, you could get the door open, locked or not." Echo raised his eyebrows, surprised. Omega grinned devilishly. "Oh, yeah, Echo. You haven't seen that side of me at all, Ace."

"I'm intrigued," he murmured, a mirthful light in his dark eyes.

* * *

"Be careful what you wish for," she retorted, blue eyes sparkling with mischief. "Anyway, one night when I was working late, I needed to take a break, so I snuck into several offices and hid some key manuals—EVA training manuals, simulation data packs, nothing really important, just stuff to make life awkward. Stuff that I knew was needed the very...next...day. At which time, I sat back and watched chaos run crazy through the Astronaut Office. Along with about half a dozen astronauts."

"Did they catch you?"

"Me?! I think you're forgetting who you're talking to, Ace. No, I was smooth. I made it look like the stuff had just been misplaced. So I laid low for a couple more days, then struck again."

"And?"

"This time I picked just a couple of guys and totally rearranged their files. Please to note, at no time did I actually TAKE ANYthing. Nothing was missing, just...reorganized."

"Hell, Meg, you are wicked."

* * *

"Now, Echo! What a terrible thing to say about your best pal!" Omega pretended to be hurt. "Para...paranoia," she forced out the word, "was setting in at this point. 'Cause by this time, see, the corps knew a prankster was among us, but nobody knew who. So three-quarters of the office became practical jokers in self-defense. 'Do one to others before they do one to you' was the rule of the day, and trust me, it WASN'T golden! Almost everybody got hit. Grease on the doorknobs, hot pepper sauce in the coffeepot, stuff hook-and-loop'ed down, one gal even brought in a cake frosted with that chocolate laxative. Did you know I'm a sniper-level marksman with a water rifle?"

"Aha! Is that where you got so good with a gun?" Echo chuckled.

"No, pickin' off groundhogs in the fields on Daddy's farm," Omega replied with a smile. "Skeet and trap helped, too. But...well, let's just say I polished my guerrilla warfare skills while I was in the Astronaut Office. And you'd never believe all the places you can fit a water balloon. The really funny thing was, I played it so straight-laced the rest of the time, it never occurred to anybody that the jokester was actually me."

"You've gotta be kidding." A skeptical Echo glanced at her.

* * *

"Nope." Omega looked pleased with herself. Echo grinned.

"Maybe I should be calling you 'Slick Meg' instead of baby."

"Oh, I dunno," Omega grinned back. "I kinda like 'Legs.' It sorta appeals a little more to my vanity."

"I...see," Echo deadpanned. "Really? I can't imagine why." It was all he could do to keep a straight face at Omega's indignant expression.

"Just for that, see if you get within a light year of me in that black bikini," she retorted.

"Whatever." Echo shrugged, feigning indifference as he watched her irritation with amusement. He stopped dead when he saw something like deep pain flash through the blue eyes, and realized with a sudden shock that the 'vanity' was all an act.

Oh damn, he thought, disturbed. *I was teasing, and I actually hurt her, instead. Now she believes...what? That I think she's unattractive?! Oh HELL no! But I got no way to redact it without coming across all wrong. Shit.*

"So, uh...what happened next?" he changed the subject quickly. Omega blinked a couple of times, apparently trying to shift mental gears.

"Um...well, a couple of the guys decided to risk putting their heads together, and finally wised up. See, one of 'em was dating a police detective, and they got her involved. She got a kick out of it. Started dusting for fingerprints."

"Uh-oh."

"Uh-oh is right. I was caught, and didn't even know it. Seems they spread the word on the quiet, and that night after I went home, the entire corps converged on my office."

"Ohhh shit."

"Yeah. The next morning, I had to go straight to the flight surgeon's office for medical testing. I couldn't have breakfast 'cause of the tests, so by the time I got to my office, I was starving, and all I could think of was a cup of coffee and something—anything—out of the vending machine.

"So I get to my office, fish out my key, and start to unlock the door. But the door's not locked; it's not even latched. I touch it, and the door creaks open like the sound effect from a Boris Karloff movie. 'Eeerrrrrrrk.'" She broke off long enough to mimic the eerie creaking from a door hinge, and Echo snorted, before she continued. "I think, 'Oh, no, I've been got. Well, as long as they left me my coffee cup, it'll be okay.' But they didn't leave my coffee cup. They didn't leave my chair...my desk...my table...my books, documents, filing cabinets, or bookshelves. They even took the curtains at the windows."

"Bare...bare walls?!" Echo gasped, about to expire with laughter.

* * *

"Not...exactly." Omega made a face as she recalled the incident. "After they got my office down to bare walls, they proceeded to re-decorate it...with festoons of toilet paper."

"They rolled your office?!"

"Yep. And then flung what was left on the rolls out the window. The upper-story window. Flapping in the breeze. For the entire Center to see."

"Mm-ha-ha-hah!" Echo chortled. "Damn, but they gotcha good!"

"Yeah. And I had to track down all my stuff on my own, too."

"Did...heh...did they at least...mmph!...hide it all in the same place?"

"...No."

Echo slapped the blankets with both hands, nearly beating them into submission, laughing uproariously the whole time. The left wrist tweaked, and he grunted, grabbing it...then promptly resumed laughing as hard as before.

"Well, Meg," he finally got out, "if a prankster ever shows up at Headquarters, I'll know what to do: Get Romeo and India to help me move everything out of your quarters and hide it."

"Assuming we ever get back," Omega breathed under cover of Echo's laughter, glancing at her wrist chronometer.

* * *

"Okay, guys, coming up on our sector of the Orion Nebula," Dog, in the pilot's seat of the *Lysistrata*, a swift, heavily-fortified but small corvette class spacecraft, called to Alpha Eight. "Kako, I want you in the navigation chair, running sensor scans and looking for any signs of an S.O.S. signal. Monkey, you're in the co-pilot's seat, on weapons."

"Ve are zhe Alpha Line team," Kako noted. "Zhould not ve be giving zhe orders?"

"Don't sweat it, Kako," Monkey said, soothing. "Neither of us is half as experienced at interstellar travel as Dog is. AND he's experienced at search and rescue. I vote we let him run with this."

"You haff a good point, Monkey," Kako said with a nod. "Yes, ve vill do zhat. Zhank you, Dog, and pardon me—I am still new to Alpha Line, and I am learning."

"Not a problem, Kako," Dog said with a smile. "I'm not standing on any sort of protocol, only my experience, and trying to make sure we three are sitting in the seats best suited to us and our respective skills. I just want to help find your missing chief and his partner. Echo and I go back a ways."

"Were you a volunteer too, then? To come on this mission, I mean?" Monkey wondered, as he and Kako took their respective stations and strapped in.

"Yup," Dog verified. "And damn glad to do it. Okay, here we go, guys. Dropping out of warp near the first system in 3...2...1..."

The star field outside the main port shifted as the saucer exited its

Alcubierre warp bubble. A yellow-white star nearby shone brightly, even as it illuminated several small planets and a large gas giant.

"HOLY SHIT!" Dog exclaimed, grabbing the controls. "HANG ON, GUYS! MONKEY, BRING UP THE SHIELDS AND GET A TARGET LOCK! WE GOT COMPANY!"

"Vhat?!" Kako said, spinning in his chair.

"Dammit! CORTIANS!" Monkey growled, fingers dancing across the weapons console. "Romeo was right!"

Just then, several green beams lanced through space nearby; Dog threw the ship into high-velocity evasive maneuvers barely in time to avoid them.

"Monkey, you got that target lock? Any of 'em will do!"

"I got three out of six, Dog!"

"Take as many shots as you can! Fire at will! I'm gonna concentrate on getting us out of here!"

"Roger that! Firing trans-warp boson cannons at will!"

Purple beams shot from the *Lysistrata* as Monkey fired at the cluster of half a dozen Cortian ships. All struck home, and immediately one of the alien craft shuddered and drifted to one side. But the others kicked in the interplanetary drive and began to pursue the *Lysistrata*.

"Ohhh, this ain't gonna be fun," Dog muttered. "Guys, you're Alpha Line. Do we try to evade and continue searching, or do we get word to Fox on what we've already found?"

"I am already preparing message for Fox," Kako noted. "I am not picking up any distress signals or S.O.S., so zhere is not immediate sign of Alpha One in wicinity. ZHERE! Message avay."

"Barely in time," Monkey snarled, looking for specific locations to target on the enemy vessels. "They just threw up a jamming field."

"I got it off before zhey did, I zhink."

"Yeah, I saw it," Dog confirmed. "Unless you guys have any better ideas, I'm voting for getting the hell outta here and heading for the nearest PGLEIA facility, then making sure our other search craft are warned...or get backup, whichever."

"Do it," Monkey ordered, disabling another Cortian ship. "I've only managed to get two Cortian ships dead in space out of six; those were lucky shots, and they're way the hell bigger than we are. We're seriously outgunned in this little runner."

"Zhis does not bode vell for Alpha One," Kako opined.

"No, it doesn't," Dog agreed. "Hang on...engaging cloak...couple evasive maneuvers to confuse 'em...going into Alcubierre warp...NOW!"

The *Lysistrata* shot away from the young stellar system, leaving the Cortian vessels behind in moments.

Chapter 10

"Yeah, Fox, Romeo, we got a situation," Monkey said. The *Lysistrata* had lost the Cortians when she cloaked, ducked, and immediately went into warp, and thus reached the Eta Orionis system in safety, where there was a small PGLEIA office and dry dock—the same one that had heard the enigmatic partial distress call.

"Lemme guess. Cortians?" Romeo said, pulling a face. Beside him, Fox shot the younger, chocolate-skinned man a mildly shocked look.

"Bingo," Dog said. "Right in one. A party of about a half a dozen Cortian ships. Not small ones, either. And they were on the lookout. That was a search pattern, or I'll eat my tie. I'd lay odds they weren't the only ones there, either."

"Farkakt!" Fox grumbled. "I was worried it was them, but I thought I hid it better than that."

"You did, Fox," Romeo said in surprise. "I didn't even know you were considerin' that, boss-man. This was all my own hunches I was playin'. Hey, aw damn, man, you don't suppose...?"

"I hope not, Romeo," Monkey said, shaking his head. "Way I figure it is, they didn't get 'em or they wouldn't still be there looking."

"Point," Fox noted. "Which means our boy and girl are either hiding, not there, or..."

"Yeah, it's the 'or' that we're worried about," Dog agreed. "What do you want us to do?"

"Didja warn the other two ships?" Romeo asked.

"Yeah, we did that right away," Dog said. "While we were en route here, to the Eta Orionis facility. Stealth ciphered, no less. We didn't wanna risk drawing attention to them, or us."

"Good." Romeo nodded. "What'd they do?"

"Peeled off the search. One had already started but hadn't encountered Cortians; the other one with the far-side grid section was still en route, close but not arrived yet. They're gonna rendezvous with us here, and wait for orders."

"Even better," Romeo decided. "They don't need t' be taking th' chance—there's other ways t' look, that don't either put more of Alpha

Line in danger, or risk leadin' th' Cortians right t' Alpha One. Y'all are outnumbered an' outgunned, like this."

"Exactly," Monkey agreed. "We actually went three-way stealth-ciphered on the comm and discussed it among the three ships, and that's the conclusion we all reached, too."

"Nice job," Fox murmured. "Good heads on your shoulders, all around. Romeo, you've got something in mind, son. What is it?"

"Meg had a thang in her hip pocket, just in case somethin' went down in Chicago that 'uz way bigger than what we were expectin', Fox," Romeo said, jaw firmed. "Have you ever seen her major backup plan, Alpha Omega Destruct Black One?"

"Ohhh, farkakt," a perturbed Fox said again, raking a hand through his salt-and-pepper hair. "Yes, I have. Do it. I'll ready the Fleet, and have Bravo and Lima prepare my flagship. You get the rest of Alpha Line together."

"Take about five minutes, Fox," Romeo said. "I already got 'em all on standby. Guys? Y'all stay there at th' dry dock. We gonna bring a shitload o' backup."

"Copy that," Dog confirmed. "*Lysistrata* standing by for a shitload of backup."

* * *

"I don't have long, Pul," Fox said on the ciphered interstellar comm. "But the news isn't good. Our very first search team encountered a goodly-sized task force of Cortian vessels, all at least the size of the *Trindak*, as soon as they dropped out of warp. Some half a dozen vessels, and that's just the ones they saw immediately. And THEY fired first. Without hailing or even attempting to communicate."

"Oh, damnation," Pulgey Entiyti grumbled. "Were there any casualties?"

"Not on our side," Fox noted, "and the Division One ship didn't stick around long enough to find out about the Cortians, though I gather they did incapacitate at least one enemy vessel. I've only had a verbal debrief, and that was short. And they haven't had a chance to submit a report yet, so I don't know details."

"No sign of Echo and Omega?"

"Not yet. But they really didn't have a chance to actually LOOK."

"Understood. What are you going to do?"

"I've arranged to get some serious automated monitoring in the region of the nebula, on the frequencies most used by the Cortians per the intel I have, and verified that there's a small damn fleet there, estimated some forty or fifty vessels of various sizes, most quite large, and apparently engaged in a search. You get three guesses as to what—or who—they're looking for, and the first two guesses don't count."

"Alpha One," Entiyti snarled. His horns stood straight up for a moment, then crossed along the top of his head, in his anger.

"Yes. But as my Alpha Line members pointed out, the Cortians are still searching, which means the Cortians don't have 'em, and THAT argues that they're hunkered down somewhere in the nebula, maybe on an unknown planet or something."

"Assuming they survived to do so," Entiyti murmured, and Fox's face fell.

"Assuming they survived," he admitted. "We're hoping they did."

"So what are you going to do now, Franz?"

"I'm calling a Level 1 Division One Maximum General Emergency, and then I'm mustering the Fleet," Fox decreed. "I'll take the flagship out, and we'll meet the Cortians head-on, with the main body of the Fleet. But Alpha Two is going to head up a smaller task force to search for Alpha One. The last thing I want to happen is for them to lead the Cortians right to Omega and Echo, though, so hopefully the rest of us can function as something of a diversion."

"...I see." Entiyti frowned. "Are you certain, old friend, that this is a wise move?"

"I don't see that I have another choice, Pul," a determined, but defensive, Fox declared. "I refuse to let those bastards have two of my top Agents, let alone my designated successor in this job! Aside from bonds of friendship, aside from the morality of the situation, have you considered what knowledge resides in those two minds? Knowledge that is classified PGLEIA information, at the highest levels? Knowledge that pertains to planetary, to Division One, security? To GALACTIC security?"

"Ah! You are right! DAMN the Cortians to twelve levels of destruction by the Maker Itself! What a dilemma!" Entiyti shook his head in intense irritation. "Very well. What would you have me do, Franz?"

"For starters, call a Level 1A Galactic Emergency. Since we're under a Level 1 Division One Emergency, effective pretty much five minutes ago, that should give you the protocol to do it."

"In the circumstances, and based on the information you have just presented to me, I believe that to be wise. Yes. Consider it done, five minutes after we end this call, if not sooner. What else?"

"How long will it take you to gather a couple of fleets?"

"Division fleets?"

"Whatever you can get me, but as big as you can manage."

"Mm. I suspected that was coming. Some few hours to perhaps a couple of days, my old friend. And most likely trending to the longer time frame. We have not had occasion to do this in many a long cycle. I assume one fleet is to back you up, and the other, what...to blockade Corta?"

"Exactly! And you might want to call in additional, in order to increase patrols along the shipping lanes. Because they're pirates, after all."

"Excellent point. All right, then. As soon as we end this call, I will notify the Council, issue the appropriate orders, and begin to muster fleets sufficient to do as you ask. I think it is, after all, high time the Cortians learned some limitations. I will have to obtain approval from the Council at large, which is not currently in session; but I think this is worth invoking the emergency referendum protocols. And I think I can guarantee that the vote will go as we wish."

"Pul...you're not going to...?"

"No, no, Franz. You know me better than that. I throw my weight about when appropriate; this is not one of those times. No, I am simply aware of some other matters which will easily shift the balance in our favor. I had intended on sending you the reports soon, in any event, in order to get your feedback and advice on the matter. You need not concern yourself with it for now; I will tell you later, when you have the time, and the concentration, to spare."

"Good. Thanks, Pul. Keep me posted, but be aware that I might be in the middle of a firefight."

"Do not get yourself killed, Franz. You are 'family,' too."

"I don't intend to," Fox replied, eyes hard. "But I do intend to take out some Cortians. And if it should come to that, I'll take a lot more with me, tsu aldi rukhes."

* * *

"Suud, it is good to see you again, my old friend," Entiyti said scant hours later, as Suud Guurn, the Reptoid that had succeeded Franz Levy as Entiyti's chief bodyguard, entered the formal Office of the Ennead Chairbeing at Entiyti's emergency summons. "How is your life?"

"It is very good, milord Pulgey," Suud noted with a broad, toothy smile—the same smile that Echo remembered so vividly from their first encounter, so many years earlier. "My mate has presented me with many hatchlings, and they are wonderful. I delight in my family and the comforts of home life. It is good to see you again, as well. But you have not summoned me in such haste to exchange pleasantries. I was your strategic and tactical advisor during your last years on the Ennead, and now you chair it once more. I can only assume you have need of my counsel again."

"You assume correctly, Suud," Entiyti said, growing serious. "You have, perhaps, heard of the Cortian incursions, particularly in Division One?"

"Yes, I have," Suud averred. "Is our old friend and colleague Franz all right?"

"He is...but two of his Agents, the two the Cortians originally targeted and nearly killed, may not be. And as Franz considers them part of his extended family, and they are also his top Agents...AND they have gone missing on what should have been a simple training run...we suspect Cortian involvement." Entiyti broke off, pondering for a moment. "What I did not tell Fra— er, Fox, is that I have been receiving reports from other Divisions of marauding alien vessels, looting, pillaging, and kidnapping from the Outer Arm to the Tethanoid Nebula. And the descriptions—of both the spacecraft, and the aliens crewing said spacecraft—match the Cortians."

"So there is a high likelihood we have a considerable force of brigands plundering the shipping lanes and planets of the Coalition."

"Precisely. The situation is serious enough that Franz has declared a Level 1 Division Emergency. And he has convinced me to declare a Level 1A Galactic Maximum General Emergency, into the bargain."

"They are coming after the Coalition, then? Is this an invasion?"

"Of sorts, in all probability. And just as high a probability that they have gone after Alpha One."

"WHAT?! Alpha One is the team they attacked? Echo and his partner?"

"It is."

"Damnation," the Reptoid cursed. "He was a good boy, become a good man."

"Exactly." Entiyti's horns crossed in a subtle display of his wrath. Suud scowled in his turn; it was not a pleasant expression. Suud had been with Entiyti at the First Contact, when Earth had become a member of the Coalition, and had been the one to discover a very young Alex Bryant sneaking up on the clandestine meeting site. After some initial misunderstanding of the boy's capabilities, he had come to like the youth, and they had kept in touch over the years, even as Echo grew into a formidable Agent. "But even worse is the fact that Echo is Franz' declared successor as Director... with all the information he knows. And Omega will, in turn, succeed Echo as leader of Alpha Line. There is knowledge in those two minds that, if forcibly extracted, could put the entire Coalition at risk. It would certainly reveal weaknesses in our system that the Cortians would be able to exploit."

"So what do you wish of me, Pulgey?" the Reptoid asked.

"The Cortians come from the Sagittarius Dwarf Elliptical Galaxy. You may know it as Divulsus Sagittarii, or Dsssllss Twngsss, in our own tongue. But Echo and Omega appear to be missing in the vicinity of the Great Hunter Nebula, and a task force of Cortian vessels has already fired on a PGLEIA Division One search craft in that region of space. Covert observations indicate some fifty or so Cortian vessels in the nebula already, so they have a fleet of their own in play. So in turn, Fox plans to lead the Division One Fleet out, in an attempt to drive off the Cortians and rescue his people...but he has requested assistance from the Coalition in the doing. Assistance that it is only reasonable that we provide, given the situation. The Ennead agrees, and a swift, but official, remote emergency vote has already taken place in the full Council, even though it is not formally in session. Given the extent of the depredations, it was not hard to pass the resolution." Entiyti frowned. "So we must also consider the Cortian homeworld, for it does no good to take one group into custody if the home system only sends out more."

"You require several fleets," Suud realized.

"I do. Two, to be precise. As large and as well-armed as can be managed. One to send to assist Franz...and the other to blockade Corta. Feel free to pull from any and all Divisions EXCEPT Division One, for they will already have their hands full. Actually, I need three—one to guard the shipping lanes—but it seems the formal PGLEIA branch of the Coalition already had that in work, pulling from their various divisions."

"I see." Suud pondered for several moments, considering the logistics. "Will you be personally commanding one of the fleets?"

"I have not yet decided," Entiyti sighed. "Truthfully, I desire to do so, but I realize my position means I should likely remain here..."

"Let me know what you decide, as soon as you can," Suud said. "As for a timetable: It cannot be done immediately."

"Oh, I know that, my friend. But how long do you estimate it will take, if it is done with utmost urgency?"

"Can you give me two days?"

"Emdalian, or...?"

"I should prefer Coalition days."

"No sooner?" Entiyti frowned.

"Perhaps. I can but try."

"Do it, then. As big and as well-armed and -shielded as you can muster. You have two Coalition days—no more. Whatever you have assembled at the end of that time will be sent out. Notify me as soon as you are ready."

"It will be done, Lord Entiyti."

Suud left the Office of the Ennead Chairbeing in haste.

* * *

It took more time to get the fleet organized and offworld than Fox wanted; after all, so many spaceships launching would attract attention from Earth's media if they were not exceptionally careful. In the end, however, nearly a full Division day later, Fox took a shuttle to the *Genesis*, his official flagship, a large, powerful star battleship outfitted with the latest tech and stationed at the L2 point dry-docks on the lunar far side. Lima attended him, and Bravo stayed at Headquarters to assist in coordinating and relaying information.

"Not that I have to like it," Bravo had noted in mildly-irked resignation.

"No, son, but it's your turn," Fox pointed out. "You came with me last time I went off-planet, and Lima stayed. And your job is just as needful. You know that. Besides, I need to make sure that one of you will survive, in case something happens to the *Genesis*, so the directorship can be properly handed over."

"You don't think..." Bravo paled.

"This is, for all intents, war, Bravo. I just don't KNOW, son. I hope not. But I WILL take every possible precaution to safeguard the position for my successor...whoever it winds up being." He sighed. "Right now, it doesn't look like being who I'd hoped, in any event."

* * *

Zebra came along on the *Genesis*, as part of the medical contingent; Zarnix headed Medical at Headquarters, and stayed behind to prepare it for an influx of injured.

The fleet rendezvoused in the extreme outer solar system near the dwarf planet Eris, and Fox took the command chair—the bridge of the large vessel *Genesis* did indeed resemble that common to certain science fiction series, as Omega had once observed, but that was because it was a fairly logical layout. However, unlike those same fictional spacecraft, the *Genesis'* bridge was buried deep in her core, surrounded by many layers of protection. Lima moved to his side, electronic tablet in hand, ready for any orders the Director—and in these moments, Fleet Admiral—might have. In front of him were helm, navigation, and weapons control, the positions' officers code-named Übermut, Cast, and Boy, respectively; to his left sat communications officer Sail; to his right, Zebra sat as medical officer and advisor. His security chief, Zero, stood ready behind him. Uncle, the chief engineer, tended to stay in the engine room, though there was usually a dedicated open comm channel directly to her, whenever Fox took the *Genesis* out.

Glancing over his left shoulder, Fox barked, "Sail, open a comm channel to the fleet."

"Opening comm, sir," the communications officer replied.

"Division One Fleet, this is Director Fox," he declared in calm, even tones. "By now, you all know about the events leading up to this mustering of the fleet. The Cortians cannot be allowed to continue their depredations in our Division, in our Galaxy. By all indications, they have attacked Alpha One, the chief and assistant chief of the Alpha Line, while they were on a peaceful training mission. We do not yet know the status of Alpha One. It is possible, though unlikely, that they have been captured; it is more likely that they are in hiding, stranded...or dead. The reason we believe this is because the Cortians are searching the Orion Nebula, their last known position; if Alpha One had been captured, it is improbable that the Cortians would still be in the area at all, let alone in the numbers GALINT would indicate. I have assigned a small task force of vessels to perform a detailed stealth search centering on Alpha One's last known coordinates, and this task force is being commanded by Alpha Two, and largely staffed by a subset of Alpha Line members. The rest of us will take on the Cortian fleet."

Fox paused, and looked at the viewscreen, knowing the camera beside it was transmitting his image.

"This is a serious task, my friends. The Cortians are not only pirates and marauders, but slavers. You need to know this going in. Do not think mercy will be shown you, should your ship be taken, and yourselves captured; it will not. My intent is that no Agency vessel should be captured by the Cortians, let alone her crew; and to that end, I am hereby issuing standing orders that heroic measures will be undertaken to rescue the crew of any disabled Division One vessel in the upcoming actions. I will not have our people enslaved...or worse." He paused. "I also wish it known that, should I find myself in extremis, I will not allow the Cortians to take me alive. I strongly recommend you consider the matter individually yourselves, each of you, and make whatever decision you deem right in the eyes of yourself and your personal deity, if you have one."

The bridge of the *Genesis* was silent for a long moment. Then, slowly, each crew member began to nod in agreement. No dissent was heard over the communications channels.

"Good," Fox murmured. "Now that you all understand our situation, know that we may not be alone in this. I have requested and obtained promise of assistance at the Coalition level; Interim Chairbeing Pulgey Entiyti is even now mustering his own forces to send to our aid. The intent is a joint operation, taking on what appears to be the majority of the Cortian fleet, currently located in the Nebula, while another fleet blockades Corta, their homeworld. Unfortunately, I have not heard from Lord Entiyti since then, and I do not have a timetable for when we will be joined by the Galactic Fleet. But we cannot wait; every hour that passes is an hour in which Echo and Omega may be discovered and captured. And aside from considerations of morality and friendship, as Echo is next in the chain of command, and Omega is also in that chain, there may be considerable security risk to our Division and our respective worlds.

"And let me add that I am very grateful to the other worlds in the Division for your participation in this mission. If you have not yet encountered the Cortians, rest assured, you would, and soon, and not in a pleasant fashion. In the course of gathering intel sufficient to plan this operation, I have discovered that, while remote systems on the Outer Arm, systems largely not part of the Coalition, have long endured their attacks, the Cortians appear to have grown quite bold. They are now running deep into the Milky Way Galaxy for their raids. And they are not content merely to attack shipping. Several homeworlds, in the Third and Fourth Divisions most notably, have been ravaged, according to several official reports, with possibly women and children taken to be sold...though it is my understanding that they were rescued before the miscreants could get far with them. It is time to put an end to it, once and for all, if it means our lives." Fox turned to Lima and nodded; Lima swiped across his tablet several times. "The planning and strategy for this operation has just been sent to your vessel commanders, in a ciphered blip. It will not be easy; this pirate race is quite skilled at evasion and guerrilla warfare. But we can wait no longer. All ships, prepare to depart for the coordinates contained in the master plan in five minutes. Director Fox out."

He nodded at Sail, who killed the comm link.

"All right, then," he said aloud. "Let's get ready to go kick Cortian ass, people."

* * *

Lydhuu Raiit was an Ergisol, once in Lord Entiyti's employ, who took over from Suud Guurn as Entiyti's chief of security when Suud became head of the Coalition military, some years prior. But upon his retirement from the Ennead, he had reduced his staff, and she had decided to move into teaching security and military strategy for PGLEIA's various university branches. Now she, like Suud, found herself back in Entiyti's office, brought in by a classified emergency summons which overrode all other matters. Entiyti had just finished explaining the situation to her. She sat for a few moments, thinking over the briefing material. Finally, she looked up at Entiyti.

"Very well; all seems in proper order. So. You want me to go with you to the Great Hunter Nebula, sir? To advise you as you command the fleet?"

"No, Lydhuu. I want you to LEAD the fleet."

"But why aren't you...?"

"Because I am, once more, head of the Ennead," Entiyti explained, "and while I do have a very good grasp of politics, you have a much better grasp of military strategy, my friend. There are three Coalition fleets about to go into play, Lydhuu, about to go into war—the Alef Fleet, the Bet Fleet, and the Division One Fleet, which is already moving out as we sit here talking. And I want three of the best strategic heads I know at the top of the chain for each fleet. My former security chief and principal bodyguard, Franz Levy, known these days by his PGLEIA code, Fox, is personally heading the Division One Fleet. Suud Guurn, who succeeded him as my chief of security, will be commanding the Bet Fleet, which is going to Corta to blockade it and put an end to their rampage; he is also assembling the Alef and Bet Fleets for us. And I need someone I know and can trust to take Alef Fleet to back up and support Fox and Division One. And that someone succeeded Suud in her turn." He gave her a lopsided smile. "I have always had excellent taste in chief bodyguards."

"Wait. You want me...to be an admiral?" Raiit practically gasped, and sat down hard in the visitor's chair best suited to her personal anatomy; given she resembled nothing so much as a seven-foot-tall June bug, few humans would have recognized the particular article of furniture as a chair.

"I do," Entiyti said with a calm nod. "At least for now. We have not needed to muster a fleet for war in many a long year; there is no longer a qualified officer for a multi-world fleet in what passes for a chain of command. More, these fleets will be somewhat haphazard, pulled from multiple Divisions, as well as quite a few volunteer ships from various worlds' independent navies. They have never worked together in this fashion, and they want welding into a coherent force—which no one from their ranks has been willing to volunteer to attempt. You, however, are eminently qualified to lead this fleet, you are well respected in the appropriate circles, you have my backing and endorsement, and you will be able to work with Fox upon your arrival, so you will have experienced colleagues with whom to work. I think that you are the only other being in this hour with the wherewithal to do this. Will you do it, my old friend?"

Raiit was silent for a moment, considering. Finally she looked up.

"Brief me. Tell me everything that is happening—everything, no matter how insignificant it seems—and precisely what needs doing," was all she said.

* * *

The Division One Fleet, fully cloaked and virtually undetectable, sliced through space en route to the Orion Nebula. The battleships led the way, accompanied closely by the space-based equivalents of aircraft carriers. These latter carried small, swift craft like the *Lysistrata*, corvettes designed for extra stealth and speed, but not as much capability to operate at long distances in battle scenarios—it was a tradeoff, speed versus distance; you could have one or the other, but not both. And while the corvettes had done well on the preliminary search, in the upcoming conflict, they would need speed, and the support of the spacecraft carriers, which latter also carried a large contingent of destroyers, intermediate-sized and -ranged war vessels.

Behind the warships were the fleet support craft—hospital ships, emergency rescue craft, repair and engineering support, and the like. Given the usual brevity of most space battles—space being an inherently inimical environment, anything that opened the enemy to that environment tended to end the fight instantly—a full supply line was usually unnecessary.

But the number two medical officer in Division One was not stationed in any hospital ship. Zebra was assigned, per her request, to the flagship *Genesis*. And currently she was seated on the bridge. Fox considered this, rubbing his hand over his chin. Then he rose, stretched, and turned toward her.

"Bubeleh," he murmured, keeping his voice very low, "are you sure about this? We can still get you behind the lines."

"I'm sure," she averred. "I know you. You're going to take the lead on this, so this is where I'm going to be needed."

"But...well, shouldn't you be in the sick bay, then?"

"I'll head there as soon as I know I'm going to be needed there," Zebra responded, expression firm; Fox knew her mind was made up, and short of giving her a direct order—which he reserved the right to do, if he felt it needful—he wasn't going to change it. "Meanwhile," she continued, "I really want to watch this. I've been talking with some of the other physicians, especially after this whole thing with Alpha One and Omega getting so badly burned and all, and we've realized...well, we don't really KNOW

238

what is required of the agents who do field work. I figured it was about time at least one of us learned."

"Ah," Fox said, suddenly understanding. "All right. Just...be careful."

"I could say the same to you."

"You could, but there is still a difference: I am trained to do this, and I have many decades of experience in it. You have neither, meyn gelibte. And should we come under attack, as almost certainly we will, getting from here to sick bay could prove problematic, at best."

"Okay, fair enough," Zebra relented. "I'll be really careful, I promise, honey."

"Then I am satisfied," Fox decided, offering her a smile. "Pay attention, use your common sense, MAKE SURE YOU ARE ARMED—"

"I am," she replied, calm. "My 'piece,' as you and some of the others call it, AND my backup. Concealed carry, so it doesn't upset my patients, but they're on me right this instant. And I've been keeping up my certification on my sidearms, too. I planned to request a ride-along, at some point," she confessed, "and probably still will, so I figured it made sense to get back in the range, so I'd be ready if something went down, and not a hindrance. Just because I'm a doctor doesn't mean I won't need to be in the field at some point, or protect my patients from an Alien Big Bad."

"Ah. And now I understand your firearms questions in recent weeks. Very good. You will do fine, then. You are exceeding competent, meyn teyere, with a most excellent head on your shoulders."

"As Meg likes to say, 'I try,'" she said with a grin.

"As Echo is wont to respond, 'You do pretty damn good at it, baby.'" The Director glanced at the helm chronometer, then sighed. "Time to get with it," he murmured. "We are not far out, now."

Zebra nodded, and Fox turned back to the command chair.

* * *

"Ship to Fleet, stealth cipher," Fox told Sail, as he resumed his seat.

"Copy, ship to Fleet," Sail replied, turning to his console and entering commands. "Cipher channel open. Go, Admiral."

Fox drew a deep breath, then plunged in.

"This is Director Fox to the Division One Fleet. We are getting close to the nebula, and you know what that means: All hell is going to break loose at some point. I will not lie to you; this is going to be dangerous. We may well lose some of you, though I hope and pray not. I, myself, may not survive it. Let me reiterate, however, that I would rather not survive than be taken prisoner by the Cortians.

"Let me also remind you that, while we are here to help locate and hopefully rescue...or at least recover...Alpha One, that is far from the ONLY reason we are here. By now, the various reports of Cortian raiders throughout the galaxy will have reached all of you. To my knowledge, and according to the reports I have received from PGLEIA headquarters on Aleancë, we have been able to successfully account for everyone taken captive without the necessity to presume anyone has been sold into slavery. However, that accounting has in large measure produced dead bodies, not rescues; apparently the Cortians do not overmuch like high levels of resistance. It seems more tractable captives are to their tastes. The sole exception has been the cache of women and children I mentioned earlier; those were largely rescued alive and...relatively...unharmed.

"Of the few rescues that have been effected, debriefing indicates maltreatment ranging from beatings to attempted rapes—a few of the latter may have succeeded; I am still waiting for more detailed reports. This latter is apparently in an attempt to produce breeding stock. Starvation and dehydration seems common, in an effort to break the captives. Do not—I repeat, DO NOT—allow yourselves, your crewmates, or any other members of this Fleet to be apprehended by the Cortians, if at all possible. Merciful death is likely preferable."

Fox paused and drew a deep breath, letting it out in a sigh that was audible on the comm.

"The plan remains the same. As I mentioned before, GALINT indicates that the Cortians are some forty to fifty ships strong, possibly more, scattered in small groups of three to six ships throughout the nebula, in a pattern consistent with a search grid. They are most likely looking for Alpha One. If they find Alpha One before we do, it will most certainly NOT be a rescue. Our Fleet plan will be bait-and-draw: Attack their small groups, and draw off these vessels from their search, by making it too dangerous for them to continue. I fully expect this to end in a fleet-to-fleet battle. We will take casualties. A mentsh tracht und Gott lach. But we will do our best to put a stop to this." He glanced at the helmsman, an agent code-named Übermut. "Helm, do we have a first target?"

"Aye, sir," Übermut responded. "Send coordinates?"

"Please."

"Coordinates to Fleet," he replied, hitting a couple of keystrokes.

"Your helm and navigation will now have our first targets," Fox announced. "Three ships detected on long-range scans, in the very near vicinity of where GALINT showed one Cortian flight to be, one hour prior to our departure from Earth. Time to engagement in twelve minutes..." He glanced at Cast.

"...Mark," Cast declared, watching the chronometer.

"Prepare for first engagement," the Director said. "Fox out."

* * *

The Cortian ship *Nixar*, along with her sister ships *Kurav* and *Wurtag*, searched their designated sector of the gas cloud, looking for the renegade slaves known as Echo and Omega. The Cortian Amalgam had issued a bounty on their heads only a couple of cycles previous, as a result of the actions of the pair, which had led to the destruction of *Trindak*, the revelation of Corta's slaving and piracy operations to the galactic neighborhood as a whole...and the probable destruction of the *Pindar*, as well, judging from the debris which had been found drifting through the star-forming region.

As a result, an implacable slave hunt was now going on through the gigantic gas cloud complex. Upon retrieving the two slaves, forcible breeding would take place; the male would be executed immediately upon completion of breeding. The female's execution would be delayed until it was determined if she bore children; if not, her eggs would be harvested and she, too, would be killed. If she did become expectant, she might survive long enough to give birth, if she gave no trouble. Otherwise, the fetuses would be harvested and she would be left to bleed out.

(Navigator! Any sign?) the *Nixar*'s commander, one Hyo by name, demanded.

(No, Captain!) the navigator responded. (There is no sign of them on sensors anywhere. There is not even any residual signature that might indicate they ever passed through.)

(Damnation,) Hyo grumbled. (It is as if they vanished into the space-time continuum. Is there NOTHING that your sensors detect?)

(No, Captain. I am sorry, but they...wait...)

(What? What do you see?)

(I...am uncertain as yet, Captain. I have never seen this before. Ah! It is gone...)

(You are my most experienced crewman at the search and seizure,) Hyo noted. (If you do not recognize it, no one else will. What did it resemble?)

(I...am not sure.) The navigator looked up with an earnest, but concerned, expression at his commander. (For a brief moment, a...'spirit'... seemed to flit across the core of the Great Spiral, as seen from our location. That...is the closest I can come to describing it.)

(Communications! Any reports from the *Kurav* and *Wurtag*?)

(Negative, Captain. They have seen nothing. They also have not seen traces of the rogue slaves. They recommend moving to the next grid segment.)

(Hm. We are not that far, as matters go, from the gravitational singularity near the center of the star-forming region,) Hyo recalled. (Perhaps it was a spacetime distortion wave, produced by that object. Or a simple gravitational lensing.)

(That may well be, Captain,) the navigator decided, relaxing somewhat. (I will keep a watch out for additional...incidents; perhaps we can get more data to determine what it is. It might even prove to be something we can imitate, to better hide ourselves.)

(An excellent notion, Navi—) Hyo broke off, his beak gaping in horror.

In front of the *Nixar*, and between her and the core of the Milky Way Galaxy, an entire fleet of some 75 ships uncloaked.

(Evasive action! Break and run!) Hyo barked...just as the *Nixar* shuddered.

(Too late, Captain!) the navigator replied, shocked. (They have engaged multiple tractor beams!)

(Issue distress call!) Hyo ordered.

(Done, sir,) the communications officer observed, fatalistic. (But you know we are on our own.)

* * *

"All ships in position?" Fox queried.

"Affirm, Fox," Sail replied.

"Helm confirms," Übermut said.

"Also Weapons," Boy noted.

"Ship to Fleet."

"Go, Director," Sail indicated.

"Division One, this is Fox. On my command, uncloak. Designated ships will initiate tractor beam lock simultaneous with uncloaking."

"Fleet confirms, Fox," Sail murmured moments later.

"Uncloak!"

The specialized, fresh-from-R&D sensor scrambling devices, along with the standard cloaking mechanisms, of some seventy-five PGLEIA warships deactivated at once. They formed a veritable wall on the Sun-ward side of the trio of Cortian ships.

"Cortian frequencies," Fox ordered.

"Go, sir."

"Cortian ships, this is Director Fox of the Pan-Galactic Law Enforcement and Immigration Administration, Division One, aboard the flagship *Genesis*. You are under arrest for unlawful incursions in Pan-Galactic Coalition space. Stand down, and you will be taken into custody."

* * *

(Arrested?) the helmsman wondered. (For trading in their space?)

(They do not see things as we do, helm. They are unenlightened,) Hyo said, shaking his head. (They consider the escaped slaves to be in league with themselves, according to the High Amalgam.) He glanced at the communications officer. (Any response from the rest of the fleet?)

(No sir.)

(You are likely right, and they will not come. However, stalling for time never hurt.) Hyo clacked his beak. (Open a response channel.)

(Done.)

* * *

The speaker on the bridge of the *Genesis* suddenly issued forth in Cortian, and the translator automatically rendered it in English.

"*Genesis*, this is Captain Hyo of the Cortian ship *Nixar*. We do not recognize your authority."

"You will acknowledge it voluntarily, or you will be forced to acknowledge it," Fox replied, in the tone of voice that had cowed beings from the Crab Nebula to the Outer Arm.

"I think not."

"You stand outnumbered, twenty-five to one. Do you think you have an advantage?"

"We do, or you would not ask that question. In any event, the moral high ground is ours. We seek two rogue slaves, who have caused great damage to the Cortian Amalgam. They will be retrieved if still alive, and suitably punished for their deeds...after appropriate measures are taken to harvest their genetics."

Fox felt himself pale. He glanced around the bridge, seeing similar horrified expressions on the agents' faces. Suddenly cold fury ignited within.

"The hell you say," he growled. "Those two 'rogue slaves' are our colleagues! They have ALWAYS been free beings of worth, and they are NOT under your jurisdiction or power! Now SURRENDER at once or face the consequences!"

"Go to the underworld and copulate yourselves," came the rude response.

Fox stood and turned from the viewing screen.

Suddenly the three Cortian vessels opened fire.

* * *

(What do you think they would do to us if we surrendered?) the helmsman, a relatively young Cortian, asked, seeming anxious. Hyo wondered at so young and inexperienced a Cortian being aboard a vessel of this type, realizing with some indifference that he was unlikely to get any older.

(What would we do to them?) the captain asked, shrugging. (Is that what you would wish for yourself?)

(NO.) The response was firm.

(Then we will not allow them to do it to us,) Hyo replied. (Open fire, all batteries.)

* * *

Zebra watched and listened in horror as her lover tried to negotiate with beings who wanted no part of the negotiations. She heard the fate the alien race intended for her friends, a couple whom her lover considered family, one of whom was the oldest human friend he still had alive.

No wonder Omega once told me that she was tough because she had to be, she thought somewhat absently. *This is the kind of shit she deals with every day. Every...damn...day. I don't think I could handle it. Not like that.*

She jumped, alarmed, when the Cortians opened fire on the Division One Fleet, but she needn't have worried—Fox 'hot-rodded' his vehicles, ALL his vehicles, for a reason, and this was why. The *Genesis* contained the most powerful force field generators available anywhere in the galaxy, as well as the largest power plant for its class—all non-standard, by the time he and his chief engineer got done tinkering, sometimes in their off hours, sometimes not. It was extremely unlikely that anything, even a planetary defense system, could penetrate her shielding.

When Fox rose and turned his back on the bridge viewscreen, their eyes met, and she saw sadness there. *He hates what he's about to have to do,* she realized.

"Fox to Fleet. Take 'em out," he growled then.

And some two dozen ships of the Fleet opened fire on the three Cortian vessels, at his command.

There was a blinding flare of light, and when Zebra could see again, there was...nothing. Where the Cortian ships had been was nothing but an expanding cloud of metal and plastic vapors.

She swallowed hard, and met Fox's eyes again. *He watched my reaction,* she observed with a shock. *Through the whole thing, he watched ME. And those gorgeous hazel eyes of his look...worried. He thinks I'll think less of him for this.*

"No, honey," she whispered, only loud enough for him to hear. "You gave them every chance. And what they'd do to Omega and Echo if they caught 'em..." She shook her head, closing her eyes. One lone tear escaped despite herself, and slid down her cheek. Gentle, familiar fingers wiped it away, and she opened her eyes to look into those same hazel eyes, which were warm. Fox was not smiling, not exactly, but there was a look of relief on his face.

"Thank you, bubeleh, for supporting me," he breathed, and she nodded.

The bridge was quiet as he turned back to stand beside his command chair.

"Division One Fleet, move out to the next target," he ordered.

* * *

"Okay, y'all," Romeo said from the flight deck of the saucer *Odyssey*. "Search teams, stand by for departure."

245

The *Odyssey* was the interstellar equivalent of a naval destroyer—swift, maneuverable, well-armed and -armored, with considerably more range than a corvette due to its larger size. It was not, however, nearly as big as Fox's flagship, which was a proper battleship of some considerable size, capability, and crew complement. The *Odyssey* had five sister ships, all carried on a spacecraft carrier, the *Columbia,* hanging near the back of the fleet, more nearly in the supply chain than with the warships.

Visible outside the flight deck's main viewport, the hangar deck of the spacecraft carrier cleared of activity; in the near distance of the huge volume, large payload bay doors opened onto interstellar space.

"Standing by," five responses came back.

"Activating maneuvering systems," Victor, the *Odyssey*'s pilot, murmured.

"An' cloak, an'...GO," Romeo ordered.

Six ships on the hangar deck of the large craft vanished.

Five minutes later, the giant bay doors slowly closed.

Columbia moved forward, linking up with the rest of the warships.

* * *

"Look, Meg, I'm more restless than you are," Echo remarked three uneventful days after their initial story-swapping episode. They still lay stranded in their chilly cocoon within a frigid, slowly-dying spacecraft. "At least you can move around; with these busted legs, I can't. But you know we use less energy when we're resting. And that means we consume less food, less water, and less oxygen. All of which either is, or soon will be, in short supply. 'Cause the air scrubbers have gotta be goin' by now, too."

"I understand that," Omega replied, annoyed despite herself. "I don't mean to complain. It's just that I'm also colder when I'm resting. I got on one 'a your t-shirts, as many of my shirts as I could layer, two of your shirts on top o' that, AND I've already put on my Suit jacket over top of everything else. You've got my robe, in lieu of bein' able to put on your Suit jacket with that bum shoulder. I slit several of your tees down the front so you could get 'em on, and slit the shoulder seam on that shirt you're wearing. Not to mention pinning up your trousers legs. We got socks on top of socks on top of socks. I got on so many pairs of socks I can barely get my shoes on, even unlaced! There's nothing else left for us to put on."

"Yeah. And it's still cold."

"Yup. And besides, I'm not tired."

"I know," Echo sighed. "Neither am I. All we can do is lie around. We're not doing any sort of activity to make us tired."

* * *

"Echo..."

"Yeah?"

"What if...Fox doesn't come?" Omega's voice was hesitant. Echo glanced sharply at his partner.

"He'll come, Meg."

"Echo, they may not even know anything is wrong."

"We're overdue. Fox will know."

"Can we be sure he won't think we're taking a couple of extra days to train or explore?"

"Meg," Echo pointed out, as reasonable as he knew how to be, "would you do that without checking in first?"

"Well, no..."

"Would I?"

"No."

"Do you think Fox doesn't know us well enough to realize that?"

"No."

"So what are you worried about?"

* * *

"So how far overdue are we?" Omega retorted.

"Going on a Division day and a half, now."

"Uh-huh. The batteries are nearly dead. I had to drape the console with some of our blankets to keep the frost off the controls. Our food's all gone, even the snacky stuff. The drinkable stuff's almost gone, and it's frozen solid, anyway."

"Meg," Echo asked softly, concern on his face and in his voice, "have you given up?"

* * *

"No—it's just...I..." Omega's voice trailed off. Her soft blue eyes, dull and despondent, stared listlessly at nothing.

Depressed, Echo concluded, studying her. *All this shit is way too soon after the Cortians torched her. She's not strong enough yet. Mentally or physically. It woulda been fine—SHE woulda been fine—if it had just been*

247

the original training mission...but the Cortians had to go and attack. I guess I should have considered something like that might happen, given how the Trindak *didn't wanna give up. And I'm betting the head injury isn't helping her mental state, either. Damn.* His next words were gentle but firm.

"Meg, you're tired, whether you realize it or not. At least lie down and try to relax."

"If you say so." She shrugged and curled up.

"Good night, Meg." Echo clicked off the flashlight.

No answer.

"Meg?"

The sounds of restless stirring were the only response he got.

"Meg, baby, are you mad at me??" Echo asked, surprised.

"NO! I'm just going stir-crazy!" Omega exclaimed in patent frustration.

The flashlight clicked back on, and Echo watched as his partner fought to get comfortable less than an arm's-length away. Then he reached under one of the pillows.

"Here," he said quietly, handing her his paperback and her father's Bible. "Your eyes are a lot better, and you've been doing all right. Read for a while. Maybe you can unwind a little bit."

Omega reached for the books, and opened the Bible as Echo settled back down to rest. He had almost drifted off when a nearly-inaudible noise—a sigh, or perhaps a sniffle—caught his attention. He rolled over to look at his partner.

Omega's head bent over the Bible, unaware of Echo's scrutiny. Her face was crumpled, her cheeks tear-stained. Despair was written in her face, her posture, her entire attitude. Just then, she dragged a surreptitious hand across her face.

"Meg??" Echo whispered, shocked. She looked up, no longer even trying to hide the tears.

"Echo, remember when I told you I wasn't...completely back to normal?"

"Yeah?"

Omega gestured to the open Bible and sighed. "I can't read it."

Echo watched in grave concern as a despondent Omega reached for the flashlight. Their nest of blankets went dark, and the two Agents lay, inches apart, isolated in the blackness, mulling over their future...assuming there was one.

Chapter 11

"...I am here, milord, in response to your urgent summons," Suud said as he strode swiftly into Pulgey Entiyti's office. "The fleets are coming together swiftly now. What do you require?"

Entiyti looked up from his computer screen.

"Ah, Suud, my friend. No, it is not what you can do for me, but what I can do for you. Did you bring your tablet?"

"I did, milord, at your injunction."

"Good. Put it in ciphered communications mode and stand by a moment." Entiyti commenced typing a command on his virtual desktop keyboard, even as Suud adjusted the classification settings on his tablet. "All right...sent," Entiyti noted, hitting the <enter> key.

Suud watched as a file appeared on his device and was automatically opened. He scanned through it with a practiced eye, then glanced up at Entiyti in surprise.

"You jest, surely," he declared.

"No, my friend, I do not," Entiyti said, shaking his massive head. "The Ganotians grew exceeding tired of the Cortian raids on their worlds. So the Coalition provided some of our newest members a bit of assistance, and consequently they were able to ambush and destroy a flight of some three or four pirate vessels...capturing crew in the process. We have Cortian prisoners in Coalition custody, and they are being interrogated by all legal means possible. Including some of the most skilled Deltiri interrogators the Arcturans could send us." He nodded at the tablet. "That report is the result. I recommend perusing it in detail before leading out Bet Fleet."

"Are you still considering leading Alef Fleet?" Suud looked up long enough to ask.

"No, I will be remaining here," Entiyti murmured with a wry, and somewhat regretful, grin. "Much though I should wish it, I have decided to let wisdom prevail and send Lydhuu Raiit out at the head of the other fleet."

"Oh, that is an excellent choice," Suud said.

"I thought you would find it so. You designated her your successor, when you moved up. It is high time she moved up, as well." Entiyti waved a claw at Suud's tablet. "What do you make of that?"

"I do not know, as yet. I need to read this in detail."

"Then read, old friend, read."

* * *

Report on the Interrogation of Cortian Prisoners Captured by Ganotian Law Enforcement

Interrogator Pr't'k of Arcturus VII, presiding

PGC Custody Date 10/198/114328

PGC Reporting Date 10/203/114328

In the recent altercation in Ganotian space which resulted in the destruction of the Cortian vessel Etelren *by Ganotian law enforcement, three subjects were captured/rescued/resuscitated as a result of destruction of their vessel and subsequent ejection overboard. Subjects include one off-duty navigational/helm officer; one propulsion engineer; and one slave minder. Two, possibly three, other Cortian vessels were also destroyed, but no survivors were recovered from those craft.*

Subjects hail from the Cortian system in the Sagittarius Dwarf Elliptical Galaxy aka Divulsus Sagittarii. This system is located on the outskirts of the rather sparse Terzan 7 'young' globular cluster; overall, this cluster is considered metal-rich per astronomical terms, though this is really a catch-all designation of all elements heavier than hydrogen and perhaps helium, so it does not necessarily speak to the resources of the cluster as a whole.

The Cortian system itself is a small system, numerically speaking, containing only a couple of planets. These planets are widely set, however, and so volumetrically the system can be said to be extended. The system's coordinates, as well as several scaled maps, as extracted directly from the mind of the navigator, are in the file appended.

The main star is designated Khula by the system inhabitants; it is an F2 Vm, a yellow-white Main Sequence star of modest size with increased metallicity corresponding to the rest of the Terzan 7 cluster. It has one rocky planet well interior of the inmost boundary of the habitable zone; this planet is quite similar to Mercury in the Sol system, and is uninhabited, and generally uninhabitable by any but a few known extremophile species.

Khula also has one gas giant, a large brown dwarf called Orge, ~0.07 average stellar masses. Orge is not in Khula's habitable zone either, being well outside it at nearly 0.015% of a light year distant, but it has many sat-

ellites. It sustains some irregular primitive fusion (principally deuterium, with some lithium-7), thus it creates its own habitable zone. There is only one satellite in this habitable zone: Corta.

The system as a whole is really a binary stellar system of sorts, with the primary being Khula, and the secondary, Orge. The system is fairly isolated, on the edge of the globular cluster, and itself does not have many resources; what resources may be in the system are likely buried deep in the gas giant Orge, and therefore unreachable. Corta itself is decidedly poor in resources, including water, and much of it is desert or mountain, or both. Living conditions have always been harsh, with historical evidence of widespread piracy, raiding and slave trade on the homeworld, among and between various population groups.

This only ended some few millennia ago, it appears—if it actually has ended, as seems improbable to the interrogation team. The change in the status quo at that time evidently occurred due to influence from outside the system. It is most probable that another race visited Corta in a first-contact envoy and was betrayed; their ship, or more likely ships, were thus captured. The particular race involved has been lost to time, though there is some speculation—by the interrogation team, and by certain Cortian researchers, according to our prisoners—that it may have been an extremely early Edeptan exploratory mission, and this may be one reason Edeptis turned inward thereafter, as well as why it has been so predated upon by the Cortians, who likely came looking for more tech.

In any event, Corta learned how to build starships from the captured ship(s), and this offered inducement and capability for the Cortians to explore outward. Already prone to piracy, raiding and slave trade on their own world in order to survive, they became interstellar pirates and plunderers after learning from the captured ship(s).

The Cortians do not appear to be overly creative as a species; there seems to have been little in the way of modification to the schematics and overall design of those original captured spacecraft, even after all this time. Due to the scarcity of resources, apparently the original tiny flotilla of spacecraft was used to raid neighboring systems, obtaining sufficient metals and other materials to build more. Over time, it occasionally fell to them to be able to commandeer a ship of another race, thereby enlarging their fleet by ones and twos.

That said, in vessels they have themselves constructed, which now comprise more than 99% of their fleet, often inferior substances are used in ships' systems considered less essential, and habitation space—crew cabins and the like—are Spartan in the extreme. This is to minimize the need for specialized spacefaring alloys, hyperdiamond fiber conduits, and other difficult-to-obtain materials. Consequently, all Cortian space vessels are of comparable size, shape, and capability; if a weakness can be found in one, it can be exploited in all.

There is no evidence of anything other than a kind of self-centered practicality behind the Cortians' choices of targets for their marauding.

Edeptis has been a repeated target, partly because of their isolated location on the galactic outskirts, and partly due to their advanced medical and other technologies, as well as certain abundant natural resources. The pacifistic nature of the Edeptans also makes them a preferred target for enslavement. Private communiqués from Lord Pulgey Entiyti indicate that his acquaintance with their legendary healer Doron comes from having once saved him from attempted enslavement long ago, which serves to confirm this theory.

Earth was recently targeted due to that system's relative youth in the galactic community, the Cortians presuming a certain naiveté of which advantage might be taken; this more so as Agent Echo has a significant reputation in galactic circles, making him what the Cortians refer to as 'a prime acquisition.' The rapid rise of his protégés, Agents Omega and Romeo, may simply have added to the desirability. The fact that the Cortians' subterfuge was seen through by Agent Omega was a decided misstep, as was the continued hounding of Agent Echo, resulting in the unexpected—to the Cortians—loss of the Trindak.

The Ganotian Confederacy appears to have been another miscalculation, as their reputation for starship technology attracted the Cortians, who failed to take into account their species' obduracy and disapprobation to unlawful incursions. This very strict adherence to law and morality is largely incomprehensible to the Cortians, who tend to view such beings as weak, and do not understand how it can be used to strengthen a people, as on their own world any such attempt tended to limit the options of the population group in question. The fact that the Ganotian cloaking technology appears to be a significant blind spot in the Cortian sensor arrays proved to their advantage. We recommend negotiations to procure this technology and retrofit all PGLEIA vessels at the earliest opportunity.

Any and all future interactions with this species should be conducted with these matters in mind. The Cortians have a long-established way of life that has included conflict, invasion, piracy and raiding, and slave trade for the majority of its existence. It is, in their view, the most logical means of taking advantage of the few resources they have had available to them, dating back to their own prehistory. It has resulted in very loosely-aligned governmental structures on Corta, which often reorganize, depending upon who has the advantage at any given time. Likewise ship hierarchies are flexible; if the captain fails in a raid and loses the respect of his crew, he is apt to be assassinated, and one of the other high-ranking officers will take his place, as determined by which officer has the greatest support among the crew. It is a kind of rough democracy, but not a stable one.

Also note that the society is highly male-dominated; though often possessed of considerable intelligence, the females are viewed as a resource for breeding, and therefore highly controlled with that specific purpose in mind. An ability to appeal to, and organize, the female substructure may well meet with some success in destabilizing the planetary governmental structures, at least in select regions of the planet.

* * *

"This...is interesting," Suud murmured, finally coming up for air, to find Entiyti watching him.

"Yes, it is, isn't it?" Entiyti agreed. "Do you remember our rescuing Doron?"

"Just barely. I was scarce past my hatchling stage when it happened, and at that time, I still spent most of my time in the galley, cleaning; it was not until some months later that you promoted me to cabin boy and steward. If memory serves, you had not yet even met Franz. But I do recall the unpleasant birdlike beings with yellow feathers, though I had not associated them with the Cortians until this moment."

"Ah yes, I recall now. You were indeed very young when you came to work for me."

"Yes. But it was a good experience. You, and later Franz as well, taught me much. Speaking of whom, have you sent this to Franz?" Suud waved his tablet at Entiyti, denoting the report just finished.

"Yes, I have. And to Lydhuu, as well. I sent it to them both, scant moments before you arrived, under URGENT header."

"And what was Franz's reaction?"

"I fear I have not heard back from him," Entiyti admitted, horns wilting in the Draconan gesture of worry. "By the time I received it, let alone sent it, he would have been well on his way to the Great Hunter Nebula at the head of the Division One Fleet, possibly even engaging Cortian ships already. I doubt he has time to reply to me. But I had hopes it would provide him some intelligence that would ease his task."

"Very good," Suud agreed with a nod. "I believe I saw quite a bit of worthwhile intelligence there, myself."

"Something you can use in the blockade?"

"Several somethings, if I am not mistaken."

"Excellent."

"What about the cloaking technology?" Suud wondered.

"I got on that at once," Entiyti confirmed. "Given the assistance we provided to the Ganotians, they agreed promptly, and we have already arranged to purchase units sufficient for the two fleets you are gathering. They should arrive in your dry-docks within a few hours, at most."

"That is VERY good." Suud pondered. "What about Franz's ships?"

"He did tell me not to worry," Entiyti recalled. "It seems the Earth research and development department has already developed a new sensor-scrambling technology that Echo used to excellent effect against the *Trindak*, when it attempted to capture him the second time. As soon as matters went to hell there, Fra-er, Fox ordered the principal battle vessels in his fleet retrofitted. The refit was completed scant hours before the fleet departed the Sol system. And...he has sent the technology to us, as well. It is being installed as we speak, in as many PGLEIA spacecraft as can be managed, before your departure."

"Oh, that is most excellent, milord," Suud realized, nodding. "Is there anything else you require?"

"No. That is all I wanted," Entiyti murmured. "If you need to go finish preparations, and I know you do, you may go, my friend."

"Thank you, milord."

And Suud was gone.

* * *

"Time to check your leg, Echo," Omega said quietly, some little time later, as she clicked on the flashlight in their cocoon. "I probably need to change the packin' by now. At least I found that extra container of batteries for the light, so I can see what I'm doin'. I just can't keep it on TOO long, 'cause they won't last indefinitely."

"All right," Echo sighed. "I'll get the packing ready. This gets old."

"Don't it, though."

They dug around in the kit together, and while Echo prepared the packing, Omega gave him another dose of antipathogen, and a partial dose of painkiller—different ones this time; the supplies were rapidly depleting, and ALL of the analgesics were entirely gone, though Omega had managed to eke out the painkillers for Echo by dint of giving him half, then thirds, of a dose. They had run out of sterile gloves long since, during what Omega had taken to calling "Echo's siege," the extended fight with infection in his leg, so she simply sanitized her hands with a small quantity of rubbing alcohol, then hissed in pain until it evaporated from the gauze wrapping her burned fingers. Echo watched, biting his lip.

"Damn," he muttered as she finally slipped off the splint, "see if I forget to strap in again."

"Tell me about it. If I hadn't undone the shoulder straps, I prob'ly wouldn't have this hinky on my noggin. There," Omega said, delicately removing the contaminated gauze with forceps, and disposing of it in the special bin for medical waste which she'd brought up from the ship's tiny surgery shortly after they'd crashed; it was now so full that she was starting to have to cram the used items into it. "How does that feel?"

"Okay, I guess. How does it look?"

"Mm. There's still a little infection in there," Omega remarked, studying the injury intently. "Gimme that anti- um, antibiotic hypo."

"Here," Echo handed it to her. "What are you gonna do with it?"

"Dribble some of the medicine directly in here," Omega said, fitting action to statement. "There we go. It doesn't hurt, does it?"

"No...it actually feels kinda good, I think. Warm, sorta."

"Okay. Now I'll put the new packing in."

A passive Echo watched in silence as Omega skillfully treated his wound, completely focused on caring for his leg while causing him as little pain as possible. Occasionally she glanced up at his face to see how he was reacting, then nodded to herself when she saw he was relatively comfortable, and resumed her work.

Damn, he thought, hiding a smile. *This woman never ceases to amaze me. She's caring for me every bit as well as India could in the circumstances, I think, but unlike most doctors—India excepted, as well as a few others like Zebra, I suppose—there's nothing indifferent or disinterested about her care. She'd do it for any other agent, I think. But she's being especially careful now, 'cause it's NOT any other agent she's working on, it's ME.* Warmth filled him. *Brains, heart, and beauty. Meg's got it all. Well,* he amended, *she's fighting with the brains thing right now, I guess, what with the head injury and all. But we'll get it worked out.*

"Okay, that's got it," Omega said, leaning back. "Let's get the splint back on, and then I think you're good to go for a while." ·

"Thanks, Meg," Echo said in a soft tone, watching her face. Omega shrugged, the barest hint of a smile on her features.

"You're welcome, Ace. Hope I didn't hurt you too much."

"You didn't hurt at all," Echo remarked, quiet. "Not even a twinge, even with only a third the usual amount of painkiller. Some of the medics back at Headquarters could take lessons from you, Legs."

"Well, I s'pose it makes a difference when the man I'm workin' on is my...best buddy." She smiled slightly and glanced down, seeming pleased.

"And that best buddy appreciates it." Echo grinned, all the while thinking, *I knew it.* "But does that mean somebody else might be in for a torture session?" he teased, then caught himself and stopped when he realized what he'd said. *Aw shit. Open mouth, insert foot.* He glanced away. "Sorry, baby. Bad choice of words."

"Oh." Omega waved a dismissing hand. "Don't worry about it. I took it the way you meant it, and didn't even consider it any other way, 'til you said something. And don't go worryin' about puttin' things the wrong way, just because of what happened a long time ago. If I knee-jerked over every little thing, I'd have gone crazy way back yonder." Then she gave him a stern look. "Anyway, do you really think I wouldn't be careful, whoever I was working on? It's just that, knowing you like I do, I can kinda...be MORE careful."

"I know, baby. Ease up about it, Meg. I was joking, it was a bad attempt, and I know it. I'm sorry."

"I know you were," she replied with a sigh. "I'm sorry, too. I guess I just don't feel very joky right now..."

* * *

"Awright, there's a reason we got th' heavily-cloaked stealth ships, guys," Romeo noted on the ciphered comm to five other small craft. "We're gonna search f'r Echo and Omega while Fox an' the fleet keep th' Cortians busy. You all got your sections o' th' search grid, so max out your sensor suite an' let's go find Meg an' Echo."

"*Aeneid* here. Roger that, *Odyssey*."

"*Iliad* copies."

"*Republic* affirms."

"*Halcyon* copies."

"*Organon* here. We copy."

"All right...GO."

No response came back from the cloaked ships, and nothing indicated that anything had moved. But Alpha Two knew that the hunt had begun. Romeo, in the co-pilot's seat, glanced back at India, sitting at the navigation station. She pursed her lips and nodded. He turned to the man in the pilot's seat.

"Okay, Victor, let's get with it."

"On it," the experienced pilot said, ginger head bobbing once, voice tight. "We'll find your colleagues if they're still alive to find. And maybe even then."

Both members of Alpha Two winced.

* * *

"...Grid block four complete," India murmured, as she studied her console display. "No sign of 'em."

"Moving to grid block five," Victor noted.

"Roger; grid block five," India acknowledged.

"I show no Cortians in this block," Romeo observed, studying the weapons-specific sensor suite.

"Good," Victor murmured. "There used to be a small group of Cortians in this block, according to the GALINT data. Looks like Fox and the others have drawn 'em all off the hunt, then."

"Thank God," India breathed, studying her sensor display. "Okay, lessee...no, dammit. I got nothing. Grid block five complete."

"No joy?" Victor asked.

"No joy."

"Damn. This may take longer than I figured," Victor grumbled.

"Maybe the others will have better luck," Romeo offered.

"Maybe. Okay. Moving to grid block six," Victor said, and they all sighed.

* * *

The next targeted flight group was some light year, give or take, deeper into the molecular cloud complex. The Division One Fleet drove onward, cloaked once more with the sensor-scrambling tech, and surprised the second small flight of enemy craft. This time, there were five.

The Cortian curses and epithets were somewhat different, though no less colorful; their responses, essentially identical to the first target.

The final result was the same.

"Lather, rinse, repeat," Zero observed from the security console.

"Exactly, zun," Fox agreed.

"At this rate, we might as well mop 'em all up and go home," Lima decided.

"Unfortunately, matters are unlikely to continue so well," Fox observed, as they continued toward the third designated target, a cluster of four ships, according to intelligence information. "At some point, the Cortians are going to decide to gang up on us and try to stop us, in order to ensure that THEY get hold of Alpha One, and not us." He drew a deep breath. "And when that happens, all hell WILL break loose."

"Is that why we keep cloaking, and why we're hitting the targets kinda randomly?" Fox's young assistant wondered.

"That is precisely why," Fox confirmed. "And why only selected ships are uncloaking each time. We want to keep them guessing, to an extent. But if they don't show up for this third target, I plan to keep at least part of the fleet uncloaked en route to Target Four. That way, the rest can see us coming, but they'll get a completely incorrect idea about how big our force is." He turned to Sail. "Did the search team get off?"

"They did, sir, quite some time back," Sail verified, "and the *Columbia* is now alongside, and fighting with us, as needed."

"That's good news. Now if the searchers can find Echo and Omega, even better."

"Amen, sir."

"Stand by for the code."

"All over that, sir. But, um..."

"Yes, Sail?"

"I just want to get this straight, sir," Sail murmured. "If the search teams can't locate Alpha One, the code is, 'Nisht gut.'"

"Right. It means 'no good.'"

"Okay. And if the teams locate Alpha One, and they're all right, the code is 'Mayn prom iz ful mit vengers,' right?"

"Exactly."

Behind Fox, Zebra snorted an unexpected guffaw through her nose, then clapped her hands over her mouth and nose. The corners of Fox's lips curved up slightly, but this time he did NOT translate the phrase.

"And if...they only recover the..." Sail broke off before he said the word 'bodies,' then finished, "that code is, 'Ikh hobn keyn vengers,' correct?"

"It is." Fox nodded, but did not explain or translate; unfortunately, though he had had numerous language courses, Sail did not reach Echo's level of expertise, and had never studied Yiddish. So poor Sail was none the wiser when Fox turned away.

* * *

"Aw, honey, I can't believe you did that," Zebra breathed when he moved to her station, his back to the rest of the bridge to hide his grin.

"Why not? I get a kick out of that British series, too," Fox pointed out, sotto voce. "And you saw Omega and Echo both double over laughing at the sketch that last night, in our quarters."

"Yeah. I guess they'd appreciate it, either way," she decided. "But damn, Fox! I nearly blew out my sinuses on that!"

"Sorry, bubeleh," he chuckled, then returned to his command chair.

* * *

No other Cortians showed up to rescue Target 3, though Sail indicated there was considerable emission of a peculiarly modulated variety, shooting through the spacetime continuum in the nebula.

"I'd say they definitely know we're here, sir," he told Fox.

"A logical conclusion, that," Fox agreed.

So Fox had the corvettes remain in the spaceship carriers, all of which cloaked; fully two-thirds of the battleships also cloaked, leaving a few battleships interspersed among the destroyers. The destroyers were rather smaller than the Cortian ships, but the battleships were roughly the same size, so this was a deliberate effort on Fox's part to cause the Cortians to underestimate the size of their fleet, by a substantial margin.

"But I want all ships on full alert, all hands at battle stations, force fields up and ready," he ordered. "Chances are, they will try to ambush us, or form some sort of pincer maneuver to try to envelop us—at least, those of us they can detect."

"Is that why you have the uncloaked ships slightly in advance of the cloaked ships?" Zebra wondered.

"Just so, meyn teyere," he affirmed. "The Cortians will focus on the uncloaked ships, likely approaching from the sides and rear; and when they attack, then the bulk of the fleet will uncloak and attack, thereby—hopefully—pinning them between the two forces."

* * *

But the Cortians were not so subtle. As the Division One Fleet approached the locus determined earlier for the fourth target flight, some fifty Cortian ships abruptly uncloaked, directly in the Fleet's path...and promptly and without preamble, opened fire.

"UNCLOAKED SHIPS, TARGET AND OPEN FIRE! FIRE AT WILL!" Fox yelled into the comm. "Corvettes, remain cloaked, infiltrate, and snipe! Spacecraft carriers, release all corvettes now, then bring your main guns to bear! Remaining cloaked ships, try to flank the Cortians! Pin them down if possible! Don't forget to use tractor beams!"

"FOX!" Sail cried. "The ship from Va'du'sha'ā took a hit! The *Arb'd'rb* got hit by three Cortians at once, and it locally overloaded their force field! They're calling a mayda—"

A brilliant blue-white flare lit the starboard side of the viewscreen, temporarily saturating that portion of the screen. The bridge complement either blinked or averted their eyes, holding up hands and arms to block the blinding light.

"Tell me that wasn't," Fox demanded.

"It was, sir," Cast reported, voice quiet. "The *Arb'd'rb* is gone."

"Farkakt, verdammt, merde, glagaram, and argdun!" Fox cursed. "Search for survivors!"

"Sensors show no life forms in the debris, sir," Cast advised. "I will continue to scan, but..."

"Boy!" Fox addressed his weapons officer.

"Yes sir!" she replied. "Already targeting the three ships responsible!"

"Lock with tractors! I want them sitting ducks, dammit!"

"Tractors locked, sir! Open fire?"

"Fire at will! And keep firing until the bastards get a taste of their own medicine!"

"Firing!"

Moments later three large explosions shoved Cortian ships aside, slamming large pieces of shrapnel into several of the remaining ships and damaging them; one began to drift to starboard, venting gases overboard as she did.

"Good job, Boy!" Fox exclaimed. "Target the two craft at ten o' clock!"

"Targeting! Tractors locked on target!"

"Fire!"

* * *

Lima eased back to Zebra's side, the better to stay out of the way, yet nearby in case Fox needed him. Slightly uncertain—he was too young to have seen action during the Klydonian invasion—he glanced at the physician.

Zebra gazed back, not sure if he was looking for reassurance, or simply general comment. So she opted for the latter.

"Well...here we go," she murmured.

"Yeah, really," Lima muttered. "Damn."

"To hell, pretty much, yup."

* * *

The temperature continued to drop within the derelict *Trojan Horse*. The two Agents inside her struggled silently against hunger, thirst, and the frigid cold which now invaded even their blanket refuge as they waited for the rescue that it seemed would never come.

Echo, forced into relative immobility by his injuries, still weak from the infection, and not as warmly dressed as Omega, grew more chilled by the moment. When, despite his best efforts, shivering set in, he concentrated on concealing that fact from his already-anxious and depressed partner.

262

But Omega's acute senses picked up the slight movement in the darkness.

"Echo?"

"W-what?"

"You all right?"

"Yes."

Her hand snaked through the pitch-blackness to touch his back, and he tensed, trying to still his shivering. But the tautness of his muscles only accentuated the motion.

* * *

"Echo! You're shivering to death!"

"I'm f-fine, Meg."

"No, you're not." Omega inched over to her partner, still resting her hand on his back. "It's expo-ex-"

"Exposure."

"Yeah, that. You're chilled to the bone." She paused. "Echo, we don't have any more covers to pile on..."

"I t-told you, I-I'm fine."

"Hush." Omega closed her eyes for a moment in the dark, then fit herself close against Echo's back, pressing into his torso and snaking one arm around his chest. "I'm gonna make like a heater. How's that?"

* * *

"Mm. You're warm..."

"Well...more or less."

After a few minutes, Echo's shivering abated.

"Better?" Omega asked softly.

"Yeah. Thanks."

"You gonna be okay?"

"Yeah, Meg. I'm warm again. You can go back to sleep."

"Wilco." Echo felt her settle down and snuggle against his back.

"Meg? I said you could...go BACK to sleep..." he murmured in an understanding tone. In truth, he would have preferred nothing better than to curl up with her again, but he was also very aware that that had thrown her off mentally, earlier, while in essentially the same position, and he didn't want to press the matter quite yet.

"I am, Echo," Omega responded, seeming puzzled. "Oh—you mean move back where I was and go to sleep..." Echo didn't reply, and after a

263

moment, Omega moved away.

He stifled the sigh.

* * *

But the temperature continued to plummet, and finally the two Agents were forced to huddle together for warmth inside their nest.

"D-damn," Echo muttered, trying to keep his teeth from chattering, "it's j-just a little ch-chilly in here." He wrapped his arms around his partner, pulling her close, into his body, where they could better share heat.

"Maybe a little b-bit," Omega agreed, shivering herself now as she pulled the covers as close around them as she could manage; they both knew that the smaller the air pocket, the easier it was to keep it warm. "Fox b-b-better get it in gear, before we both t-turn into ice c-cubes. What time is it?"

"We're at least three d-days overdue."

"Earth or D-division?"

"Division, I th-think. I'm not real sure, 'cause I lost track while I was f-f-feverish."

"How long would it t-take for them to get from—?"

"T-two or three hours, m-maybe, at maximum." Echo's reply was quiet. "We're not that f-far."

"Oh."

"How are you d-doing?"

"C-cold. Hungry. Want s-s-somethin' to drink. Head hurts fit to split open. 'Sides that? Okay," Omega replied, obviously reining in her annoyance for his sake.

"Head hurts pretty b-bad?" Echo repeated, pulling his shivering companion even closer.

"Uh-huh."

"Meg, tell me what...you thought of my p-picture." The non-sequitur made Omega blink.

"What?"

"You know—the p-picture I made for you with the...s-s-sensors, the one you wanted," Echo explained, a slight hesitancy in his own speech. "Tell me what you t-thought of it."

"I liked it-t. I t-told you, it was g-good."

"But tell me what that...that as-astronomer's eye s-saw."

"Well, uh...there...there was..." her voice faded. "Aw. Echo, I didn't think you'd e-ever make fun of me." Omega's low voice was reproachful.

"What?!"

"You know my h-head's still...messed up. Why are you askin' me s-stuff like that? I...I can't tell you. Not any m-more. I'm not sure why..."

"I'm not...ridiculing you, Meg, I swear," Echo said, his own speech thick, and slower than usual. "I'd never do that to you, baby. I was trying to...check s-something out. I didn't want to s-s-say anything if it wasn't really h-happening, but...I'm starting to have p-p-problems too. It's just a lot more n-noticeable...with your head injury. Meg, the air's going b-bad."

* * *

"Entering grid block twenty-three," Victor called off. "We are getting way the hell too close to the battle lines, guys. We need to be careful, or we're gonna get some unwanted attention. Clear?"

"Clear," Romeo replied. "No Cortians in the grid blo— wait."

India and Victor tensed.

"'Wait' what?" Victor demanded. "We got enemy sighted?"

"Damn," India murmured, "you can see the explosions and stuff from here. Have the battle lines shifted toward us?"

"Yes, they have. That's my point," Victor replied, becoming impatient, as his stereotypical red-headed ire flared. "Do we have enemy sighted or not, Romeo?!"

"Not exactly," Romeo decided, studying his display with intensity. "I'm reading a Cortian signature, but no life forms, an' nothing big enough t' be a ship...hang on, lemme figure this out..."

"Are. We. In. Danger?!"

"Naw, man. I'm not even reading power. I think...I think I maybe got ship debris."

"Lemme see." Now past impatient, Victor leaned over Romeo's near forearm and studied the readouts. Ginger-toned eyebrows shot up. "Huh. I see what you mean, now. It's characteristic of their alloys and manufacture, but there's nothing there bigger than a car body panel."

"Yeah," Romeo agreed.

"Romeo? Are you thinking what I'm thinking?" India asked.

"That they got in a fight with one a' the Cortians, took it out, but got hit themselves?"

265

"Exactly."

"Then yup, I'm thinkin' what you are." Romeo adjusted the sensor scan. "India, babe, ramp up the gain on your sensors as high as it'll go, an' let's scan this area real careful-like."

"You think they're probably around here someplace, then?" Victor queried.

"Someplace, yeah." Romeo nodded. "I thin—"

"Romeo! I got something!" India exclaimed. "And I think it's an automated mayday! But it's awfully weak. It just suddenly snapped on!"

"Follow it!" Romeo ordered Victor, who immediately bent over the helm.

"Tracing signal," he said. "Keep a sharp watch out for Cortians; now would be a really bad time to get snuck up on."

"Roger that."

A few short translation maneuvers served to triangulate and establish signal direction via varying signal strength, and the *Odyssey* homed in on the automated distress beacon.

"Looks like...a protoplanet in the cloud ahead, maybe...?" Victor wondered then.

"Yeah, I see it, an' concur," Romeo murmured.

"GUYS!" India cried. "I got lifeform readings on it!"

"WHAT?! How many? What kind?" Romeo demanded.

"I got two, and they're human! They're coming from the middle of a wrecked spacecraft, and..." India adjusted some controls, "...yes! Encrypted identification code shows it's the *Trojan Horse*! We found 'em!"

"WAHOO!" Romeo shouted. "Send coordinates t' th' helm, while I get a message sent! Victor, swoop in fast! India, be ready! We gotta move quick t' get 'em outta there before a Cortian ship sees their transmission!"

"On it!" two agents exclaimed at once.

* * *

The two Division One Agents lay snuggled close together, as still and relaxed as they could manage to be, trying to consume as little oxygen as possible while keeping each other warm. The air scrubbers had gradually ceased functioning as the ship slowly died, and the atmosphere was now becoming rapidly depleted in oxygen, while becoming loaded with excess carbon dioxide. Alpha One began to pant, the oxygen in the cabin air no longer sufficient for their bodies' needs. Nausea built, and from time to time one or the other retched briefly, though nothing came up; the lack of food and water meant their bellies were empty of anything to purge.

"Echo...I can't...c-can't think...head...m-my head..."

"Hold on, honey. Just...h-hang on."

"Echo, they're...not c-coming. Not in time...for us."

"Are you t-tired, Meg?"

"No...b-but yes..."

"What...what do...you m-mean?"

"Give me...your h-hand." Omega found the hand that Echo extended in the dark, and laid it against the side of her head. "Tired here."

Echo's shoulders slumped in despair as he let his hand slide back over the silken hair, caressing gently, careful not to catch his fingers in the tattered, bloody gauze that still wrapped her head.

It's time, he thought, reaching a private conclusion. *We don't have long left now. It's time to 'fess up. At least that way, she'll know, before... before we...*

"Meg, listen," Echo murmured, pulling her close. "I...I want you to know something. Something important...well, it's important t-to me, anyway. I haven't said anything be-because...well, because I wasn't sure how you'd react. You s-see, I—"

Suddenly an alarm sounded, low-pitched and distorted. Both Agents went on alert, sitting up and staring at each other.

"Echo?! Is it—?"

"I'm...not s-sure, Meg. Cold's affecting...the electronic b-buzzer, but...I think it's...the p-proximity al-arm."

They scrambled up as best they could, wrapping in blankets, and Omega struggled, gasping for air, to drag a flashlight-wielding Echo over to the helm and help him into the pilot's seat. Together, they pulled the blankets off the console, then looked at each other.

"Here goes...the last...of the b-battery power, Meg," Echo said, powering on the sensor display.

"It's all right, Echo. Not m-much...anything else left, anyway. This'll end it...one way or an-another. What's it say?"

Echo studied the readouts intently, then turned to Omega, a wide smile on his face.

"YAHOO! About d-damn time! It's Division One, Meg! There's a ship in cl-close, and...wow! Even with the sensors nearly dead, I'm reading a huge b-battle a few astronomical units from our location! Fox is out there with...damn, all of Alpha Line an' m-most of Division One, it looks l-l-like!" Echo turned back to the console and worked to ensure a mayday transmission signal got coaxed from the nearly-lifeless equipment. After a couple of minutes, text popped up onscreen in reply, and Echo read it aloud for his companion's benefit.

* * *

A-1:

Odyssey *incoming. F & Co. fighting Cortian fleet. Battle lines moving this way.*

Be ready. Move fast.
A-2

* * *

"Okay, Meg, that's why...they're l-late. There's a battle going on upsstairs...and they had to fight their way th-rough. We're gonna have to—" Echo turned toward the co-pilot's chair. It was empty. He turned to survey the flight deck with the flashlight. There was no sign of Omega. "Meg? B-baby, where are you?"

'I'm not going home, Echo.' The memory of her voice suddenly surfaced in his mind.

Echo paled, and his head spun; then, despite the bad air, he bellowed at the top of his lungs.

"*MEG*!!"

Omega burst from the doorway out of the flight deck, using her cell phone as a flashlight and skidding to a stop on her knees before Echo, who was panting heavily from the exertion of the shout.

"What?! What's wrong??" she panted in the toxic atmosphere, trying not to gag as her stomach rebelled at the extreme activity in the depleted air.

"What...were you d-doing?"

"Getting your s-stuff together. Gotta be ready...when R-romeo an' India get here."

"What about your s-stuff?"

Omega shrugged.

"Meg, you're c-coming back home with me." Echo made sure his tone

268

brooked no argument.

"Why?" Omega asked simply. "I'm not much good as an...an Agent like this. Can't b-be anything else if you can't...brain b-bleach me."

"You already are s-something else—to me. I tho-thought you'd accepted X-ray's old j-job," he said in a low tone. *Among other things...I hope,* he mentally amended. *Eventually.*

Omega studied Echo's eyes for a long, tense moment, apparently seeing in them something of the desperation he felt—and which, in that moment, he didn't try to hide from her—then she nodded.

"Yeah, I did. All r-right, Echo. I'll go with you. I can be your p-pal, if...if nothing else. But you have to d-d-do something for me."

"What?"

"If they can't f-fix me, don't let 'em p-put me in the room with the little w-window."

Echo looked into the face of the woman in front of him, dimly-lit by console lights and flash. He saw the loyalty, the caring, the trust—and the dread—written there. Thinking back over the last month's events, Echo suddenly realized with a shock just what Omega had been willing to go through for him, and how much she was now depending on him to do the same for her.

She cares, he grasped. *She cares with everything she's got. Maybe not the way I want her to, at least not yet—maybe not ever, like that, though I can hope—but in her own way, she loves me to pieces, as us Southern types say.*

He nodded confirmation of her request without another moment's hesitation.

"I p-promise, Meg," Echo said in a low voice, holding out his hands, palms up. "I won't let you b-be a 'lab rat'. If the medics c-can't make you well, I'll...t-take you away."

"All right. That's ok-kay, then." Trusting, Omega laid her hands in his, and he squeezed them gently.

"Now g-go get your gear together, too," Echo told her.

* * *

The minuscule, cloaked *Lysistrata* zipped through the nebulosity, darting between the larger vessels, plunging deep behind Cortian lines to fire their main cannons, before dashing through and away. She and her

269

sister-class corvettes caused considerable damage to the Cortians in this fashion. The Cortians apparently had no comparable tactic, as all of their starships seemed to be of a similar size and design—big enough to carry significant numbers of slaves and stolen goods, but small enough to be relatively maneuverable and easy to hide in, say, an asteroid field. But they were no match for the Division One corvettes.

So the tiny three-man *Lysistrata* did more than her fair share of carnage to the Cortian fleet.

Until she zagged when she should have zigged.

A green beam painted the *Lysistrata*'s propulsion unit, and the little spacecraft shuddered, losing the drive and much of her power. The cloaking systems failed at the loss of power, and she became visible across the spectrum. Momentum carried her into the battle's no-man's-land, where friction with the nebula's gas and dust took effect—the *Lysistrata* gradually came to a near-stop, drifting slightly, dead in space. Seconds later another green beam grazed the craft; a small explosion rocked her frame, and the aft hull split, white puffs of freezing atmosphere escaping into what was, for human lungs, essentially vacuum.

* * *

On the flight deck—which was almost all there was of the crew compartment in the pint-sized vessel—Dog dug frantically in the emergency stowage, hauling out three special suits. Monkey leaned on the comm button, yelling into the microphone, even as their ears popped at the rapid pressure drop.

"MAYDAY! MAYDAY! *LYSISTRATA* HAS BEEN HIT! WE HAVE LOST PROPULSION, AND ARE VENTING ATMOSPHERE! MAYDAY! MAYDAY!"

"Here," Dog said, handing Kako and Monkey one suit each. "Emergency pressure suit. Get it on as fast as you can, while you can!"

As the three agents scrambled to don the special suits which would keep them alive—provided the Cortians didn't target them again—an incoming message annunciated, somewhat distorted by the decreasing atmospheric pressure in the cabin.

"*Lysistrata*, this is Comm Officer Sail aboard Division One flagship *Genesis*. We copy mayday, and Fox is diverting to your location. Set your airlock to emergency boarding. We will be there momentarily to effect rescue."

"Thank God," Monkey murmured, fastening the pressure suit and initiating its power, as Dog, already in his suit, moved to the airlock hatch to adjust its settings.

"Vhat you said," Kako agreed, voice slightly muffled by the pressure suit. "I just hope zhey do not hit us again before zhe *Genesis* can arrive."

"We're good," Dog said, peering out the airlock port. "Here comes the *Genesis*, and if I'm reading that little flash of Cherenkov radiation right, they just extended their shields to include us."

"Hallelujah," Monkey declared. "Kako, buddy, grab your gear bag from stowage and let's go. Dog, man, I'm recommending you for Alpha Line when we get home."

"Sounds good to me," Dog agreed.

* * *

Romeo and India had the Division One pilot bring the rescue ship *Odyssey* in fast, landing and emergency-docking to the airlock of the *Trojan Horse*. But when the airlock hatch opened and Romeo stepped into it, the first thing he saw were the remnants of a tattered, acid-eaten spacesuit piled on the airlock floor. Wide black identifying stripes encircled arm and thigh; the Division One and Alpha Line patches adorned the shoulders and neck cowling—what was left of them. The Greek letter Ω was inscribed in black on the left breast.

"SHIT! India, girl, get your medikit and get ready!" he called over his shoulder. "Echo an' Meg may not be in too good shape. I just hope they're both still alive."

"On it!" India called back, right behind him. She, too, spotted the spacesuit's remains. "Oh, hell. No..."

* * *

When the inner airlock hatch opened, Alpha Two found Alpha One huddled together on the deck on the other side, pale, shivering, gasping for air, nauseated, wrapped in blankets and bloody gauze.

"Oof," India murmured, "the air's really bad."

"Yeah, stand in th' flow from th' hatch," Romeo advised. "I ramped up th' air on th' *Odyssey* 'fore we came over, 'cause I was worried 'bout this. Did a stint on a sub once, an' hadda deal with scrubber problems. I made sure we'd have positive pressure b'fore we boarded."

"Good job," India agreed, and Echo nodded, giving the younger Agent an approving thumbs-up, but didn't waste breath trying to talk.

Gently, Romeo and India helped their friends and colleagues into the rescue craft.

"Careful...wi' Echo," a panting Omega told them once she got in the airlock, "both legs are...broken."

"Aw, damn," Romeo said, wincing, as he carefully eased his ex-partner onto an antigrav stretcher. "Been there, done that. You got it, pretty lady."

"India," Echo said quietly, trying not to gasp for air as Romeo maneuvered the stretcher through the hatch, "check out...Meg's head...right away."

"I will, just as soon as we get you two aboard the *Odyssey* and lift off," India replied, taking the two small gear bags from a wobbly, weak Omega, wrapping an arm around her waist, and assisting her toward the sleeping berths. "Is it a concussion, do you think?" she asked the astronomer-turned-Agent.

* * *

Echo and Omega looked at each other, both at a loss to know exactly how to answer the physician's question. Finally, as they entered a sleep cabin, Omega ventured a response.

"It's, um...kinda broken..."

It was Romeo's and India's turn to glance at each other, puzzled.

"You mean you have a skull fracture?" India verified.

"I...I don't know. I just..." a nervous Omega stammered, fidgeting.

"India," Echo interrupted, trying to ease his partner's discomfort, "Meg, well...she took a really bad bump when we crashed, and...she's having trouble with...higher-order brain function."

Romeo laid Echo on a bunk in one of the *Odyssey*'s port sleeping berths, strapping him down securely, and India put Omega in the bunk next to him.

"So...you can't think too well, Meg?" India asked softly, putting their gear in a nearby locker.

"No. I get...get con...con—" Omega shot a glance at Echo for help.

"Confused," Echo filled in quietly, and India and Romeo stared at him, then turned shocked gazes on Omega as they grasped the degree of her deterioration. Omega's face crumpled slightly, and her partner realized that she was fighting to keep from bursting into tears. Echo closed his eyes to hide his pain, just as another agent with freckled face and flame-red hair appeared in the cabin door.

"But, Meg," Romeo protested, "you're a Ph.D. An astronaut..."

"Was, Romeo," Omega whispered. "Was..."

"Got 'em strapped in?" the strange agent asked then. "We gotta go before we get spotted."

"Yeah, Victor," India replied. "We're coming." Victor headed forward again as she spread blankets over the two Agents, who were still shivering. "You guys rest a while and get warm. Stay strapped in; it may get bumpy. I'll come back when we're in the clear."

* * *

Alpha Two disappeared though the doorway. Omega turned her head to face Echo.

"That's why I didn't want 'em to see me," she said in a low voice. "That, right there. I jus' wanted 'em to think of me the old way. I don't want anybody feelin' sorry for me."

"We don't pity you, Meg. We...hurt for you." Echo's eyes were pained.

"They didn't do that to you. You're hurt, too." She shook her head and stared at the deckhead as they felt the spacecraft lift off. "If it had been anybody but you that asked me, Echo...I'd still be down there right now."

* * *

"Damn!" Echo exclaimed as the ship rocked again. "We're taking a real beating."

The spacecraft had left the surface of the protoplanet at maximum ascent speed, breaking orbit and heading into interstellar space. It had also, apparently, inadvertently headed squarely into the middle of the space battle which still raged between the Cortians and Division One. It made acute, high-velocity maneuvers, and occasionally the shielding took a hit, both from beam weapons and explosive shock waves, which latter propagated through the cloud complex's medium at varying degrees of effect, depending on said medium's local density. Echo was glad, in his current condition, to be strapped down. He was also glad that the well-oxygenated air of the cabin had lessened his anoxia symptoms, otherwise he—and Omega—would have been retching with considerable violence.

To his surprise, Omega unstrapped and sat up.

"I'm gonna go see what's happening. Maybe I can do something." She swung her legs over the side of the bunk, just as another impact shook the craft, and Echo put out a hand to help her brace herself.

"Meg, be careful. Don't fall and bash that head again. That might be REALLY bad."

"I know. I will be." She adopted a wide stance and exited the sleep cabin, stepping cautiously and holding to the bulkhead hand grips and any other makeshift handholds she could find.

* * *

When Omega entered the *Odyssey*'s flight deck, she saw a battle raging outside. At least four dozen or more Division One spacecraft were visible through the main view port, as they engaged about the same number of Cortian vessels in the midst of the Orion Nebula. No quarter was asked or given; ships on both sides took an incredible beating. Nearby, one Cortian ship exploded, its fragmenting warp generator temporarily distorting space in its near vicinity before the warp collapsed, creating a second detonation.

"Ooo. That's not good..." she muttered. India, in the navigator's chair, turned at the remark.

"Meg! What are you doing here?!"

Omega didn't answer, staring at the view out the cockpit window and struggling to keep her feet as the ship rocked again. Suddenly she turned and ran out of the room.

"What the hell was that about?" Romeo asked, worried.

"Beats me," India replied, just as concerned. "Maybe she flashed back to the crash and it spooked her."

"You guys wanna shut up with the Freud and help me get outta here, before we all become part of the nebula?" Victor interjected, voice tight.

"Sure, man," Romeo said, shooting the pilot an intense, irked glare. "Let's target this guy..."

* * *

"Echo!" Omega cried, appearing in the door of the sleeping berth. "I got an idea, but I need your help."

"Meg? Can you...think...again?" Echo began struggling to sit up, automatically responding to his partner's urgency.

"It's a little better with the good air, yeah," she said, unstrapping him and helping him sit up. "Now we gotta figure out how to get you up front with me."

"Umm...this is a Jupiter-Three class starship...check the little science lab, aft, for a rolling desk chair."

"Gotcha. Hold still. Whatever you do, don't fall outta the bunk until I get back. Well, uh, don't fall outta the bunk at all, actually." Omega vanished, reappearing moments later dragging a wheeled office chair. "It was strapped down. Here, Ace, let's get you in this while I tell you my idea..."

* * *

Omega and Echo burst into the flight deck, using the desk chair like a wheelchair for Echo. His feet rested on the wheel struts, his hands gripped the chair arms, and Omega 'drove' as if their lives depended on it.

"Meg, show 'em where to target!" Echo barked orders. "Romeo, move over so I can get to the comm."

"Whassup?" Romeo asked, moving aside to make room for Echo.

"Meg had an idea, and it's a good one," Echo said, leaning over the console and activating the comm.

"It, uh, it comes and goes," Omega explained. "My head, that is. Um. Anyway, I r'membered the fight Ace and I had with these guys b'fore we crashed. We took out their ship. Pull up a...a..." She drew a blank on the word, and glanced at Echo in distress.

"Diagram," Echo said briefly, filling in her sentence while keying in a coded message. "Victor, isn't it?" he addressed the copper-haired agent.

"Yeah," the pilot responded, brusque, concentrating on his flying.

"Victor, bring up a sensor schematic of the Cortian ships for her."

"All right," a harried Victor replied, short. "But we're in the middle of a battle, in case you haven't noticed, so this had better be damn good. I don't have time to listen to some brain-damaged dumb blonde otherwise."

At the statement, a very small sound that might have been a suppressed gasp of anguish came from Omega's vicinity. Echo stopped everything, glaring at the pilot with a dangerous light in his eyes. Romeo recognized it as his 'Yellowstone stare.'

"You want to start over and rephrase that?" Echo's voice was low, quiet. Victor glanced in uncertainty past a furious Echo at a shocked Alpha Two.

"Do you know who this is, Victor?" India asked softly.

"Yeah, man," Romeo continued. "This is Alpha One, Alpha Line's chief and assistant chief. That team reports directly to Fox. They're the bosses on this ship now—rankin' Agents. And the pretty lady here ain't no dumb blonde. She may be blonde, and she may have a bump on the head, but she's still got more brains in her than you an' me put together." A shy Omega gave him a grateful, hesitant smile.

"Riiight. Gimme a damn break," Victor muttered, still maneuvering frantically through the battle. "I've read the reports. That may be Echo—emphasis on 'may,' because she called him Ace just now, not Echo, an' Ace is a legit phonetic alphabet code name—but this woman sure isn't Omega."

"Hold on," India said, holding up one hand and scowling. "Just who the hell exactly did you think we were coming to rescue?"

"Thought you said one of the Alpha Line ships went down on that planetoid in the fight," Victor replied, curt.

"Yeah," Romeo said, "but it wasn't THIS fight, an' it was the chief an' assistant chief!"

"Cut the crap. I already told you, I know this isn't Alpha One. Now, as I'm the pilot and you're not, *I* am the ranking agent in a dogfight, and I'm telling you to sit down, shut up, and help me. You two," he gestured to Alpha One, "get back in the berths and lie down, like Agent India told you to, to begin with."

* * *

Just then an alert communiqué came in on the priority channel.

"*Odyssey*, this is flagship *Genesis* for Alpha Two."

Romeo hit the comm.

"*Genesis*, this is Alpha Two Romeo. Go ahead."

"Romeo, this is Monkey; I'm helping Sail coordinate all the comm. We got your coded signal about the eels, but it broke up a little, and since I'm Alpha Line, I took this communiqué. Fox is asking if you got 'em. He wants a status. For that matter, you know how I feel about 'em, so I wouldn't mind knowing, either."

"We got 'em," Romeo replied, shooting a hard glance at Victor. "They're pretty banged up, but they're both alive."

"That's good news!" Monkey's voice exclaimed over the comm. "Well, not the banged-up part, I guess. Anything...permanent?"

India leaned over the microphone.

"Monkey, this is India. I...can't answer that quite yet. I need to get 'em to better diagnostic equipment than I've got here."

There was a pause on the comm. In the background, Fox's voice could be heard murmuring, "That doesn't sound as good as I'd hoped. But at least they're still alive. EVASIVE ACTION! Fire at will!" Another pause, then Fox's voice came directly over the comm.

"Fox to Echo, do you copy?"

"Echo here, Fox. Whatcha need, Boss?"

"Just to hear the sound of your voice, alter khaver. In your estimation, how badly are the two of you hurt?"

"Hard to say, Fox," Echo sighed. "I got a couple thoroughly busted legs and a messed-up arm—shoulder AND wrist—so I got splints and slings all over; but it's nothing that won't heal well in time, I think. Meg... took a pretty good blow to the head. It didn't miss the temple by much."

"Damn. And that's a highly vulnerable area."

"Yeah. In my estimation, about an inch, inch and a half down, and we could've lost her...again. And it's not..." Echo broke off, looking for a diplomatic way to put things that wouldn't embarrass his partner. He finally settled for, "Uh, it's giving her some issues."

"Hm. Oh wait, I get it. She having cognitive problems?"

"Some, yeah. We've been working on it. Like she's told me, it comes and goes, depending on certain conditions. The burns don't help, from where she had to go EVA for repairs and didn't get finished and back inside before the acid rainstorm hit."

"Damn. Well, just take care of yourselves until we can get you back to Headquarters and the medlab. Before you go, though, do either of you have anything for me? Any observed weaknesses in the enemy ships, any combination moves, anything I can use in this verdammt battle?"

"We might, Fox," Omega murmured then. "I got some ideas, but I need to show 'em to Romeo..."

"Why, Fox? What's up?" Echo wondered.

"We got telepathic-interrogation intel out of some captured pirates that all of the Cortian ships are basically identical where it counts," Fox explained. "If you find a weakness in one, you can exploit it in all of 'em. So I thought, given you're still alive to tell the tale..."

"Aha. Well, that's some good news," Echo decided. "Okay, Boss, have everybody keep an eye on us for a few minutes, and let's see what we can do. Either it'll work, or it won't."

"Copy that. Meanwhile, you know the drill, here. Once you've tried whatever you're gonna do, get the *Odyssey* the hell out of the battle zone as fast as you can. I want the four—wups, five; sorry, Victor, I forgot Alpha Two isn't pilot-rated yet—I want the five of you back on Earth and Alpha One getting patched up, not crashing again. Or worse."

"Roger that, Fox," Echo replied...before Victor could.

* * *

"Send word to Aleancë," Fox told Sail, who shared his console with Monkey for the time being. "We have Alpha One, and they will survive."

"Roger that, Director." Sail nodded as his hands flew over his console. "That's some news I'll be happy to pass on. Anything else?"

"Affirmative. Send a heads-up to the Fleet to watch the *Odyssey* in the next few minutes for possible tactics and Cortian weaknesses, like Echo just recommended."

"On it, sir," Sail noted. "And Monkey, thanks for the assistance, dude."

"You're welcome," Monkey declared, taking another message and passing it to the proper channels.

* * *

"Zebra, bubeleh?" Fox turned to his lover.

"Yes, Fox, Alpha One should be all right," she told him, anticipating his question. "Oh, we might have to be a bit delicate with Omega's head wound, but given that enhanced constitution of hers, coupled with the new techniques Doron showed us, I think she'll be fine in no time."

"That...is what I wanted to hear," he said, stifling a sigh. "There are not many humans alive with whom I go so far back as Echo, and Omega..."

"Might as well be your daughter; I know," she said, understanding. "Just like Echo is as much son as friend. Don't sweat it, honey. I'll see they're taken good care of."

"I know you will. Now, let's see about getting this band of miscreants mopped up so you can go do just that. Helm! Move into position to assist *Odyssey* in clearing the volume if needed."

"Helm copies..."

* * *

Four sets of eyes stared holes into Victor as he dodged and swerved through space.

"Awright, awright," he grumbled. "So that's Echo, the Alpha Line chief. So who's the blonde chick? You really can't tell me that's Omega; I know about the tesseract puzzle record, and her multiple degrees, and all that shit. Hell, the whole Agency has heard about 'that shit.' But this woman? No way. She can't even string together coherent sentences half the time. Not to mention, she has NO scarring, but I heard Omega got caught under a Cortian craft's ion drive..."

Omega winced; Echo's face hardened into glacial granite. His body seemed to expand even as Omega withdrew, almost flinching away from Victor.

"I am telling you: This lady," Echo said, very, very quietly, "is my partner and assistant department head, Agent Omega. She has sustained potentially severe head trauma, almost certainly has a skull fracture, and while she is not functioning at her normal capacity, that does not mean she is incapable." Victor opened his mouth to protest again, and Echo responded in a voice that was deceptively soft, "You just heard Fox acknowledge us as Alpha One. AFTER hearing BOTH of us speak. Think very carefully before YOU speak again. Do you really want to get put on report as soon as we land?"

Victor stared at the injured man, who suddenly seemed a lot less injured...and backed down.

"Good. Now do as she says," Echo ordered, in an unequivocal tone of command. A couple of keystrokes later, Victor was back to evasive maneuvers as Omega scanned the computer image on the transparent heads-up weapons console display. Meanwhile, Echo was busy preparing a general-broadcast ciphered message for the PGLEIA Division One Fleet.

"Here!" Omega pointed at the computer display, which now depicted the external schematic of a Cortian spacecraft. "That's the place! When I hit it right here, it started spreading out from there. Boom, boom, boom." She traced her memory of the detonations with her fingers on the diagram. "Then we hit it over here," she tapped the image, "and it blew up. But you gotta be way back when you do, 'cause it blows up hard. That's why we crashed—we got hit, by, by, um..."

"Shrapnel," Echo finished for her. "Some serious, big-ass shrapnel."

"Yeah," she agreed. "That."

"Aaall riiight!" Romeo exclaimed, seeing and grasping the sequence she meant. "I see it! I'm all over this one, Meg! Let's party!"

"Message away," Echo declared just then. "It's all yours, junior." Echo grabbed the edge of the console and used his hands to shove himself well back, out of the way, and Romeo slid back into the co-pilot's chair, selected a Cortian ship, and commenced targeting where Omega had indicated.

"You wit' the plan, Victor?" Romeo asked. "You saw that, right?"

"Yeah, I'm on it," Victor replied, curt, concentrating on his course while trying to avoid being hit. "It does look like it might work. Coming around...fire at will."

"Right here, Romeo," Omega said, pointing out the main port. "See? Over there. Right below that strut-thing."

"Got it. Eat trans-warp boson cannon, ya bastards!" Romeo said, firing. Chain-reaction detonations shook the targeted vessel as they watched. Romeo glanced over his shoulder at Omega. "What next, pretty lady?"

"Now put one right here." She pointed at the schematic. "Over near that shuttle hatch, in the, um, oh! In the radiator field. But stay way, way back."

"Got it," pilot and weapons officer said simultaneously.

Moments later, the Cortian vessel's constituents had joined the nebula, imperceptibly enriching it in heavy elements. Several very large chunks of bulkhead flew past, but the *Odyssey* was far enough away that they proved easy to dodge.

"Look!" India cried, pointing out the cockpit window. "The other Division One ships saw what we did!"

* * *

One at a time, the Division One Fleet took out more and more of the Cortian ships. Occasionally two or more PGLEIA craft would team up to target a Cortian vessel, hitting it in a one-two punch that was so swift and lethal, the enemy craft had no chance to react before it was an expanding mass of gas and debris.

Suddenly the majority of the Cortian fleet pulled back, retreating at speed out of the area; the Division One Fleet turned to pursue. Then the incoming message alert tripped.

* * *

Pan-Galactic Ennead Governing Body to Division One Agency of planet Earth:

We have received the Alpha Line Alert and have dispatched multiple fleets to Corta and the Great Hunter Nebula at maximum velocity as support and backup. Fleet A should be arriving at your locus momentarily, flanking the Cortians per your transmitted communiqués. Your forces will be escorted safely home, your wounded assisted and cared-for, and the Cortians will be handled according to the dictates of intergalactic law. Salvage efforts will also commence on the planetesimal, and any and all recoverable equipment and materiel from the Trojan Horse *will be returned to Sol system. Commendations to Alpha One Agents Echo and Omega for this notification of further violation, and for their excellent teamwork against multiple Cortian attacks.*

Lord Entiyti sends his personal greetings and congratulations to Director Fox and Alpha One.

Ennead out.

* * *

Echo folded his arms and looked at his partner with a satisfied smile. Behind him, Alpha Two beamed, and Victor gawked in astonishment.

"Good job, Legs," he told her. "That was some fine analysis, there, baby. You're an Alpha Line Agent of Division One—the creamiest of the crop—whether your head is at a hundred percent or not."

Then he watched with satisfied amusement as the others did double-takes at the new nickname, and Omega fairly glowed.

Chapter 12

"Get ready to break formation and pursue," Fox ordered, as more and more of the Cortian ships were destroyed. "They'll tuck and run very soon."

"Orders relayed, sir," Sail reported. "All ships ready for pursuit."

"Good. I don't want any more of these bastards to get away than we can help," Fox confirmed, never taking his eyes from the heads-up tank display of the battle. "All of the reports I've been getting indicate that the sons of bitches have been wreaking havoc across the entire galaxy. It's time they were stopped." He drummed his fingers on the arm of his command chair, and Lima, at his elbow, noticed. The younger man leaned forward.

"Is everything all right, Fox?" Lima asked. "You seem...worried."

"Not worried, exactly," Fox admitted. "I had hoped to get assistance from the Coalition on this fight, and despite the message from Aleancë, I've not seen..."

"SIR! Long range sensors indicate another group of starships on approach!" Cast, the navigator, cried. "We're picking up their ciphered identification beacons only because they're tight-line beaming them! Identification indicates they are NOT Cortian, and at least some of them DO have the sensor-scrambler technology; most likely it's a Coalition fleet!"

"Now THAT is the second-best news I've had all day!" Fox exclaimed. "Expand display to include!"

Cast hit several keystrokes, and the holographic tank display expanded, to depict a third group of ships approaching at speed, shifting positions to form a giant hemisphere, its maw centered on the scene of Division One's current battle.

"Aha!" Fox exclaimed. "Fleet comm, now!"

"Fleet comm, sir!"

"Director Fox to Division One Fleet! A Coalition fleet is currently inbound to our aid! Pull up their ID beacons in your tanks and tactical displays! Prepare to form the other half of the hemisphere on my command!"

* * *

Admiral Raiit had received all the information Lord Entiyti had to hand, by the time the Coalition Alef Fleet left the rendezvous point just outside the Aleancë system. What she didn't have was specific details regarding where the battle was taking place. And the gigantic Orion Molecular Cloud Complex would take some time to search, if it came to that.

That proved easy to rectify, however; as Alef Fleet approached the cloud complex, even in stealth mode, passive sensors picked up sufficient data that a full, three-dimensional schematic of the battle could be raised in the virtual tank on the bridge of the *Dutzel*, Raiit's personal flagship.

"It looks as if the Division One Fleet is doing reasonably well for itself," Raiit noted from her seat on the command platform. "There appear to be quite a few derelict Cortian ships, yet not so many PGLEIA ones."

"True," her first officer, a Wintourn named Alva Sigusmund, remarked while studying the layout of vessels. "Which argues that Division One has been mightily busy, and has some very skilled pilots. But it is still an even match and— by the Maker! What just happened?!"

In the holographic tank, the Division One Fleet had abruptly reformed its structure, and begun systematically taking out Cortian ships at a great rate; second by second, more Cortian ships exploded, expanding into the cloud complex itself.

"Aha. Someone found a weakness and shared it with the others," Raiit observed. "The Cortians are about to— COMMUNICATIONS! Open a ciphered channel to Alef Fleet!"

"Open, Admiral!"

"Coalition Fleet Alef, this is Admiral Raiit! Assume flanking hemisphere, radius half a million klicks! Accelerate to emergency speed! Stand by for battle stations! GO!"

A slight g-force was felt as the *Dutzel* accelerated in response to her order.

"Admiral Raiit? What is it?" Sigusmund wondered.

"Look at the tank, Alva," Raiit murmured. "The Cortians are being decimated. They are about to break and flee."

"Yes. There they go," the helm officer, a purple-haired Chesharilzi named Peter Rogersen, remarked.

"Envelop!" Raiit cried. "All ships! Battle stations! Raise shields and decloak! Comm! Open a channel on Cortian frequencies!"

"All ships in place, decloaked, Admiral! Channel open!" came the reply.

"Cortian fleet, this is Pan-Galactic Coalition Fleet Alef, commanded by Admiral Lydhuu Raiit," she announced. "You are surrounded. Stand down and surrender, and you will be spared." Glancing at the comm station, she drew a tibial spur across what passed for her neck, and the communications officer—Raiit hadn't had time yet to learn her name, but the segmented felinoid was good—killed the link. "Director Fox," Raiit barked, and the felinoid nodded, hitting several buttons.

"Fox here," the Division One Director's voice responded. "I heard the broadcast. Lydhuu, is that you?"

"It is indeed, my old friend and teacher," Raiit said, clicking her mandibles in a friendly fashion. "No time for long greetings. Have your ships form the other flanking hemis—"

"Way ahead of you, whippersnapper," Fox replied, the sound of a grin in his voice. And Raiit watched, pleased, as the Division One forces filled in the other half of the surrounding sphere, with the remaining handful of Cortian vessels grouped in the center. "Did you get the message from Agent Echo regarding the tactics for taking out their ships?"

Raiit swiftly glanced at the felinoid, who was now carrying on an urgent conversation with Sigusmund. Sigusmund looked up and nodded, then gestured at the felinoid and pointed to the helm and weapons officers. The felinoid trilled, hit several buttons on her console, and looked up. Fractions of a second later, the weapons officer was grinning wolfishly—the fact that he was a lupinoid helped—and the helm was nodding as he studied the information.

"We have it, Fox," Raiit averred. "Sigusmund, make sure the rest of the ships get it."

"Already on it, Admiral," Sigusmund replied.

"Don't expect 'em to surrender, Lydhuu," Fox added. "They're damn stubborn sons of bitches."

"Well, farkakt," Raiit grumbled, and Fox laughed.

"I see I rubbed off on you," he noted.

"Yeah, yeah," Raiit continued to fuss. "How do you want to handle this, Fox?"

"Would you like me to take the lead, where the Cortians are concerned? I've had more experience with them..."

"Much appreciated," Raiit agreed immediately. "I'll watch what's happening, and ensure my fleet doesn't let anything through, fore or aft, if we can help it.”

“Good girl. All right, stand by.”

* * *

“Cortian frequencies.” Fox gestured to Sail.

“Go, Director.” Sail hit several buttons and nodded. Fox narrowed hazel eyes, gripped his chair arms, and leaned forward instinctively.

“Cortian fleet, this is the Division One Fleet, commanded by Director Fox,” he declared. “We are working in cooperation with Coalition Fleet Alef, commanded by Admiral Lydhuu Raiit. You are surrounded. Stand down and surrender immediately, and the Pan-Galactic Coalition will show mercy. This is not a request.”

The chittering snap of Cortian came over the inbound-message speaker, and the translators rendered it, “Go to hell.”

Abruptly, green beams lit up the center of the circle, targeting PGLEIA craft in both fleets. The Cortians unleashed a barrage of space-to-space missiles as well. Some found their mark; several ships in both Coalition fleets shuddered and drifted aside.

“CLOSE RANKS!” Fox barked. “Medical ships, attend the hits! Division One Fleet, FIRE AT WILL! Take these bastards out!”

* * *

“CLOSE RANKS!” Raiit cried. “Medical craft, attend the casualties! ALEF FLEET, OPEN FIRE! Caution on your alignments—we don’t want to hurt our own with friendly fire!”

The center of the sphere became a hellish inferno.

* * *

The Cortian fleet was gone within moments.

A very few—perhaps a half-dozen or so—feigned disablement, venting gases overboard to drift themselves out of the concentrated fire and close to Coalition forces, before suddenly ‘reviving,’ attacking the nearest PGLEIA craft, and darting through the opening thus provided, into the gas and dust clouds beyond.

Designated Coalition spaceships shot off after them, determined to run them down and capture them, though it was inevitable that a couple would escape.

* * *

“And that’s that,” Fox told Raiit on holovid from the privacy of his personal cabin aboard the *Genesis,* when it was all over but the mop-up. "I'm sure there are still some ships out there, but they'll be scattered, and if Suud has matters well in hand at Corta—"

"And I am sure he does," Raiit observed.

"No doubt, or I'd disown him as my protégé," Fox chuckled. "But with the home planet taken care of, I don't think we'll have many more problems out of them. Oh, maybe the odd lone pirate here and there, but those should get handled pretty quickly, once they try to make that first raid, after this."

"I wonder what the Ennead intends to do with their system," Raiit considered.

"If I understood Pulgey aright, there's going to be an attempt to...I suppose 'rehabilitate,' is as good a term as any," Fox said, shrugging. "Not that I'm holding my breath, personally. It sounds like, given the lack of adequate...ANYthing...on the homeworld, the whole 'rob Peter to pay Paul' way of life is rather...ingrained."

"Indeed, and I should not bet against you," Raiit agreed. "Oh, before I forget, did you find your people? Alpha One?"

"We did," Fox nodded.

"Are they...all right?"

Fox winced.

"More or less," he decided. "Somewhat the worse for wear, I gather, and I have some fears for Omega's rather unique brain—it seems she likely suffered a skull fracture and severe concussion, with associated cognitive difficulties—but they are alive. I'll have to wait and see what the prognoses are. But let me note that THEY are the ones responsible for showing us the particular vulnerability in the Cortian spacecraft design that we all were able to exploit so effectively." He nodded, commending. "BOTH of 'em, not just Echo. In fact, I gathered it was Omega's idea, and Echo simply helped her show the others on the *Odyssey,* as well as notify the rest of the fleet to pay attention, while she was helping target a Cortian ship. It seems when they were attacked during their training mission, she was the one who figured out and hit the targeting points on the attacking Cortian ship while Echo flew the ship and put her in position to take the shots, and they flatly destroyed it, all on their own, with a much smaller vessel. It was the unexpected force of the resulting explosion, combined with some rather large pieces of debris, which resulted in their craft's going down on the planetoid, and not anything the Cortians did."

"That bodes well, then."

"I'm hoping so, yes. Listen, speaking of such things, would you mind taking control here, Lydhuu? My number two medic is aboard the *Genesis* here with me, and I need to get her back to Headquarters to assist Zarnix, the head of Medical, with all of our casualties."

"By all means, go, Franz," she murmured. "We have this. Take your wounded and go home. We can even provide escort if needed; Lord Entiyti ensured there would be sufficient ships for the after-action policing, as well as assisting your people. Do you have any personal messages you would like for me to deliver?"

"Give Suud my greetings, and to you, Suud, and Pul—thank you," Fox said, sincere. "A lot more would have gotten away if not for you and your fleet, and it was high time Corta stopped terrorizing half the galaxy. And it was only going to get worse."

"Exactly so," Raiit agreed. "For myself, you are more than welcome, Fox, and I am sure the others will say the same. But I will pass on the messages, nevertheless." The Ergisol clacked her mandibles in lieu of the smile her kind could not show, and Fox smiled in return. "The next time you are on Aleancë, come by my office at the University and we shall have a cup of roffl together. Off with you, now."

"Right away, Admiral, and I will," Fox chuckled, before punching an open channel to the bridge. "Helm, we have Admiral Raitt's orders. Set course for home."

* * *

Many light years away, in a slightly different galaxy, a similar fleet closed in on its target.

"Open a subspaced, coded cipher to Bet Fleet," Suud ordered.

"Opening cipher comm," his communications officer noted. "Comm open, Admiral. You may begin."

"This is Suud," the Reptoid announced into the air, certain his comm mic would pick up and transmit his statements. "We are approaching the Cortian system. All vessels will maintain stealth mode when exiting warp. Blockade formation A-1-B-2 will be executed upon arrival. The flagship will take the lead, as per prior plans. Initiate collision avoidance protocols and remain cloaked until I give the order. All ships relay receipt and compliance to flagship communications officer, effective immediately. Suud out." Then he turned and looked at the comm station.

One panel of that station was exclusively devoted to an array of red/green lights, a small label beside each one. Initially dark, they all immediately lit red at the conclusion of his communiqué. Now they began turning green by ones and twos; moments later, all were green. The communications officer, a Deltiri named Kk'l'kn, turned to him.

"All ships affirm, sir," he said.

"Good," Suud murmured, and turned back to the viewing screen. "All crew, prepare for arrival. Battle stations."

"Battle stations, aye," Kk'l'kn reiterated, sending the order over the flagship's internal comm.

"Helm? Time to warp exit?"

"Time to exit warp bubble in five, Admiral."

Suud sat in the central chair and drummed his claws on its arm. The faint ticking noise was the only sound on the bridge as the *Sslthsd*—or as humans knew it, the *Devil Dragon*—approached Corta at maximum speed.

* * *

Five minutes later, the fully-cloaked Coalition Fleet Bet dropped out of warp in the sparse Cortian system. Immediately the *Sslthsd* and her followers initiated full sensor scans of the system.

What they found was...depressing.

The distant brown dwarf/stellar dwarf binary system, located on the edge of the relatively young Terzan 7 globular cluster, had little in the way of planets, and the star and brown dwarf were separated by some six astronomical units. As per intelligence information gleaned from the captured Cortians, the main star, Khula, had only one planet orbiting around it, a hellish Mercury-like rocky planet far too close to its star to be in the habitable zone. The brown dwarf Orge, however, had several satellites, and thanks to its impressive mass, some 75 times Jupiter's, somewhat irregularly sustained primitive fusion, largely of deuterium, generating a rudimentary habitable zone of its own. And this was where they found the Cortians' homeworld, the sole satellite within Orge's rude habitable zone.

Corta itself was immediately obvious; it was the only body in the system capable of supporting life—and even that appeared tenuous. It was a very unappealing planet, displaying wan shades of brown and gray to the universe at large, with a few relatively small bodies of shallow gray-green water which looked...dirty. Even the foliage appeared sparse and sere.

This, combined with what Suud knew of the Cortians' history from the interrogation of the captured pirates, explained much to the canny Reptoid.

So, he considered, *I will give them every opportunity to do this the easy way. Somehow I do not believe they will take it, but at least I will have tried.*

* * *

"All ships in position," Suud murmured.

"Confirm all ships in formation A-1-B-2," Kk'l'kn said moments later. "All Coalition craft still cloaked, and in stealth mode."

"Good," Suud replied. "Open a general broadcast to Corta, across all known frequencies. Broadcast override—and activate the translator; I want everyone on that damn planet to hear me."

"Roger; broadcast override protocol engaged, sir. Translator active. You may proceed."

"People of Corta, this is Admiral Suud Guurn of Emdali commanding Bet Fleet of the Pan-Galactic Coalition of the Great Spiral," he declared. "Both your planet and your entire system are currently blockaded. Surrender at once, and send the top four leaders of each nation to the coordinates I will designate, or face the consequences. Your continued marauding and depredations of the Great Spiral and its inhabitants will no longer be tolerated."

He drew a clawed finger across his throat in the universal 'kill it' gesture, and Kk'l'kn ended the communications feed, then sat silently for long moments; Suud knew that the communications officer, specifically chosen for this position, was using his telepathic abilities to 'read' the state of Corta's inhabitants. After several moments Kk'l'kn nodded to himself, then checked the comm console for messages before turning to Suud.

"They do not believe you, sir," he informed Suud. "As you expected."

"Fleet comm," Suud ordered.

"Fleet comm open, sir."

"All ships, stand by. Remain cloaked until I give the order."

Within seconds, red lights had all turned green.

"All hands, battle stations. *Sslthsd*, decloak," Suud told the helm. "Maximum shielding."

"Maximum shielding; decloaking, sir."

Fractions of a second later, Corta unleashed its entire planetary defensive armament upon the now-visible *Sslthsd*.

* * *

The Loteran ship, *Wuff Plugnor*, followed close behind the flagship *Sslthsd*. Its Hypothenemoid bridge crew stood ready for imminent action; Captain Voytak's executive assistant, Vulbin, waved his prehensile antennae in the air.

"But doesn't this plan put Admiral Suud at risk?" he worried. "He has set the *Sslthsd* as the bait..."

"Do not fear for the Admiral," Voytak noted, calm, settling his carapace more firmly into the command couch. "Suud Guurn is as wily as they come. Only his mentor, now known as Director Fox, is wilier. Did you get a look at the *Sslthsd* before we jumped into warp?"

"Yes..." Vulbin observed, uncertain.

"Did you note how very large it was?"

"Um, yes?"

"There's a reason for that, larva. The *Sslthsd* has the biggest damn force field generators the Admiral could manage to cram into it. And the power plants had to be big enough to drive it, the weapons, AND one of the hottest warp generators he could find. That ship will handle the entire combined defensive weaponry of Aleancë without blinking, then turn around and zap every defensive position it can find."

"Grubdrfrutz," Vulbin said blankly. "Oh! Forgive me, Captain!"

"Heh. Nothing to forgive, larva," Voytak chuckled. "Your carapace is barely hardened yet; I'd have been surprised if you had reacted any other way."

"Thank you, sir."

"At any rate, Admiral Guurn planned this from the moment he received the assignment from Lord Entiyti. He has nothing to fear, nor do you. Our admiral will be fine when this is all over. And given his plans, I expect we all will be. The Cortians, most probably not, however."

* * *

Green beams danced and scintillated about the *Sslthsd*, rising up from the planetary surface below.

But none reached the *Sslthsd*'s hull, expending their energies on her powerful force fields.

Several Cortian ships, orbiting their homeworld, likewise opened fire on the lone flagship, adding missiles to the energy beam weapons, but they were no more effective; all fell short of the ship's hull.

"Planet-wide comm, override protocol," an irritated Suud snapped.

"Go, sir."

"I am not foolish enough to come here in a spacecraft that is incapable of withstanding planetary-level weapons bombardment," he growled. "I will repeat my demand: Surrender at once and deliver your leaders, or we shall retaliate."

"Incoming message, Admiral."

"On audio."

"This is Tke, spokesbeing for Emperor Nda," the lone voice said, a haughty air behind it. "We do not recognize your authority, and your single ship does not impress us. Surrender and you will be taken captive. Refuse, and we will destroy your ship, and yourself along with it."

"You are welcome to try...again," Suud taunted. "We will in no wise surrender."

"Then you will be destroyed," Tke replied...

...And the planetary beam weapons, as well as all nearby Cortian ships, opened up once more.

* * *

But Suud had indeed chosen his ship well, and outfitted her with as many of the most powerful field generators the Coalition possessed as he could cram within her hull. More, he had taken another page from Franz Levy's book, routing a kind of circuit through the fields, so that the energies being expended upon them actually shunted through higher dimensions into a collector, thence into a kind of battery helping to power the field generators; the more the Cortians fired at the *Sslthsd*, the longer her force fields would last. There was entropy involved, of course; that was the way of the universe—only a fraction of the energies made it to the *Sslthsd*'s battery. But it was enough, and the technique still served its purpose: Their shields were not even stressed, even after fully five minutes of the attack.

"Admiral to Fleet," Suud murmured to Kk'l'kn, who nodded.

"Go, Admiral," came his reply.

"All ships, this is Suud. Target one or more of their beam weapons sites, or one of their ships, while they are firing, and stand by."

"All ships targeting and standing by, Suud," Kk'l'kn said moments later.

"Steady...steady," Suud muttered. "Wait for my order..."

Just then, the continuously-firing planetary beams stuttered, their vivid green paling, as the decidedly limited energy sources powering them ran low.

"ALL SHIPS—UNCLOAK AND FIRE AT WILL!" Suud shouted. "Target secondaries—dry-docks, manufacturing facilities, power plants, and military installations!"

* * *

Low Cortian orbit lit up with the unleashed energies of fully two hundred fifty vessels of war, now revealed in the Cortian system. Aurorae lit the planet from pole to pole, and spilled into the magnetosphere of the brown dwarf around which it orbited. Titanic detonations illuminated the planet's surface for hundreds of miles in all directions.

Three minutes later, all weapons barrages ceased, as all primary and secondary targets had been obliterated.

* * *

The aurorae remained for several hours, as the plasmas produced by the extreme energies slowly dissipated, draining away from Corta's magnetosphere into that of Orge. During this time, Fleet surveillance revealed rioting and uprisings across all continents.

Five hours after the crippling strike, several messages came up from Corta. None utilized standard communications protocols of any sort; all came from civilians. One came from a female Cortian. All contained the same message:

"We surrender unconditionally. We have our former leaders in custody, awaiting your instructions. You may take them prisoner or execute them, as you wish."

Suud studied the missives in silence for long minutes.

"Bring up the penal ships," he finally ordered. "Have the deposed Cortian leaders taken into custody at once. Prepare for standard interrogations. Have the Deltiri interrogators standing by."

"And the rest of the Fleet, sir?" Kk'l'kn asked. Suud pondered only briefly.

"Cloak and resume stealth mode," he decided. "They no doubt have more ships out there, somewhere. Eventually they have to return home."

"At once, sir."

Chapter 13

"...And we've taken care of the skull fracture," India told Echo. She was sitting beside his hospital bed in the medlab at Division One Headquarters, discussing Omega's condition, several days later. An IV with a certain familiar lavender solution ran into his arm. His legs were encased in lightweight, high-tech removable casts. "It was only a hairline fracture."

"But there's no sign of brain damage?" Echo verified.

"No."

"Well, that's good," he remarked, relieved.

"Mm. Yes and no," India hedged. "She's still having a few cognitive problems, Echo. But we don't know where they're coming from. If we knew, we could always resort to the same regeneration bath we used after the Cortians burned her nearly to death in their ion drive. But we can't fix it if we don't know what's wrong."

"Oh," Echo replied, deflating a bit. *Well, shit. That's exactly what Meg said, back on the protoplanet, dammit. Exactly what she was afraid of.* "Where is she now?" he wondered.

"Tests."

Echo frowned.

"It's all right, Echo," India soothed. "We'll get her back to normal. We just need to find out what's causing the problem. We'll run some tests, put her under observation for a while..."

"No."

"What?" India asked, caught off guard.

"How long before I'm on my feet?" Echo asked, ignoring the question.

"Mm...late tomorrow. Damn, but I wish we'd had this stuff for Romeo's multiple fracture! Anyway, the bones in your legs will be completely knit back by then, and the laceration from the compound fracture fully closed up, though us medics would like to see you keep a cane handy for a few days, to minimize stress on those legs. Why?"

"Get Fox in here when he can," Echo told India. "Tell the medics they have until I'm released tomorrow to get as much data as they can to find out what's wrong with Meg."

"But, Echo!" India protested. "It's not that simple..."

"Tomorrow," Echo said firmly. "Where are they bunking her?"

"The observation room."

"No. Put her in a regular room."

"Echo, there aren't any regular rooms available. The battle with the Cortians filled up the lab. Half of Alpha Line is in here, and a whole bunch of field agents from other departments, too. Thank God we didn't actually lose anybody in the department; Zebra says it's almost as bad as it was during the Klydonian invasion. And we DID lose people, elsewhere in the Division. One entire ship blew up, the one from Va'du'sha'ā, with all hands lost!"

"Aw, damn."

"Yeah. Besides, Meg needs to be observed—"

"No. Move another bed in here, then."

"Echo, I really don't think—"

"India," Echo said quietly, "I have my reasons. And I will pull rank if I have to. You know I don't like to do that, but..."

The two Agents stared at each other for long moments, then India capitulated with a nod.

"All right. I'll go get Fox."

* * *

"Look, Fox," Echo explained, once that worthy had managed to break away from the more administrative aspects of mopping up after a space battle, "I'm not going to tell you all that. You could give me a direct order, and I still wouldn't do it. First off, I don't KNOW exactly what happened. We talked about it a couple times while we were marooned. The first time she didn't say much, 'cause the Cortians were overhead and she was already agitated and upset; the second, we were trying to fill the time while the ship died around us and we waited for rescue, so she told me a smidgen more... not a whole lot, because we were in a damn depressing situation, and, well, that was about the time we decided to start swapping funny stories, I think, just for the morale boost. But what little she told me..."

He shook his head, then sighed, and somehow Fox didn't think it was in regret for keeping mum. Echo continued.

"I'm sorry, Fox, but she said it in confidence, and I'm not comfortable breaching that confidence, even with you—at least until she gives me

295

permission, which she hasn't, yet—for ANYBODY. And Meg herself is just not ready to talk about it. She may never be, to tell the truth, and I can respect that. It's still just too damn painful even to remember, from what I could gather from her reactions to my questioning—which, when I started realizing just how bad it had been, I tried to keep...discreet and, and...gentle, I guess you could say. Best I could, at least. You know what I mean: Not pressing her, giving her an out so she didn't have to answer, glossing over things, stuff like that." Echo sighed again, and raked a hand through his hair. "But I do know she feels really strongly about never again being in a situation where she feels like a prisoner being experimented on."

"But Echo," Fox expostulated as he sat in a visitor's chair beside the bed, "it's for her own good. The medics are trying to help her. And she's not a prisoner."

"I didn't say she was. I said she FELT like one. Okay Fox, I think I'm gonna tell you this much, 'cause I'm starting to decide maybe you need a general picture. That way, you can ensure nobody puts a foot in what sounds to me like a damn deep pile of shit, buried in Meg's psyche." Echo jabbed an index finger at the door of his hospital room, and Fox recognized he meant the medical team caring for Omega. "I want your help, here. I need your support and backing on this. For Meg's sake."

"All right, Echo, that's fair," Fox agreed, considering the matter. "I understand. And I'll ensure Zebra gets a heads-up, if you want me to. But discreetly, without revealing Omega's deepest secrets."

"Good, an' yeah, that's exactly what I want. Okay." Echo nodded, seeming satisfied.

"So tell me, zun. Give me that general picture."

"You, of all people, aren't gonna like it."

"Oh no. You don't mean..."

"Uh-huh. She compared her kidnapping and 'enhancement' as a child to being in a concentration camp under Joseph Mengele. AND she termed it a...vivisection. While conscious. NO anesthetic. He took her apart and put her back together! And she FELT it all, Fox!" Echo's face had contorted with sympathetic pain.

* * *

"Damn." Even Fox's face registered mild shock. "Oy. I wondered, even suspected...but I didn't expect it to be THAT bad. Concentration camp

296

victim, in spades, complete with sadistic experimentation...but SHE survived it..."

"Exactly. And now has to live with the memories of it."

"I see. You know, this lends a whole new face to how she was able to hold up after the Cortians toasted her."

"Yeah, it really does, now you mention it," Echo realized. "And she actually referenced that, herself—she thinks Slug tweaked her so as to be able to 'not go crazy,' as she put it."

"Yes, and I have considered—wondered—that myself, a few times. I know I have discussed it with Zz'r'p, and may have mentioned it to you."

"Yeah. But Fox, 'not going crazy' doesn't equate to 'not caring.' So stop and think a minute. Can you imagine what kind of mental scars she's got, where none of us can see?"

"And she's probably one of the most...sensitive...agents I have." Fox nodded. "Omega's tough because she has to be, to do the things she has determined she will do, not because it's her nature. Yes. I'm beginning to see the problem."

"I promised her, Fox," Echo told the Director, as earnest as he knew how to be. "She's trusting me to take care of her, not to let her be a 'lab rat'—to use her phrasing. And I swore I'd do it. You KNOW me, Fox—I don't go back on my word. Not to anyone. And above all, not to her."

* * *

"Yes, especially given how you feel; all right, I can understand that, and agree with it," Fox said, sympathetic; he had come to realize, in recent weeks, just how much this particular department chief cared for his partner.

More, the Director considered it a potentially excellent match, with largely positive ramifications for the Alpha One team, and was in Echo's corner. The fact that Fox strongly suspected Omega of having similar feelings for Echo—feelings that she was afraid of admitting, BECAUSE OF what had been done to her—only encouraged the Director to support the notion.

Especially since, until Earth is ready to know about the galactic government, we're essentially a society apart from the rest, he thought, *with no option but to choose our loved ones from within our own ranks...or bring them into those ranks, if we can.*

"What are you going to do, alter khaver?" Fox asked then, keeping his voice gentle.

Echo sighed.

"For starters, I want her out of the observing room. I get that there's no more rooms, because of the battle, so...bring another bed in here and put her here with me."

"A 'co-ed' hospital room?!"

"C'mon, Fox," Echo remonstrated. "After what we've just been through? Busted up, bedding down on the floor of the flight deck, trying our damnedest to doctor each other enough to stay alive, huddled together for warmth? Do you really think sharing a hospital room is gonna faze either of us, at this point?" Echo jabbed a finger at the wall, where a bundle of white cloth draped, tied back. "We've got curtains, Boss, if the docs have to strip one of us or something. Besides, I think it might help her morale, which I'm sure is in the toilet, about now."

"I...suppose so. All right. I'll contact Zebra and Zarnix, and see that it happens. What else?"

"The medics have until I'm released tomorrow to get as much data on Meg as they can," Echo told him. "If they've figured out how to fix the problem, fine. Go to it, and more power to 'em. If not, I'm taking Meg and leaving."

"There's a problem with that plan, old friend," Fox reminded him. "We could set the two of you up in a new life—together, I presume," and Echo looked at him impassively without answering, "if we could brain-bleach Omega. But the same 'enhancements' that made her extract your promise made her immune to the brain bleacher."

"I know. I thought of that." Echo nodded. "It won't be necessary—any of it—if I just take her to the Ranch."

* * *

"Aha, I see now," Fox remarked, eyebrows shooting up in understanding. "Not a retirement—"

"Right. Reassignment to heading up a field station together. Meg grew up on a farm, and lived in Texas for several years, enjoying it, from all she's said to me. She should adapt fine. And if, later on, the medics figure something out..."

"Yes! That will work. I'll start the paperwork, just in case. Do you have a recommendation for your replacements as Alpha Line's leaders, as if I didn't know?" Fox asked. *Didn't we just go through this a couple weeks ago?* the Director pondered, stifling a sigh. *And here it is, back again. Damn it all to hell. And back. Twice.*

Echo smiled then, and Fox thought he detected more than a hint of regret in the other man's expression at the thought of replacement.

"Romeo and India, of course," Echo said.

"Of course." Fox didn't even try to stifle that sigh. "I'll get the paperwork ready for that, too."

"Okay, Fox. Listen...thanks."

"I will miss you both, zun."

"I know. The feeling is mutual...on both sides of Alpha One," Echo said, then hesitated. "Or, well, what used to be Alpha One..."

"Don't cross that bridge quite yet, zun. We can always hope. There's still a little time left. Let's wait and see."

* * *

A silent Omega, clad in a black medical jumpsuit, followed the medic into the hospital room and climbed into the second bed, across from Echo, which had been moved into the room shortly after Fox's departure, earlier. She stretched out on her back and stared bleakly at the ceiling as the medic pulled the covers up over her, then departed. Echo, who had been sitting up in bed watching the television, immediately grabbed the remote and muted the TV before turning to his partner.

"Meg?" Echo queried, concerned.

Wordlessly she turned her head to look at him. The despondent sapphire gaze told him all he needed to know...about the continued lack of a diagnosis, about her mental state, her emotional state, her overall outlook. *And none of it is good,* he thought. *Damn.*

"How are you making it, baby?" he continued, cocking his head to one side, trying to evoke the sympathy he felt in his expression and gestures, so she could see it.

Omega shrugged, turning her attention back to the ceiling.

"Are the acid burns healing okay?"

Omega held up her hands to show him undamaged palms and fingertips.

"Good. How about the shoulders?"

She nodded and gave him a thumbs-up, but still said nothing.

299

Echo was silent for a bit, considering his morose partner, and pondering how to word what he intended to tell her. Then he spoke again.

"Meg—I get back on my feet tomorrow. I'll have to use a cane for a few days, but I'll be mobile again."

"Oh—that's good," she murmured finally, turning to look at him. She reached for the bed controls and elevated the head in order to converse with him easier. "You really hated not being able to get up and go on your own."

"Well, yeah, but I had a good set of substitute 'Legs'," he teased. "Listen, Meg...I know you're pretty miserable..."

"I hate it," Omega said in a low voice. "They tried to put me in that room. Well, they DID, until India came in and told them you said no."

"I'm sorry. I didn't know they'd bunked you there, baby, I swear. I only just came out of regen last night, and was too groggy to..."

"Nah, it's okay, Ace. I was keepin' up with you," Omega averred. "I knew you were out of it, an' that you were healin' good. They actually took you out early, I think, 'cause they had some idea that they wanted to try with the IV meds, an' not keepin' you under so long that you'd lose muscle tone an' junk. 'Cause they just wanted the bones to knit back fast, not to rebuild half a charcoal briquette, like they hadda do with me."

"How long was I in?"

"Division day an' a half, about," Omega replied, waggling a hand in the air to invoke an approximation. "They said you were healin' up great. Me, on the other hand? Not so much. They poked and prodded at me all day today, an' yesterday, an' the day before that, and they still don't know what's wrong."

"Damn. Well, can you put up with it until I get out of here tomorrow?" Echo asked.

"Why?"

"If they can figure out what's wrong, they can patch you up. If not, I'll come get you tomorrow and—we'll leave."

"The medlab?" she asked, confused.

"New York," Echo clarified.

"Won't Fox stop—?"

"I've already talked to Fox, and I've cleared it with him. He understands. He's setting it up now, just in case."

"Where will you take me?" Omega's voice was very quiet. Her face had paled.

"Some place I think you'll like." Echo smiled, trying his best to be encouraging. *What's wrong?* he thought, perturbed. *That should be perking her up like a well-watered flower.*

"Then what will you do?" Omega asked, turning her attention back to the ceiling without reacting to his expression.

"What do you mean?" Echo responded, puzzled, both at her question and at her downcast responses.

"Will Fox find you a new partner?"

"Why do I need a new partner?"

Omega's eyes shot back to Echo's face.

"You...you're not...I'm not...?" she stammered.

Suddenly Echo understood.

"Aw, Meg. You thought I was going to take you away somewhere, then leave you there and come back here?"

"Well, you are the top Agent, an' Fox's suc-successor, and—"

"Omega," Echo quieted her, and she blinked at his unaccustomedly-formal address, "I would never abandon a friend who needed me. Let alone the best and most devoted friend I've ever had in my life."

Omega flushed, smiling slightly, before a confused look crossed her face.

"Wait. Then...we're leaving the Agency?"

"No. We're going to run an Agency field station."

"What?"

"We'll be able to keep doing 'stuff' together, as you put it. We'll be able to keep working with aliens. We'll even be able to take space flights occasionally," Echo told her. "How does that sound?"

Omega's face suddenly lit up with a shy smile. *Finally,* he thought, relieved.

"It sounds good to me, Echo," she said, and he smiled back at her. "Are you sure, though, Ace? It will be...quieter...than what you're used to..." She shrugged. "Than what WE'RE used to."

"I'm sure, Meg. Stick it out until tomorrow afternoon with the medics. Then, one way or another, it'll be over. I promise you, it'll be over."

* * *

The medics woke Omega deliberately, and Echo incidentally, quite early the next morning when they came to take Omega for yet more tests. She sighed softly and scootched out of bed. Echo motioned her over to his bedside.

"Meg, they're trying to help you," he told her. The medics nodded silently in agreement.

"I know, Echo, I know. And it's never really bugged me THAT much before, whenever Zebra would give me my checkup every year. I mean...it bothered me, because I always had all of these tests where they poked me inside and out, and it took all day, and all that. But this...is different. A LOT different. There's a problem, they dunno what it is, and...well, it's just..." Omega shrugged.

"It reminds you too much of the kidnapping when you were a kid, doesn't it?"

Omega studied the floor intently, as Echo and the medics watched in silence.

"Yeah," she finally confessed, without looking up. "It's all the same kinds of pokin' and proddin' I got before Slug...set to work on me. An' to him, all I was, was a lab rat. I know these guys don't really mean it like that, but..." She sighed; the dejection was obvious. "I can't help it. I wish I could forget it all, but...I can't. It just...brings it all up again."

Echo glanced past her at the medics, who were casting startled, puzzled glances at each other.

"How about it, guys?" Echo asked them. "Ease up on the professional curiosity and improve the bedside manner for my bestest buddy here, okay?"

"Fair enough," the chief shift medic, whom Echo didn't recognize, said. "We'll try to be a little more considerate, Omega. We didn't mean to open old wounds."

"It's not your fault," she said with another sigh. "There's only so many ways you can do what India calls 'eval tests.' Just...help me get through this, all right?"

"How can we do that?" one of the other physicians asked. "What do you need us to do different?"

"Um, well, maybe don't be so distant?" Omega suggested. "Crack a joke with me once in a while. 'Splain what you're trying to do, what the test is supposed to tell you. Just...don't ignore me while you're testin' me. That's what Slug did. I think 'Shut up' was his favorite phrase, see."

"Ohhh, damn," the third physician muttered. "Guys, we been doin' this all wrong, for her."

"Maybe we can fix that," the second medic remarked.

"That'd be kinda nice," Omega said, wistful. "R'member, I was a scientist too, so, um, maybe sorta just treat me like one o' the gang? So okay, I can't think good now, but maybe you can still act like I can, I dunno. Tellin' me what you're doin' an' why is a good start, I s'pose."

"You've got it," the chief shift medic said, offering a slight, friendly smile. "All of it, to the best of our ability. C'mon, let's go see if we can figure out how to patch you up."

* * *

Romeo came by with a titanium cane and a Suit for Echo later that day, and stuck around to help the still-stiff Agent prepare to leave the med-lab. Romeo handed Echo a battered duffel bag as he finished dressing.

"What's this?" Echo asked, opening the bag and looking inside.

"Your gear from the *Trojan Horse*," Romeo replied, as Echo pulled out a worn, black leather-bound book, then sat down heavily. "Echo? Sumthin' wrong?"

"No, hot shot, everything is...fine now. Or it will be, some kinda way. How's Meg? Have you or India heard anything? She hasn't been back to the room since the docs took her out, early this morning." Echo replaced the Bible in the gear bag.

"India says they don't know any more than they did."

"You've talked to her recently?"

"Yeah. She gave me your cane, like maybe ten, fifteen minutes ago. Said to tell you she'd already adjusted it to your height an' all."

"Oh. Tell her thanks, okay?"

"Will do, man. But naw, they ain't got Meg's problem figured."

"All right." Echo sighed. "I was kinda hopin' they'd get it worked out in time. Oh well. You got Meg's stuff?"

"No. India was takin' it to her. Said to tell you they'd meet us in Fox's office."

"Okay. Let's go."

"Echo? What's goin' on?"

"You'll find out soon enough, junior."

* * *

The distaff members of Alpha One and -Two were waiting with Fox in the Director's office when Romeo and Echo arrived. Echo was taking it slowly, gingerly testing out his legs and leaning on his cane as he went, but generally moving relatively well.

"Hey, pretty lady," Romeo greeted Omega as he moved to India's side. "How's it goin'?"

"Hi, Romeo," Omega said, subdued. "It...goes."

"Hi, Meg," Echo murmured. "Ready?"

"Hi, Echo." Omega's face started to crumple, and she looked away. "I'm sorry. I'm so sorry."

"For what?"

"You should stay here. Let me go, and you stay here."

"Why?"

"You belong here. You're the department chief. Fox needs you," Omega said, and Romeo and India listened, open-mouthed in shocked surprise, to the conversation. An impassive Fox watched, silent.

"You want to break up the team, Meg?" Echo asked, his voice quiet. "I thought we were in this for the long haul, pal."

"No, Echo, I don't," Omega said, obviously struggling to stay in control. "But I didn't want the a-alien genes stuck in me, either. I didn't want my family killed by Slug. I didn't want to smash my head against the console. I'm used to not getting what I want..."

"Wait jus' a damn minute, here," Romeo broke in. "You two are talkin' like you're leaving."

"They are," Fox answered for Alpha One.

"What?!" India exclaimed, as Romeo's jaw dropped. "Why?"

"So Omega won't feel like a prisoner of the medlab," Fox replied. "And so she'll feel useful, not pitied."

"I don't get it," Romeo said, confused. "Th' medics are just tryin' ta help 'er."

"Romeo, you don't know what it's like to be ex-experimented on," Omega said in a low voice, and the office fell silent. "Never again."

"L'olam lo 'od, tekhter," Fox declared, quiet but firm. "If anyone here understands the meaning of those words, I do, Omega. Never again. And because I do understand, along with Echo, I will do my best to help you keep that vow."

* * *

They were all silent for a long moment.

"Come on, Meg," Echo finally said. "It's already settled. Let's go."

"I'll see your things get sent on," Fox told the former Alpha One team, before Omega could respond.

"Thanks, Fox. Romeo, India," Echo said, holding out his hand, "we'll see you one of these days, Meg and me."

"...Echo, man," Romeo said blankly, staring at the outstretched hand. Finally he took the hand and shook it. India grasped it in turn, then Alpha Two hugged Omega. "Stay cool, pretty lady," Romeo told her, his voice wobbly.

"Take it easy, girlfriend," India whispered. Omega could only nod; her throat was choked with unshed tears.

"Ready?" Echo put his free arm across his partner's shoulders, and she nodded. "All right. Let's head downstairs to Grand Central Station. There's a maglev waiting for us."

"...Okay," Omega murmured.

* * *

The five Agents exited the Director's office. As the word spread rapidly, various aliens and members of Alpha Line straggled into the Core, in order to tell their friends and leaders goodbye. Echo turned to Romeo and India, jerking his head at the assembled Alpha Line, as the startled and uncertain department struggled to set itself in something approximating ranks, when half their number was still in the medlab.

"Take good care of 'em, guys," the former department chief noted.

"Us?!" India exclaimed.

"Yep. You."

"Oh, maaan..." Romeo moaned. "We are SO not ready for that job."

"Sure you are, Romeo. You'll do fine," Echo said. "Fox will help, 'til you get used to it."

"NO, Ace!" Omega exclaimed then. "We can't do this. *I* can't do this. NO. Just...no. You've gotta stay here."

"Why?"

"'Cause this is where you wanna be. It's where you're s'posed to be.

305

You know it, and I know it. I'm just sorry I can't help you with it any more." She hung her head. "But if you get, um, a new partner, it'll be okay. You can keep doin' it—you can keep runnin' Alpha Line, an' keep bein' Alpha One."

"Hold on a minute, here. Guys," Echo addressed the others, "can y'all give us a few minutes alone? Meg and I need to have a private chat. There's some things she doesn't understand. Things I never got around to telling her, that she needs to know about, now."

"Sure thing, Echo," India murmured, waving the others away, and giving the pair plenty of elbow room to talk.

* * *

When everyone except himself and his partner had moved out of earshot, Echo turned to Omega, ensuring his back was to their potential audience; several Agents, including Fox and Alpha Two, were quite skilled at lip-reading. *Not that I expect 'em to do it,* he considered. *But accidentally? Sure. And I want this talk to be just me an' Meg.*

"Look, baby, it's like this," he explained. "Alpha One—or, well, at least this partnership—is us. You and me."

"Well, it's the Alpha Line chief an' his, um, partner."

"No, it isn't," Echo explained, earnest. "I realized something early on, babe. I realized you and me, we've got something special in the way of a partnership. Oh, sure, we have our disagreements an' shit, but not even Romeo and India have a partnership with the capabilities you and I have together, and they're going spousal with it."

"Ooo. They're gettin' married? Oh, wait, they can't do that yet..."

"Right, they can't, not until the Council sees fit to approve the addendum to our charter. But it turns out that they filed the paperwork for what's called a 'life partnership' right after you and I left to take Doron home. Once that goes through, that makes 'em pretty much as good as, at least within the Agency. My point is, Meg, Alpha One has been specifically defined as you and me. Omega and Echo. Echo and Omega. Not one or the other, but BOTH."

"But you...how...?" She blinked at him, startled and confused. "Is it a life thingie, too? I didn't..."

"No, it's not; not unless we ever decide we want it to be. But back when you left to go find yourself—after we found out about Slug's programming, well. It hit me upside the head, pretty hard, that I'd had the perfect partner, at least for me, right beside me...and I had to let her go. We've got the ideal partnership, you and me. So I went to Fox and I told him so. He tried to talk me out of it, tried to set me up to train another partner, because frankly, nobody expected you to come back..."

"Aw." Omega hung her head. "But you didn't. Get a new, um, partner, I mean."

"No, I didn't. Because that was when I told him that I didn't want another partner, nobody could measure up to you after that, and that was my final word on the subject. If you didn't come back, Alpha One as an entity, a team, would cease to exist, and I'd take a desk job, running the department." He paused, and gave her a slight smile. "And you, of all people, know how stubborn I can be. Finally Fox gave in, 'cause there was no convincing me otherwise."

Omega stared up at him, wide-eyed. "You...you mean..."

"Exactly. So Fox and I put together some special paperwork, and created the first in a new category of partnerships—so far, the ONLY one in that category. From that day on, Alpha One has been defined as consisting of two people, and two people only: you and me. No substitutes, and no replacements." He took her gently by the shoulders. "Stop and think, baby: If anything happened to me, would YOU want to get another partner?"

"No." Her face closed, crumpling slightly, and a wash of warmth went through him.

Wow. The very idea hurt her. Maybe, if I take it slow and give her plenty of time to adapt, he thought, *we might actually manage that life partnership now. Damn if this is the way I wanted it to happen. But she's still 'my Meg,' even if certain mental abilities have gone away.*

"Okay, then. So would you expect me to feel any differently?" he asked her.

"I...I guess not," she admitted. "An'...an' you already were ready t' do it that time."

"Right. And this time, I won't be going to a desk job. We'll still be doing real, good work for the Agency, Meg, field work, not paperwork. Not that paperwork is bad; it has to be done, it's just...not us, to do nothing but. So we'll be doing another kind of field work. It'll be different, sure, but it's good, legitimate work all the same."

"But...but," Omega tried, "you could still do the Alpha Line stuff,

Ace."

"How?"

"We...could stay here, an', an' you could do the Alpha Line stuff, an' I'll..."

"Stay cooped up in the little room with the window all the time?" he finished for her. "The one that you hate? Do you really think I'd condemn you to that, baby—condemn you to life as a subject in the medlab, the best buddy I think I've ever had in my life—just in order to stay on as a department chief? Do you think I'm the sort of person to covet position and power?"

"No." She scrunched her lips together, and Echo recognized it as a hidden smile.

Good, he thought. *Even with the messed-up head, she knows me better than that.*

"Okay, then," he continued. "We follow my plan, the one I been workin' on for a little bit now, and that way, we'll be together, and we'll both be happy."

"Not as happy as when we was, um, were, Alpha One."

"Maybe, maybe not," Echo admitted. "But happier than one of us sittin' in an office pushing paper, and the other cooped up in an observation room like a lab rat."

"Yeah..."

"So do you trust me to have worked something out?"

"Yeah, Ace," Omega agreed, nodding. "I always trust you. You know that." Her expression finally relaxed, and she almost smiled. Almost.

"All right. Let's do this."

"...Okay."

* * *

The former Alpha One team rejoined their companions. Slowly the five worked their way through the Core toward the elevator, as other agents from different departments came up to make their farewells to Echo and Omega, including Madrid of the Weapons Development and Testing department, and Sugar from Diplomacy. The gauntlet of friends and colleagues was a painful one, though in an emotional sense, rather than physical.

However, just as they reached the elevator, it opened, disgorging a frantic medic with a special medscanner.

"THERE you are! Thank God I caught you before you left!" Quickly, the medic ran the scanner over Omega as a startled Meg stood there blinking, then activated a cell phone. "That's an affirmative, Zebra! Tell Zarnix we got a positive!!" She closed the connection, and exclaimed, "We got it! WE GOT IT! We know what's happening to Omega!"

* * *

"...It's that same concept of mental circuit-breakers you guys came up with after the original Cortian attack, Echo," Zebra explained.

Both Zebra and Zarnix had met Fox, Alpha One, and Alpha Two in the small 'Director's conference room' just off the Core, and opposite the Alpha Line Room. Across the way, in the Alpha Line Room itself, clustered as many of that department's members as could get there, waiting for word on their leadership. The rest, down in the medlab, were linked in via cell phone...those that were conscious enough to do so.

"Okay," Echo said, waiting for more.

"...Omega's circuit-breakers popped, Echo. All of 'em," Zebra declared.

"Every last blessed one, as nearly as we can determine," Zarnix added in a murmur. "Absolutely fascinating."

"Huh?" Romeo said.

"Explain, you two," Fox commanded.

"Omega's injuries to that uniquely-wired brain of hers caused it to gradually—or suddenly, depending on conditions—shut down higher functions as a protective measure against permanent damage," Zebra elaborated. "The more stress to the physical, organic brain structure, the more high-level function was reduced."

"Oh! That's why, when Meg was rested and kicked back, not worrying..." Echo began.

"She was probably able to think fairly normally," Zebra finished for him, and Echo nodded. "She had a helluva concussion, and a hairline skull fracture, but in an ordinary, regular human, the same injuries wouldn't have produced the same kinds of dramatic effects."

"It's because of the way her brain has been restructured," Zarnix added. Echo and Omega both winced slightly at the choice of words the two medics used.

"Would y'all mind talkin' like I'm in th' room?" Omega grumbled.

"Just because I can't think like I usually do doesn't mean I'm not here, or can't understand."

Both of the medics flushed, embarrassed.

"Damn. I'm so sorry, Omega, honey," Zebra apologized, laying a gentle hand on the other woman's shoulder, before pulling her into a brief hug. "We got way the hell too clinical, I guess. It's been a hard job, trying to understand what happened to you, and we've both been face-down in galactic neurological research, in addition to studying all the test results. You, of all people here, know how that has a tendency to make your thinking go dry as dust!"

"Yeah, I do," Omega admitted. "Okay. 'Pology accepted. Go 'head."

"All right," the physician went on. "So basically, to continue and extend that whole electronic analogy, the bump on the head knocked some wires loose and caused, um...a short, I guess. Autonomic functions detected it and started shutting down nonessential activities to prevent...overheating." Zebra shrugged.

"And as conditions deteriorated in your spacecraft," Zarnix added, "more and more 'circuit breakers' began to trip, as Omega's nervous system—her whole body—had to operate with fewer and fewer resources. Echo, you became aware of your own mental deterioration as the atmosphere grew bad, correct?"

"Yeah, I did," Echo confirmed. "But my system is apparently a lot less sensitive to those kinds of stresses than Meg's is."

"Well, at least when there's already a brain injury," Zebra corrected. "Maybe not so much otherwise; she's always seemed pretty damn tough and resilient, to me. But in any case, based on your reaction, you can imagine what it was doing to her."

"Okay, I get it. And it sounds like you've explained what happened. But in my mind, the important question is this: is she permanently...'shorted out'?" Echo asked, unable to hide his worry...and in the circumstances, not trying that hard to hide it.

"No," Zebra and Zarnix answered in unison. Zebra turned to Omega. "You need rest, honey, mostly physically; and plenty of time for the concussion to heal. Echo told us about your being able to temporarily override his pain impulses—albeit at the cost of higher functions—as well as your 'dream' detailing his original partner; I'd guess that 'short circuit' caused you to pick up random memories from Echo during REM sleep and incorporate them into your dream. Mental static. Or you may have done some of that 'overlapping' shit like you did before the Cortian arrival, and during Echo's emergency trip to Doron's homeworld; either way, it amounts to the same thing. You may find that happening off and on until you heal, but I don't think it's anything to worry about."

"So Meg will be back to normal soon?" Echo asked, hopeful.

"Absolutely," the female medic responded with a reassuring smile. "With a little TLC from her close friends—her family, as Fox and I have taken to calling it—and some rest, Omega should be fine in a few more days. You two don't need to go anywhere. I'd lay money that, in a week's time, you'll both be slave-driving Alpha Line as hard as ever." Zebra smiled. "Do you concur, Zarnix?"

"I do, Zebra," the alien chief medic replied. "Though I suspect it may take a bit longer than a week. But it will happen! I prescribe plenty of protein, no jarring motions to the head, nothing to increase intracranial pressures, and lots of rest."

"Rest?!" Omega almost wailed. "I have to rest?! You've gotta be kidding! I'm stir-crazy already!"

"Looks like the tables have turned, Legs." Echo grinned.

"Don't think you can just pick up and go, either, Echo," Zarnix warned. "You may be able to walk around now, but those legs of yours are not nearly ready for a marathon yet. Plus, based on Omega's debrief and your blood tests, you're recovering from a VERY severe infection—you are fortunate you still have that leg. If it were not for Omega's skill and determination, you probably wouldn't, and you might not even be alive. AND your rotator cuff is still healing from microsurgery, so make sure you use the cane in the OTHER arm. Don't forget, or I expect you'll regret it immediately, if not sooner! So...yes. You need rest, too. And plenty of it."

"Hah!" Omega exclaimed, grinning devilishly; Echo looked irked.

"It could've been a lot worse, Echo," India offered in her soft voice. "Considering the condition she was in, in my professional opinion Omega did a damn good job of taking care of you. And vice versa, I should add. Her acid burns in particular were nasty. But you really could have lost a leg—even your life—if you'd developed sepsis. See, if gangrene had set up in that compound fracture before you were rescued, then gone into septicemia—or hell, even just the original infection had gotten into your bloodstream—you wouldn't have made it to rescue. And from what I saw, it probably would have, without Meg caring for you. Just take it easy for a few days, and be thankful."

"Yeah," Romeo agreed. "Damn, dude, y'all CRASHED. Hard! And you're still alive to talk about it."

Echo jammed his hands into his trouser pockets and compressed his lips thoughtfully; Omega stared into space, contemplating things unseen. Then they both nodded.

"Fair enough," Echo said quietly.

"Yeah," Omega murmured.

"Excellent," Zebra averred. "Proper perspective has been achieved."

"Indeed," Zarnix agreed.

"I'll place Alpha One on indefinite sick leave, Echo," Fox said. "That okay with you?"

"Sure, Fox, whatever you think," Echo conceded. "Um, actually, you should probably be asking Alpha Two..."

"Naw, man," Romeo declared. "Me 'n' India talked with Fox about that while you an' Meg were talkin' in private. He wasn't gonna put the paperwork through until we all saw y'all off on the maglev, and that suited us fine. In fact, it's what we 'uz gonna tell 'im to do, if he hadn't already had th' idea first."

"What Romeo is saying, guys," India elaborated, "is that the transfer of leadership never went through. Alpha One still holds the management of Alpha Line, and that's the way we like it."

"So you...an' we," Omega murmured, trying to wrap her mind around it, "Echo an' me are still...?"

"That's right, Omega," Fox concurred. "Echo is still the department chief, and you are still the assistant chief. To be honest, I think everyone is happy about that...ESPECIALLY Alpha Two."

"Damn straight, skippy," Romeo affirmed. "One of the things I learned while y'all were gone: I ain't near ready f'r that job yet, an' I know it. One 'a these days, maybe. But not any time soon."

"Exactly," India agreed. "And you already know I don't WANT to be in the chain of command, so it's all good."

"Thanks, y'all," Omega breathed in gratitude.

Echo glanced at each face, opened his mouth to speak, closed it again, swallowed hard, then dropped his gaze to the floor, remaining silent. Omega laid a gentle hand on his arm, and he shot her a brief, warm glance, but still said nothing. The others, including Zebra and Zarnix, maintained a respectful silence, recognizing that Alpha Line's chief was too deeply moved to speak.

After a few moments to gather himself, Echo merely jabbed his thumb at his partner, then nodded. The others were easily able to interpret the message: *What she said.* Everyone in the room—except Echo—smiled; Echo pressed his lips together and kept his gaze down.

"Wanna go home now, Ace?" Omega asked her partner in a soft voice, after a few moments.

"Yeah, that sounds good, baby," he agreed, voice only marginally rough. "It'll be nice to sleep in my own bed for a change. The deck of a spacecraft gets kinda hard after a while. And awful damn cold."

"Amen to that," Omega avouched.

* * *

After Alpha One's departure, India addressed the chief and assistant chief of Medical.

"You guys saw their debrief items about the shipboard medikits, right?"

"Yes, India, we did," Zarnix confirmed.

"And so I had a kit yanked from a similar starship out of Penn Station," Zebra noted, "and brought straight to us, so we could take a look. Echo and Omega are damn right—those medikits need reworking."

"What do you mean, bubeleh?" Fox wondered.

"Just that they had what Echo termed 'a crap-ton' of different pharmaceuticals," Zarnix explained, "but not a whole lot of any one thing."

"When it should be a limited number of pharmaceuticals with wide-spectrum usage, and a crap-ton of those," Zebra finished. "The exact inverse of what's actually in there. I've already put in recommendations with Ship's Stowage to increase the pharmaceutical supplies on the spacecraft, especially any that Alpha Line are using. And I'm working out exactly what the inventory needs to be."

"'A honkin' big bottle of Rejuvic,' as Omega put it, for one," Zarnix noted.

"Yeah," Zebra agreed.

"That works, then," Fox decided.

"Guys, y'all want us t' go over t' the Alpha Line Room an' tell 'em what's goin' down?" Romeo wondered. "Or do you wanna tell 'em, Fox?"

"Why don't we three go over together," Fox suggested, "and let Zarnix and Zebra get back to the medlab? I'm sure the other physicians will welcome their assistance with the other patients, now that Alpha One is squared away."

"Oh, we neglected no one, Fox," Zarnix replied. "But yes, we do need to get back."

"Then let's all head out, and spread the good news," Fox decided.

* * *

Echo was still learning to negotiate with a cane on his newly-healed legs, so his progress was slow as Alpha One headed across the Core toward the corridor to the agents' quarters. Omega hung back with him, choosing to walk at his side and prepared to offer assistance if it should be needed.

Consequently they were just reaching the archway into the corridor when the cheer went up from the Alpha Line Room.

Startled, they both spun; Echo's shin tweaked, and he staggered for a moment, but Omega steadied him quickly.

Inside, the Alpha Line Agents could be seen, leaping up, whooping and yelling in delight. Romeo stood at the front of the room, India beside him, both beaming from ear to ear. Behind them, Fox stood silent, arms folded, lips compressed to hide the smile. He glanced out the door and spotted Alpha One, raised an eyebrow, and shot them a thumbs-up.

"I think they're happy we're not goin' anywhere, Ace," Omega murmured.

"Sure sounds like it," Echo concurred. "Damn, what a racket." Then he chuckled. "Well, that's what family's all about, I guess."

"Yup," Omega agreed. "C'mon, Echo. Let's go home."

"I am so there, baby."

"Not yet, you ain't. We got a long way to go yet."

"Sorry." Echo huffed.

"Aw. I'm just pickin' at ya, Ace."

"I know. I'm just frustrated, Meg."

"Want me to go find ya a desk chair an' push ya? Like I did on th'

Odyssey?"

"I dunno. From the sound of the noise comin' outta the Alpha Line Room, we might wind up in the middle of an office chair race or something."

"Yeah, no. Zebra would 'bout have a cow..."

Chapter 14

Nearly a Division week later, Omega, casually dressed in black jeans and t-shirt, long silver-blonde hair down and loose, slouched on the black leather sofa of her quarters. TV remote in hand, she was channel surfing, bored stiff, when she heard a knock behind her. She dropped her head back over the arm of the couch to stare whimsically, upside-down, at a similarly-clad Echo, standing in the 'back door' between their adjoining quarters. His cane was in hand, but he no longer had to lean on it; he only kept it handy because the medics were still insisting on it.

"Hi, Echo," she greeted him. "Come on in. What's up? Please tell me something's up," she begged with a grin.

"Hi, Meg. I've got something for you," Echo said, with the barest hint of a smile at his playful partner. He bent over and picked up something that leaned against his side of the wall, then stepped forward into her apartment, holding up the object. "A little present. What do you think?"

Omega audibly caught her breath, rolled over onto her stomach, and rested her chin on her forearm as she gazed at the large color image of the Orion Nebula that Echo had coaxed from their ship's sensor scan. It was matted and framed in jet black, the perfect mate to the telescopic image of the nebula that Omega had made with her rooftop observatory and given Echo, and which was still the only adornment on his walls. Her eyes grew distant as she lost herself in the depths of the image.

"...Echo to Omega. Do you copy? Come in, Omega."

"Oh!" she said, jerking herself back to Earth with a start. "Sorry about that."

"May I take it that you like it?"

"It's gorgeous!" Omega enthused. "Look over there at the end of that filament—a protostellar object. That big bright patch of hydrogen emission..."

"The astrophysicist is back." Echo grinned. "Welcome home."

"Thanks." She smiled. "Good to be back—to stay."

"By the way, speaking of which: All of the data we sent back on the system discoveries, to include all nomenclature, has been reviewed and approved at the Coalition level," Echo told her. "And the salvaging operations found our flora samples in the *Trojan Horse*'s stowage. They've been taken to the Pan-Galactic Coalition's Special Advisor for Exobiology on Aleancĕ for analysis. And the Special Advisor is twelve kinds of excited. It's saying this may open up new lines of inquiry about the other sentient plant races, like the Dendroids."

"Really?" Omega asked, delighted. "Cool."

"I thought you'd like that."

"What about the medals from Edeptis? Have we heard anything back from Geology yet?"

"Yeah, as a matter of fact, I got a message from Fox to contact 'em. Well, actually, they wanted to get you to contact 'em, but when they found out you were still on sick leave, they asked Fox for instructions 'cause they didn't want to bother you, and then he called me, and then I...well, you get that idea."

"Ha! Yeah, okay."

"So anyway, it turns out that our medals are in fact corundum—sapphire, specifically, like you figured. And there's more: both medals apparently came from the same crystal, which was honkin' big. Corundums are real long, hexagonal columns, right?"

"Pretty much, yeah. They're in the hexagonal crystal system, and are often found in long columns, but they can come in modifications of that shape, like barrels, tablets, and double pyramids. A tablet, though, is really just a truncated column, so same difference."

"Okay, it was one of the tablet-like columns, they think. Might have been a barrel, I guess. Anyway, that thing was originally, by their estimates, nearly four and a half inches across, and, to accommodate the thicknesses of the medals, probably at least an inch and a half thick. Likely closer to two or three. And that only counts the segment that the medals came from; it may well have been a lot longer."

"Damn! That's way the hell bigger than that star sapphire they found over in Sri Lanka awhile back. And that's the biggest sapphire ever found on Earth!"

"Yeah. I told Fox, and he was delighted. He's gonna discuss it with Pulgey, who had some slight familiarity with Edeptis from years ago—Doron is the physician who healed Fox, way back when, after all—but could never convince 'em to join the Coalition back then. He agreed with my idea that the gemstones were likely one reason the Cortians were fixated on Edeptis—that, and their technology; pirating any or all of it would make for some lucrative subsequent 'trade' for the Cortians."

"It sure would. Damn 'em."

"Yeah. And now Fox is all kinds of excited, and has Sugar doing double-duty, negotiating trade agreements with Edeptis, in addition to the Ganotians. I dunno if they got diamonds on Edeptis or not, but diamonds aren't the only gems with a blood trade on Earth, after all."

"Wow. Even better."

"Yup. We should get the medals back in a couple days, unharmed. Oh, and your trophy blaster from our first Alpha Line mission?"

"Yeah?"

"Was recovered, repaired, and is waiting for you in the armory room. I gave the salvage team a heads-up that it was important to you, and they brought it straight back to your buddy Madrid, who personally handled the reconstruction."

"YAY! So I didn't lose it after all?!"

"Nope. I took a look at it, and it looks great—not that I'd expect differently from Madrid's work. Of course, when the Weapons Lab was done rebuilding and repairing it, it was back to standard config, so I took the liberty of modifying it to run 'hot,' like you and I prefer. That okay with you?"

"Sure was! Thanks, Ace!" Omega offered him a happy smile, and he returned it.

"So. Do you want this hung on the wall?" he asked, waggling the framed image.

"Yeah, I do. Where do you think I should put it?"

"Mm...what about back here, kinda behind the couch? Or over there, over the entertainment center?"

"...Back here, I think. I like the idea of being able to look up and study it," Omega said. "Besides, you've got yours over your couch. They're a set. Like their owners, I guess."

"Okay," Echo said, letting the remark pass and leaning the picture against the chosen wall. "I'll go get a hammer." He disappeared through the back door, into his own quarters.

"You're gonna use a hammer and nails? I thought you'd use that special adhering plate that R&D came up with a while back, so you don't have to put nail holes in the walls."

"I tried to do that with mine," Echo called back, "but the frame is too heavy for it. But I like the framing and matting, so hey."

"Fair enough, then, and I like it too. If you'll hang it, I'll fix us something to eat. It's almost time for first lunch."

"Deal," Echo's voice floated through the back door, accompanied by the sounds of rummaging. "But you have to double-check that it's hanging straight. I hate that. I'm good at it, but I hate it. Now where did I put the damn thing? It oughta be right here..."

"Oh!" Omega called, as she got up and headed for her kitchen. "I think I used it last, Echo. Maybe I didn't put it back in the right place. Are you in the study?"

"Yeah..."

"Look in the middle drawer of your tool cabinet. That's where I put it."

"Aha, you little bastard! There you are!"

"Great." Omega got out a sauté pan. "How does stir-fried chicken with black bean sauce for lunch sound? With steamed rice?"

"That sounds good," Echo said, coming into her quarters and slipping surreptitiously into her bedroom. He carried the hammer in one hand, and a black, leather-bound book in the other.

"I take it, you found the hammer?" her voice floated from the kitchen.

"Yeah," Echo replied, emerging quickly from Omega's bedroom, carrying only the hammer. "Where exactly do you want this?"

He pulled a finishing nail out of his jeans pocket, surveying the wall judiciously. Omega stuck her head out of the kitchen door, pointing with the tip of her chef's knife.

"Center it about there." She ducked back into the kitchen.

"Okay. How's lunch coming?" He positioned the nail and raised the hammer.

"Everything's chopped, an' I already got the rice in to cook. Gimme a few minutes to stir-fry it and let the sauce 'make,' and it'll be ready," Omega called over the sound of the hammer. "Sounds like your shoulders are back to normal."

"Yep," Echo replied, hanging the picture on the wall, then stepping back to eye it judiciously. "I took a nice long workout in the gym this morning, too. Complete with a brief run on the treadmill. It was still a really light workout, especially compared to what we usually do, but damn, it felt good." He straightened the frame. "I missed my spotter, though."

"Must be nice," Omega's voice responded from the kitchen. "Sorry I couldn't be there to spot for you. The medics still won't let me do anything high-impact or likely to raise intracranial pressure."

"Oh? I'll tell Fox, then. I thought they were gonna release you today," Echo said.

"No, not quite yet. Zebra said they wanted to err on the side of caution. After all, I only got one brain. An' it runs everything."

"Well, she's got a good point, I suppose. And I'm kinda fond of your brain, to tell the truth. So it's better if it works right, I guess. Especially since we've already experienced it NOT workin' right. An' I know how much that upset you. Come on out and check this when you get a minute."

"Be right there. Just dishing up lunch."

"Mm. I knew it was smelling good in here."

"Here you go," Omega said, coming out of the kitchen and handing Echo a plate and chopsticks. "Grab whatever you want to drink out of the fridge; the chocolate stout is in the door rack if you want one. I know it's supposed to be served 'warm' but I like it just a little cooler. Oh, perfect, Echo. You hung it exactly where I wanted it. And it's straight. Thanks."

"You're welcome," Echo said, exiting the kitchen with a couple of diet Cokes in addition to his plate of food. "You wanna sit at the table, or in front of the TV?"

"Whichever."

"TV, then. There's a game on I want to watch." Echo sat down on the couch, put the drinks on the coffee table, and patted the seat beside him. Omega joined him with her plate, as he grabbed the TV remote and flipped the channel.

"Wrong time of year for football," she remarked with a teasing grin, as they popped open their drinks and began eating.

"Never said I hated baseball," Echo responded, waving at the television with his chopsticks. "It's an early-preseason exhibition game."

"Who's playing?"

"New York and Atlanta."

"Woo-ooo-ooo-ooo!" Omega exclaimed, karate-chopping the air.

"I wonder who you're rooting for?" Echo deadpanned.

"Well, I am from within rock-chunkin' distance of the place. What about you?" Omega asked. "Who's your team in this one?"

"Atlanta." He shrugged, a slight grin on his handsome face.

"Good! I wasn't sure, though. You've been in New York a long time. Now, if it was Houston..."

"We'd both be goin' nuts."

"That's an affirmative, Houston," Omega grinned. "Is lunch okay?"

"Mm-hm," Echo responded, deftly wielding his chopsticks to rapidly deplete his supply of the savory dish. "I've said it before, lotsa times, but I'll tell you again, anyway—you're a damn good cook, baby."

"Thanks. I like to experiment, try new stuff. The scientist coming out in the kitchen, I suppose. You're pretty darn good in the kitchen, too, Ace. Not that you haven't heard THAT before! Seriously, though, that Greek dish last night was to die for. If I don't start gettin' a little more exercise soon, I'm liable to start lookin' like a toasted marshmallow. Swing, batter! Yeah! Outta the ballpark!"

"Nice hit," Echo agreed. "Bases loaded, too. That brought in a few runs. Toasted? Marshmallow I understand, but...why a toasted marshmallow?"

"Marshmallow dressed in black," Omega replied succinctly, a twinkle in her eye. She waved a hand at her clothing.

"Oh. Ooo, really bad, Meg," Echo editorialized on her joke as she laughed, and he grinned despite himself. "So when ARE the medics gonna let you go active again?"

"It's gonna be a couple more days, they said this morning. I'm probably okay now, they just want to make sure. Did you get some more counseling for the nightmares?"

"A little bit. I...think it's helped, some. I'm...gonna keep doing it for a while, I think."

"Good. And the brain bleaching?"

"No," Echo replied, jaw firming in a stubborn response. "YOU can't forget, so I'm not gonna disrespect what you did for me by erasing its memory. I'm just not, baby. So please, don't even go there."

"Aw." Her face crumpled slightly.

"Don't try to use emotional stuff to change my mind, either," he said, voice suddenly gruff.

"No," she murmured, glancing down. "That's not what I meant, not what I was trying to do, Ace. I..." Omega shrugged. "I'm, I'm touched, and, and honored, that you feel that way about it."

"Well...okay, then." He thrust his jaw forward, shot her a sidelong glance, then shoveled in the last of his chicken and rice.

"All right. 'Nuff said, I guess. Yell if," Omega shrugged again, "well, if there's anything I can do to help that situation. And you know you're always welcome to wake me up, or, or just come check on things...or whatever. 'Cause I get that."

"Okay; thanks. But I'll try not to disturb your sleep any more than I can help, baby; you've earned the right to a good night's sleep, I dunno how many times over."

"The feeling's mutual, ya know."

"Yeah, I know."

They were silent for a time, watching the game and finishing their lunch.

"So...sounds like you got a good case of cabin fever?" Echo asked after several minutes.

"Oh, HELL yes, Ace. A rip-roaring good case."

"Well, hang in there. Fox has got an assignment waiting for us when we're ready," Echo told his partner.

"Okay. But in the meanwhile, I've gotta find a way to keep myself occupied for a couple more days," Omega sighed. "I'm runnin' out of ideas, Echo. And I'm BORED."

"Hm," Echo murmured, thoughtful. He got up, took Omega's empty dishes with his own into the kitchen, plopping them into the dishwasher, then emerged, hands on hips, considering. "Wait here. I've got an idea." He disappeared into his own apartment, and Omega distantly heard the sound of a one-sided conversation. When Echo reappeared in the back door, he was grinning.

"Slap on some sunscreen and let's go, Legs."

"Where?!"

Echo pointed at the television. "I'm taking my closest friend over to the stadium in Queens to see Hotlanta whip up on New York. If we drive the 'Vette and 'hurry,' we can catch the bottom of the second."

* * *

Alpha One made a day of it. After watching Atlanta's baseball team beat one of the New York teams, Echo and Omega cruised over to Manhattan, grabbed hot dogs from a street vendor for second lunch, then prowled the Metropolitan Museum of Art for several hours. Afterward, they got a bite to eat for dinner at a nice Italian restaurant run by a Gurguv from Dekken, and discussed baseball and art.

"So which did you like better, Echo, the baseball game, or the Met?" a curious Omega asked, skillfully twirling up a forkful of pasta.

"Mm, I know what you probably expect me to say," Echo remarked around a mouthful of lasagna.

"Oh? What?"

"The ball game."

"But you're actually going to say—?"

"Both."

"Both? You don't like one better than the other?"

"Do you?" Echo asked bluntly.

"Well, it does depend on my mood, I guess."

"Exactly."

"So what's your favorite part of the Met?" Omega queried. "I really enjoyed the sculpture garden on the roof."

"Yeah, I like that, too," Echo agreed, "but today I really got into Gauguin's stuff. Wishful thinking, to an extent."

"That tropical theme after we nearly froze our asses off on the protoplanet?" Omega grinned, and Echo chuckled.

"Hell yeah!"

"The sunshine in the stadium did feel good today, didn't it?" Omega agreed, and Echo nodded. "Thanks for getting me out...in...in more ways than one, Echo." The look of gratitude in the blue eyes made Echo glad he was sitting down; his knees felt unaccustomedly wobbly.

"Well..." Echo began, somewhat uncomfortable. "It took both of us, working together, to get off that protoplanet."

"That's only part of what I'm talking about, and you know it," Omega offered in a soft tone. "You were willing to go the distance to keep me from feeling like a lab rat. From feeling pitied. And from making a very bad mistake back on the protoplanet."

"And I'm alive and I've...still got my legs," Echo replied in a low voice, intensely grateful. "Both of 'em. You were exhausted, in pain, and not able to think clearly, Meg. It's all right. We're even, I think."

The friends were silent for a while as they ate, content in each other's company. Then Omega spoke, in a casual, serene tone.

"Well, Ace, whaddaya wanna do tonight?"

"Aw, shit, Meg, I don't know—how 'bout a movie?"

"Okay. There's a new *Trek* sequel out..."

"Damn. You wanna see that guy again?" Echo wasn't sure whether to be jealous or not.

"Yup. I like his work. Besides, he reminds me of my best buddy." Omega grinned. Echo settled a bit at her response.

"Well, since you put it like that..."

* * *

They came home laughing and joking together after the movie, which even Echo had to admit had been exciting enough to rivet his attention. Echo fired up his quantum light storage sound system, leaving the volume low, and he and Omega chatted of matters consequential and not, late into the night, until Omega began to yawn prodigiously.

"Time for you to get some rest, Meg," Echo said then, raising his recliner to an upright position and lowering the footrest.

"Yeah, I guess so," Omega said, sitting up and swinging her feet off Echo's couch. "But it goes for you, too. We're both still gettin' over being so banged up."

"I won't argue that, at all," Echo said, stretching. "See you in the morning, baby."

"Good night, Ace."

* * *

As Omega climbed into bed a little later and reached for the switch on the nightstand lamp, she noticed the book with the black leather cover nudging a certain pink resin block, inside which was a preserved rose blossom. Instead of turning off the lamp, she picked up her deceased father's Bible.

A sheet of paper fluttered out, landing on the blanket. Omega picked up the handwritten note. The handwriting was bold, precise, and after all this time, very familiar.

* * *

Ω—

Thought you might like this back. After all, it's your father's, and I know how much it means to you—on a lot of levels. I've taken good care of it, but it's not the right time for me to have it. For now, it still belongs to my best buddy.

—E

* * *

Omega smiled and replaced the note carefully in the Bible, laying the book reverently on the table. Then she picked up the resin block containing the rose, pressing her lips to it before setting it beside the old Bible, and extinguished the lamp.

But as tired blue eyes drifted closed, the dark bedroom dissolved into a lush, tropical garden.

* * *

The abundant foliage, in shades of blue and green, was profusely dotted by colorful blossoms. The blue sun shone down warm and bright, making Omega much too hot in her black Suit.

"Meg? You ready?" The question came from behind, and Omega turned to see Echo, flanked by Romeo and India, standing and watching her, waiting expectantly.

"Sure, Echo," she responded, then pointed behind him. "But I think somebody wants to talk to you first."

Echo glanced over his shoulder, then smiled and turned to greet the figure that emerged from the undergrowth. Romeo and India came to stand beside Omega as Echo exclaimed, "X-ray! Good to see ya, ol' buddy!" Echo grabbed the other man's hand and clapped him on the back.

"Hi, Echo!" the older, gray-haired agent replied with a smile. "It's been a while."

"Yeah, it has." Echo was silent for a moment, then extended one hand back toward his colleagues. "X-ray, I got some folks I want you to meet..."

"I know. That's why I'm here," X-ray responded as Romeo, India, and Omega moved forward. "Great recruits, Echo. You did a fine job there, pal. And the new department is really something to behold." X-ray held out a hand to India, who grasped it firmly and shook. "India, nice to meet you. Medic, detective, and Agent all rolled into one. Strong and cool. Keep it

up." India smiled, and he moved on to Romeo. "Romeo, I'm X-ray, Echo's first partner."

"Pleased to meetcha, X-ray. I was—"

"His second. I know. Good man. Thanks for helping him out, when he needed somebody beside him. Piece of advice for you, Romeo: You've got heart, son. Hang onto it. This job can beat it out of you, if you're not careful. Don't let it. And hang onto her. As hard as you can." X-ray gestured to India. "I learned the hard way, it's...too easy to take the path of least resistance sometimes. Don't. 'Cause that's the way to lose everything. Do you understand?"

"I...think so, sir," Romeo said, glancing at India.

"Good." X-ray moved on to Omega.

"X-ray, this is—" Echo began.

"Omega, your current partner," X-ray finished. "The Agent who finally replaced me. Exceeded me, really."

Echo and Omega both winced.

"X-ray, I didn't mean— I never intended—" Omega began to protest.

"Quiet there, Angel; I didn't take it like that, nor mean it like that," X-ray said with a gentle grin, then he sobered as he studied her. "You've sure been through a lot, honey," he remarked thoughtfully. "But still, you always come out on top, scrappin'. Do you like his jokes?" X-ray jerked a thumb over his shoulder at Echo. Omega grinned.

"Oh, yeah."

"Does he like yours?"

"I...think so."

"I do," Echo averred over X-ray's shoulder, matching her grin. The elder agent nodded.

"Good. You remind him to stop and just enjoy looking at the stars with you once in a while, don't you? Smell the roses, all that?"

"Yes..." The soft answer came, not from Omega, but from Echo. X-ray and Omega glanced at him, then X-ray nodded and returned his attention to Omega.

"Good. That was something I couldn't do. He was just too focused on mission ops for me to break through. Of course," X-ray sighed, "I was responsible for TEACHING him the mission ops, so I suppose it's my own damn fault." X-ray turned back to Echo. "Is she good to have at your back *in a brawl?"*

"I wouldn't have her as a partner if she wasn't. You know that." Echo was matter-of-fact. Then he frowned, brow creasing in something like distress. "X-ray, listen. I'm not trying to replace you, pal, it's just—"

"It's all right, Echo," X-ray said, soothing. The older man held up a staying hand. "I understand, and it's okay. They're here for you, and I'm not—not any more. I had to do what I had to do, and you had to let me. And now you have to do what's best for you and the team. You've got good people around you, son: friends, buddies you can count on. People you really CARE about, and who care about YOU. Family. Just like I do—and did. And your new 'best buddy' there," he gestured at Omega with a grin, "well, I think she'll do real well in my old job. Probably better than I ever could, and in ways I never could, if you'll both ease up and let it happen." Then X-ray elbowed Echo in the ribs. "But take my advice: I liked the black bikini a lot better," he murmured in a sly tone. Echo grinned for a moment, then turned to look at Omega.

"Thanks, pal," he said softly, and Omega was uncertain if Echo was speaking to her or to X-ray. Or perhaps both, *she considered. When Alpha One turned back, X-ray was gone, replaced by a lovely petite, dark-haired woman. Echo looked truly shaken for the first time since Omega had known him.*

"Hello, Echo." The woman's voice was pitched low and soft.

"...Hi."

"Surprised to see me?"

"Yeah, a little."

"Uncomfortable?"

"Some." Echo shrugged. "It's good to see you, though..." he said quietly, a warm smile lighting his features.

"Let go, Echo," the woman told him. "It's time to move on."

"But—" Echo blinked, caught off-guard, and the smile faded. Omega watched, puzzled.

"No buts. You know I'm correct, Echo. I was never the right one for you." The woman looked deep into the brown eyes, then glanced over Echo's shoulder at the other three Agents, and nodded. "Good. Excellent choice, hon. You always made the important decisions that way. Enjoy the chase, Echo." She turned to go.

"Wait." Echo laid a hand on the woman's arm.

"Echo, let go..." the woman said, with infinite tenderness. "It's all right. Let go. You're in good hands. Right where you belong."

Echo looked down into her soft dark eyes for a long moment, then slowly, hesitantly, released her arm, still studying the woman's face. Her eyes darted meaningfully over his shoulder, and he automatically followed her gaze with his own, as she locked that gaze with a pair of confused blue eyes. In that instant, Omega saw the woman take several steps backward and fade into the shadows beneath the trees. There was a bright streak upward, and when Echo turned back around, the woman was gone. He stood for long minutes, staring into the empty foliage, then his head tilted back, and he looked into the sky.

"Goodbye..." he murmured softly. "Goodbye." Then Echo came to stand beside Omega.

"All right, guys," Echo said then. "Time to move on."

Omega glanced to her side at Romeo and India, who nodded silently, then back to Echo.

"Ready when you are, Ace," she said.

"Then let's go."

"Where?" Romeo asked. Echo pointed ahead.

"Forward."

* * *

Omega woke up early the next morning. Shortly after she rose, a phone call from the medlab came in. She answered it and chatted with Zebra for long moments, then thanked her profusely and disconnected the call. But her mind was on the previous night.

So she wrapped her black silk robe—now free of bloodstains—around her body over her pajama top, shoved her feet into her house shoes, and wandered into the kitchen. There, she made coffee, poured a mug, and sat thoughtfully at her dining table for a long time. After a while, a knock sounded at the back door, and she called, "C'mon in. Coffee's ready in the kitchen. I made a pot today."

A sleepy Echo, clad in black jeans sans shirt, barefoot, hair rumpled, eyes barely open, wandered through on his way to the coffee. From the waistband of the jeans peeked the top of what looked to be black silk knit boxers; Omega realized he was experimenting with sleepwear again, like he had promised her before the crash. She hid a gentle smile of appreciation in her coffee mug.

"Thought I smelled chicory coffee this mornin'," he muttered then.

"I thought I was the one with the enhanced senses," she said with a grin, "and you aren't even awake yet. Yeah, I made some, special today; a whole pot, 'stead of the pod brewer. I wanted to celebrate a little, 'cause Zebra called, and the medlab is definitely releasing me for duty again day after tomorrow!"

"Really? Good. 'Bout damn time."

"Tell me about it. The cream's still in the fridge, by the way."

"Already got it."

"Want some breakfast?"

* * *

"Not yet," Echo said, bringing a steaming mug and coming to sit down at the table across from Omega, running his fingers through that sleep-rumpled hair, disarranging it further. "Give me a few minutes to wake up, first." He sipped the hot liquid for a few moments. "Mm. That's better."

They sat staring at the tabletop, both lost in thought, then said simultaneously, "I had a weird dream last night..." They looked up at each other, startled, then grinned.

"Zeta Aurigae Four?" Omega asked, and Echo nodded.

"Were Romeo and India there?" he asked.

"Yep. And X-ray," she replied, and he nodded again.

"Sounds like we might've had the same dream," Echo decided. "The medics said you might do that."

"Sorry." Omega bit her lip.

"No big deal. I trust you." Echo shrugged, unconcerned; their recent adventure had laid to rest any fears that she might invade his privacy, even inadvertently. "What did X-ray say?"

"He seemed interested in how well I fit his old job description, mostly. Oh, he also gave Romeo and India some advice..."

"Yep. Same dream," Echo said quietly. "He approved."

"Do you think he really would?" Omega asked, chewing her lip. "In real life, I mean."

"Yeah, I do."

"Echo...there was somebody else there," Omega said, voice and face thoughtful, and Echo stiffened despite himself, wondering what she had picked up on from his dream. "Somebody I didn't know—but you did," she remembered. "A pretty brunette. She kept telling you to let go of something. I...didn't get it."

"Never mind, Meg. Let..." Echo caught himself, then went ahead, "let it go. It was...only meaningful to me. Don't worry about it."

* * *

"Well...is it okay?" Omega knit her brows in concern, watching him. It had not escaped her attention that Echo had tensed at mention of the woman, and she had a sneaking suspicion she knew why...and who the woman had been.

"What do you mean?" Echo asked.

"Was it time to let go? And did you?" she pressed, worried for him.

Echo considered his empty coffee cup intently, face drawn as if in pain. Omega struggled to hide her own emotions, which were decidedly mixed. *After all, he's still grieving her, and he's never gonna look at ME like that,* she thought. *I just hope he gets to the point where he can move past her, a little bit. Where it doesn't hurt him so bad.* His next words confirmed her suspicions.

"Yeah...I think so. Started, at least. I thought I was a lot farther along, but...oh well." He stood abruptly, picked up both mugs, and took them into the kitchen. Then he switched off the coffeepot, and covered the carafe. "Go get dressed."

"What about breakfast?" Omega rose from the table, startled.

"We'll grab something out." Echo headed for the back door.

"Where are we going?" Omega called from the door of her bedroom.

"Shopping," floated, enigmatic, from Echo's quarters.

* * *

The next day, about mid-morning while Omega was watching a movie, Echo came by her quarters. She immediately hit the pause button on the TV's remote control.

"Oh, hey Ace," she said, sitting up straight as he walked through the back door, clad in his Suit. "What's up? I expected you to be at your desk in the Alpha Line Room."

"I was," Echo said, offering a slight grin as she adjusted her gray sweatshirt and tugged her black jeans straight. "Don't sweat it, Meg; I've seen you in more, uh, disarranged clothes than that. But speaking of, do you feel like putting on, say, a polo shirt with those jeans and coming with me to see Fox?"

"Huh? What's up?" she wondered, standing and heading for the bedroom. "I'm still on medical leave for one more day, you know."

"I know. And so does he. Evidently he's just got some follow-up information that he thought we'd both like to hear. So he asked me to swing by and see if you'd mind joining me in his office for a few minutes. Only I figured you'd be more comfortable in the Director's office if you were dressed up a little more than a sweatshirt."

"You figured right," she agreed, coming out wearing a black polo shirt, neatly tucked into her black jeans. A discreet silver chain and tiny star earrings, the latter a Christmas gift from Romeo, accessorized the outfit. "Will this do?"

"Great," Echo said with a smile. "You look terrific. C'mon, let's go."

* * *

"There she is!" a cheerful Fox exclaimed, as Alpha One knocked at the open door of his office. "I kept meaning to come by for a visit, Omega, just to see about you, but I have been so damned busy with paperwork in the aftermath of the Battle of Orion, I've barely gotten home to sleep! Come on in, you two. I cannot say enough how glad I am to see you both on your feet and looking good."

"Thanks, Fox," Echo murmured with a smile. "Believe me when I say it's good to be on my feet."

"And you, Omega?" Fox wondered. "How are you doing, tekhter? I hear from Zebra that the medlab will release you to duty in the next day or so."

"That's the plan, Fox," Omega said, happy. "I go back to work tomorrow. It's only light duty for now, but I'm feeling good, and frankly, I'm ready for a little work! Sitting around the house all day gets old fast."

"I'd bet it does, meyn khaverte. And that highly intelligent brain? Is it also doing well?"

"It's doing great, Fox," Omega said with a wide smile. "Thank the good Lord."

"Amein to that."

"So what's up?" she asked.

331

"Nothing incredibly urgent," Fox noted. "But I thought, under the circumstances, the two of you would like to know about the latest missive to come down from the Ennead—from Pulgey, specifically."

"Oh? What's wrong?" Echo wondered.

"Nothing, actually," Fox told them with a smile. "The Coalition has taken care of some planet named Corta."

"Lemme hear," Omega practically growled. "I'm so sick of them, I could chew nails an' spit bullets."

"And she's not the only one," Echo added, unamused. Fox chuckled; it was a grim sound.

"Make that three," he added, "four if you count Zebra, and five, counting Pulgey. We can probably add in all of Alpha Line, the Ennead, the Ganotians, Edeptis, half a dozen other Divisions...well. Anyway. I don't know if anyone told you, since the *Odyssey* was ordered to exit the battle as soon as it could fight its way out after rescuing you two. But Pulgey himself arranged no less than THREE Coalition Fleets, as it turned out; I'd only really asked for two...though I did recommend three. One, under the command of the PGLEIA minister, was sent out to help patrol the galactic trade lanes, and was largely composed of several Division fleets working together. Another came to the Orion Nebula to relieve the Division One Fleet. Mop-up went pretty damn fast after that. Not one of the damned Cortian ships would surrender, though, so we essentially wiped 'em out. Oh, a handful may have slipped into the nebula to hide, so I'm sure space navigation will still have the odd Cortian pirate slavers to deal with for some little time to come. But that fleet, at any rate, is no more."

"Good," Echo snarled.

"That," Omega agreed.

"As for their homeworld, my old friend, colleague and successor, Suud Guurn—you remember Suud, Echo? Yes, I thought you would—led yet a third Coalition fleet to Corta and blockaded the whole damn system... not that there was very much of one. It turns out that Omega's original surmise, back before the *Trindak* arrived, was entirely right: The system is small and poor, taken on its own." He shrugged. "It stands to reason they'd be desperate enough to resort to raiding, piracy, and slaving."

"Fox? I'm curious," Omega admitted. "If you have time, tell us all you know about that system."

"I'm with her," Echo confessed. "My curiosity's up, too."

"Okay, you asked for it," Fox said with a slight smile. "Here, have a look at this."

He passed a printed document across to them, and putting their heads together, Alpha One read it simultaneously. It was the report on the Cortian prisoners that Entiyti had sent to his Fleet Admirals, and Fox waited patiently while Echo and Omega perused it in detail, watching as their expressions slowly changed. Scowls softened, becoming expressions of interest; Omega's eyes widened as she reached the astronomical details contained therein.

She and Echo exchanged glances; Echo raised an eyebrow, and Omega nodded, then tapped the page and pointed to a particular location. Echo re-read the section, then nodded. They bent their heads back over the paper and continued reading.

Finally Echo flipped over the last page, and Alpha One sat back in their chairs, thoughtful. Brown eyes and blue stared into space, considering, for long minutes. After a few more moments, Omega came up for air and made an observation.

"Interesting," Omega murmured. "So I'd think that the majority of any resources the system has would be buried deep inside Orge."

"And you'd think right, according to the follow-up report Pul sent me," Fox confirmed. "The Corta system as a whole is dirt-poor. There's a dozen or so other large-ish moons or planets—depending how you want to define 'em—orbiting Orge, and apparently those have been mined into Swiss cheese. There's so little left that the engineers on Suud's flagship wondered how the hell they hadn't gravitationally collapsed into rubble."

"Damn," Echo muttered.

"Yeah," Omega agreed. "So...how the blazes do they manage to create fleets of starships? How did they manage ONE, to begin with?"

"In as far as we can tell," Fox elaborated, "likely another race, maybe from elsewhere in the Terzan 7 cluster—though there's speculation it was Edeptan—visited Corta on a first-contact embassage and was probably hoodwinked by the Cortians. They outmaneuvered greater tech, probably with sheer, merciless ferocity. If I had to guess, I'd say the embassage was probably enslaved—those that survived the capture—and the ship or ships taken by the Cortians. Who knows what happened to the embassage, the poor bastards. But it was the ships the Cortians wanted. They probably analyzed 'em, learned how to fly 'em, how to build 'em, all of that. And those spacecraft became the core of their first interstellar fleet," Fox observed. "From there, they started spreading out through the cluster, raiding and pillaging. The relative richness of the rest of the cluster, combined with the proximity of other star systems, made it an enticing way to operate. Evidently they get their shipbuilding materials from their raids, at least whatever they can get their hands on. You saw the assessment of the crew quarters."

"Which might also explain why they didn't want us exploring anything in the *Trindak* other than what they were willing to show us," Echo surmised. "It would have been a dead giveaway that Corta wasn't the dream world they were purporting."

"Good point," Omega agreed. "Especially if the slave quarters were even worse."

"Ugh," Echo murmured. "I have a feeling that, if you hadn't stopped matters, Meg, I might have had an up close an' personal tour of those."

"Most likely," Fox agreed. "And the fact that their homeworld political system already operated in that fashion, just on the basis of trying to obtain needed resources, made the whole 'interstellar pirate and slaver' thing a logical next step for them."

"And once they'd managed to gain sway over the cluster, they moved out into their entire galaxy," Echo extrapolated. "Not that it's that big."

"Exactly. And then started raiding along the edges of ours, to the Edeptans' grief."

"Then decided to strike deeper," Omega decided. "Because Division One isn't exactly near the center of the Milky Way, and volume-wise, it's one of the larger Divisions, which in this case means a relatively low population density..."

"Right. But you two pissed 'em off royally," Fox informed Alpha One. "Not only did you thwart their getting their hands on what they considered prize stock, you took out TWO of their top-of-the-line starships—assuming the Cortians really have such a thing, I suppose; in any case, starships are valuable resources to 'em—AND you revealed their true nature to the entire damn Coalition."

"Then helped incorporate two more systems—at least one of which was favored for raiding—into that Coalition," Echo added. "Not to mention upgrading that system's defensive infrastructure."

"Precisely. So the two of you were at the top of the Cortian Most Wanted List. But I'm not sure either of you would have survived long," Fox added. "There might have been some, ah, 'forced breeding' attempts, but Pulgey and I are ninety-nine point a whole buncha nines percent sure that you wouldn't have lived more than five minutes past that."

The three were silent for long moments, none of them particularly wanting to speculate on the details of that scenario.

"So...what did the Coalition do to 'em?" Echo wondered then.

"Yeah. I remember reading a Heinlein book in high school," Omega recalled, "where something similar happened, and it was a really nasty punishment..."

"Oh, where they shunted the planet—but not their star—into another dimension?" Echo asked.

"Yeah, that's the one."

"Well, we don't have the capability to do THAT," Fox pointed out, "at least, not yet. Though I think Pulgey would cheerfully have done it, if we had! No, Suud blockaded Corta and issued an ultimatum, which Pul had helped him put together. It was in two parts: the first part was unconditional surrender and taking their leaders into custody, and the second part didn't get made until that happened...which took a bit, I gather. Anyway, the second part was offering them assistance if they would quit their marauding ways. There was even an offer of provisional membership in the Coalition, provided Corta proved itself willing to abide by galactic law first."

"I bet I can guess what happened," Omega murmured.

"Yep. They fired their planetary defense guns," Fox noted. "Twice. Took out several of Suud's ships by accident; they were all cloaked, since he was using my old 'bait and target' tactic. He was NOT amused, I can assure you. Five minutes later, Corta had no planetary defense guns. They also had no more military installations, spaceports, interstellar-capable craft—in orbit or otherwise—or spacecraft construction and manufacturing facilities. At least, not in the system. Then he demanded—and got—their planetary leaders." Fox nodded to himself, satisfied. "I always knew Suud would make a damn fine security chief one day. I just never dreamed it would be for the whole galaxy."

Echo snorted.

"Tell him good job, and thanks, for me, okay?"

"I surely will, alter khaver," Fox said with a grin.

"Ditto. So what happens next?" Omega queried.

"Oh, several nexts have already occurred, while the two of you were recuperating," Fox said. "The Cortian system has been quarantined, essentially permanently, unless we get a very specific capitulation message, which doesn't look like coming, at least any time soon; what passed for governmental entities—Corta had multiple nation-states—devolved into the worst kind of chaos, with rioting and looting rampant. Suud said there was even a nuclear exchange between the two biggest countries."

"Shit," Echo breathed.

"Yes," Fox agreed. "The Joint Coalition Fleets have set up a prison-planet perimeter around the system; no unauthorized craft are going in or out of Corta for a very long time. Any ships that got away from us at the Orion Nebula are completely on their own now."

"But with so few resources...?" Omega began.

"Don't worry, Omega; neither the Ennead, nor the Pan-Galactic Coalition as a whole, is committing genocide. Note I said 'unauthorized craft'? Automated supply ships will be sent in periodically to provide the needed resources for the people to survive. Perhaps not to thrive, but there will be enough for all to survive, though Pul has some ideas as to how to do it so as to force them into cooperation, instead of thievery and the like. The system is being closely monitored; there will never be too little...but there will also never be too much. The only way they can have more is to earn it themselves by working for it; even the supplies will be tagged such that, if raiding, theft, or piracy occurs, the supplies self-destruct, one way or another. And the cargo ships are evacuated to space, so anyone who attempts to stow away won't make it to orbit." Fox shook his head. "Pulgey is sick of their shit, and intends to put a stop to it, whatever it takes."

"Whoa," Omega said, silver-blonde eyebrows shooting up. "Okay, I get that."

"The planetary leaders were formally arrested and tried on all KINDS of charges; convictions, across the board, occurred three Division days ago. The executions occurred early this morning," Fox finished the litany. "I wanted to wait to tell you two until that all went down. Besides, I..." he broke off, and glanced away. "I wanted to wait until you were both a bit stronger before I dumped all of it on you."

They were silent for a moment.

"We...appreciate that, Fox," Omega murmured, sapphire gaze soft. "Thanks...for everything."

"What she said," Echo added, voice a bit uneven. "You're about the oldest friend I've got, Fox, and...well."

"Exactly, Echo," Fox replied, hazel eyes meeting brown ones. Then he turned his gaze to Echo's partner. "And just because I haven't known you nearly as long, yung froy, don't make the mistake of thinking you're an afterthought with me. Because you'd be dead wrong."

"Is anybody an afterthought with you, Fox?" Omega wondered with a small smile.

"In the Agency? Not if I can help it," Fox answered, then he sighed. "Anyway, I...thought you'd both want to know. Sorry for disturbing your time off, Omega."

"If I know her, Fox," Echo began.

"And you do," Fox interjected.

"...I'd bet she was glad for the 'disturbance.' She's been about to bounce off the walls, ready to get out and about."

"But even when I go back on duty, it's supposed to be 'light' duty," Omega reminded the two men, glum.

"All right," Fox decided. "In that case, I think I know just the assignment for when you come back online. Scamper on back to your quarters for now, and behave, so I can GIVE you that assignment. Echo, make sure she goes back where she's supposed to go."

"All over it, Fox," Echo said, grinning. "C'mon, baby, let's get going."

Alpha One rose, and as they headed for the door, Echo added to his partner, "You still game for that outing tonight?"

"You mean dinner and the comedy club? You know it, Ace!"

"Good. Afterward, what say we hit that rooftop bar in the hotel over on North 12th?"

"Ooo! That sounds like fun!"

"I thought you'd like that idea. You loved the view from up there, the first time we went. And it should be warm enough now that we can go out on the terrace to sit and unwind and just talk, get some fresh air, and enjoy the view."

"I am so there!"

"You're not tired of yakking at me, after all that time we spent doing nothing but, on the protoplanet?"

"Aw, hell, Ace, why would you think that...?"

Their voices faded as they descended the ramp to the main floor.

In their wake, Fox smiled.

"Well, well," he murmured to himself. "That appears to be progressing nicely. I'll have to remember to update Zebra tonight..."

* * *

Alpha One's evening out went well; the pair came back rested, refreshed, and closer than ever.

Bright and early the next morning, the medlab crew gave Omega one last, quick once-over, then Zebra smiled, as she looked over her patient's chart.

"Go back to your quarters and Suit up, girl," she said, "then go report to Echo. You're back on duty."

"WAHOO!" Omega whooped.

"Easy, now! Remember, I want you on relatively light duty for a few more days, yet."

"Oh—Fox said he had an assignment for us," Omega remembered. "He seemed to think it would be a good one, something I could do without violating medical whatevers..."

"Yeah, he checked it out with me the other night," Zebra confirmed, "and I'm good with it. Just be careful, and if there's anything heavily physical to be done, let someone else do it. Actually, I think Alpha Two might be going along with you on that mission, because I told Fox I'd like Romeo there as physical backup for you both, and India there to keep an eye on you two for a couple days yet. That okay with you?"

"Yeah, it's good."

"All right. Go get dressed and report for duty, girlfriend."

* * *

A delighted Echo welcomed his partner into their joint Alpha Line Room office, made her a cup of coffee from the new pod brewer, and saw her comfortably settled into her own desk chair.

"This feels a lot more normal," he decided immediately. "Good to have you back, baby."

"Good to be back," Omega said with a grin, sipping her coffee...which was prepared exactly the way she liked it, without her having to lift a finger.

Omega was the last of the department to be released from medical care; all of the other casualties had been healed using established medical techniques or Doron's new regeneration procedures, and subsequently released for duty. But Omega's head injury had been such that she had had to heal largely in the old-fashioned method, so it had taken some time. Consequently, over the course of the day, various Alpha Line teams straggled through the meeting room, some reporting in, others making a pretense of reporting in. All were there in actuality just to welcome their assistant department chief back to work.

Echo watched with hidden affection as Alpha Eight stopped by just in time for the afternoon snack, with a fresh pastry from the bakery down the street, bought expressly for Omega. Having just made a fresh cup of coffee, Omega was delighted, thanking them profusely, and promptly tied into the gigantic cinnamon bun.

Abruptly it occurred to Echo to wonder if Monkey was after his partner again, at least in some fashion, and the slight smile on his face vanished as he chewed his lip in concerned thought.

Just then, Monkey turned, extracted a plump, glazed cruller—one of Echo's favorites—wrapped in parchment paper, from the bag...and handed it to his department chief.

"Here, boss," Monkey murmured. "Don't think we're not glad to see you back, too. You just got back on duty before a lot of the rest of us! Damn, big guy, you two be careful, all right?"

"We do our best, Monkey," Omega murmured, "but thanks for worryin' about us."

His concern alleviated, Echo likewise nodded his thanks and accepted the cruller, launching into its consumption with alacrity, to Kako's and Monkey's pleasure. Mouth full, he waved a hand at the pod brewer, then at the guest chairs by way of invitation, and Alpha Eight made cups of coffee, pulled out their own pastries, then joined their leaders for a convivial afternoon meal.

Alpha Two had already been by long since with hugs and good wishes, and had in fact been the first—after Echo—to welcome Omega back. The

Alpha Three Enigma Team had been next; then there was a fair deluge of partnerships, as the word spread. Even Alpha Seven—Tare and Yankee—stopped by with greetings, though Yankee's were somewhat grudging; he still had not forgiven Omega for a particular abortive kiss the previous Christmas. But there was still a certain relief in the eyes of both Agents over the return of both of their department's leaders.

"And that's that," Echo told Omega at the end of their shift, as they shut down their computers and rose to leave the office. "Life is as back to normal for us as it ever gets around here. And I dunno about you, baby, but I am glad of it."

"Amen to that," Omega agreed. "Let's get outta here."

"Done. Wanna go out, or fix dinner at home, or...?"

"Ace! After I spent so long stuck at home, what do YOU think?!"

"Right. Which restaurant, then...?"

* * *

"All right, ladies and gentlemen," Fox said the next day in his office, where Alpha One and -Two had assembled, "I have an assignment perfectly suited to two Agents just off medical leave, and their backups. Very little chance of any physical altercations for a change, just some smooth interaction in a nice location, with plenty of off-time to sightsee if that sort of thing interests you—and I know it does, for all four of you. So. The lot of you, get any gear you need in addition to your travel kits, and head for Penn Station. There's a spacecraft waiting for you in Hangar Bay 12. The Diplomatic department has requested your presence in the Ganotian Summit as soon as we could spare you."

"Where we goin'?" Romeo asked.

"Zeta Aurigae Four," Alpha One said in unison, grinning.

"You two look pleased with that," India noted.

"Yep," Echo said succinctly.

"Let me ask you this, India: Did you pack a swimsuit in there, perchance?" Omega chuckled, pointing at the small kits each of them carried. A small rectangular bulge showed in the side of Omega's kit...right next to a perfect square.

"Nooo..." India responded, thoughtful.

"Whoa, baby!" Romeo whooped in glee. "The Eden planet!"

"Oh!" India exclaimed.

340

"That's it," Omega said, grinning from ear to ear.

"Never mind, Meg," Echo said, grinning as well. "There's no time now. Romeo and India will just have to do their shopping when we get there." He patted his own kit. "You and I are set, at any rate. X-ray would approve, I think..." Omega laughed, but Romeo and India looked puzzled. "Let's go," Echo finished.

"Have a good trip, children," a benevolent Fox said, following them onto his balcony as the four headed for the elevator. "Try not to break anything this time!" he called after them.

"Including strings," Echo murmured to his partner, straight-faced, and Omega snickered.

"You know it, Fox!" Romeo exclaimed as the elevator doors closed on them.

* * *

"Hey, who's flyin', anyway?" Romeo wondered then.

"Echo, I guess," Omega shrugged. "He's the only one qualified to do it."

"Not quite," Echo remarked. "Didn't anyone tell you, baby?" The elevator disgorged them into Grand Central Station, and they walked through the departure gates.

"Tell me what?" Omega responded as they climbed into a maglev car labeled 'Pennsylvania Station' and strapped in.

"According to Division regs, 'Any pilot-candidate who has completed all requisite training, but has not yet passed the required certification exams when he or she is thrown into a combat scenario, with or without an experienced pilot also at the helm, is automatically certified as a Division One Agency pilot.' You finished your principal training. And you were in no less than two battles. In the pilot's seat for the first one, at that, even if I was doin' the flying—because you were essentially designating the targets for me, and managing fire control into the bargain. That put you in command. Congratulations, partner." The maglev doors opened onto the Division One Pennsylvania Station spaceport, and Echo pointed at the awaiting saucer in Hangar Bay 12, directly across from the maglev station. "That's the *Calypso*, and she's all yours, Meg. Try not to crash her on any protoplanets, okay?"

The hangar echoed a delighted whoop, and three grinning Alpha Line

Agents ran to catch up with the fourth as she danced exuberantly across the hangar bay toward the waiting ship.

342

Author's Notes

And now it's time to thank the usual suspects. Mom & Dad, husband Darrell (who, as always, does a bangin' cover!), my beta readers Evelyn Hively Zinn, Dr. James K. Woosley, and Larry Bauer. Add to that list, Nitay Arbel and his wonderful, ongoing assistance in helping me maintain Fox's essential Yiddishness. I dunno what I'd do without any of y'all; your support is tremendous.

Guys, you have NO IDEA what sort of brainstorming goes on when I'm writing a story like this one! You just can't imagine. "What kind of alien ritual ceremony might the Edeptans perform over Alpha One...ooo, that could work...but now what do they LOOK like...?" Yeah, that. And yes, if you've finished the book you know EXACTLY what I'm talking about!

And a special thanks to Larry, who provided a NASA story for Omega to tell Echo while they waited for rescue. He's an old friend and colleague from my NASA days, and while my particular control center console position rarely made for a lot of fun or funny stories, he saw quite a few. (He actually gave me 2-3 more that I didn't use! They may find their way into later stories.) That said, the practical joke war actually did occur to me, when I was in graduate school, in a slightly modified form—meaning it didn't escalate for as long before I got caught, but my office really did get emptied and rolled overnight. And either the professors helped, or they simply chose to sit back and watch, I was never quite sure which.

So yes, I really do have such a mischievous, and sometimes inconvenient, sense of humor. Now you know where my books get it!

Speaking of mischievous humor, this particular book really MUST thank the creators of the webcomic, *Two Lumps*. (http://twolumps.net/) If you've never read it, it's an ongoing story revolving around two cats, Russian Blue litter mates, created by J. Grant and Mel Hynes, and based on two cats they owned at the time of the comic's creation (the cats have since passed on). Being a serious cat person myself, I love the comic and read it regularly, and it is one of the independent comics I recommend to friends. Ebenezer has a genius intellect and is a very serious cat. His brother Snooch gives very credible indication of intellect as well, but is far less inclined to apply it, being a rather decided slacker, as well as over-fond of Mom's booze. His vocabulary is distinctly lacking relative to Benny's, so when, in a strip posted in 2016 (http://twolumps.net/d/20160829.html), Snooch misheard Benny's reference to "incipient diabetes," and rendered it instead as "sapient dire beets," I howled with laughter for probably 5-10 minutes! I had tears streaming down my cheeks. When I could finally stop laughing, I KNEW that had to go into a Division One story! And with James' and Mel's full, properly-obtained permission, the story of sapient dire beets is now contained within this tome you hold! James, Mel, I sincerely hope you get a kick out of it!

~Stephanie Osborn
Huntsville, AL
May 2017

About the Author

Stephanie Osborn is a former payload flight controller, a veteran of over twenty years of working in the civilian space program, as well as various military space defense programs. She has worked on numerous Space Shuttle flights and the International Space Station, and counts the training of astronauts on her resumé. Of those astronauts she trained, one was Kalpana Chawla, a member of the crew lost in the *Columbia* disaster.

She holds graduate and undergraduate degrees in four sciences: Astronomy, Physics, Chemistry, and Mathematics, and she is "fluent" in several more, including Geology and Anatomy. She obtained her various degrees from Austin Peay State University in Clarksville, TN and Vanderbilt University in Nashville, TN.

Stephanie is currently retired from space work. She now happily "passes it forward," teaching math and science via numerous media including radio, podcasting, and public speaking, as well as working with SIGMA, the science fiction think tank, while writing science fiction mysteries based on her knowledge, experience, and travels.

For more, go to http://www.stephanie-osborn.com/.

A sneak peek at *Texas Rangers*, Book 6 of the Division One series, by Stephanie Osborn!

"Oh, man. This. Is. Great!" Omega enthused, that evening after dark had fallen at last on a companionable, cheerful day of vacation explorations. "Look at that sky! Fantastic seeing!!"

"I take it this is a good night for observing?" Echo deadpanned as he watched Omega efficiently set up and align the telescopic equipment. Earlier, he had helped her unload it from the packs on the horses, then extract the various pieces, at her instruction, but they had decided that this time, he should sit back and watch as she performed the setup, because she had a specific way she wanted the equipment assembled for the observing session. Now, the soft sound of loosely-hobbled horses grazing rose nearby—there was neither fence post nor tree nor bush sturdy enough, or close enough, to tether them in that location.

"That, Echo, is an absolute understatement. Not only are we way out from any city and the light pollution from 'em, the air is dead calm, clear, and there's no moon tonight, 'cause it's in new phase. And there's almost no scintillation."

"Say what?" Echo had started spreading out a blanket, intending to lie down and relax while Omega worked at the 'scope, but he paused to look at her in intense curiosity. "Scintillation? Dammit, I should remember that from your class..."

"Twinkling," she answered. "If the air along the line of sight is really still, the star won't twinkle much at all. That's good, because a twinkling star jumps all over the place in the telescope focus. And no, I didn't cover that in class, because the class didn't focus on observational astronomy. Well, I guess celestial navigation from space is a kind of observational astronomy, but it's different from this." She waved a hand at the telescope. "I wanted to make the class something that would be of use to Division One agents, and ground-based observational astronomy of this sort really isn't in y'all's purview. I already got the comments at the end of class, but if I get more interest in it from serious hobbyists in the Agency, I'll look at putting together a 200-level class in it."

"Oh, okay. That makes sense. And yeah, I might just wanna consider taking a class like that; I have to admit, hanging out with you has kinda got me curious about it. What are you gonna look at tonight? Anything you can show me?" Echo asked as he stretched out and settled down on the blanket, folding his arms behind his head and gazing skyward.

"I'm picking up where I left off a year and a half ago—before you, and Cartman the big purple bulldozer, came crashing into my world, trashed my setup, and made life interesting," she teased as she worked. "I finally managed to reconstruct my observation schedule and most of my data. I was studying compact-object binaries—regular stars circling black holes, or neutron stars, and such. Photopolarimetric analysis. It's not much to look at, I'm afraid. Most astronomical research isn't very spectacular to see. When I'm done, I'll try to pull up some more fun stuff for us to look at." Omega flipped a couple of switches, then booted up the laptop and inserted a data chip. "All right, let's see...yeah, my old observing order will still work... there. Let 'er rip." After entering some commands, Omega came over and sat down beside Echo on the blanket, stretching sore muscles. "Mmh; I'm still stiff. And gonna be stiffer, I expect. Anyway, that's got it. I'll check it in a while and make sure everything's okay."

"You're not gonna stay with it?"

"Nah. I got it all automated now. What did you do with the snacks?"

"In the right-hand saddlebag on Spirit."

"Wasn't that your old horse's name, Ace? The one you were riding when you came upon the First Contact?"

"Yeah, it was."

"This isn't the same horse, is it? I mean, did you have the Agency acquire him, like they did my farm?"

"No, he's not the same horse," Echo said, quiet. "But I did have the Agency acquire him, yeah. The original Spirit died, oh, ten or twelve years ago. When this one was foaled, I was...notified...and they let me name him." He shrugged. "His full name is...lessee...Spirit Echo, I think it was. He's a registered quarter horse, just like the original Spirit was, so the name had to be a little bit different. He looks a good bit like him, though."

He deliberately failed to mention that Spirit had sired Spirit Echo—if sophisticated extraterrestrial genetics technology were factored into the siring. Spirit had been gelded, and when the decision was made to do *in vitro*, then implant the fetus in the donor mare, they'd had to reconstruct Spirit's genetic contribution. However, Echo had a suspicion that might not be a good topic to discuss with his partner at the moment, given certain conversations the previous evening about her own genetics. So he conveniently neglected to bring up the subject, to avoid spoiling her cheerful mood.

"I actually came out here a couple times during his training and helped out with it," he continued. "It...helped. Me, I mean; I dunno that it made any real difference in his training. But I kinda feel like he's more or less my horse."

"Should I have maybe not brought it up?"

"Nah, it's okay. I actually meant to tell you earlier, but I forgot."

"Okay. Listen, I got some serious munchies goin' now..."

"You're kidding," Echo teased with a grin. "You mean after another huge ranch-hand dinner, you're hungry again?"

"Aw, shuddup. That's why we brought the snackies, silly. Want anything?" Omega asked as she got back up to track down Spirit, and the right-hand saddlebag.

"No, thanks. Not yet. Probably later, though."

"Okay."

Echo lay silently on the blanket, looking up into the jewel-encrusted heavens, trying to identify the stars and constellations his partner had taught him. Out here, away from the lights of the city, there were many more stars visible, and he found it more challenging, as well as more interesting. After a while, it occurred to him that Omega hadn't returned. He glanced at his watch, then sat up and looked around.

There were Spirit and Celeste, still contentedly grazing, complete with saddlebags, but Omega was nowhere to be seen.

"Meg?" Echo called into the warm Texas night.

"...Ssshhh..." came faintly through the dark.

After a few moments, he spotted Omega creeping along, low to the ground, between the two horses. Every instinct in Echo screamed a warning as she worked her way silently back to him. He opened his mouth to speak, but she put a finger to his lips and leaned forward.

"Follow me," she breathed in his ear, "but stay low, and be dead quiet."

Omega started back the way she had come, and Echo followed closely, imitating her actions. A short distance past the horses was a slight rise they had ridden past on the previous afternoon, just before racing across the field beyond, and she headed up it, dropping onto her belly as she neared the edge of the ravine on the other side. At the edge, she carefully parted some low scrub, and motioned him close to look through.

At the bottom of the ravine was a small group of beings, maybe eight or ten, only a couple of which appeared human. They sat clustered in a circle, discussing in low tones the map which one of them held. Blonde head and brown bent together in the darkness for long moments, watching and listening, then Echo touched his partner's shoulder lightly and began worming his way back the way they had come. Omega followed suit. Once back at their own 'campsite,' he turned to her.

"Pack up your telescope, Meg," Echo said quietly. "Our vacation just ended."

Don't miss any of these highly entertaining SF/F books by Stephanie Osborn!

The *Division One* series by Stephanie Osborn:

Alpha and Omega

A Small Medium At Large

A Very UnCONventional Christmas

Tour de Force

Trojan Horse

Coming soon:

Texas Rangers

Stalking in the Night

Break, Break, Houston

Alpha and Omega (ISBN: 978-0-9982888-0-2 ebook/ 978-0-9982888-1-9 print) by Stephanie Osborn

Dr. Megan McAllister was already a pretty unusual human—NASA astronaut, professional astronomer, polymath—when she encountered the man in the black Suit that night in west Texas. What Division One Agent Echo didn't know, when he recruited her to the Agency, was that she was even more special.

But he'd find out, soon enough.

Stephanie Osborn, aka the Interstellar Woman of Mystery, former rocket scientist and author of acclaimed science fiction mysteries, goes back to the urban legend of the unique group of men and women who show up at UFO sightings, alien abductions, etc. and make things...disappear... to craft her vision of the universe we don't know about. Her new series, Division One, chronicles this universe through the eyes of recruit Megan McAllister, aka Omega, and her experienced partner, Echo, as they handle everything from lost alien children to extraterrestrial assassination attempts and more. [First book in the *Division One* series]

* * *

A Small Medium At Large (ISBN: 978-0-9982888-2-6 ebook/ 978-0-9982888-3-3 print) by Stephanie Osborn

What if Sir Arthur Conan Doyle was right all along, and Harry Houdini really DID do his illusions, not through sleight of hand, but via noncorporeal means? More, what if he could do this because...he wasn't human?

Ari Ho'd'ni, Glu'g'ik son of the Special Steward of the Royal House of Va'du'sha'ā, better known to modern humans as an alien Gray from the ninth planet of Zeta Reticuli A, fled his homeworld with the rest of his family during a time of impending global civil war. With them, they brought a unique device which, in its absence, ultimately caused the failure of the uprisings and the collapse of the imperial regime. Consequently Va'du'sha'ā has been at peace for more than a century. What is the F'al, and why has a rebel faction sent a special agent to Earth to retrieve it?

It falls to the premier team in the Pan-Galactic Law Enforcement and Immigration Administration, Division One—the Alpha One team, known to their friends as Agents Echo and Omega—to find out...or die trying. [Second book in the *Division One* series]

* * *

A Very UnCONventional Christmas (ISBN: 978-0-9982888-4-0 ebook/ 978-0-9982888-5-7 print) by Stephanie Osborn

It's Christmas in NYC, but for Alpha Line it's anything but a Silent Night: The Agency has a mole, leaking classified information to toy manufacturers and film producers alike, and the Agents are in danger of losing their anonymity. To complicate matters, the Prime Minister of Lambda Andromedae III, complete with entourage, has arrived to negotiate a new trade agreement with Earth. Worse, the more paranoid Division One field agents look at Omega's recent history with the Agency and suspect they have identified the mole!

Simultaneously, the discovery of a grim countdown in the most incongruous place possible—the Christmas tree at Rockefeller Center—augers the threat of horrific events on Christmas Eve itself.

Meanwhile, Omega is struggling to adjust to her very first Christmas in the Agency, made more difficult by the exposure of parts of her past long hidden from her conscious mind.

Will Omega be able to refute the accusations, or be punished for crimes she did not commit? Will the internal conspiracy expose the Agency? Or

351

will efforts to thwart it see Echo—and Fox—caught up in the accusations as well? What is the meaning of the countdown to Christmas Eve, and will any of Alpha Line survive it? [Third book in the *Division One* series]

* * *

Tour de Force (ISBN: 978-0-9982888-6-4 ebook/ 978-0-9982888-7-1 print) by Stephanie Osborn

Alpha One is participating in Omega's very first First Contact diplomatic operation. Unfortunately, it's going to split up the team—the Cortians, a race from the Sagittarius Dwarf Galaxy, have stringent requirements, and that narrows down the list of "candidate exchange students" to...Echo. ONLY Echo. PGLEIA's top Division One Agent, the man being groomed to be the next Director...and Omega's partner. A plum assignment, for the pick of the crop.

But Omega doesn't see it that way, though she can't—or won't—explain why. She is determined to stop the mission from going forward. At any cost.

Why is Omega trying to scuttle a diplomatic mission? What is she seeing that more experienced Agents aren't? Why won't the others listen? Is something bigger, more menacing, happening to her—to them? Will—CAN—Alpha One survive? [Fourth book in the *Division One* series]

* * *

Trojan Horse (ISBN: 978-0-9982888-9-5 ebook/ 978-1-947530-00-3 print) by Stephanie Osborn

After returning the healer Doron to his homeworld of Edeptis, Echo takes Omega on a training run to make her a Pan-Galactic Coalition-certified starship pilot—celestial navigation, extra-vehicular activity, emergency repair, planetary surveys, the whole grand tour. And he secretly delights in seeing Omega's joy at finally fulfilling a childhood dream.

But when the Cortians show on the scene, intending to take Alpha One into custody for crimes against the Cortian Amalgam, the resulting space dogfight severely damages the *Trojan Horse*, causing it to crash on a primitive protoplanet. Both Echo and Omega are badly injured, and it will take both of them working together to survive in the wreckage, while more Cortian vessels search for them overhead, and Fox and the rest of Alpha Line try to fight their way through to rescue their friends and colleagues. [Fifth book in the *Division One* series]

* * *

The *Burnout* series by Stephanie Osborn
The Fetish
Burnout: The mystery of Space Shuttle STS-281
Coming soon:
Escape Velocity

The Fetish (ASIN: B007YATGG8) by Stephanie Osborn

In *Burnout: The mystery of Space Shuttle STS-281*, Dr. Mike Anders buys a small spaceman fetish from a Zuni elder at a trading post. But there's a story behind this little lapis spaceman carving. What is it, and how did it come to be?

* * *

Burnout: The mystery of Space Shuttle STS-281 (ISBN: 1-60619-200-0) by Stephanie Osborn

How do you react when you discover the next shuttle disaster has happened...right on schedule?

Burnout is a SF mystery about a Space Shuttle disaster that turns out to be no accident. As the true scope of the disaster is uncovered by the principle investigators, "Crash" Murphy and Dr. Mike Anders, they find themselves running for their lives as friends, lovers and coworkers involved in the investigation perish around them.

* * *

Sherlock Holmes: Gentleman Aegis series by Stephanie Osborn:
Sherlock Holmes and the Mummy's Curse
Coming soon:
Sherlock Holmes in the Wild Hunt
Sherlock Holmes and the Tournament of Shadows

Sherlock Holmes and the Mummy's Curse (ISBN: 1-51888-312-5) by Stephanie Osborn

Holmes and Watson. Two names linked by mystery and danger from the beginning.

Within the first year of their friendship and while both are young men, Holmes and Watson are still finding their way in the world, with all the troubles that such young men usually have: Financial straits, troubles of the female persuasion, hazings, misunderstandings between friends, and more. Watson's Afghan wounds are still tender, his health not yet fully recovered, and there can be no consideration of his beginning a new practice as yet. Holmes, in his turn, is still struggling to found the new profession of consulting detective. Not yet truly established in London, let alone with the reputations they will one day possess, they are between cases and at loose ends when Holmes' old professor of archaeology contacts him.

Professor Willingham Whitesell makes an appeal to Holmes' unusual skill set and a request. Holmes is to bring Watson to serve as the dig team's physician and come to Egypt at once to translate hieroglyphics for his prestigious archaeological dig. There in the wilds of the Egyptian desert, plagued by heat, dust, drought and cobras, the team hopes to find the very first Pharaoh. Instead, they find something very different... (First book in the Gentleman Aegis series)

Sherlock Holmes and the Mummy's Curse is a Silver Falchion Award winner.

* * *

The *Displaced Detective* series by Stephanie Osborn:
The Case of the Displaced Detective: The Arrival
The Case of the Displaced Detective: At Speed
The Case of the Cosmological Killer: The Rendlesham Incident
The Case of the Cosmological Killer: Endings and Beginnings
A Case of Spontaneous Combustion
Fear in the French Quarter

The Case of the Displaced Detective: The Arrival (ISBN: 1-60619-189-7) by Stephanie Osborn is a SF mystery in which brilliant hyperspatial physicist, Dr. Skye Chadwick, discovers there are alternate realities, often populated by those we consider only literary characters. Can Chadwick help Holmes come up to speed in modern investigative techniques in time to stop the spies? Will Holmes be able to thrive in our modern world? Is Chadwick now Holmes' new "Watson"—or more?

And what happens next?   [First book in the *Displaced Detective* series]

* * *

The Case of the Displaced Detective: At Speed (ISBN: 1-60619-191-0) by Stephanie Osborn

Having foiled sabotage of Project: Tesseract by an unknown spy ring, Sherlock Holmes and Dr. Skye Chadwick face the next challenge. How do they find the members of this diabolical spy ring when they do not even know what the ring is trying to accomplish? And how can they do it when Skye is recovering from no less than two nigh-fatal wounds?

Can they work out the intricacies of their relationship? Can they determine the reason the spy ring is after the tesseract? And—most importantly—can they stop it? [Second book in the *Displaced Detective* series]

* * *

The Case of the Cosmological Killer: The Rendlesham Incident (ISBN: 1-60619-193-4) by Stephanie Osborn

In 1980, RAF Bentwaters and Woodbridge were plagued by UFO sightings that were never solved. Now, McFarlane, a resident of Suffolk has died of fright during a new UFO encounter. On holiday in London, Sherlock Holmes and Skye Chadwick-Holmes are called upon by Her Majesty's Secret Service to investigate the death.

What is the UFO? Why does Skye find it familiar? Who—or what—killed McFarlane?

And how can the pair do what even Her Majesty's Secret Service could not? [Third book in the *Displaced Detective* series]

* * *

The Case of the Cosmological Killer: Endings and Beginnings (ISBN: 1-60619-195-0) by Stephanie Osborn

After the revelations in *The Rendlesham Incident*, Holmes and Skye find they have not one, but two, very serious problems facing them. Not only did their "UFO victim" most emphatically NOT die from a close encounter, he was dying twice over—from completely unrelated causes. Holmes must now find the murderers before they find the secret of the McFarlane farm. And to add to their problems, another continuum—containing another Skye and Holmes—has approached Skye for help to stop the collapse of their own spacetime, a collapse that could take Skye with it, should she happen to be in their tesseract core when it occurs. [Fourth book in the *Displaced Detective* series]

* * *

A Case of Spontaneous Combustion (ISBN: 1-60619-197-7) by Stephanie Osborn

When an entire village west of London is wiped out in an apparent case of mass spontaneous combustion, Her Majesty's Secret Service contacts The Holmes Agency to investigate. Once in London, Holmes looks into the horror that is now Stonegrange. His investigations take him into a dangerous undercover assignment in search of a possible terror ring, though he cannot determine how a human agency could have caused the disaster. Meanwhile, alone in Colorado, Skye is forced to battle raging wildfires and tame a wild mustang stallion, all while believing that her husband has abandoned her. Who—or what—caused the horror in Stonegrange? Will Holmes find his way safely through the me taphorical minefield that is modern Middle Eastern politics? Will this predicament seriously damage—even destroy—the couple's relationship? And can Holmes stop the terrorists before they unleash their outré weapon again? [Fifth book in the *Displaced Detective* series]

* * *

Fear in the French Quarter (ISBN: 1-60619-202-7) by Stephanie Osborn revolves around a jaunt by no less than Sherlock Holmes himself—brought to the modern day from an alternate universe's Victorian era by his continuum parallel, who is now his wife, Dr. Skye Chadwick-Holmes—to famed New Orleans for both business and pleasure. There, the detective couple investigates ghostly apparitions, strange disappearances, mystic phenomena, and challenge threats to the very universe they call home.

It was supposed to be a working holiday for Skye and Sherlock, along with their friend, the modern day version of Doctor Watson—some federal training that also gave them the chance to explore New Orleans, as the ghosts of the French Quarter become exponentially more active. When the couple uncovers an imminently catastrophic cause, whose epicenter lies squarely in the middle of Le Vieux Carré, they must race against time to stop it before the whole thing breaks wide open—and more than one universe is destroyed. [Sixth book in the *Displaced Detective* series]